JOEY

CHICAGO RUTHLESS: BOOK 2

SADIE KINCAID

RED HOUSE PRESS LTD

For all of my wonderful readers, and most especially for any of you who've ever felt like you've never quite fit in.

It doesn't matter.

Why waste your time trying to fit in when you're so capable of shining all on your own?

All my love, Sadie xx

CONTENT WARNING

This book is intended for mature readers and contains scenes of graphic violence as well as those of a sexual nature.

PROLOGUE

MAX—AGE 20

"She's fucking dead, D." I stare at my best friend Dante in horror as the bottle of brandy I drank last night threatens to make a sudden and violent reappearance.

His older brother, Lorenzo, stands behind him, his finger-tips on the girl's neck, checking for a pulse we all know he won't find. Her lips are blue, for fuck's sake.

"Calm down, Max," Dante says in that cool, calm tone I've come to know so well. On any other occasion it might actually work on me, but not today.

I look past him, my eyes searching Lorenzo's face for a sign that she isn't dead. Maybe she passed out from too much vodka and cocaine, maybe—

His eyes leave her face and lock on mine. "We'll take care of it," is all he says.

"No!" I shake my head and rake my hands through my hair. "We can't fix this. I fucking killed her, Loz," I shout.

"Keep your voice down," Lorenzo whispers angrily. "I said we will take care of it."

I look down at her face again. Her ash-blond hair fans over the pillow, and the covers are pulled up over her naked body,

1

protecting her modesty. Apart from the blue tinge to her lips, she looks like she's sleeping. But the dark purple bruising on her neck—that I don't even remember putting there—is unmistakable.

Bile burns the back of my throat. I'm a fucking monster. I don't even remember taking her to bed, let alone fucking her and wrapping my hands around her goddamn neck. But that's my thing, right? Choke them until they almost pass out? It makes the orgasm more intense. I've been into it since I first discovered the pleasure that can be found between a woman's thighs. I've never attempted it while drunk off my ass before though. I never let it go too far.

Until now.

I stare at her. Nineteen years old. A life full of promise snuffed out by one careless act. My head spins so hard, I sway on my feet.

"Max! I asked you if anyone saw you coming in here together?" Dante asks, and I realize I must not have heard him the first time. *How long has he been speaking to me?*

I shake my head. "I don't know. I was out of it. I don't even remember bringing her in here. I don't remember …" The words stick in my throat, and I almost choke on them. I've killed plenty of people before, and I've taken great pleasure in causing people pain. But this is something so much worse. I completely lost control, and I am a man who thrives on control.

Dante places his hands on my face, turning my head so I'll focus on him instead of the dead girl in my bed. "It was an accident, compagno."

Compagno? How the fuck can he still call me his friend after what I've done? "I killed her, D."

Lorenzo checks his watch. "It's not even ten yet. We can take her to the funeral home and incinerate the body before anyone even notices she's missing."

I blink at him. "This is Fiona Delgado we're talking about. You don't think her father is going to lose his fucking shit when he finds out his only daughter has disappeared? Everyone knows she was here last night."

Lorenzo scowls at me. "And I am Lorenzo fucking Moretti, and if I want her to disappear then she will. Bruce Delgado will believe whatever the fuck I want him to."

I swallow the knot of emotion that seems lodged in my throat. "I can't ask you to do that for me. If anyone finds out ..." It's one thing to take out our enemies or to kill in the interest of business, but to strangle a girl to death during sex is on a whole other fucking level.

"They won't," Dante assures me.

"You're our brother," Lorenzo adds. "And this was an accident." He says the last words with such conviction that I almost believe him.

ONE

TWELVE YEARS LATER
JOEY

"**G**ood girl," Max says with a smirk as my right foot connects with the pad. I'm grateful that my cheeks are already flushed from the workout because those words coming from his perfect mouth have me about to melt into a puddle.

I, Joey Moretti—a one hundred percent card-carrying feminist—would gladly drop to my knees and crawl to this man if he told me to.

"You're not done yet." He nudges me with the pad, waiting for me to kick him again. Because our workout isn't even half over. He works almost as hard as I do in these training sessions —pushing me to my limits and making me faster and stronger every time.

I hit him with another roundhouse, and his grunt of approval causes warmth to pool in my center. I doubt I'd work even half as hard for any other trainer, but Maximo DiMarco isn't just any trainer. He is the reason I get out of bed every morning. He's one of the most feared men in the city, but to me, he is sweet and funny and kind. And the fact he has a body that looks like it was chiseled by the gods themselves, not to mention the most incredible dark brown eyes I've ever seen in my entire life, doesn't hurt either. But he's also my older brothers' best friend, the right hand of the Cosa Nostra, and as off-limits to me as any man can be.

"You tired already?" He chuckles, tapping the side of my head.

"No," I lie. My desire to make him proud overrides any pain or fatigue that I feel during his grueling workouts.

My brothers arranged for him to teach me some self-defense, and in return I get a little more freedom. I also get to drool over a shirtless, sweaty Max every Monday, Wednesday, and Friday, and those mornings are the highlight of my week.

"Harder, Joey. I know you got more than that," he says, bouncing on his toes as he moves effortlessly around the ring—like he's not the size of a mountain.

I lean back like he taught me, swivel my hip, and strike the pad with as much strength as I have left in me.

"That's my girl," he says, and my breath catches in my throat. Sometimes I wonder if he does this on purpose. I mean he must know I have a huge crush on him. It's kind of a running joke with my two sisters-in-law. And my overprotective brothers tolerate it because they know without a doubt that Max would never cross that line. Which is a damn shame if you ask me.

"Okay, kid. You got two minutes to take a quick water break, and then we do a little conditioning."

I groan. Conditioning is code for torture. Burpees and mountain climbers and all kinds of other insane exercises that Max makes me do at the end of my workout.

"You should enjoy this while you can. Your new trainer won't take it so easy on you," Max says with a laugh and hands me a bottle of water.

I blink at him. "New trainer?"

CHAPTER ONE

"Yeah. Didn't Dante tell you?"

Dante is my older brother. The chosen one. Head of the Cosa Nostra and, along with our oldest brother, Lorenzo, a giant pain in my ass.

I frown. "No. I don't need a new trainer."

"Trust me. This one is way better than me."

"Nobody is better than you," I blurt, and my face flushes with heat at my admission.

"Joey." He narrows his eyes before taking a gulp of his water. "You sure you can't think of anyone who'd be better at teaching you self-defense than me?" He's teasing me now, but I'm not in the mood for his games. All I can focus on is the fact that I'm losing him.

"No."

"Your half sister is an MMA fighter," he reminds me with a satisfied smile, as though that makes losing him easier somehow. "After her fight this weekend, she's taking a little break. So she's gonna train you instead. Dante said he was going to tell you."

"He and Kat were a little busy last night." My nose wrinkles at the memory. "They were practically dry humping in the kitchen after they came home from their date."

Max rolls his eyes.

"Did he guilt trip Toni into doing this? 'Cause I know this house isn't her favorite place to be." I don't know my half sister that well. She was born around the same time as Dante, to my father's mistress at the time. She never lived with us, but she used to spend holidays here and she was nice to me. In fact, she used to braid my hair and come up with fun stories for me. But she moved to LA with her mom when I was four and she was thirteen, and I never saw much of her after that. Dante is the only one she's really close to. She and Lorenzo never got along. It's as though he finds her existence an insult to our mother's memory, but it's not Toni's fault she was born.

"No, he didn't guilt trip her. She offered her time. Now that your father's no longer around, she's much happier about being here. I think she's been feeling kind of lonely since she left LA. Even her and Lorenzo are getting along a little better."

"Hmm," I mumble, looking down at the floor.

Max nudges my arm. "You're gonna be trained by an MMA champ, Joey. You'll be able to knock me on my ass by the time Toni is through with you."

I sigh. "I guess."

"You don't sound very happy about it."

I look up at him, annoyed at the tears pricking at my eyes. I hate being vulnerable. But Max won't judge me. He never does. "I'll just miss you training me is all."

"I'll still be here all the damn time," he says, bumping his arm against mine and making my insides melt like butter on hot toast.

"Yeah."

"Now drink up because you got thirty seconds left before we start again. We leave everything in the gym, right?"

"We leave everything in the gym." I repeat his favorite mantra as my heart breaks a little at the realization that soon he'll be leaving me in the gym too.

TWO

MAX

"You staying for dinner?" she asks, her eyes wide and shining. I spend a lot of time looking into Joey Moretti's deep-brown eyes. The way they sparkle with flecks of amber when she's happy or mad fascinates me.

Her eyes are a safe zone. Because if I were to let my gaze drift lower, I might let it linger on those insanely perky tits of hers, or the way the perspiration on her back runs down the channel of her spine, slipping beneath the band of her yoga pants and down to her juicy ass.

And then I would have to stand here with a raging boner. I swear, these workouts test my willpower like nothing in my life ever has before. I could say I have no idea why I agreed to them, because they're pure fucking torture—but I've always been a sucker for punishment. Spending time with her is the most exquisite kind of torture there is. She's the one woman I can't have and the one woman I want more than any other.

"Max?" she says with a frown.

"Huh?"

She places one hand on her hip and rolls her eyes like a

spoiled little brat. What I wouldn't give to discipline that sass out of her. "Dinner?"

No, I can't stay for dinner. I need to get home and take a shower. During which I will jerk off to the image of your ass in those pants.

"You can shower here," she offers, and for a horrifying minute, I wonder if I said that out loud. "You know, 'cause you're kind of sweaty." She wrinkles her nose, a mischievous smile playing on her lips.

A grin tugs at the corners of my mouth. "Well, working you out is a tough job, Joey."

Her eyes darken with heat. This would all be so much easier if she didn't look at me that way. Because I know for certain she likes me too. She's had a crush on me for years, and her brothers tolerate it because they trust me to never act on it. But that gets harder and harder to do with each passing day. I spend so much time thinking about slipping my hand into her panties and finding out how wet I make her that it's become a huge distraction. I know that I get to her. I just don't know how much.

"I can't. I have somewhere I need to be," I tell her, and the hurt on her face makes me wish that I hadn't. She masks it well though, and if I didn't pay such close attention to her, I probably wouldn't have noticed it. But I pay far too much attention to her. I practically stalk the girl, and I do it under the guise of looking out for her on behalf of her brothers.

"A date?"

"No."

She grabs her towel off the floor and turns on her heel, swaying the finest ass I've ever seen as she sashays toward the door. "Well, whatever it is, have a great time."

I watch her leave, drinking in every detail of her before she disappears from view. Maybe I *should* go on a date and get her out of my head. Except it never works. I've fucked countless women this past year, and there wasn't a single time I didn't imagine it was Joey I was fucking instead.

I check my watch. Shit! I really do have somewhere to be.

THOUGHTS OF JOEY and her perfect ass continue to invade my thoughts when I pull into the parking garage at my apartment building an hour later. I take my private elevator to the penthouse apartment, and when the doors open, she stands there waiting for me, chewing on her fingernails and bouncing on her tiptoes. Anxiety radiates from her like heat from an open fire. She hates being left alone, and while I don't keep guards at my home because I prefer absolute privacy, this place is still safer than Fort Knox.

"You said you'd be back at five," she says, accusing eyes searching my face.

I check my watch and sigh. "It's like ten past."

"You know how much I worry, Max," she whines. "You're all we have." She rubs both hands over her rounded stomach, and a wave of guilt washes over me. She's right.

I take two steps forward and wrap my arms around her. "I'm sorry, okay? I would have called to say I'd be a little late, but I was on the bike."

"Those things are dangerous, you know." She sniffles, pressing her head against my chest.

That makes me laugh. "Pretty sure everything I do is dangerous, Kristin," I remind her. That makes her laugh too, a soft chuckle that vibrates through her entire body.

I drop my arms to my sides and she looks up at me, her eyes wet with unshed tears. She's far too young and innocent to be here with me. "If anything ever happened to you ..." she whispers.

"It won't."

"I'm making dinner," she says, changing the subject before things get too tense.

I arch an eyebrow at her. "But you can't cook."

"I'm learning." She swats my chest. "I'm following a recipe. It's called chicken parm for dummies. It will be amazing. I swear."

"Hmm," I murmur, unconvinced. "Didn't you follow a recipe the night before last and almost burn down the kitchen?"

Her cheeks turn bright red, and she looks down at the floor. "I didn't realize you had to take the plastic thing off the chicken. I've learned my lesson. This time it's all fresh stuff. No plastic packaging involved."

"Well, in that case, I'm looking forward to it. Let me grab a shower and then I can help out."

"That would be great." The huge smile on her face makes her look so desperate for my affection and makes me feel guilty for leaving her alone all day. I'm about to apologize for that a second time when she grabs my hand. "The baby's kicking!" she squeals, placing my hand on the side of her stomach and pressing gently. "You feel it?"

There's a soft tap against my palm. Then another. *Wow!* "Yeah, I feel it."

"How cool is that? He's gonna be so strong, you know? Just like you are." She blinks up at me, fluttering her long dark eyelashes.

"Naw, just like his mom," I tell her with a wink. She throws her arms around my waist and buries her face against my chest again. I drop a soft kiss on the top of her head.

"Thank you, Max," she whispers.

I CHEW on another mouthful of the worst chicken parm I've ever eaten in my life, then wash it down with a gulp of soda.

"It's bad, isn't it?" Kristin eyes me from across the table.

The truth would hurt her feelings, so I lie. "It's fine." I rarely eat at my place as a rule, preferring to spend my time at the Moretti mansion. But since Kristin walked into my life, that's not always an option. "Besides, you don't have to cook. We can get takeout."

"I'm trying to be healthy though. For this little guy." She rubs a hand over her stomach and smiles.

"You still haven't heard from your father?"

Her smile fades in an instant. "Nothing." She looks down at her half-eaten plate of food.

I drop my silverware and scrub a hand over my beard. "And there's nothing else you can think of? Something he might have said? A clue as to where he might have gone?"

She shakes her head. "I wish there was, but I've gone over our last conversation so many times in my head. All he told me was that he had to take care of something because if he didn't, we would never be safe. He said if he wasn't back in two days —" She swipes her cheek, whisking away her tears, and takes a deep breath. "He told me the only person I could trust in the whole world was you, and he told me to give you that message. That was it."

I've never had any cause not to trust Dante or Lorenzo Moretti, and while their father was a cruel man who never once let me forget how much he did for me by taking me in when I was fourteen, his sons are nothing like him. They are like brothers to me. Still, my brow furrows. *My dad says you can't trust the Morettis. They turned you against your real family.* That's the message she's referring to. The one her father asked her to pass along if she ever had cause to come to me and ask for help.

Six nights ago, she turned up on my doorstep and did exactly that.

THREE

JOEY

"This house is so cool," my best friend Monique says as she wanders down the hallway. "Like everything is so tasteful and"—she runs a hand over the gold handrail of the huge marble staircase—"expensive." She acts as though this is her first time seeing my house, but she's been here at least a hundred times.

"Hmm." I shrug. I barely notice any more. The house is massive, and it has everything a person might need, I guess. Huge gardens, a pool, state-of-the-art gym with a boxing ring, a home theater, game room, library. You name it. But what my best friend sees as luxury, I see as my overprotective brothers' way of making sure I have as few reasons as possible to leave the house.

"Your house is amazing," I remind her. I'm actually jealous of it. She lives in a beautiful four-bedroom house with a pool. But best of all, she lives with her mom, who's hardly ever there, whereas I'm constantly surrounded by my family. Living with my two brothers and their wives makes it hard to get any privacy.

We make our way upstairs to my room, and Monique

brushes her fingertips over the furniture and expensive artwork along the way, an expression of awe on her face. "Is this one new?" She stops in front of a painting of a ballerina, a Degas, in the hallway. It cost my brother a small fortune.

"Yeah. Lorenzo bought it for Anya." I swallow the ball of sadness that lodges in my throat.

"I bet it cost a fortune. She's so lucky."

I don't tell her that my wonderful, funny, kind sister-in-law isn't lucky at all. She has terminal cancer, and we all have to watch her grow sicker and weaker by the day.

"You're all so lucky, Jo," she says with a wistful sigh. "I can only imagine what it's like to be a Mafia princess."

A Mafia princess. I fight the urge to roll my eyes. I can never tell if that's an insult or a term of endearment from her lips. She's called me that for as long as I've known her. We've been best friends since we started high school, but even after all these years I can never quite figure out if she's being nice or bitchy. That was probably what drew us to each other. I was just like her back then. We walked around Mercury High like we owned the goddamn school.

"You're not exactly a peasant, Mo," I say with a sigh. "Your dad left you and your mom with a fortune."

"It's not an endless pot of money though." For a second, there's a glimmer of something in her eyes that looks a lot like sadness. But she tosses her long blond hair over her shoulder and it's gone.

Her mom does travel a lot. She's always at some five-star resort in the Caribbean or somewhere exotic, and I suppose that eats into a fortune pretty quickly. Still, Monique has no idea how good she has it. She has so much freedom and independence, and I would trade this gilded cage for a little more of that any day of the week.

Monique lies on my bed, feet up against the wall as she twirls a tube of lip gloss between her fingers.

"Lex said she'll meet us at ten. She's bringing that douchebag, Nyx, with her too."

Rolling my eyes, I continue to apply my makeup. Monique thinks any guy who isn't into her is a douchebag. "He seems nice to me."

"Ugh, he has a freaking ponytail."

"Lex likes guys with long hair though. Besides, I'm pretty sure she's not interested in him for his ponytail." I grin. Lexi told me her new friend-with-benefits is amazing in bed, not that I'm going to tell Monique.

She laughs. "You think he's got a huge dick?"

"Maybe."

"Nah, he doesn't," she says, shaking her head.

I arch an eyebrow in amusement. "How would you know? You seen it?"

"No, but I know his type."

"And that is?"

"Nice guys." She shudders. "They're only nice to girls because they have tiny dicks."

I gape at her reflection in the mirror, incredulous. "You're saying guys are only nice if they have small dicks?"

She gives a casual shrug. "Either that or they don't know how to use them."

"Jesus, Mo, your logic is so fucking twisted sometimes," I snap, feeling defensive of our friend. Lexi's happier than I've ever seen her, which is probably why Monique is being such a bitch.

"Oh, lighten up, Jo." She releases a dramatic sigh. "Since when did you become such a fucking bore?"

I close my eyes and suck in a calming breath. I guess she isn't

17

wrong. This is the kind of shit we used to talk about all the time, but that was back in high school. We're past that now, aren't we? "Lex seems happy, is all. If she likes the guy, it doesn't matter how big his dick is, right?" I say, trying to defuse the tension, because Monique and Lex are the only girlfriends I have.

"Not that you'd know anything about that though." She snorts a laugh, and I roll my eyes, sorry I ever confided in her that I'm still a virgin. Ever since I did, she's made it her one-woman mission to get me laid.

I toss my makeup sponge at her, and it bounces off her forehead. "Just because you've been dicked down more times than you can remember ..."

Monique sits up, swinging her legs off the end of the bed, a wicked grin on her face. "Jealous?"

"Uh, no."

"We'll get you some good dick tonight, I can feel it."

"I'm not looking for that." I sigh and go back to my mascara. "Well, not exclusively."

That makes her laugh out loud. "But if a nice fat dick were to present itself?"

"Depending on who it was attached to, maybe I'd consider taking it home." I laugh too.

Monique gasps. "Can you imagine your brothers' faces if you brought some stray home from the bar?"

"God, no," I say, shivering at the thought.

"You can always use my place. In fact, you could stay over?"

"I can't tonight. I watch Gabriella on Saturdays."

She huffs. "So, have a week off. She's not your kid, not your responsibility."

I actually love taking care of my niece on Saturday mornings, and I was the one who suggested the arrangement. She's five months old and I adore the beautiful little smooch. Plus, it allows Dante and Kat to sleep in and spend some time together, and that always puts my brother in a great mood. Which is a win for me because it makes him so much easier to manipulate. "It keeps Dante off my back," I say, if only to avoid any more accusations that I'm boring. "And if we're going to that new club tomorrow night, I need to keep him sweet."

"Fine," she says with a roll of her eyes. "If we can't get you some good dick tonight, we'll definitely get you some tomorrow."

"You're obsessed with dick."

"No." She gets off the bed and puts an arm around my shoulder, leaning down and checking her reflection in the mirror. "I'm worried about my best friend still being a virgin at the age of twenty-two."

"It's not that unusual," I say.

"It is, Joey, and if you don't pop that cherry soon, guys are going to think you're a freak."

I stare at my own reflection. I'm not a freak, am I? As much as I hate to admit it, Monique is right about one thing. I need to have sex with someone soon, preferably before I spend the family fortune on batteries. I'm pretty sure I could keep Energizer in business all on my own.

"Which hotties will be accompanying us tonight? Is Max tagging along?" she asks, seductively chewing on her lip. I wish I knew how she does that—she can switch from looking sweet and innocent to looking like a goddamn porn star in less than a second.

"Henry and Ash will be with us. No Max," I say, trying to keep my disappointment out of my voice. I can't go anywhere without armed guards—it's one of the conditions my brothers attached when they conceded to allowing me more freedom.

"Ash is hot though," she says with a pop of one perfect eyebrow.

I look at her like she's lost her mind. "He's like forty or something."

"Hmm. Imagine all that experience."

Ash has worked for my brothers for as long as I can remember. With his icy blue eyes and blond buzzcut, I can see why she'd be attracted to him, but he isn't my type. I wrinkle my nose and she rolls her eyes. "Of course, he's not *Maximo*." She rolls his name on her tongue, dramatically clutching at her chest.

"Oh, stop." I stand up and smooth my hands over my minidress. "Do I look okay?"

She tilts her head to one side and appraises me. Monique's leather body con dress is way more revealing than my long-sleeved one. She looks hot, but then she always does, with her huge boobs, huge lips—both of which I happen to know are gifts from the local plastic surgeon rather than anything her momma gave her—and long blond hair. She could roll out of bed in a pair of pajamas with stale morning breath and still pull any guy she wanted.

She flutters her eyelashes. "I think Max would approve."

I give her a playful shove. "Will you stop going on about Max."

"But you are so hot for him, girl. You practically drool when you talk to him."

"I do not," I insist, grabbing my heels and slipping them on. "He's like a third big brother. It could never happen."

"Whatever you say." The smirk she gives me makes the hairs on the back of my neck stand on end. Max would be just Monique's type. I mean, who wouldn't be into him? Tall, dark, stacked. Muscles and tattoos for days and more than a hint of danger—he's a freaking walking wet dream. And even if he isn't her type, she'd fuck him just to get one up on me. *Note to self— remind the great Max DiMarco that your friends are off-limits.*

CHAPTER
FOUR
MAX

My phone buzzes in my hand and Dmitri Varkov's name flashes on the screen. I've been waiting for his call. I tap the screen to answer, looking at the Chicago skyline through my apartment window. "Tell me where we're at."

"He's gone underground. Still not prepared to go down quietly," he replies.

"Well, we never expected him to," I remind him. Dominik Pushkin was the head of the Russian Bratva for over twenty years. I doubt he ever expected his leadership to be challenged, particularly because he has two capable sons, and especially not by Dmitri Varkov.

"I know that, but I didn't anticipate him putting up the fight he has. I've lost a dozen good men already."

Rage prickles beneath my skin and my right hand balls into a fist. We also lost two men last week, but that's the nature of our business. "You're trying to take over as the new head of the fucking Bratva, Dmitri. What the hell did you expect? That he'd just roll over and hand you the keys to his kingdom?"

"No!"

"If you're getting cold feet and you need us to handle this ourselves—"

"No. I can handle it," he says.

"You know that Dante and Lorenzo can't be seen to let this go. This is their father's murder we're talking about."

"I know, Maximo. There's no need for any of you to get more involved than you already are. Let me handle this my way."

I pinch the bridge of my nose, trying to stave off the tension headache that's been building for the past few hours. Dmitri is in a tenuous position. Having the backing of the Moretti brothers can be both a blessing and a curse. The Morettis rule Chicago, and their seal of approval basically grants Dmitri permission to challenge the top. But there's an added complication that makes this a fine line for him to walk—the new head of the Bratva can't be perceived as a lackey to the Sicilian Mafia. An alliance is good for business, but Dmitri needs to prove that he's equally powerful standing alone. And Dante and Lorenzo cannot allow Pushkin to evade their wrath much longer, not after they openly accused him of murdering their father, Salvatore Moretti.

He didn't. Dante killed Sal himself after he discovered the sick, twisted shit his father was involved in for years.

But that secret will remain locked within the Moretti compound. Family business is family business. Besides, the lie is a great excuse to get rid of that piece of shit.

"I underestimated the support he'd have with the other families. I had to be careful about uncovering the evidence with everything that was involved," he says pointedly.

He means *everyone*, not everything. More specifically, one person. Salvatore Moretti. Things would've have been easier for Dmitri if he could have exposed his former boss's full role in the sex trafficking ring much earlier. It would've turned most of the other families against him immediately, but because Sal was involved in the whole fucked-up situation, he had to be discreet about it.

"Both Dante and Lorenzo appreciate your discretion in keeping their father's name out of any scandal."

"I gave them my word."

Dmitri is a man of his word. And he's a hell of a lot easier to work with than his predecessor. Hell, I actually kinda like the guy. But this is business, and given the stakes involved, I can't allow any leniency. If he can't bring Pushkin to us soon, then we will be forced to find him ourselves. And that really won't look good for him.

"Do you have any idea where's he's hiding?"

"I'm working on it. Now that I've been able to reveal what Pushkin was involved in without implicating Salvatore and they've all seen the proof for themselves, things should move more quickly. His sons have gone to ground too. They're running scared. It won't be long before we find them and deal with them."

"Good."

"I have some leads to follow tomorrow if you're interested in tagging along?"

I rub a hand over my jaw. "I can't. I have some shit to deal with."

"I'll keep you informed then."

"Before you go, I wondered if you could look into something else for me." I don't have a lot for him to go on, but I need answers fast, and he's well connected.

"Sure. What is it?"

I recall everything Kristin told me about the father of her baby. "I'm looking for a guy. I only have a first name, but I think he's probably Bratva."

"Is he local?"

"No. New Jersey. At least he was there around six months

ago. I don't think he was from there, but he definitely operated around those parts."

"His name?"

"Jakob."

"Anything else?"

"Tall. Shaved head. Twenty-four. Russian." I don't tell Dmitri about his dreamy eyes, killer smile, or abs for days—which were the only other details Kristin gave me.

"Why do you think he was Bratva?"

"Just a feeling." Everything about the way she described him, his tattoos, his paranoia, the way he disappeared at a moment's notice, his money, it all screamed Bratva.

"I'll ask around, but it's not a lot to go on. Unless he's someone high up, then maybe I can trace him."

"If you could get me a name and a location, I'd appreciate it."

"Anything I should be concerned about?"

"No. Just helping out a friend."

"I'll see what I can do. And I'll keep you updated on Pushkin."

I end the call and stare out the window. Kristin's situation is a problem I could do without right now. With everything going on for Lorenzo and Dante, I need to pick up the slack, but instead I'm distracted looking for Kristin's father.

And then of course there's my other distraction. My constant, makes my cock twitch just looking at her, sarcastic, spoiled brat, ray of utter fucking sunshine of a distraction. I open the app on my phone and stare at the small blue dot on the screen.

That's her. Joey Moretti. My girl. At some bar with her friends. I didn't stick around after her workout today to see what she chose to wear to go to said bar, but I can guarantee it was short and tight. The best outfit she could find to show off her perfect long legs. The amount of time I spend tracking her movements is borderline obsessive. But what else can I do? Knowing that she's out there without my protection. Knowing that some jackass is probably salivating over her right now, thinking he might have a shot with her. Thinking about touching her. Actually touching her.

Rage bubbles up in my chest and sears through my skin at the thought of another man putting their hands on her. I stare at the dot on the screen. She has two armed escorts with her. They're some of her brother's best men. She's safe. She's also in a bar with dozens of guys who would love to fuck her.

Grabbing my cell, I stuff it into my pocket and walk into the den to grab the keys to my bike.

"Are you going out?" Kristin asks. She's curled on the sofa, watching a movie on her laptop even though I have a huge TV.

"Yeah." I swallow the knot of guilt. She's perfectly safe here, and I can't babysit her all the time. I still have a life to live while I'm helping her out. "I have somewhere I need to be."

She frowns at me. "You have a date?"

"Not that it's any of your business, but no."

"When will you be back?"

I glance at my watch. It's a little after ten, and Joey usually heads home around midnight on Friday nights so she can be awake and ready for Gabriella on Saturday morning. "Two hours. Maybe three. Don't wait up."

"You know I will anyway," she says with a sigh.

"You shouldn't though, Kristin. I'm more than capable of looking after myself and you are safer here than anywhere else in the world. I promise you."

"I know. I just ..." Her throat contracts as she swallows.

She's *just* a pregnant and terrified eighteen-year-old who just lost the only person in the world she's been able to depend on. And while Uncle Vito might be a piece of shit for having an affair with his brother's wife—my mom—and running off with her, he's still Kristin's father. I may have only known about my baby sister for a week, but she deserves a better big brother than the one she got.

I close my eyes and sigh. Joey is fine. She's safe. Me going to that bar and watching her for the next few hours will only end the same way it always does—me frustrated, with a raging boner and only my hand to fuck.

Tossing my keys back onto the sideboard, I walk to the sofa and flop down beside Kristin. "What are we watching?"

"*Bridesmaids*," she says with a smile.

"Then can we at least watch it on the TV instead of this tiny ass screen?"

She picks up the TV remote from the table beside her and hands it to me. "Sure."

CHAPTER
FIVE
JOEY

"Oh fuck me, it's MoJo," a familiar voice shouts.

"Toby Fiore!" Mo shrieks, arms thrown wide, almost knocking me out of the way as she lunges for the guy standing behind me. Toby was our friend in high school. Actually, he was more like our obedient puppy dog the way he used to follow us around. Mo never really had much time for him, so I figure her reaction has more to do with the six cocktails she's knocked back in the past hour than happiness at seeing our old friend.

However, when I spin around to say hi too, I realize why Mo's so happy to see him. It seems our buddy Toby grew up while he was away at college. Gone is the skinny boy with the shy smile and braces, and in his place is a fine ass man with muscles and stubble and twinkling hazel eyes.

Mo's literally hanging off him with her arms around his neck. He rolls his eyes at me. "Hey, Joey," he mouths over the loud music.

"Hey."

When Mo finally lets him go, I give him a quick hug. "It's

good to see you," he says with a smile, revealing perfect white teeth. I guess those braces really paid off.

"You too. I haven't heard MoJo for a long time." I laugh, recalling our high school nickname. I kind of hated it, but Mo loved it. The moniker stuck with us right through to our senior year.

He laughs too, brushing his dark hair out of his eyes.

"Toby, come buy me a drink." Mo tugs on his arm and pulls him toward the bar.

"You want one?" he asks, looking down at my almost-empty glass.

"Sure. I'll take a rum and coke."

"Rum and coke," he repeats, his eyes fixed on mine. Wow. Toby has really grown up. He went away to Berkeley, and rumor had it he was going to stay in California because he got a job with an accounting firm. I wonder if he's only here to visit his family. It will be nice to catch up with him if he's in town long enough. He and I had a lot in common when we were younger. He was a good friend.

Lexi sidles up to me, nudging my arm while I watch Toby and Mo disappear into the crowd. "Wow. Toby got hot."

"He was always cute," I remind her.

"Yeah, but now he is h-o-t, hot." She waggles her eyebrows at me. "You think he's back for good?"

"I dunno."

"He used to have it so bad for you. You remember?" She giggles.

"No. We were just good friends," I insist, although I do remember the way he used to look at me with those puppy dog eyes of his. But I was always more interested in assholes back then.

"He lurves you," Lexi says, sniggering.

Nyx comes over and wraps an arm around her waist. "Come dance with me, babe."

Lexi bites on her lip and stares at me, her huge brown eyes wide and pleading.

"Go dance," I tell her. "I'll wait here for Toby and Mo."

It's MIDNIGHT, and it's time to go if I'm going to have enough energy to look after Gabriella tomorrow. Mo and Toby appear deep in conversation when I approach to let them know I'm about to leave.

Toby checks his watch. "Actually, I need to head out too. You need a ride?"

"Nah. I got my armed escorts." I gesture toward Henry and Ash who are standing about twenty feet away from me, where they've been all night. I'm so used to them now, I usually forget they're there.

"Of course you do," he says with a smile. "You mind if I grab a ride with you then? I won't need to bother my dad's driver."

"Sure. But what about you, Mo?" Lexi and Nyx left a half hour ago, and I don't want to leave her here alone.

She links her arm through Toby's. "I'll come too. You can drop me at home, right?" she asks me.

"Of course." I take her other arm and we walk out of the club with Henry and Ash.

When Henry pulls the car to the curb outside Mo's house, I tell her good night and lean over Toby, giving her a quick kiss.

"Night," she says, but then she focuses all her attention on Toby, and I smile to myself. The poor guy has no chance. "You wanna come in? I have beer and nachos."

"I really have to get home. I have an early thing tomorrow."

He shrugs, a sad expression on his face, like he really would rather stay here with her.

Mo's face falls. She's not used to being turned down. "Fine," she huffs. "Maybe next time?"

He nods agreeably. "Maybe."

Mo climbs out of the car, and we watch to make sure she's safely inside before Henry drives off.

Toby doesn't make any attempt to scoot into Mo's now-empty seat. Ash glances back at the two of us. "Your place, Toby?"

Toby looks at me and arches an eyebrow. "Um."

I offer a casual shrug. "I only have waffles."

"Now waffles I can get with." He laughs.

"Home then?" Ash asks me with a grin.

"Yes please." I settle back in my seat and turn my attention back to Toby. "So, tell me, are you home for good?"

TOBY AND I sit opposite each other at the huge wooden table in my kitchen, fresh waffles covered in syrup in front of us. "This reminds me of back in high school. We always had waffles after we snuck home from a party," he says, looking around the room. "This place has barely changed."

"Hmm." I wrinkle my nose. "It's the same and completely different."

"I was sorry to hear about your dad."

I feign a well-practiced smile. My father was a monster and my life is way better without him in it. But I don't tell Toby that. "Thanks," I say instead.

"You sure your brothers are going to be okay with me being here?" He glances at the door as though he half expects them to burst in here any second and break his arms and legs.

"Relax, Toby, we're just eating waffles."

"I know." He grins.

"It's so good to have you back. I missed you," I say honestly. He was such a good friend to me back in the day. And now that he's back in Chicago for good, it will be nice to spend time with him.

"I missed you too, Joey. Now, I've bored you with every single detail about my time at Berkeley, so you have to tell me what it was like going to school in Italy."

I roll my eyes. "You make it sound way more exciting than it was."

"I bet it was cool." He stuffs a piece of waffle into his mouth and syrup runs down his chin. He licks it off, staring at me like I'm the most fascinating person in the world as he waits for me to talk.

"Well, there was this one girl I really liked, Cherry. She was from England, but her parents sent her to St. Agatha's because she was such a handful. Some of the stuff she used to get us into ..." I snicker, remembering the time she caused a riot in the cafeteria just so we could sneak out and go to the beach.

Toby leans forward, arms resting on the table. "So, tell me."

CHAPTER
SIX

JOEY

"I forgot to mention Toby Fiore was back home. Did you and he have a chance to catch up?" Dante arches an eyebrow as he spears a strip of beef filet with a fork while balancing his daughter on his lap.

I resist rolling my eyes. "You know we did." I'm well aware that Ash and Henry inform my older brothers of almost every move I make. I've tried to stop letting it get to me and accept that it's an inescapable consequence of being a Moretti.

A slight frown furrows his brow. "Yes, I know he came here last night. I was just making conversation, Joey. I don't want details."

I wrinkle my nose. "There are no details to give. He's my friend, D."

"I wasn't suggesting ..." He sighs and shakes his head. "Where is this club you're going to tonight?"

"Downtown. It's new. They offered to put me and the girls on the guest list. We get a VIP booth and everything."

"Hmm." He narrows his eyes.

"What?" I set my silverware down, ready to argue my case if he starts pulling any of his sexist, overprotective bullshit.

"I don't like people using you for free publicity is all."

"Free publicity?" I frown.

"Yes."

"How am I free publicity?"

"You're Joey Moretti," he says, scowling. "Everyone in this city knows who you are. You think they gave you a free booth out of the goodness of their hearts?"

I shrug, unbothered. "Whatever the reason, it sounds like it'll be fun."

He closes his eyes and sucks in a breath that makes me wonder what he's thinking. I know he'd rather I stay home where he can keep a closer eye on me, but that's not the life I want to lead. "Henry and Ash will go with you."

"Of course."

"Is this going to be your life now? Partying and going out with your friends every night?"

"I go out two or three nights a week, Dante," I say with a sigh. "I'm twenty-two, it's what young people do."

"I know ..." Gabriella starts to fuss, and he bounces her on his knee. "But you could do so much more."

I lean forward in my chair. "Such as?"

"What do you want to do?"

Narrowing my eyes, I stare at him with suspicion. Is this a trick question? "I want to work in the family business."

I expect him to laugh at me, but he regards me with curiosity. "You do?"

"Yes."

"Okay." He takes another bite of his steak.

"What?" I blink at him. I must have slipped into an alternate universe.

"I said okay. Let me speak to Lorenzo and see where he thinks would be a good place for you to start. Unless you have an idea of what you'd like to do?"

"Are you serious?"

"Yes."

"Fuck me," I mutter.

"Don't curse in front of my daughter," he says with a slight frown.

"Sorry, but this is pretty epic, D. I mean, you've never once given me any indication that I could work with you and Lorenzo."

Dante shrugs. "Well, things are different now."

They sure as hell are! "I don't know where I'd like to start yet, but I'll think about it. And I'll consider your and Lorenzo's suggestions about it too." As much as they drive me crazy, my brothers *are* the family business, and they know it inside and out.

"Okay."

I lean on my elbow, watching him as he eats and smiles at his daughter. "Thank you, D."

He waves his hand dismissively, unaccustomed to my gratitude. "It's about time you did something to pay your way around here."

"Did Kat do something freaky to you before she left or something?"

"Joey!"

"I'm sorry, but you're in an exceptionally good mood." I laugh, and Gabriella giggles too, like she understands what I'm saying.

"I'm always in a good mood, aren't I, sunshine?" he says to his daughter, who squeals in response.

"D?" Max's voice drifts through the open doorway, and I smile to myself. Any day I get to see Max's fine ass is a good day.

"In here," Dante shouts, and a few seconds later, Max walks through the door, dressed in jeans and a shirt with rolled-up sleeves, looking way finer than any man ought to look. He eyes Dante's steak.

"You want some lunch?" my brother asks, nodding down at his plate.

"No. I already ate. I spoke to Dmitri last night, just wanted to give you an update."

I know Dmitri Varkov is in the middle of a takeover and that the man he's trying to oust is the same man my brothers pinned our father's murder on, but I'm not sure what Max and my brothers have to do with it. I lean forward in my seat, curious to know more.

Dante's brow furrows into a frown. "Give me fifteen minutes to put Gabriella down for her nap and then I'll meet you in my study."

I guess he isn't quite ready to involve me in *all* the family business just yet.

Dante leaves the room with my niece, leaving Max and I alone. He sits beside me and steals a slice of tomato from my plate. "How was your night out?"

"Fun."

He arches an eyebrow at me. "Fun?"

"Yes. You know what that is, right? Something people do when they have a life."

His eyes darken. I'd like to claim I have no idea why I enjoy pushing his buttons so much, but that would be a lie. I love to get a rise out of him. Seeing that thick vein bulge in his neck and his eyes turn so dark they smolder like coal makes butterflies swirl in my stomach.

"Who did you go out with?" His tone remains cool even as his eyes burn into my skin.

"Monique and Lexi. And Lexi's guy friend, Nyx."

He narrows his eyes.

I let out an exasperated sigh. "What?"

"Monique DeLuca is trouble, Joey."

"Yeah, you've been telling me that since I was fourteen, but guess what, Max? You don't get to tell me who I can be friends with."

He grunts in response.

"Most guys love Mo." Does he? He's never had much time for her, but does he avoid her because he secretly likes her?

He scoffs. "Most guys see her as an easy lay."

"Max!" I snap. "That's completely sexist."

"How is it sexist if it's the truth? She goes home with a different guy every single time you go out."

"How do you know? You been keeping an eye on her? Wishing it was you she'd go home with instead?" How the hell does he know who Mo goes home with? And why does he care?

"Don't be ridiculous. Mo?" He snorts.

"You don't like her?"

He stares into my eyes when he answers. "Not even a little."

"You know she'd fuck you just to mess with me though?"

"Yes."

"Because you and I are friends," I add quickly, my cheeks flushing pink.

"Of course." The corners of his eyes crinkle as he fights back a smile. Asshole. "And doesn't that tell you all you need to know about the kind of friend she is?"

I want to roll my eyes so bad right now. I hate when he's right. "Anyway, Mo didn't go home with a guy last night."

"Well, there's a first time for everything."

"I did though."

His expression darkens, and I feel the heat from his gaze in the very pit of my stomach. Wow!

"You didn't. Henry and Ash wouldn't have let you go home with some guy," he says with a snarl.

How do you know that, Max? Why are you so interested in me going home with a guy? "Well, no. He came here instead." I shrug casually.

"Who?"

"Toby Fiore."

"Michael's son?"

"Yeah. I haven't seen him since high school, so he came back here and ..." I don't finish the sentence because I'm having way too much fun watching the vein pulse in his neck. What I wouldn't give to run my tongue along it and taste his skin.

"And what?" he demands. The deep, commanding timbre of his voice rumbles through my bones and goes straight between my legs. I squeeze my thighs together to give myself relief from the throbbing ache building in my pussy.

"We ate waffles and talked about our time away at college."

"You ate waffles and talked?"

"Yes. You think he'd try anything else?" I laugh. "He probably thought there were cameras watching his every move."

His dark eyes narrow, his intense stare making me feel like I'm seconds away from melting into a puddle in this chair. "Did you want him to try something?"

I probably shouldn't answer that, but beneath all the weird ass tension between us, Max is kind of my best friend. "Not last night, no. But that doesn't mean never. He is kind of cute," I say truthfully.

Max doesn't reply. He goes on staring at me, his jaw ticking. And now I don't want him thinking about me and Toby. It feels too weird. "Anyway, I'm not sure he even likes me." That's a lie, but maybe he'll buy it. "I invited him to that new club opening downtown tonight, but he said he's busy."

"Well, maybe he is. He just started working for his dad."

Toby's dad is Michael Fiore and he's been our family's accountant forever. "What accountant works on a Saturday night?"

"Your brothers' accountant works when he's told to, Joey," he says with a smile.

"I guess."

"So, this club?"

"Killers." I wiggle my eyebrows at him.

"Ah yeah. It used to be called Mika's back when Dante and I went there. But I know the new owners."

I roll my eyes. "Of course you do."

He leans forward, and I catch the scent of him, cologne and fresh air and sex. Damn, he is the finest man to ever walk this earth. "One of these days, you're going to regret rolling those eyes at me, Joey," he says with a dark chuckle. Then he takes another slice of tomato from my plate, pops it into his mouth, and strolls out of the room.

SEVEN

MAX

Anger bubbles beneath my skin and the ache in my forearms reminds me to unclench my fists. I have no fucking right at all to be pissed about who Joey spends time with, but I want to cut that little fucker Toby's throat with a rusty hacksaw.

"Hey." Dante walks up beside me. "Everything okay?"

"Hmm," I mumble as we head to his study together.

When we're both seated in his office, he eyes me with concern. "So, Dmitri?"

"He still hasn't found Pushkin, and although he assures me he's doing all he can—"

"It's not enough," Dante says, pinching the bridge of his nose.

"He knows that. I told him as much last night."

"We need him found, Max, before ..." he shakes his head in annoyance.

"He's kept your father's name out of it. He alerted the other families to what Pushkin was doing without implicating Sal in any way. Nobody's going to find out, D."

Dante nods, but worry etches his brow.

"We'll take care of it," I assure him. "And if Dmitri hasn't found Pushkin by the end of the month, then I'll just fucking find him myself."

"No. I need you here. Lorenzo needs us."

"I know." I nod in agreement. Lorenzo is spending as much time as he can with his sick wife right now.

Dante sits straighter in his chair, running a hand over his beard. "Besides, this is a Bratva problem. That was the whole fucking point of pinning my father's murder on Pushkin and backing Dmitri, so he could sort this mess out for us."

"Maybe he just needs a timely reminder of who he's dealing with?" I suggest, and not only because I believe that's true, but also because I need to do something with all this pent-up rage bubbling inside me. I could happily tear someone's head off their shoulders right about now.

Dante stands and grabs his suit jacket. "You're right. I think we should pay our friend a visit."

"You know Toby Fiore was at your house last night? With Joey?"

Dante's driving, but he takes his eyes off the road for a second to give me a wry look. "Of course I do."

"And you're okay with that?"

"They were eating waffles in the kitchen, Max. What do you expect me not to be okay with?"

"It starts with waffles in the kitchen." I say with a frown. The image of her sitting with him—laughing, flirting, smiling —burns an imprint in my brain. Did he touch her? Kiss her? She said he didn't, but would she tell me?

"And it goes where?" He laughs. "As she reminds us almost

every damn day, she's an adult. She's going to date, Max, and Toby is ..."

"He's what?" I scowl at him. Toby Fiore is an asshole. And he's nowhere near good enough for Joey Moretti.

"He comes from a good, loyal family. He's the same age as her. He's got brains. He's respectful. From what Ash said, he didn't make any moves. They're friends."

"So, you'd be happy with your sister dating him?"

He frowns at me. "He's not the worst guy she could date, Max. Actually, I think he could be good for her."

I grind my teeth together and keep my mouth shut. If I disagree with him, he might see right through me.

Dmitri's surprised to see us when we pull up at the gates of his house, but he welcomes us inside. A few moments later, we're seated opposite him and his younger brother, Kyzen, in the study.

"I wasn't expecting you, Dante," Dmitri says with a frown. "Is something wrong?"

"Just want to know where things are at with your former boss," Dante replies.

Dmitri glances at me before he looks back to Dante. "As I told Maximo last night, it is proving more difficult than I'd hoped to find Pushkin. He has a lot of friends."

"Even after everything they've found out about what he was involved in?"

"The tide is turning against him, slowly. People have accepted that I've taken over, but Pushkin has many allies. He was their leader for over twenty years," he reminds us in his slight Russian accent.

"It's turning too slowly," Dante says.

"We are doing everything we can," Kyzen pipes up.

"Did I fucking ask your opinion?" Dante asks, a deep scowl furrowing his brow.

"We can only work with what we know," Dmitri interrupts, shooting his brother a warning glance. He's always been much more levelheaded than his younger sibling. "I promise you that we will deliver him to you soon. Everyone knows he is the man in the frame for killing your father," he says pointedly.

Dmitri doesn't know Dante murdered his own father, but I suspect he knows that Pushkin didn't do it either. The two men were in business together for years. Still, he's never pushed for more of an explanation than the one Dante gave him months ago. He was already preparing to orchestrate the takeover and having the Morettis' backing to do so escalated and fortified his plans.

"And this is why I can't sit back while you chase your fucking tail trying to find him, Dmitri," Dante snaps. "I cannot put my father's death to rest until we have vengeance on the man who killed him." Dante and Lorenzo have played the dutiful role of mourning sons perfectly and managed to convince the entire world that Pushkin killed Sal, but there's only so long his death can appear to go unpunished.

"I understand," Dmitri says with a solemn nod. "But I swear to you that I am doing all I can."

"Do more," Dante says calmly, but the threat in his tone is implicit.

"It would be a hell of a lot easier if we could have blown the whole trafficking ring wide open from the start," Kyzen retorts. "But instead we had to protect your family name."

Dante turns in his seat, but he doesn't have time to respond before I'm on my feet. I grab Kyzen by the throat, pull him up, and squeeze until he struggles to breathe.

Dmitri stands too, but Dante signals him to sit his ass back down and he does.

"You ever speak to Mr. Moretti like that again, you piece of shit, your brother will be cleaning your tongue off his carpet. You got that?"

He glares at me even as his face turns purple, but he nods his understanding, and I drop him back into his seat.

"We've been friends for a long time, Dmitri," Dante reminds him. "There's no reason to waste this opportunity to strengthen our alliance, but if you don't deliver some results soon, I'll be forced to take matters into my own hands."

Dmitri bristles. He knows that could make him look weak after he openly challenged Pushkin for leadership. "I will find him."

"See that you do." Dante stands, and I follow him out of the study. There's nothing left to say.

"You going to stick around when we get back to the house?" he asks me as we reach his car.

"I wasn't planning on it." I promised Kristin I'd do more to look for her father today.

"I haven't seen much of you this past week."

"I know. The new casino deal is keeping me busy." That isn't a complete lie. We're in the process of buying our own casino, and it's occupied a fair bit of my time, partly because the current owners, Ralf and Micah Strauss, are resistant to selling outright. They want to form a partnership, but that shit isn't gonna happen.

"It should settle down soon," he says, opening the car door. "I got a Skype meeting with Ralf later tonight to discuss final terms. Until then, you just keep putting the pressure on where you can."

"Gladly." I'm happy to put pressure on anyone at any time if it might help relieve some of the tension that's plagued me lately.

~

I press my boot against the neck of the man on the ground until his cries for mercy are cut off by his desperate gasps for breath. I train my eyes on the man in front of me instead—the one who's currently pissing his pants—and wrap a hand around his throat.

"Do not make me ask you again, fuckface. When was the last time you saw Vito DiMarco?"

Tears run down his cheeks. Pathetic asshole. "I-I don't know any Vito—" I squeeze harder and he wheezes. He's lying. Kristin gave me his name. Or at least the nickname he goes by —Monty. She told me he was from Chicago but used to occasionally visit them in New Jersey. A little digging led me to this guy—a lawyer named Montgomery Lincoln; he's married with four kids but has a penchant for men with tattoos and shaved heads. Much like the one writhing beneath my boot.

"If you lie to me again, I will snap your friend's neck and then you'll have a hell of a job explaining his naked corpse to your wife when she gets home. Now tell me when you saw Vito."

"I-it w-was over a year ago."

"Where?"

"New Jersey. At his house." He glances down at his lover who's turned a mottled shade of dark purple beneath my boot. Loverboy is running out of time, and Monty knows it. "I don't have it. I swear. I don't even know where it is."

Now I'm getting somewhere. "Have what?"

"The recording. Isn't that what you're looking for?"

What fucking recording? "Who does have it?"

"Vito. He keeps it in a safe in a storage locker somewhere. I don't even know where. If anything happens to him and he doesn't check in with the storage company on the first of every month, they send it to me. That's the deal."

"And then you?"

"I send it to the press."

"The press? Not the police?"

He wheezes, and I decrease the pressure on his throat. "Vito said the police would bury it. The guy on the recording is a big deal."

"What is on the recording, Monty? And you got about forty-five seconds before his neck snaps under my foot."

"A murder," he blurts out, glancing at his lover and then back at me. "I don't know who's on it though, I swear."

I lift my boot off the throat of the man on the floor. "Do not fucking move," I warn him.

He rubs at his raw skin and nods his understanding.

"So Vito has evidence of a murder. But you don't know who it involves?"

"No. I swear to you. He said it was safer if I didn't know. I just know the guy involved is big. I was just going to be the middleman."

"You know who the victim is?"

"No."

"Was Vito blackmailing this guy? The killer?"

"No. Well, not for money. To keep his family safe."

I let go of Monty's neck and push him back on the bed. "You have any idea at all who's on that recording?"

"Given who Vito is and who his brother worked for, my best guess would be a Moretti."

Who his brother worked for. The reminder of my father feels like a punch to my gut.

"His brother has been dead for eighteen years. Vito left Chicago before that. How long has he been sitting on this recording?"

"Ten or eleven years."

"Why do you think it has something to do with the Morettis?"

"Because he was in Chicago the night it happened and there was nobody bigger in this city than Salvatore Moretti. And now his sons too." Monty shudders. It's obvious he has no idea who I am. "Do you work for them? Is that why you're looking for the recording? Have they found out? Have they taken him?"

I shake my head. So many questions. I should just shoot Monty and his naked lover right now. Let his wife come home and find the pair of them in each other's arms. "No. I don't work for the Morettis. How are you involved in this?"

"I used to be Vito's lawyer. He came to me that night. Rambling about how he was going to show his nephew who the real traitor was."

"His nephew?"

Monty nods.

Me.

Monty Lincoln just bought himself and his buddy a reprieve.

"If that recording ever finds its way to you, you contact me and only me. You got that?"

"I d-don't have your number," he stammers. "Or your name,"

"I have yours. I'll send you a number you can reach me on later. Someone has taken Vito, and right now you're the only man I know who can help me. But if that recording ends up in the press, Monty"—I take a threatening step forward—"I will make you watch while I murder your wife. Then I will carve out your heart while it's still beating and feed it to your orphan children for dinner. You understand me?"

His face turns gray, and he puts a hand over his mouth, gagging. "You ... you won't tell her about this, will you?" He looks at the guy on the floor.

"I have no interest in the fact that you're fucking around behind your wife's back, but I am *very* interested in anything to do with Vito DiMarco. That's all you need to be concerned about right now."

I walk out, leaving Monty to help his friend off the floor. I have more questions now than I did when I got here, and I'm wound tighter than I was a few hours ago.

What the fuck is on that video? Why did Uncle Vito tell Monty he wanted to show me who the real traitor was? And how could my uncle possibly think he isn't the traitor to the DiMarco name when he screwed around with his brother's wife and then fucked off to New Jersey when shit got hard? Vito was always good at blaming other people for his failings. Salvatore Moretti might have been a cruel and twisted piece of shit, but he always had my back when I needed him.

Walking to my bike, I dial Kristin.

She answers on the first ring.

"Hey, how are you doing?"

"Good, I guess," she says. "Did you find out anything about my dad yet?"

"Maybe. Do you know anything about a storage locker he has?"

"No. Why?"

"Did he ever mention a video recording of someone?"

"No, Max. Is that why someone took him? A recording?"

"I don't know. I'm still looking into it." I sigh, scrubbing a hand through my hair.

"When will you be home?"

I shake my head. I'm too wired and pumped up to go home right now. I need to do something about all the rage burning up inside of me before I explode. And I need to see *her*. I can't get her out of my fucking head.

"I'll be a few more hours yet. Don't wait up for me, okay?"

She sighs. "Okay."

"You're safe there, Kristin," I remind her.

"I know."

"I'll see you in the morning."

"Bye, Max."

EIGHT

MAX

When I get to the new club downtown half an hour later, Henry and Ash are positioned near the entrance, their eyes trained on Joey. I follow their gaze to where she stands with two other girls and a group of older guys. Way older guys.

"Who the fuck are they?" I ask as I approach.

Henry keeps his eyes on Joey while Ash turns to me. "No idea, Boss. Look like city types. They've been talking to the girls for about a half hour now. Bought them a few drinks."

"Have either of you spoken to Joey?" They're supposed to keep their distance when she's out with her friends, but I like them to actually check in with her at least once every few hours.

Henry nods. "I checked in on her about ten minutes ago. She said she was fine and having a good time."

"Hmm." I chew on my lip and watch her. One of the guys leans close and whispers something in her ear that makes her laugh. His hand dusts over her hip and my chest tightens. "You two can finish up."

"You sure, boss?" Ash asks.

"Yeah. I can take it from here."

"You wanna go grab a bite?" Henry asks his buddy.

Ash agrees and they head out, leaving me to stand alone at the bar and watch my girl. Too busy having fun with her friends and flirting with the guys who are old enough to be her father, she doesn't look over and notice that her security detail has changed. I glare at the one who keeps touching her—brushing her arm, bumping her hip when he talks to her, resting his hand on her shoulder. He's at least twenty years older than her, and he's going to lose that fucking hand if he puts it on her one more time.

"You here alone?" a soft voice says, giggling in my ear. I turn my head and find Monique standing beside me.

"Hey, Mo," I give her a disinterested nod and return my attention to Joey and the piece of shit who's practically salivating over her. She smiles at him, and he cups her chin in his hand. Does this jackass actually think he gets to kiss her?

Monique puts her hand on my arm. "You want a drink?"

"Nope. I'm working."

"Are you Joey's bodyguard for this evening then?" she whispers, her lips close to my ear.

I shrug her off. "What do you want, Monique? Shouldn't you be over there with Joey having fun?"

"Nah. Those douchebags she and the girls are talking to are assholes."

Well, at least we can agree on that. "Who's that other girl? I've never seen her before."

"That's Amy," Monique says with a dramatic sigh. "Lexi invited her out. They went to college together. You want a mint?" She takes a small tin out of her purse.

"Is that your pickup line?" I ask her with a smirk, keeping one eye on Joey and the douchebags.

She laughs, then holds the breath mints in front of my face. The design catches my attention, and I take the tin from her, studying it. *Elena's Erotic Arena* is printed on the top of the lid in neon pink.

"What the hell have you been doing at a sex club in Racine?"

She opens her mouth and then closes it again in an incredibly rare display of being lost for words. Her cheeks turn bright red. "I w-wasn't. My boyfriend lives above the place." She snatches the tin out of my hand and shoves it back in her purse.

She disappears into the crowd, and I roll my eyes. I don't give a fuck if she visits a sex club. As long as she doesn't take Joey with her anyway. Speaking of ... I turn my attention back to Joey and almost lose my shit when I see that asshole put his hand on her fucking ass and squeeze it. I barge through the crowd until I'm standing right behind him. Joey sees me first and her eyes widen. All the while, that fucker's hand stays on her ass. My fucking ass.

Grabbing him by the hair, I yank his head back and grab his wrist, twisting his arm behind his back until I feel the satisfying pop of his shoulder dislocating. His agonized scream makes me grin menacingly. I shove him and he drops to the floor.

"Max!" Joey reprimands while his two friends come at me.

"You really want some too?" I say with a snarl as they hold their fists up like they have a snowball's chance in hell of landing a punch.

They look at me and then at each other before they crouch down and help their friend instead.

"What the fuck, dude?" one of them says as the fucker struggles to sit up, his arm dangling at an unnatural angle.

"Any of you ever touch her again, and I will tear every one of your limbs from your fucking bodies and wrap them around your throats."

"What the hell are you doing?" Joey shrieks as bar security surrounds us. They all know me—or know *of* me—so they focus on the asshole and his two buddies rather than me.

I grab Joey by the arm. "Say goodnight to your friends. You're leaving."

She opens her mouth to argue, and I glare at her. I guess she recognizes the look in my eyes because she rolls hers and says goodnight to her friends, who stare at me with an equal measure of wariness and amusement. Marching Joey through the crowd and out the back exit, I feel the rage vibrating through her body.

We step into the cool night air, and as soon as I release my grip on her, she spins on her heel and slaps me across the face so hard that I bite my lip. Running my tongue over the inside of my mouth, I taste blood. *Brat!*

"What the hell was that?" she shouts.

"He was old enough to be your father."

Her beautiful face twists into a scowl. "So? He was just talking to me."

"He was holding onto your fucking ass like it was his personal property."

She folds her arms across her chest. "You are unbelievable, you know that? I was just having a little fun. It was harmless."

"It's not harmless when he wants some sort of payback for the drinks he's been buying you, because that's what guys like him are about, Joey. It's not harmless when he's trying to get you back to his place for a quick—" I rake my hands through my hair. She's too distracting and I've said too much already.

"A quick what, Max? A quick fuck?"

Her sneer shreds the last sliver of restraint I have. I push her against the wall, making her gasp as I press my body against hers, flattening her next to the cool brick. She stares up at me with those huge brown eyes, rough breaths fluttering against her full pink lips. My cock strains against the zipper of my jeans. I know she can feel me. She rocks her hips, grinding herself on me. Before I can think through the consequences of what I'm doing, I wrap a hand around her throat. "You want to be fucked, Joey? Is that it?"

Her breath catches. Her beautiful tits shudder against my chest. "You're too afraid of my brothers to fuck me."

"You think?" My free hand coasts down her body, over her ribs and the curve of her hip, making her shiver.

Her dark eyes burn into mine. "Yeah."

I grip the edge of her short dress and she lets out the softest and sexiest little moan I've ever heard in my entire goddamn life. Yanking it up, I push my hand between her thighs and brush my fingertips over the tiny scrap of fabric covering her pussy. It's damp. And I am fucking done for. I squeeze her throat a little harder. "Are you wet?"

"Yes."

"Why? Because that jackass was touching you?"

"What do you care?" she snaps, and her smart mouth makes my cock throb.

Curling the tips of my fingers around the soft material, I tug her panties aside and gently caress her bare pussy. It's so fucking smooth. Either freshly shaved or waxed—like she really was looking to get fucked tonight. "Or is it because I'm touching you?"

"Fuck you," she spits.

Blood thunders in my ears. I shouldn't do this. Not with her. I should go back inside the bar and do this with someone, anyone, other than Joey Moretti.

"You want me to, huh?" I taunt, dusting the pads of my fingers over her swollen clit.

She groans, rocking her hips for more friction. "You wouldn't dare."

I press my forehead against hers. One hand still wrapped around her slender neck, I slide two fingers between her folds, biting my lip to stifle the groan that rumbles through my chest. She feels like hot liquid silk.

"Oh, fuck," she whimpers.

"You like that?"

"Y-yeah."

Slipping my hand farther into her panties, I circle her entrance and her entire body quivers. When I push a finger inside her, her back bows off the wall and she cries out into the darkness. Her pussy squeezes me, snug and hot.

"You're gonna have to be a little quieter, baby girl, or someone might hear us."

I know this club. Nobody has access to this alleyway unless they come through the fire exit we just came out of, and the bouncers wouldn't dare come out here after me. Still, I don't want to draw any attention to our illicit activities.

She sinks her perfect white teeth into the plump bow of her lip and gives me a faint nod.

"You're so fucking tight, Joey," I groan as I work my finger a little deeper.

"Do you always talk this much?" She raises her eyebrows in a challenge, wrapping her arms around my neck. "I knew you didn't have the balls to fuck me."

Spoiled little brat. I squeeze her throat a little tighter as I pull my finger out of her and unfasten my belt and zipper. "So, you just want to be fucked, is that it?"

Her eyes flash with heat. "Do you have a condom?"

"Nope." I shake my head. "Do you?"

Her throat constricts as she swallows. "In my purse." She glances down at the small square of leather that rests against her hip.

That pisses me off even though I should be proud of her for being responsible, but nothing I feel about this girl is rational. "I guess you'd better get it then."

She hesitates, making me frown. "I'm on birth control, Max," she whispers. "And I trust you. If we don't need one, then that's okay."

Holy fucking fuck! I guess if I get to fuck her just this once, I should feel her the way nature intended. "I always wear them, Joey. I'm clean."

"So am I."

With my cock in one hand and the other wrapped around her slender throat, I lose all sense of logic and reason. "Wrap your legs around me," I command.

Uncharacteristically for Joey Moretti, she does as she's told, holding onto my shoulders and wrapping her long legs around my waist until the crown of my cock is positioned at her entrance. Her breath hitches as she stares into my eyes. Waiting for me to fuck her. My cock throbs, desperate to feel her around me. I slide in just a little, forced to go slower and gentler than I intended because she's so fucking tight.

"Max," she hisses, her eyes fluttering closed as I stretch her open. Her molten, silky heat squeezes me tight, causing all the blood in my body to rush south.

I pull almost all the way out. The tip of my cock is slick with her arousal, making it a little easier to push back in again, but it's still a struggle. I'm a big guy and I have six piercings, five along my shaft and one in the crown. It's a lot to fit inside a tight pussy and this isn't the ideal place to fuck. It would be so much easier if I could lay her down somewhere and spread her wide open. Then I would sink inside her to the hilt.

I brush my lips over her skin, sliding my free hand to her ass and pulling her leg higher to get a better angle. "Let me inside you, baby girl."

"I'm trying," she whimpers, but she shifts the angle of her hips, which allows me to push deeper.

"Good girl," I grunt, lips pressed against her ear.

Her pussy muscles clamp around my cock in response, squeezing me tight as she moans my name. So, my spoiled little brat has a praise kink.

"You're so fucking wet, Joey. You like my cock in you?" I growl, even though I can barely get halfway inside her tight little cunt.

Wet heat slicks over me as she whimpers and mewls.

I run my nose along her neck. She smells so good, a mix of cotton candy-scented perfume and hot, fresh sweat mingled with the scent of sweet cum dripping from her pussy. My mouth finds hers, and I lick her plump lips. She opens them on a soft moan, allowing me to slip my tongue inside and taste her. I'll certainly regret this later because she tastes sweeter than anything I've ever experienced. Decadent and sinful. I tongue fuck her mouth, claiming it for my own as I claim her pussy, swallowing every whimper and moan that I wring from her incredible body.

Sliding my hand between our bodies, I find her swollen clit and rub it firmly as I pick up my pace, driving my hips and managing to sink deeper with each thrust. I'm feral with the need to get as far inside her as possible, but I still can't get all the way in.

I rock my hips, setting as punishing a pace as I can. She winces every time I manage to dip a little deeper, but her pussy grows slicker and looser with each thrust. Her legs begin to shake, her breaths growing faster and harder as her walls squeeze me tight. My girl is on the edge. I break our kiss and she pants for air.

"Oh fuck, Max."

"That's it, baby girl. Come hard for me. I want to feel you on my cock."

Her eyes roll back in her head and her skin flushes with heat and pleasure as she lets go for me. Legs trembling and breathing ragged, she drops her head onto my shoulder while I fuck her through her climax. Her wet pussy flutters, milking my cock, and when she sinks her nails into my shoulder muscles a few seconds later, I drive into her one last time, groaning her name as I grind out my own orgasm.

"Fuck, Max, that was ... intense."

I hum my agreement, unable to speak because I'm breathing so hard. Sliding out of her, I look down and the sight of my blood-streaked cock knocks the remaining breath from my lungs.

My hand is still wrapped around her throat, and I tilt her head upward until her dark eyes meet mine. "Joey, please tell me you're expecting your period."

Her brow knits into a frown. "What? No, why?"

I release my grip on her neck and lower her legs to the ground before I look down again, hoping this time my dick won't be covered with what I think it is. "You're bleeding."

"It's okay. That happens the first time, right?"

Holy fuck, I'm going straight to hell. "Please tell me I didn't just take your virginity behind a dumpster in an alleyway?" I plead.

"I could tell you that, but I'd be lying." She drags her bottom lip through her teeth and blinks up at me, her face so full of fucking innocence while her body is all sex and sin.

"Fuck, Joey," I snap, my tone sharper than intended as I tuck my bloodstained cock back into my jeans.

"I-I thought you knew," she whispers, hurt flashing in her eyes.

I brush her hair back from her face. "Of course I didn't know. If I had, I never would have ..." I shake my head and sigh, sliding my hand to possessively palm the back of her neck.

"You would never have what?" She gives me a defiant glare

as she fixes her dress, but I don't miss the tremor in her voice or the slight tremble of her bottom lip.

I would have taken you to bed and fucked you properly. "I would have made sure it was a little more memorable, baby girl. I wouldn't have been so rough with you if I'd known you'd never ..." I pinch the bridge of my nose.

"It was pretty memorable to me," she whispers.

"How is it even possible, Joey? How can you be a virgin?"

"Seriously, Max? The girl who can't breathe without someone watching over her? When exactly would I have found the time to have sex, let alone find someone crazy enough to risk my brother's wrath?"

I guess she has a point. "But I thought ... maybe in Italy?"

She lets out a sarcastic laugh. "In the convent school? Where Lorenzo had me locked down tighter than a prisoner in a maximum-security facility? Oh yeah, plenty of opportunity to get my rocks off there."

My cell vibrates in my pocket, interrupting our conversation. I take it out and frown at the screen, and for the first time in my life, I ignore Dante's call. "I need to get you home."

She rolls her eyes. "Of course you do."

We wind through the streets of Chicago, Joey straddling the bike behind me, her arms wrapped tightly around my waist. If I had the choice, I'd drive as slowly as possible. In fact, I'd prefer to not take her home at all. But no doubt her brothers have learned that I dismissed Henry and Ash and want to know where she is, especially since I didn't take Dante's call. So instead, I drive full throttle, her thighs gripping my hips.

CHAPTER
NINE

MAX

We pull into the driveway of her family's gated mansion, and Joey climbs off my bike, handing me her helmet. Her face is unreadable. We should talk about what just happened. I should take care of her. I just took her virginity in a dark alleyway next to a dumpster. I should be fucking ashamed of myself—so why aren't I? Why is my cock hard at the thought of how good she felt? How wet she was for me. How fucking incredible she smells.

"Night," she says coolly, then spins around on her heel and strides away. Her ass sways seductively as she walks into the house, reminding me that she was never mine to touch and she never will be.

I look down at the floor and every muscle in my body screams for release. I need to beat the shit out of someone. Or fuck her until neither of us can walk.

"I thought you were heading home earlier?" Dante asks, snapping me from my thoughts.

I look up to see him standing in the doorway, watching me intently with his hands stuffed in his pockets. Can he see what I've just done? Does he know simply by looking at me?

"You coming in for a quick drink?" he asks.

I take off my helmet and kill the engine. "Sure."

"Everything okay with Ash and Henry?" he asks as we walk down the hallway to his study.

"Yeah." I glance around, wondering where Joey went. Straight for a shower so she can wash me off her body?

"Max?" Dante says and I realize he's been talking to me.

"What?" I blink at him.

He frowns. "I asked why you brought Joey home."

I shrug. "I called to check in with the guys. Joey was ready to leave so I offered to bring her home."

"You spoil her," he says with a soft laugh. He assumes she asked me to bring her home, which has happened before. Joey loves my bike. "You never could say no to her."

I force out a laugh. *If he only fucking knew.*

Dante sips his Scotch while we discuss our Russian friends and the recent change of Bratva leadership.

He checks his watch and mutters, "Fuck." With a shrug, he gives me a small smile. "Kat will be wondering where I am."

"No worries, D. Can't keep the wife waiting. We'll talk more tomorrow." I can't help but grin, amazed at how much he's changed since he met his wife. I never thought I'd see Dante Moretti bow to the whims and desires of a woman. His world begins and ends with Kat and Gabriella, and I've never seen him so happy and fulfilled.

Dante downs the last of his Scotch and stands up, heading toward the door.

I get up to follow him but stop. "Hey, you mind if I go check on Joey?"

He turns and frowns at me over his shoulder. "Why, something happen tonight?"

"No. Nothing really, something to do with one of her girl-friends, but I kind of snapped at her." I shrug, the lie falling easily from my tongue. *How long will it take for him to see through me?*

Dante laughs softly, shaking his head at me. "I'm sure she'll forgive you."

"Yeah, you're probably right. But I'll check on her anyway."

We part ways in the hallway, him going toward his bedroom while I go to look for his sister. I don't find her in the kitchen or den, so she must be in her bedroom. I knock on her door.

"What is it? I'm in bed," she shouts.

"It's me. Can I come in?"

The answering silence is almost too long for me to handle before she finally answers. "Sure."

Walking inside, I close the door behind me. She's lying on the bed, still dressed in her clothes from earlier. Still smelling of me.

"What is it, Max?" she asks, sighing.

"You don't think we need to talk about earlier?"

She crosses her arms over her chest. "I think you said all you had to say."

"I barely said anything, baby girl." I lie beside her on the bed and can hardly resist the temptation to run my hand over the bare skin of her arm.

"You said enough about regretting what happened," she says, and I hear a sob catch in her throat.

How could she think that? Fuck! How could I have let her think that? I prop myself up on my elbow so I can study her beautiful face. "I regret that I didn't know it was your first time."

"Yeah, it was pretty unmemorable, right? You said that too." She swats a tear from her cheek and glares at me.

I clench my hand into a fist, seconds away from flipping her onto her stomach and spanking her ass until she stops being such a brat.

I huff a sigh. "Joey."

"Just get out, Max," she says with a sniff. "There's nothing more to say."

She gasps when I roll on top of her, her perfect tits shuddering against my chest as I take her wrists and pin them above her head. "Fucking you against a building in that alley was incredible. I will remember your tight virgin cunt squeezing my cock for the rest of my days. But I meant I should have made it more memorable for you, baby girl."

She blinks at me, her dark brown eyes so full of emotion and longing that it makes me feel like the world's biggest jackass for playing with her heart like this—for giving her false hope that whatever this is between us can go any further. She pretends to be this tough-as-nails Mafia princess, but I see who she really is beneath the veneer of sarcasm and sass. "It was incredible for me too, Max. I'm glad you were my first."

I want to be your fucking last too. I run my nose over the soft skin of her throat and inhale her scent. She smells of perfume and fresh air and sex—and me. "Why didn't you shower when you got home?"

"I like having you inside me."

My cock stiffens. "Fuck, Joey. You're going to get me killed," I murmur against her skin. "I should have taken you home to my bed."

"I wish you could, Max," she breathes. "Tell me what you'd do to me."

I drag my teeth over her smooth flesh, making her shiver. I should leave right now. No good can come from me telling her this shit, so why can't I fucking stop myself from answering? "I would strip you bare and kiss every fucking inch of your skin. Then I'd spread your legs wide ..."

Her breath catches in her throat, and it makes my cock harder.

"And I'd eat your pussy. I'd bury my face in your sweet cunt until I made you come so hard your juices would be running over my tongue."

"Max," she groans, wrapping her legs around my waist and rocking her hips against me.

"And then the real fun would begin."

"Yeah?" She continues to work her hips, chasing the friction of my cock against her clit.

"I'd slip my fingers into you. One at first, because you're so fucking tight. And when you were whimpering and begging for more, I'd add another, fucking you with them until I could make you ready for my cock. I'd bring you to the edge, baby, over and over again without getting you off."

"Monster," she hisses as she digs her heels into my ass, pulling me closer until she's full-on dry humping me.

"You know I am," I say, trailing my lips over her throat, desperate to sink my teeth into her perfect flesh and mark her as mine. "And only when you were begging me for my cock, desperate for me to fill you up, that's when I'd sink into you. Not just half like you had earlier, but all the way. Balls deep, baby girl."

"That was only half before?" she says, panting.

"Yep." I laugh, releasing her wrists so she can wrap her arms around me.

"Max, please?" She clings to me, grinding her pussy against me as she chases her orgasm.

"I can't. I'm not going to fuck you in your brothers' house. I'm not going to make you come either, baby. But if you want to keep grinding on my cock until you get yourself off, well I guess there's not a lot I can do about that, is there?"

"Please? Nobody will know."

"I'll know," I remind her. Dante and Lorenzo are like brothers to me, and my mouth fills with the bitter taste of guilt.

MAX

Still, despite the guilt, I can't bring myself to get up and leave. Not while I have Joey's thighs wrapped around me and my cock is damn near busting through the zipper of my jeans.

"Then take me home, Max. Take me anywhere but here." She whimpers, and her eyes squeeze shut as she presses her head against the pillow. She's almost there.

Holding still, I let her use me to grind out her release. "I can't, baby." I place my hand over her mouth, stifling her soft moans as she comes apart in my arms. She shudders through her climax, her body radiating heat. And when she looks up at me through lust-glazed, hooded eyes, it takes every single bit of willpower I possess to stop myself from tearing off her panties and burying my cock inside her.

"Why not?" She blinks at me, her eyes wet with unshed tears. Fuck, she's far too young and innocent for me. I'll go straight to hell for even touching her, but I can't shake off the belief that is burned into my mind—into my soul. Joey Moretti is mine. She has always been mine.

I dust my knuckles over her cheeks. "My kind of love isn't the type you're looking for, Joey. You deserve so much more."

She narrows her beautiful eyes at me. "Who said anything about love?"

"You think that we could just be about sex? With a history like ours? I've known you your whole life. I've loved you for most of it. You think I would stop just because we were fucking?"

Tears spill over her cheeks and she swats them away. "That's a whole different kind of love you're talking about."

"Is it?"

She ignores the question, her body tensing under me. "Why do you get to tell me what I deserve? I choose my own life, Max. Don't you dare try to tell me this is for my own good." Her cheeks are flushed with outrage. She hates being treated like a

64

child, but that's not what this is. She has no idea what she's asking for. If I took her to my bed right now, I'd never let her leave.

"You make your own choices, Joey, but I can't be one of them. I'm sorry, baby." I kiss a tear that rolls down her cheek before I climb off the bed and walk out of her bedroom.

I hate that I'm hurting her like this, but better she suffers a little pain right now than a whole fuckload of it later on. Better that she never has to deal with the man I really am.

Because if I ever hurt her for real, I wouldn't be able to live with myself.

TEN

JOEY

Damn Max DiMarco!

Who the hell does he think he is, fucking me the way he did and then telling me we can't do it again? Then telling me he loves me! Of course he does, but not the way I want him to. What the actual fuck? Asshole!

I guess I should've told him I was a virgin, but then he probably wouldn't have touched me at all. It's one thing to have a quick fuck with your best friends' kid sister, but to take her virginity ... No way Max would have gone for it if he knew. He's too damn principled. Gah! Trust me to fall for a man who thinks nothing of cutting out people's eyeballs on a daily basis but draws the line at dating his buddies' sister.

I close my eyes and I'm right back in that alley. With Max's hands on me. Calling me baby girl. Squeezing my throat. Tugging my panties aside and touching me. I've gotten myself off plenty of times before but never has my body responded the way it did to his touch. The climax that man wrung from my body was nothing short of life altering. The fresh memory makes heat sear between my thighs, and I squeeze them together. I feel sore and tender, but not uncomfortably so. It's actually kind of comforting in a way—a reminder of what we did. A reminder that I'm no longer a virgin and that the man who took it from me is the same guy I fantasized about for the past six years. A man I thought would never ever go there with me.

A smile spreads across my face. Max lost control earlier. I made him do that. And if I made him do it once ...

"Hey, sweetheart, Monique is here," Kat says, popping her head around the door to the den.

"She is?" I wasn't expecting her today, but of course she'll be here to find out what happened after Max marched me out of the club.

Max! The ache between my thighs has been there all day, a constant reminder of what we did. Every time I think about what happened last night, I feel a slick of arousal between my thighs. Max DiMarco took my virginity, and it was hotter than I had ever imagined it could be. Then he went and ruined it all by being Max.

"Here let me take Gabriella," Kat offers with a smile.

I give my niece a soft kiss on her bald head. "Bye smooch."

A few seconds later, Monique sashays into the room in a cloud of Dior perfume and flops onto the sofa beside me. As soon as Kat closes the door behind her, Monique nudges me in the ribs. "So?"

"So what?"

"What happened last night after Max got all psycho on your ass?"

"He did not get psycho on my ass."

"Uh, yeah, he did. He hauled you out of there so fast."

"He was just pissed about something," I say dismissively.

"About what? Have you been naughty, Joey Moretti?" She giggles like we're still in high school.

"No. There was just some family stuff, is all. It was nothing," I insist.

She stares at me, her eyes narrowed with suspicion. "I wondered if maybe he was jealous of that guy flirting with you, but then ..." She presses her lips together.

"Then what?"

She wrinkles her perfect nose. "There's no way Maximo would ever be into you. You are so not his type."

I certainly seemed like his type when he was fucking me against a building. Monique might be one of my closest friends, but I don't trust her with this, so I simply nod my agreement even though it burns me to do it.

She changes the subject, telling me about what she did with a guy she took home from the club. Barely listening, I allow my thoughts to drift back to Max. Max with his hand around my throat. His other one in my panties. His lips on my skin. His dick in my ...

"Earth to Joey," Monique says with an overly dramatic sigh.

I blink at her. "Oh, uh. Sorry. What?"

"I asked you if you think I should go out with him."

"Do you like him?"

She rolls her eyes. "You're so juvenile."

"And you're a slut."

"Better than being a frigid virgin." She pulls a face at me.

"I thought you were hung up on Mystery Guy anyway." She's been after some super mysterious dude for months now, but she's refused to tell me his name. Every few weeks, she goes off grid for a few days because he shows up and decides he wants to spend time with her. Then he disappears again, leaving her swinging in the wind. I've never seen her like this over a guy before, so I figure he must be married, super rich, or powerful—or knowing Monique, all three.

"Keeping my options open, Jo," she says, flashing me a huge smile that doesn't quite reach her eyes. She turns away but not before I can see the hurt on her face. I guess she still has it bad for Mystery Guy.

"So are you going out with him then? The guy from the club last night?"

"Hmm. Maybe," she says with a shrug. "I could see if he has a friend for you?"

"I'm good." Well, I *would* be good if Max wasn't being all noble and shit. His whole *my love isn't the kind of love you need* deal is super annoying. What the hell does that even mean? Pretty sure I could handle a whole lot of his love.

"You should double date with us. Give you a chance to practice some skills before you meet a guy you actually like," Monique suggests.

"Isn't the idea to practice skills with a guy you like though?"

She laughs. "God, Joey, you're so naive."

My cheeks flush with embarrassment. I am so regretting that I told her I was a virgin. I guess *was* is the key word now—not that I'd tell Monique that. But I hate the way she uses my lack of sexual experience to make me feel like a child.

"You could at least get some blowjob practice in. That way you won't seem like a total loser when you finally do fuck a guy. You'll be able to keep him interested with your oral skills even if you don't know what you're doing when it comes to fucking."

I stare at her, and for a second I think she must be joking, but she's serious. "You think guys would honestly be bothered that I'm inexperienced?"

She snorts. "Guys want a girl who knows what they're doing, not someone they have to teach the basics to."

I don't think Max would make a girl feel bad for being inexperienced. I mean he didn't even know I was a virgin until I told him, so it couldn't have been that obvious.

"Yeah, I think I'll just wait, thanks," I tell her with a saccharine smile.

"Your loss."

I sit back against the sofa and smile because Monique just gave me an amazing idea.

ELEVEN

MAX

The safe in Dante's study is a huge old thing that's been around since the time of his grandfather. It was cutting edge in its day, but now it's outdated and needs an upgrade. I guess it serves a purpose though—it keeps most people out. I can't remember the last time I looked inside there. I'm not sure I've ever paid much attention to what goes in there. Money? Important papers? I have the codes to get into it. That's how much he trusts me. If he walked in here and found me with my head in that safe, he wouldn't think anything of it. And that's why even the thought of looking inside when he or Lorenzo isn't here makes my skin crawl. It shouldn't have even entered my head, but this thing with Kristin and Vito nags at me constantly. What the hell is this video recording Vito has? Do Dante and Lorenzo even know about it? Maybe I should just ask them?

I made my little sister a promise that I wouldn't tell them she exists or that she's in Chicago, but that was before I found out that my long-lost uncle could have a video of the Morettis involved in a murder. Given that I know Dante and Lorenzo so well, I figure it's probably something to do with their father. But I can't keep it from them much longer. I don't care if Kristin's father told her the Morettis can't be trusted, they're the only family I've ever had and I've never had a single reason to doubt them.

I don't look inside the safe. It would be a betrayal of their trust in me. Instead, I put the paperwork regarding the new casino on Dante's desk and leave the room, closing the door behind me. Stretching my neck, I sigh when it cracks. Fuck, I need to get rid of some of this tension I'm holding onto. It's been two long days since I fucked Joey Moretti, and I can't stop thinking about how good she felt and how good it would feel to have her again. Just one more taste.

Is she here? I usually know her every move, but I've backed off since the other night. It's the least she deserves.

"Hey, asshole." The sound of her voice stops me in my tracks.

I spin around, and she's standing in the doorway of the den, leaning against the doorframe with her arms crossed over her chest.

I stride back down the hallway toward her. "Asshole?"

She flashes me a wicked grin. "Hmm. Kinda."

"And why is that, Guiseppina?"

Her features darken. "Don't call me that, Max." She hates her full name and has insisted on being called Joey from the moment she could say the word.

"Then don't call me an asshole."

"Fine." She sighs. "Anyway, I was hoping you'd stop by. I need your help with something."

"What is it?"

She catches her bottom lip between her teeth and draws in a breath that makes her perfect tits rise and fall. I try to keep my eyes on her face, but I glance down, and she sees me do it too. Busted.

"Well, I was thinking, since you were my first fu—"

"Joey," I whisper harshly, cutting her off as I push her back through the open doorway to the den. "What the fuck are you doing?"

She laughs. "Relax. Nobody's home."

I close the door anyway to give us a little privacy. "There are guards here. Your brothers have ears everywhere."

"The guards are only ever by the front door or outside now. You know that," she says with a roll of her eyes. It's true that since Dante's daughter was born, the guards' presence has been restricted within the house. Kat insisted on a friendlier atmosphere to raise their children. But they're still here, and who knows when one might go wandering somewhere they shouldn't.

"You're going to get me fucking killed."

She puts her hands on my chest. "I would never put you in harm's way, Max. You know that. I was just playing. I'm sorry," she whispers.

I narrow my eyes at her. I have no idea if that's true. Joey Moretti likes to live life on the edge, and I'm flirting with death by even being alone in a room with her. Now that I know how good her lips taste and how tight and hot her pussy is, I'm always partially hard around her and it takes all my effort not to touch her. Fucking her in the alley the other night plays on a loop in my head. I've jerked off to the memory way more times than could be considered healthy—even for a red-blooded single man in his early thirties. "Did you actually need my help with something or are you just trying to push my buttons?" I ask, trying to distract myself.

"Oh, I'd love to push every single one of your buttons." She giggles, her hands brushing down my chest toward my stomach.

I take hold of her wrists before those hands move any lower. "Joey?"

"Yes, I do need your help. But you cut me off before I could finish my sentence," she says, pouting.

What the fuck is she up to?

"I guess it's more of a proposition than anything. You know how inexperienced I am when it comes to sex, right?"

Yes. Because I had your tight-as-fuck pussy squeezing my cock and I can't stop thinking about it. "Hmm."

"Well, I'm inexperienced in *every* way. You know what I mean? I only ever kissed a guy before you."

My cock is throbbing in my pants now and she fucking knows it. "What does that have to do with me?" I grind out the words.

"Well, you also know I trust you more than anyone."

Now my head throbs along with my cock. I let go of her hands and pinch the bridge of my nose. "What is it, Joey?"

"I want to suck your cock."

What. The. Fuck.

I blink at her, stupefied. She did not just say that. My brain must be misfiring. Hallucinating from her talking about sex while her hands are on my chest. "What?"

"I want to suck your cock, Max," she says with a sweet smile.

Fuck. Me. "Joey, you can't just ..."

"Can't just what? You *just* fucked me the other night."

"That was different."

"How? You took what you wanted. And now I'm asking for what I want."

I blink at her.

"It was just sex. I get it," she says, shrugging. "But it was good sex. At least for me. I want to try everything, Max. I want to learn. And you're the only man apart from my brothers that I trust."

"You want me to teach you how to suck cock?"

"Yes."

"Have you lost your mind, Joey?"

"Far from it. In fact, I think my reasoning is pretty solid. I need a teacher, and I figure you seem to know what you're doing. I know you'd never take advantage of me. I'm going to do this, Max. I'd rather my first time was with you than some rando from a bar."

Oh, fuck no. She isn't hooking up with some stranger. I stare into her dark brown eyes. "Are you trying to blackmail me?"

She tosses her hair over her shoulder. Such a fucking brat. Oh, the pleasure I would take in disciplining that out of her. "Not at all. Just making you aware of the reality of the situation."

I suck on my bottom lip. Am I seriously fucking considering this request? She's going to kill me. "And where and when exactly would this cocksucking lesson take place?"

"Nobody's home. Everyone's out for the afternoon. How about right here, right now?"

"You want to suck my cock here in your brothers' house?"

"It's my house too," she reminds me.

"You're out of your fucking mind."

"Then I guess I'll just find someone at the bar Friday night," she says with a flippant shrug, and my last shred of restraint and patience snaps.

She goes to walk away, but I grab hold of her wrist, pulling her back to me. "You are not hooking up with random fucking men in bars, baby girl."

Her cheeks flush with heat and she flutters her long dark lashes at me. "I don't want to, Max. But I'm almost twenty-two —a grown woman, and there's so much I want to experience.

I'd rather do it with you, but if that's not an option ..." She doesn't finish that sentence. Instead, she adds, "Please."

I can't do this with her. Especially not here. If her brothers walked in here right now, they wouldn't even question us being alone together, that's how much they trust me with her. And just like earlier with the safe in their office, even thinking about this feels like a betrayal of that trust. Except my resolve is weakening faster than ice on a hot skillet. How am I supposed to resist those huge brown eyes and those full pink lips when she pleads with me like that? I'm not a fucking saint.

Besides, this would be for her protection, right? If I do this, then she doesn't go trawling bars to find some complete fucknugget to do this with instead. If I agree to what she's asking, it will be for her benefit, not because I want to feel those soft lips wrapped around my cock more than I've ever wanted anything else my entire life. And with that, I've managed to convince myself that this is the right thing to do.

"On your knees, baby girl."

Her eyes flash with lust and she smiles as she sinks to the floor.

I open my belt and my zipper, stifling a groan at the relief of giving my aching cock a little more room. But I don't take it out yet. She didn't see me the other night at the club, and I don't want to freak her out before I've explained what's going to happen.

She looks up at me expectantly. She's a fucking paradox. So naive and innocent but with a body and mind as wicked as sin.

I rub the pad of my thumb over her cheek. "You sure you want this?"

She blinks at me, long dark eyelashes fluttering over her cheeks. "Yes." She licks the plump bow of her lips.

I pull her hair back, tucking it behind her ears so I can see her perfect face. "You'll need to breathe through your nose."

"Okay."

"I'm a big guy, you might not be able to take all of me right away, but that's okay. We're going to train your pretty little throat until you can take every last inch of me."

She draws in a shaky breath.

"Put your hands on my thighs," I command.

She does as she's told, splaying her fingers over my quads. My muscles tighten at her touch. She opens her mouth—expectant and eager. "Patience, Joey," I say with a smirk, and she narrows her eyes at me. Such a beautiful little brat.

"I didn't realize this was a lecture." She glares at me in defiance. "I thought we were having a practical demonstration."

Fuck me, this girl is dangerous. She is going to drive me to the brink of insanity, which is even more reason to establish some ground rules with her. I ignore her snark and thread my fingers through her hair, palming the back of her head. "When I hit the back of your throat, you'll gag, maybe even feel like you're choking. Tears are going to run down this pretty little face. And that's only gonna make me want to fuck you harder, baby girl."

She arches an eyebrow at me and fuck me if she doesn't see that as some sort of challenge. "It is?"

"Yes. And this is why you need to pay attention to me. Because when your hot little mouth is stuffed full of my cock and you're struggling to breathe, there's no way in hell you're going to be able to talk."

She frowns with confusion.

"If you want me to take it a little easier, you squeeze my thighs, okay?"

"Okay."

"Do it."

"Right now?"

"Yes, now."

She rolls her eyes but squeezes my thighs lightly.

"Harder than that. I'll need to feel it."

"Fine," she mutters, and she squeezes tightly, her fingers digging into my taut muscles.

"Good girl." Her breath hitches and her eyes shine. Such a slut for praise. "But if you need me to stop, you tap me instead, Joey. You got that?"

She giggles. "Like tapping out?"

"Exactly like tapping out. So try it."

"Yeah, I'm not gonna need to do that." She shrugs her shoulders, full of that Moretti confidence that makes me want to prove her wrong.

"Tap. My. Leg."

"Okay," she huffs, but she does what she's told.

"Good."

She's staring up at me, almost salivating, and it's making me crazy. This is her first time, and her eagerness is such a fucking turn on. How the hell am I going to last more than a few minutes fucking that pretty mouth?

"Oh, and Joey? One last thing." I give her a wicked grin as I finally free my cock from my boxers.

"What's that?"

"Be careful with your teeth."

She frowns at me, her eyes still fixed on mine. "I won't bite you, Max."

"I wasn't talking about that, baby girl." I glance down at my cock and she looks too, seeing it up close and personal for the first time.

"Y-you're pierced?"

"I am."

"But you weren't ... I didn't feel any ..."

"I wasn't far enough into your pussy for you to feel them properly, and if you didn't know what to expect ..."

Her tits shudder with a deep breath, and her cheeks flush pink. "How far in were you again?"

"Not even halfway."

"Jesus, Max," she hisses as her gaze flickers back to my face.

The tip of my cock is an inch from her lips, and I'm so close to having her mouth on me, it's driving me insane. "So, you still want to —"

"Yes," she insists, cutting me off before I can finish the question.

"Then go ahead, baby girl. Take whatever you can handle."

She edges forward a little, licking her full pink lips. "Use your hand first, Joey. That way you can have a little more control."

She nods, wrapping her slender fingers around the base of my shaft and squeezing hard. "Like this?"

My thigh muscles tremble with the effort of holding myself back as heat shudders up my spine. "Yes, exactly like that."

"Now can I taste you, Max?"

"Uh-huh," I grunt, anticipation burning through me. How is it that this is her first time and it's me who feels like I'm about to nut in her face?

Her tongue darts out and licks the bead of precum off the crown of my cock, flicking over my piercing like she knows exactly what she's doing.

A bead of sweat trickles down my forehead. "You sure you've never done this before?"

"No, never," she says sweetly as her tongue dances over my skin.

I bite on my lip to stop myself from moaning like a horny fucking teenage boy. I've had my cock sucked plenty of times, but never have I been more desperate to have anyone's lips around me than I am right now.

She hums appreciatively before she guides the tip of my

cock inside her soft, wet mouth and begins to suck. I loosen my grip on her hair, letting her go at her own pace for a few minutes despite wanting to fuck her throat more than I've ever wanted anything.

She looks up at me, her dark eyes searching mine as she takes me deeper.

"You're doing so good, baby girl," I tell her as my cock pulses inside her.

Her eyes shine with happiness. She's such a fucking brat the way she pushes my buttons, but she's still a slut for my praise. So desperate for my approval it scares me. Tightening my grip on her hair, I push her head forward, forcing her to take more of me, and she takes it like a champ. My girl was born to suck cock. I rock my hips, shoving deeper, and the sound of her choking sears my balls with the need to fill her with my cum. She stares up at me, tears and mascara running down her cheeks as she takes deep breaths through her nose.

"Good girl. You're taking me so well," I groan as I pull out a little and drive back in again. She gags harder, but she still doesn't tap me. I'm torn between seeing how far I can push her and wanting to protect her from the side of me that would get off on watching her struggle to breathe.

She sucks harder and saliva runs down her chin, whimpering when I tug her hair. "You're doing so good. So. Fucking. Good." I grit out each word as my abs tighten. I'm so close to filling her throat with my cum.

"Mmmf," she mumbles. Her breathing becomes harsher, and she stops sucking. I'm literally just fucking her face until she squeezes my thigh and I ease up a bit.

"Good girl," I say, rewarding her for following my instructions because I know how much that must have killed her. Joey Moretti never backs down from any challenge, and that's all this is to her. "Remember to breathe, Joey,"

"Hmm," she murmurs, and the sound vibrates through every nerve ending in my cock, making my balls tighten. Swiping my thumb over her cheek, I wipe some of her tears, smudging her makeup further. She blinks at me before she starts to suck my cock again. Her breathing evens out, and her soft moans are just as hot as her gagging.

"Fuck, baby, you're a natural at this. You know that?" I grunt as I rock my hips, chasing the high she's about to deliver.

She murmurs contentedly and relaxes her grip on my thighs. "You think you can take a little more, baby girl?"

"Mmm," she mumbles with a flutter of her eyelashes.

I drive my cock against the back of her throat, and this time she's ready for me. Her breathing remains steady even as she accepts almost every inch of me. I refrain from feeding her my entire cock. This is still her first time, and she isn't ready for that.

My fist tightens in her hair. Her succulent pink lips stretched around my shaft as she greedily sucks as much of me as she can is the most exquisite sight I've ever seen.

She will never do this with anyone but me. Never. Joey Moretti is mine. All fucking mine. My balls tighten and my cock spasms, my climax pulsing through me—all searing heat and fire raging through my core.

And my girl swallows every last fucking drop, licking me from root to tip even as I pull out of her mouth. Like she's as fucking desperate for me as I am for her.

My chest heaves and I pant for breath. Grabbing her jaw, I tilt her head up and watch, mesmerized, as she licks her lips, trying to catch the cum and spit that dripped from the sides. I catch a drop with the tip of my thumb and push it back inside her mouth. She sucks on my thumb appreciatively before she releases it with a wet pop. Fucking siren.

"How was that?" she asks. She knows it was good. She just sucked my fucking soul from my body.

"It was fucking perfect, baby girl."

"It was?"

I narrow my eyes at her. "Yes. But any man ever tries to fuck your throat like I just did, I'll cut off his cock with a rusty blade."

She sucks in a deep breath that makes her tits jiggle enticingly. "Max. You can't say things like that."

I grip her jaw tighter. She's mine, but I can't take her. I wish I could keep her for my own.

But the stakes are already way too high.

CHAPTER
TWELVE

JOEY

Max's dark eyes burn into mine as he keeps a tight hold on my jaw. Licking my lips, I taste his cum again, and my core contracts with heat and need. My pussy is aching and wet. My whole plan backfired. This was supposed to be about me gaining back a little control, but I'm even more desperate for him than I've ever been. I had no idea that sucking his cock would get me this worked up. I assumed it was all about the guy's pleasure, so why am I this wet between my thighs? I would do anything for this man. If he ordered me to strip naked and crawl to him on my knees, I'd do it in a heartbeat.

He pulls me up by my jaw until I'm standing and our bodies are only inches apart, his eyes never leaving mine.

I pant for breath. His jaw ticks. Time stands still.

"Max?"

"Nobody else, Joey. You understand me? No one ever does that to you but me."

"You can't expect me to keep that promise. You're not even my boyfriend."

His eyes narrow and anger creases his brow. "You know that I can't be."

"Why? Because you're my brothers' best friend? You know we're both adults, right?"

"It's so much more than that."

"Fine." I shrug, trying to hide the pain his words cause me. "So you don't get to tell me what to do."

His frown deepens. "Just not like that, okay? You never let anyone be that rough with you."

I swallow hard. I wish I knew what was going on in his head. How can it be that I know him so well in some ways but not at all in others? "And what if I say no?"

His expression darkens. He slides a hand over my hip and onto my ass, pulling me close until our bodies are flush. Every single nerve ending in my body tingles with nervous excitement as my breathing grows heavier. Then Max undoes the button of my jeans with one quick flex of his fingers. He dips his head, pressing those hot lips against my ear. "Then I'll never make you come again, baby girl," he says as he shoves his hand into my panties.

"Holy fuck," I groan as his fingers find my swollen clit.

He inhales sharply. "So fucking wet from sucking my cock, Joey."

I press my face against his shirt, breathing him in until he's everywhere and everything. Max DiMarco owns my goddamn soul. I whimper as his fingers slip a little further, circling my entrance. He dips a fingertip inside me, taunting me as I tremble in his powerful arms.

Warm waves of electric heat pulse through my core as he works his digit deeper, rubbing against a sensitive spot deep inside that I've never been able to reach by myself. My legs shake as my pussy grows wetter until the noise of him driving in and out of me is unmistakable. I cling to him, my fingers grasping at his shirt in an attempt to hold on to some semblance of sanity as he drives me almost frantic with the need for more of him.

"Please, Max?"

He dusts his lips over my hair. "Are you my good girl?" he says, teasing me.

"No." The word ends on a moan as he drives his finger deeper.

"Of course. You're my little slut, right?"

"Yes," I pant, and his skilled fingers bring me to the brink of a mind-blowing orgasm.

"I'm gonna teach you how to be a good girl for me, Joey." He chuckles, and then the bastard pulls his finger out of me, leaving me teetering on the edge of ecstasy.

"Max?" I gasp in protest, but he just looks at me with a wicked grin on his face.

"I told you I wouldn't make you come in your brothers' house, baby girl, and I meant it." Then he sucks his finger clean, kisses my forehead, and walks out of the room.

CHAPTER
THIRTEEN
MAX

My jaw clenches and I rock my head side to side, trying to get rid of the tension in my neck while Dante and I sit in Ralf Strauss's office and listen to him drone on about the benefits of going into partnership with him and his brother. I'm so not in the mood for this prick tonight. I have much more important things I need to be doing —such as search for my missing uncle. Part of me thinks good riddance to that particular waste of oxygen, but Kristin deserves to know what happened to him at least. And despite him being a terrible uncle to me and an even worse brother to my father, he seems to have been an okay dad to her.

And until I find out where he is, she's stuck living with me. Not that I don't like the kid—I do. But I can't continue lying to everyone about her. I hate it.

The message her father told her to give me plays on my mind constantly too. *He said you can't trust the Morettis. They turned you against your real family.* Why would he ask her to give me that specific message? I guess he actually believes that? But the Morettis are the only family I've had for a long time, and I can't keep secrets from them much longer.

"You see how this could be good for us all, don't you, Maximo?" Ralf asks, dragging me back to the conversation at hand. The same one he and I have already had.

"Like I already told you, Ralf, no."

"Dante?" he pleads.

"If Max says no, then it's no," Dante replies with a frown. "And I'm insulted that you've dragged me here tonight when my partner here has already told you his feelings on the matter."

"But I thought ..." Ralf sighs.

"You thought I was going to disagree with him? This man who's basically my brother?" Dante asks with a cock of his eyebrow.

Now I feel even guiltier about the secrets I'm keeping. Because Kristin isn't the biggest one. No, Joey Moretti claims that title. Joey and her wickedly sinful body and even more sinful mouth. I have no fucking idea how anyone who's never given head before can get it so spectacularly right on their first time. But who am I kidding? Just being inside any part of her has me fucking desperate to bust my nut like a fourteen-year-old who just discovered Pornhub. The girl is fucking addictive, and she is going to kill me. But what a way to go.

Dante pushes himself out of his chair and turns his back on Ralf. "Deal with this piece of shit, will you? I need to call Kat."

"No problem."

He walks out of the room, leaving Ralf and me alone. "I told you a partnership wasn't on the table," I remind him, and he eyes me warily.

When I push my chair back, he flinches and I suppress a smile. Walking around the desk, I grab him by the neck, pressing my palm against his Adam's apple until he opens his mouth to gasp for air. I shove three fingers inside, pushing them down his throat until he gags and tears run down his face.

"Mr. Moretti expects the paperwork pertaining to the purchase of his new casino in his inbox tomorrow morning. If it doesn't arrive by noon, then consider the deal off."

He tries to wrench free, his body struggling to get oxygen, but I tighten my grip. "You understand me, Ralf?"

His eyes meet mine, and he nods almost imperceptibly. Ralf and his brother have had a free ride in this city for far too long. They stepped on plenty of people on their way to the top and can't be trusted. The last poor fuckers who went into business with them ended up bankrupt because the Strauss brothers ran the company into the ground, bleeding it for every cent right under their business partners' noses. But because of who they were and their perceived alliance with Salvatore Moretti, no one would challenge them. There's no chance we'd ever go into business with him. When Salvatore was alive, the Strauss brothers traded off the fact that they were his enforcers for a few years, after my father died at least. However, their gravy train has come to an end. The casino is about to go under, and we're going to buy it for a quarter of what it's worth.

Ralf and Micah won't take it lying down, but I don't give a shit. I'll add them to the long list of people who'd like to kill me.

I pull my fingers out of Ralf's mouth and wipe my saliva-covered fingers on his expensive Italian suit jacket. "By noon."

He coughs, rubbing at his throat, but when I lift my hand, he recoils and gives me a nod.

I tap him on the side of his face. "Good boy."

By the time I walk outside, Dante's waiting for me in the car.

"He get the message?" he asks me when I climb inside.

"Yep. Asshole."

He laughs. "The look on his face when I asked him why he dragged me over here. He looked like he was about to shit his pants."

"He almost did after you left."

"You were right about having a face-to-face with him though. Remind him who he's dealing with. And it's nice seeing you work. You're the most effective negotiator I know." He laughs harder. "I'm so glad you're on my side, compagno."

Another pang of guilt twists my stomach. I have to tell him about Kristin soon. And stop fucking around with his sister. Closing my eyes, I lean back against the seat, but all I see are images of Joey sucking my cock earlier today. Yeah, doing the right thing and not fucking around with Joey Moretti is never going to happen.

CHAPTER
FOURTEEN

JOEY

"You're not paying attention, Guiseppina," my half sister says as she taps the side of my head.

"You're such a bitch, Antoinette, you know that?" I snap back, bouncing on the balls of my toes as I raise my guard. She knows I hate my name. Everybody knows—but I don't hate it nearly as much as Toni hates hers.

She laughs wickedly. "Oh, now you really pissed me off, kid."

"Good, maybe you'll actually bring me some heat this time," I goad her as we circle the ring.

"Such big words for such a little girl. Big brothers aren't here to protect you now though."

"You're such a bitch," I say with a scowl.

"You already used that one, princess." She jabs her left hook at me, but I duck out of the way. "Maybe you wish Max were here to protect you instead, huh?"

I launch forward, aiming my right hand at her jaw but she's way too fast for me and dodges it easily.

"Oh, I do love pushing your buttons, kid."

"Leave Max out of this," I warn her, my eyes narrowed.

"Hmm." She rolls her lips together. "No."

"Toni!"

She aims a perfect right hook at my chin, but she doesn't put any power behind it. My half sister is an MMA champion, and she would knock me on my ass if she hit me for real. Still, it grazes my face, making me shuffle back. "Remember what I taught you, Joey?" she says, all business again. "Someone comes at you like that, you duck and go for the nuts."

"You don't have any nuts."

She smirks at me. "You hit someone in the pussy, it's gonna hurt like hell too."

Even the thought makes me wince. "Ouch."

"Your mind is elsewhere today, Joey. I need you to focus, kid. I'm not giving up my time to have you half-ass it."

"I know. I'm sorry. I'm all in now. Promise."

"Good girl," she says, but that only makes me think of Max and the way he says those same words and turns me into a puddle of goo. "Okay, playtime is over. I'm gonna hit you for real now, so if you don't keep your guard up ..."

"I know." I shake my head, clearing it of all things Max. I actually love training with Toni, and I work just as hard for her as I did for Max. She's the most badass woman I know, and I can't believe our asshole father drove her away and deprived me of her influence growing up. Lorenzo wasn't always her biggest fan. It bothers him that she was born only a few weeks after Dante, and he sees her existence as an insult to our mom. I guess he's right about that, but it's not Toni's fault. At least he finally seems to be coming around.

Toni throws me a towel. She works my ass super hard, but I feel so good after our sessions—like I can take on the world.

She sits on the weight bench while I wipe away the sweat dripping down my face. "So, anything new with you?"

"Um, actually ..." I bite my lip. Should I tell her about Max? I need to tell someone. I almost told Kat last night, but it would put her in a difficult position with Dante, so I kept quiet.

"Oh, Dante told me you were going to start working with him and Lorenzo," she says with a wide smile before I can decide one way or the other. She probably thought that's what my hesitation was about. She and Dante are super close. Would she feel disloyal to him if I told her about Max and me? "You must be excited. I told him you were too smart to be wasted sitting around this house all day."

I frown. "You guys were talking about me?"

"Not in a bad way, just like in a you're-our-sister-and-we-care-about-you way." She gives me a reassuring pat on the shoulder. "Anyway, he was worried you were getting bored and lonely since you got back from Italy—"

"And he was worried I was going to get into some trouble if he didn't give me something to do?" I ask, hand on my hip. "He's unbelievable."

"Well, smart people with not much else to do tend to get into trouble," she says with a shrug. "But no, he was genuinely concerned that you needed more going in your life. Then earlier he told me you two had a chat and you're interested in the casinos. I told him I thought you'd be a good fit."

"Oh." I can't be mad at her when she's complimenting me.

"Yeah. You're sharp and you understand what makes people tick. You don't take shit from anyone." She winks. "And you're hot, and that never hurts when you're in a place that's all about image."

I blush at her open praise. "Toni!"

"You are. You got those Moretti genes," she says, tossing her blond hair over her shoulder. Toni looks nothing like me or my brothers. She's the spitting image of her mom, and she's one of the most beautiful women I've ever seen.

"Anyway, tell me ... is there anything new with you?" I ask, trying to steer the conversation away from me. "Have you seen your lawyer friend again? Emerald?"

"Her name is fucking Sapphire, Guiseppina," she says, admonishing me good-naturedly.

"I know." I bump my arm against hers. "I'm just playing with you."

"Well, I haven't seen her since I spent the night at her place. I think she's ghosting me."

"No?" My mouth drops open in horror. "Not *the* Toni Moretti being ghosted?" She scowls at me, and I laugh. She's such a player—she's usually the one to do the ghosting.

"Hey, I liked this one." She frowns, and I feel a little bad for laughing.

I put my arm around her shoulder. "Then I'm sorry. I'm sure she's just busy or something."

"Or something," she mutters. "Anyway, what are your plans for today?"

"I'm hoping to catch up with Dante. He had a meeting about the new casino last night and I was hoping to go along, but Anya wasn't feeling well and asked me to watch her favorite movie, so ..." I shrug. There will be plenty of casino deals and only a finite amount of time with Anya.

Toni gives my hand a gentle squeeze.

I change the subject. "I'm going to ask him to fill me in on what happened, then I'm going for lunch with some old high school friends."

"Including Toby?" She waggles her eyebrows at me.

"Did Dante tell you about him too?"

"Maybe," she says with a knowing smile. "So ...?"

"Nothing, really. We're friends, that's all. I think he'd like to be something more but ..."

"But little Joey Moretti's in love with someone else." She winks.

I blink at her. "W-what?"

She stands up, ignoring my question. "I need to take a shower. Catch you later, kid." She walks out of the gym, leaving me to stare after her and wonder what the hell she meant by that.

FIFTEEN

MAX

"You sure everything's okay? You seem kind of distracted lately." Dante says as we walk down the hallway toward his study.

Distracted? That's a fucking understatement and a half. "Me? No. Everything's good, compagno."

Everything is *not* good. I'm lying to his face. I need to speak to him about Vito, but the time never seems quite right. Finding out I have a sister and her showing up and telling me her father went missing, probably over some video recording, is the biggest secret I've ever kept from him.

Until Joey.

It's been two long and torturous days since I allowed her to suck my cock right here in his house. I've done my best to avoid her ever since, but I miss her like hell.

He arches an eyebrow. "You met someone?"

"Fuck, no," I snap. And right at that moment, *someone* turns down the hallway and comes face-to-face with the two of us.

"Hey, guys," she says with a flutter of her eyelashes. Her hair is pulled back into a ponytail and sweat glistens on her abs. She's wearing those tight-as-fuck yoga pants that cling to every single inch of her perfect fucking body, but that's not the most distracting thing about her today. My eyes drop to her t-shirt, which she has tied up in a knot so that her tan, taut stomach is still on display. The shirt has two words emblazoned across the front, stretched across her beautiful tits. *Tap Out.*

Girl is going to fucking kill me.

My jaw ticks as I grind my teeth together and will my cock to stop twitching in my pants.

"How was your workout?" her older brother asks.

"Great." She gives him a huge smile. "Toni is *such* a great trainer. She's amazing. Really knows how to get the best from me, you know?" *Brat!*

"No need to lay it on so thick, kid. She isn't standing behind you," Dante teases her.

Joey rolls her eyes and avoids my gaze. "Are you going over the new casino deal?"

"Yeah."

How does she know about the new casino deal?

"Cool. Can I sit in?" she asks.

"You want to grab a shower first?"

She wrinkles her nose before looking down and assessing her clothing. I can't help doing the same. I want to rip them off her and fuck her until she begs me to stop.

"Nah, I'll shower after. I'm going out with some friends this afternoon."

"Toby?" Dante asks.

Her cheeks flush pink. "He'll be there, yes. But I'm not going out *with* him."

Dante chuckles softly while my muscles tense at the thought of that douchebag being anywhere near her.

We continue walking down the hallway and Joey falls into step beside us. Once we're inside Dante's office, he takes a seat behind his desk, and Joey and I sit opposite. I try to avoid looking at her, but when I glance sideways, she gives me a wicked smile.

"Tell me how it went with Ralf last night," Joey says as she leans forward in her seat. "Was he open to the buyout, or did he take some convincing?"

Feeling like I just stepped into an alternate universe, I frown at Dante. I know I should keep my mouth shut, because this is their family business and she's as much a Moretti as he is, but I can't. "You told Joey about Ralf?"

"Yeah," he replies. "She wants to be more involved in the family business—"

"And you thought the casino deal was a good place to start?"

Dante frowns at me, unaccustomed to me questioning his methods, but those methods have never involved putting Joey in harm's way before. And he's never blindsided me like this. Usually, I know everything that's going on. I guess I've been more distracted than I thought.

"Fuck's sake," Joey mutters under her breath, but I ignore her. I'll deal with her later.

"It's not like I'm asking her to blow someone's head off, Max, but ..."

"But what?" I snap.

"She's a fucking Moretti. This is her legacy too. If she wants to be a part of the business ..."

I can't believe the change in him. The same man who sent her off to school in Italy at the age of eighteen, even though she cried and pleaded with him not to, is telling me that she can be part of the family business. "You really think that's a wise move? Putting her at risk like that?"

His hands ball into fists. "Are you seriously questioning my decision-making when it comes to my family?"

"*Your* family?" I say with a snarl at the suggestion that

somehow I'm no longer a part of it.

He bangs his fist on the desk. "Yes! *My* fucking family."

"Jeez, guys, calm down," Joey yells, but I keep my glare focused on her older brother.

"This city. All of this"—he waves his hands in the air—"is as much hers as it is mine and Lorenzo's."

"I'm not suggesting otherwise," I bark. "But it's too fucking dangerous."

"You're the one who's spent the last two months telling me how tough she is," he snaps back.

"He has?" Joey says. I glance over. Her cheeks are bright pink, but I can't think about the reason why right now.

"That's different," I say, returning my attention to Dante. "Why now, D? When all of those years you were determined to protect her, why are you letting her be a part of this now?"

"Because the man I needed to protect her from is fucking dead, Max," he shouts. "I fucking killed him, remember?"

He's talking about their father. We all protected Joey from the worst of him. But when Dante found out their father was operating a sex trafficking ring with the head of the Bratva and had known about an assault on Kat years before, he went to his house and put a bullet in his head. But Salvatore wasn't the only threat. There are too many people who'd see Joey Moretti as an easy target. Too many people who might use her to get to her brothers.

"Are you telling me you don't think she has what it takes?" he asks, and I swallow harshly.

Both their eyes are locked on me as they wait for my answer. How do I answer that? Of course she has what it takes. She's a fucking Moretti through and through. Smart and tough. I have no doubt she could be as ruthless as her brothers if necessary, but there's more to it than that.

"Max?" he says.

"She's ..."

"I'm what?" Joey snaps. "A girl?"

You're fucking mine. "She's too good for this life, D."

Joey jumps to her feet. "This is *my* fucking life, Max. It's all I've ever known. If you think I'm going to spend all my days sitting at home painting my damn nails, then you don't know me at all."

I growl at her. "I never said that."

"No? You're thinking it though, right? Just a spoiled little princess." She leans down, bringing her face close to mine as she glares at me. "Well, I am a fucking princess, Max. Chicago royalty. Heir to the goddamn Moretti empire, and don't you *ever* fucking forget it."

Then she storms out of the room, slamming the door closed behind her.

"Fuck," Dante sighs, rubbing a hand over his face as he leans back in his chair. "Why couldn't I have only had brothers?"

"It would have been easier." I sure as shit wouldn't spend almost every hour of every day thinking about being inside his brother.

"She's going to be a part of this, Max. How can I refuse her when she has a point? If I stop her because she's a woman, aren't I as bad as him?"

"You're nothing like your father."

"I know she's young and naive in a lot of ways, but with some experience, I think Joey could be an asset to our business. Don't you?"

I nod because we both know it's true. "I can't help worrying about her though, D. The kind of people we deal with ... they see women as easy targets. She could be the easiest way to get to you or Lorenzo."

"Then we have to make sure she's not an easy target," he

says with a shrug. "Lorenzo is teaching her how to handle a gun. She almost knocked Toni unconscious with her round-house yesterday."

"She's a fucking firecracker." I smile because there's no denying that. "But it's more than being able to handle herself, D. I know she's smart, but she's also too fucking naive about so many things, and that makes her vulnerable." *And that fucking terrifies me.*

"I know, compagno." He nods in agreement. "But I can't keep her under lock and key forever. So we make sure that the message is out there that anyone who touches her will die a very slow and agonizing death. Yeah?"

Now that's a sentiment I can get behind. "Yeah."

SIXTEEN

JOEY

I swat away my tears and stomp up the stairs to my bedroom. Screw Max DiMarco. I am so over him treating me like a goddamn child. Like he knows what's best for me? Asshole!

So he doesn't think I have what it takes, huh? I stand in front of my mirror and pull out my hair tie, shaking my long hair loose. He thinks I'm just a spoiled little princess, then that's exactly what he'll get from now on. He can go to hell with his overprotective bullshit and his "I can't be one of your choices, baby girl" crap.

When I'm showered and changed an hour later, I head back downstairs, hoping to go straight out and avoid Max completely, but just my luck, he walks down the hallway right as I come down the stairs.

"Joey." He glances over my outfit—no doubt thinking that my jeans are too tight or my top is too revealing. Good thing I don't care what he thinks anymore.

"I'm going out. I don't have time," I say as I breeze past him.

He catches my wrist, pulling me toward him. Goosebumps

prickle along my forearm at his touch, and I wrench away before he can notice. "Take your hand off me."

"I didn't mean ..." He frowns as he goes on staring at me like he wants to say something more but can't. Or won't.

"I don't give a shit what you meant, Max. I am a part of this family, and I am not a fucking child. Now I'm going out with my friends, people who treat me like an equal and not some pathetic little girl who can't think for herself, so get the hell out of my way."

His eyes darken. "Don't, Joey."

I step closer until we're barely an inch apart. His breathing grows heavier and the thick muscles in his neck tense. He might push my limits, but I test his too. Every single one of them.

"Or what, Max?" I whisper, running a painted nail over the buttons of his shirt.

"I am fucking warning you, baby girl," he says with a growl from deep in his throat, and I swear my pussy purrs in response. *Traitor.*

"I don't take warnings from men who have absolutely no power over me." I take a step back and smile sweetly at Lorenzo as he walks toward us. My brother just saved my ass from a pissed-off Max who looks like he's seconds away from imploding. Serves him right.

"You out again, kid?" Lorenzo asks, stepping up behind Max.

Tilting my head to the side, I grin. "Well, this is what us young, fun people do, Loz."

The vein in Max's neck grows thicker.

"Huh," Lorenzo grunts. "Henry and Ash going with you?"

"Of course. I'll be back by dinnertime. It's just a lunch thing."

"Be good," he says with as much of a smile as my oldest brother ever seems to be able to muster.

"Me?" I look between him and Max, fluttering my eyelashes and feigning innocence.

"Yes, you, Joey," Lorenzo adds before he turns and disappears down the hallway.

No way. I mouth the words so he doesn't hear, but Max sees, and that vein in his neck damn near bursts. He inches forward, his expression mutinous—

"You coming, Max?" Lorenzo interrupts whatever Max was going to say or do.

"Buh-bye now," I whisper sweetly, then I turn around and head outside where Ash and Henry are waiting.

Mo's polished off at least a whole bottle of champagne by herself and now sits beside me, complaining about how she hasn't seen Mystery Guy for five weeks.

"You should forget about him. He sounds like an asshole," I tell her, wrapping an arm around her shoulders.

"No." She shakes her head and gives her empty glass a longing look. Leaning closer, she whispers in my ear, "He's my ticket out of here, Jo."

"There are loads of guys who would kill to date you."

"But I only want him," she whines. "He has it all."

I frown at her. I've never ever seen her this torn up over a guy.

"He's so freaking rich," she sniffs.

Ah, now I get it.

Toby takes a seat on the other side of me. "You think we should get her home?"

"Hmm, maybe. She seems pretty wasted," I whisper.

He looks at my full champagne glass on the table. "You hardly drank anything at all."

"I prefer hard liquor." I cast an anxious glance at Mo, who's now draped over me, babbling about men being too difficult to understand.

"Seems a shame that your afternoon out's been ruined," he adds, also looking at Mo.

"No, it hasn't. I had a good time," I say truthfully. A bunch of us from high school got together today, and it was nice to catch up. I haven't seen most of them in years, and I much prefer being clearheaded when I'm out with people I don't know all that well, so not drinking isn't a big deal.

He arches one eyebrow. "I think you deserve a better time than the one you've had though."

I figure he's talking about me having to look after Mo, but I genuinely don't mind. She's my best friend. "No, really. I've had a great time."

He runs a hand through his hair and huffs a laugh. "Jeez, Joey. You're not making this easy."

"What?"

He takes a deep breath. "I'm trying to ask if you want to go somewhere else. With me?"

I blink at him.

"Like a date?" he adds.

"Oh."

"Only if you're free. I'm sure you're busy." His cheeks turn pink. It's kind of adorable.

I am free. Free and single. Toby Fiore is a good guy. He treats me like a grown-up—like an equal. I think he's even a little intimidated by me, which is a nice change from the usual possessive, overbearing alpha-holes I'm surrounded by.

"Yeah, I'm free."

His face breaks into the cutest, biggest smile ever. "Cool. You wanna go for a drink? Or some food? You choose."

"How about a movie?" I suggest. I rarely get to go to the movie theater, but I love it.

"Perfect."

"Let me take Mo home and make sure she's okay, and then we can go, yeah?"

He nods. "Yeah."

"I just have to call my brothers and let them know."

I don't miss the fleeting look of pure terror that flickers over Toby's face, but he recovers quickly and is soon smiling again.

"They'll be cool," I assure him. "And Ash and Henry will have to tag along too. Sorry."

"I know." He understands this life and the rules that come with it. Brushing a stray curl from my forehead, he leans closer. "But I hope that one day your brothers might trust me to look after you myself."

Aw, bless. He really is adorable. Like that would ever happen.

CHAPTER
SEVENTEEN
MAX

"You sure you can't remember anything else about when Monty used to visit? Your father never went anywhere before or after? Never mentioned a video recording or anything like that?"

"No, Max," Kristin groans and rolls her eyes. "If I knew, I would tell you."

I guess she's right. I've been interrogating the kid, repeating the same questions over and over since I spoke to Monty a few days ago. "The longer your father's missing, the more likely it is he'll turn up dead somewhere."

Her face falls and her eyes fill with tears. I feel like an asshole, but this is her reality. I've spent the past week and a half barely sleeping, trying to find out what happened to her father, but I continue to hit dead ends. Vito hid his tracks well.

"I'll do everything I can to find him," I assure her. "Sometimes we forget things though, and it can only take a word or a phrase or something insignificant to trigger a memory."

"I know. I wish I could remember something."

"And you're sure it doesn't have anything to do with the father of your baby?"

"Jakob? No way. I guess he might be looking for me since Dad made me leave before I got a chance to say goodbye, but he wouldn't take my father. Why would he?" She shakes her head. "Jakob has nothing to do with this."

"Maybe he blames your dad for taking you away from him?"

"Even if that were true, he loves me, Max. If he found us, he would have come for me, not my dad."

I rest my head on the countertop and sigh. I'm grasping for fucking straws here. My phone vibrates, rattling against the kitchen counter. I see Ash's name on the screen and answer. "Yeah?"

"I know you asked me to check in on Fred at the warehouse, but I can't tonight. If it can wait, I'll do it tomorrow."

"Why not tonight?"

"Joey's going out, so ..."

"Right." I pinch the bridge of my nose. It's not like her to go out on a Wednesday night. "Where's she going?"

"On a date."

White-hot anger sears a hole through the middle of my chest. I take a breath and count to five. "On a what now?"

Ash laughs. "Yeah, I know. Guy must have balls of iron, right? Wouldn't think that to look at him though."

My knuckles turn white as I grip the phone so tightly, I almost bend it in fucking half. "Who is she going on a date with?"

"Toby Fiore."

Toby. Of fucking course it's him. "And Dante and Lorenzo are okay with this?"

"Yup." He laughs again.

Kristin stares at me with concern, and I realize I'm scowling. *Going on a fucking date.* I'll kill him. Rip his fucking arms off his body and beat him to death with them. And I will spank her bratty ass so hard—

107

"Maximo?" Ash interrupts my murderous thoughts. "Tomorrow for the warehouse, yeah?"

My jaw ticks. "Yeah."

"Good."

"If *anything* happens tonight. Anything weird at all. If she even looks the slightest bit uncomfortable or upset or—" I take deep breaths to calm my racing heart. When I get my hands on Joey Moretti, I will remind her exactly who she belongs to. "You call me. Okay?"

"Okay, boss, but ..."

"But what?"

"Well, they're only going to see a movie and then ... well, Dante said that if she's in the Fiore mansion, she's okay to be left alone, so me and Henry won't be in there with her."

My right hand balls into a fist. "He said what?"

"He spoke to Michael Fiore first. Made him aware that Joey would be under his care, you know? That Toby kid would have to have a death wish to try anything stupid."

I growl. Michael Fiore is a traditional family man, and he's a loyal employee—who happens to have a healthy fear of his employers. Toby *would* be a fucking fool to try anything more than a kiss—but don't all horny twenty-two-year-old fuckwits think with their dicks? Says me, the guy who's foaming at the mouth just thinking about Joey—a girl I can't fucking have—going on a date. But what did I expect when I told her there was no future for us? Joey's not the kind of woman who sits around and waits for life to happen.

"I'll call you later, Boss."

"You better," I snap and end the call. Now all I need is an excuse to go to Michael Fiore's house later tonight.

EIGHTEEN

JOEY

"You have the most incredible eyes," Toby says, and that's when I realize he's staring into them. Oh, fuck. This is happening. I mean, I wanted it to, right? This is why I went out on a date with him. I know he's into me. And he's kinda cute. We got back to his house half an hour ago. His mom and dad hovered around us for a while and reminded Toby we couldn't go to his bedroom—no doubt a stipulation put forth by my brothers. I was surprised they were cool about me coming to Toby's house without Ash and Henry, but I guess they know I'm safe here with the Fiores. They have almost as much security as we do. But now Toby and I are alone in the den with the TV on in the background.

"Thank you," I whisper, shocked by how embarrassed I feel all of a sudden. I wish I wasn't so inexperienced when it comes to sex. The thought of kissing Toby makes my toes curl in my sneakers, and not in a good way. But it's just because I'm nervous, right?

Except I'm never nervous around Max. Well, not like this. I'd climb that man like a tree if he gave me the slightest bit of encouragement.

"Can I kiss you?" Toby asks, snapping me out of my thoughts about Max DiMarco.

I smile at him. He is too damn sweet. "Sure," I say with a shrug.

He closes his eyes and leans in, placing his soft lips over mine. It's not a bad kiss. He knows what he's doing, but I don't feel anything. I close my eyes too, hoping it will help me get into it more. Toby takes that as his cue to push me back against the sofa cushions, and I settle into a comfortable position as we make out.

I hear the soft ticking of a clock somewhere nearby and then a dog barking. Does Toby have a dog? Did he put it outside because I'm here? I like dogs. He didn't need to do that. Are his parents still home? They'll let the dog inside, right? Or should I ask him about it? Opening my eyes, I see Toby's are still closed. Shouldn't I enjoy this? Is there something wrong with me?

I mumble for him to stop, but the sound is swallowed by Toby's mouth. I guess he takes it as a sign I want to take things a little further because his hand slides beneath my top. I flinch like I've been burned by a hot poker and, without thinking, I shove him away. "Stop!" I pant, my head spinning. I don't want this.

"Joey?" He frowns at me. "Are you ... Did I ... I'm sorry ... I thought ..." he babbles, looking as confused as I feel.

"I'm sorry, Toby. I just—I can't right now." I shake my head, feeling like a complete idiot. "Is-is that okay?"

"Y-yeah." He nods, relief written across his face. I bet his whole life just flashed before him, as well as scenes of torture at the hands of my brothers.

"It wasn't anything you did," I assure him. "I'm just ... feeling a little queasy, I think," I lie. "I should probably go home."

"You want me to drive you?" he asks.

"No. I'll call Ash and Henry. They won't be far away."

WE STAND by his front door while I wait for my ride. I shuffle my feet uncomfortably. "I'm sorry, Toby." After I called Ash, I burst into tears for some reason. I'm such a freaking idiot. Poor Toby must wonder what the hell he's gotten himself into. No doubt he's relieved that he's about to get me out of his house.

"You don't have to apologize," he says with a reassuring smile right as the doorbell rings. "I still had a nice time. Maybe we can do it again?"

God, he's such a good guy. Why can't I be into him? "Um, yeah. Sure."

The doorbell rings again, saving me from having to tell any more lies.

"We're coming," I shout. Ash isn't usually this impatient.

"I'll call you, yeah?" Toby leans in for an awkward hug.

I mumble a quick yes against his shoulder before I untangle myself and open the front door. "Why are you being so impa—"

"Why the fuck have you been crying?" That voice sends a shiver down my spine, and Toby takes a step back.

I blink. "M-Max? What are you doing here?"

He glares at Toby, his entire body bristling with rage. Oh, shit. This looks really bad. "What the fuck have you done to her?" Max says with a vicious snarl.

He makes a grab for Toby, but I take hold of his wrist. "Max, stop! He hasn't done anything."

Max's gaze flickers back to me and he narrows his eyes as he searches my face. "So why the fuck were you crying?"

"Can we just go? Please?"

"I didn't do anything, Maximo. I swear," Toby insists, the tremor in his voice all too obvious.

Max continues to stare at me. "He didn't," I whisper. "Can we go?"

"If I find out you did anything to her ..." Max warns, not needing to finish the sentence because the threat is implicit.

"Bye, Tobe." I turn and give him an apologetic smile. Max wraps a protective arm around my shoulders, and I'm tempted to shrug him off, but I want to get off this doorstep as quickly as possible.

We walk down the drive of the gated mansion in silence. As soon as we reach Max's motorcycle, I step away from him.

"Tell me what's wrong, baby girl," he says, dusting his fingertips over my cheek. "Why were you crying if it's nothing to do with Toby?"

I shake my head. "I'm an idiot, is all."

A deep sigh rumbles through his body and we stay like that for a few beats until he breaks the silence. "You want to come for a ride with me?"

No! I want to never see you or go for a ride with you again, Max, because this is too fucking hard. "Yes," I whisper instead.

He hands me the spare helmet, and I climb onto the back of his motorcycle and wrap my arms around his waist. The familiarity of his body against mine makes me smile and want to cry again at the same time. He taps my knee, letting me know that we're about to take off and making sure I'm holding on tight. It's one of the many small ways he takes care of me. We both know I hold on to him too tightly—in every sense of the word.

And I need to let him go.

Max drives us out of the city to the woods and stops in a small clearing surrounded by trees. He kills the engine and pulls his helmet off. When he turns, I get lost in his beautiful dark eyes. He gives a jerk of his head, and I take that as my cue to climb off the back of the bike. I pull my helmet off too and he takes it from me, placing it on the ground beside his. Shaking my long hair loose, I wonder why he brought us to this spot near the woods.

"Tell me what happened with Toby," he commands in a low tone.

"After you tell me why you turned up at his house instead of Ash."

"Ash called me." He rubs a hand over his jaw. "He said you sounded upset."

I frown. "But why did he call you?"

"Because I asked him to."

"Why?"

"I've answered your question, Joey. Now tell me what happened."

"He didn't do anything wrong. It was me." I go to cross my arms over my chest, not wanting to go into this with him, but he catches my wrists and stops me.

"Come here," he says, scooting back on the seat of his bike and patting the space in front of him.

I roll my eyes, but I do what he says. Because despite everything, I yearn to be close to him. To have any part of him touching me sets my soul on fire, and like a desperate fool—and as much as I'd hate myself for it—I'd do anything for him. I straddle the bike, but he's so huge that I'm practically straddling him too.

"What happened?" he says again, his voice cutting through me like a hot blade.

I stare into his eyes. I can't help it. He has some kind of hold over me that I can't explain. I shouldn't talk to him, of all people, about this, but he's my best friend. My real best friend.

"Things were okay," I mumble. "Then we were on the sofa. We were kissing ..." I swear every single muscle in his body tenses at those words. "He wanted to fool around, I guess ..."

He narrows his eyes at me. "But you didn't?"

"I did. At least I thought I did. But then he put his hand under my top ... and ..."

"And what, Joey?" he snaps. "Did he do something to you?"

"No, Max. He was a perfect gentleman. I told him to stop, and he did. Straight away."

"Then why were you so upset?"

"Because I wanted to enjoy it. Toby is a nice guy. He's cute. He's into me. He's emotionally available. I wanted to want him, but he ..."

His hands ball into fists, knuckles turning white. "He what?"

"He wasn't you." The words burst out of my mouth, and I can't call them back, no matter how badly I wish I could. It's too late.

His eyes darken as he draws a deep breath through his nose.

"We kissed for almost ten minutes, and I felt nothing. When I'm with you, I feel—" My throat tightens, and I swallow before I say too much.

"What do you feel with me?" he asks, probing even though I don't want him to. He already has too much of me, I can't give him more. But the way he looks at me, with such longing and intensity, it breaks through every single defense I have.

"Alive," I whisper. "Like my soul is on fire. And when you kiss me—" I suck in a breath that makes me cough and stutter. "T-Toby was sweet and gentle and kind, but I don't want that, Max. I want to feel the bite of fingertips digging into my flesh, teeth biting at my skin. I want a hand around my throat."

His tattooed hand moves so fast I barely have time to blink before it's wrapped around my neck. He squeezes gently. "Nobody puts a hand on your throat, baby girl. Nobody but me.

Ever. You got that?" Wet heat pools between my thighs. He dips his head and runs his nose along my jawline as his fingertips flex on my throat. "What happens when I kiss you?" His harsh whisper sends a shiver down the length of my spine.

"I get this ache," I pant, my heart rate doubling as I gasp for breath.

His grip loosens. "Breathe, Joey."

I blink at him, his dark eyes burning into mine as I regulate my breathing.

"Where do you ache, baby girl?"

"B-between my thighs."

He arches one eyebrow. "What kind of ache?"

"Like ..." I dart out my tongue and run it over my bottom lip. "It makes me feel wet and needy."

"Yeah?" His free hand slides up my thigh until his fingers hover over the button of my jeans.

"Max," I whimper, rocking my hips.

He opens my jeans with ease, and then his hand is in my panties and my blood thunders through my veins while wetness surges between my thighs. His fingertip brushes my clit. I tremble. "Fuck, you are wet, baby," he says with a groan. "Who did this to you?"

I moan. "It's all you."

He removes his other hand from my throat and tangles it in the hair at the back of my head. Pulling my head back, he slides his hand deeper into my panties. My back arches into the pleasure, giving his wicked mouth better access to my neck. He takes full advantage, trailing his teeth over my sensitive skin and making me shiver.

"So fucking tight, baby girl," he growls as he shoves his entire hand into my underwear. He pushes a thick finger inside me, and my jeans slide farther down my hips. I almost come apart on the spot.

"M-Max, please?" I whimper as he slowly thrusts in and out of me.

"Hmm. Needy too." He chuckles wickedly. Tongue and teeth lash at a sensitive spot on my neck while he gently finger fucks me in the middle of the woods on his motorcycle.

I wrap my arms around his neck, curling my fingers in his thick dark hair as I rock against him.

"That's it, ride my hand," he commands, rubbing the heel of his palm over my clit. "My needy little slut."

"Oh. My. God!" My eyes roll back in my head as an intense orgasm crashes into me. If it wasn't for Max's arms holding me upright, I'd fall off this bike and crumple to the ground in a heap.

"You feel better, baby girl?" he asks as he pulls his hand out of my jeans. Heat blooms beneath my skin as I watch him place his finger in his mouth and suck it clean before releasing it with a wet pop. "Sweetest thing I ever tasted." He grins.

"You think you're so smooth."

He stares at me, his jaw ticking and his eyes roaming over my face. Like he wants to tell me something but he's searching for the words. "I should get you home," he finally says.

"No!" I shout the word, surprising both of us. "Take me to your place, Max. Please?"

He sighs heavily. "I can't, Joey."

"Why not?"

"Because you're Joey. Lorenzo and Dante would never forgive me."

"You can screw me in an alleyway and finger bang me on the back of your motorcycle, and that's okay? But spending the night with me is crossing the line?"

Pain flashes across his face for a split second before his brow furrows with annoyance. "Joey," he pleads.

"Ash will tell Dante and Lorenzo that I'm with you. I can say

I'm staying at your place. They'll know I'm safe. Just take me to bed. Just once?" I beg him, tears pricking at my eyes.

He stares at me for what feels like forever before he finally speaks. "You're going to get me fucking killed, Joey Moretti." Then he reaches down and snatches our helmets off the ground, motioning for me to get on the bike.

NINETEEN

JOEY

For some reason, Max drives us further away from the city—away from his penthouse apartment and north toward the river. He eventually stops his bike outside a beautiful log cabin in the woods. He cuts the engine and taps my leg, signaling me to climb off.

"Where are we?"

He frowns. "I never told you about this place?"

"No."

"Hmm." He rubs a hand over his thick beard. "I like to come here sometimes."

"Is it yours?" I look at the beautiful cabin that's currently shrouded in darkness.

"Of course it is." He laughs softly and takes my hand, leading me to the front door.

My legs are shaking by the time we get inside. This place is so secluded, I wonder if anyone even knows it's here. I doubt anyone knows we're here. Not that I'm scared of being alone with Max, but the thought of being completely isolated with him makes me more nervous than I've ever felt in my entire life.

He takes his cell from his pocket and eyes me with concern.

"I'll let your brothers know you're with me and you'll be back tomorrow, okay?"

Is he waiting for me to change my mind? Not gonna happen. "Okay."

I wander around the large open-plan living area while Max types out a text. It's so cozy. Big sofas with soft cushions. Soft rugs on the floor. A huge fireplace that I would love to see blazing in the winter.

"Do you, uh, bring a lot of women here?"

He tosses his phone onto the sofa and stalks toward me. "No."

I swallow my nerves. I'm shaking like a freaking leaf.

"Why are you so nervous, baby girl? I don't have any power over you, remember?"

Holy fuck! Why the hell did I say that earlier? I think I'm going to pass out.

"I d-didn't—"

"You need me to remind you exactly what you said?"

No. I'd like to make you forget it instead. "You know I was just mouthing off," I whisper.

He arches an eyebrow. "Just being a spoiled brat?"

"Well, isn't that all you think I am?"

Sliding his arms around my waist, he palms my ass cheeks and yanks me toward him. He bends his head low so he can whisper in my ear. "Oh, you're so much more than that, baby girl."

Before I can come back with a snappy retort, he lifts me, wraps my legs around his waist, and carries me through the living area. He kicks open a door to a bedroom, walks inside, and lays me down on the bed.

I stare up at him, my heart racing wildly and my blood thundering. I'm hot. I'm wet. And I need him so badly. I would do literally anything he told me to right now. Anything.

Max brushes my hair back from my face, his fingertips grazing over my neck as he feels for the fastening of my St. Christopher pendant. My brothers gave it to me when I left for Italy, warning me never to take it off. I rarely do—not because they told me not to, but because it belonged to my mom.

I blink at him. "Why are you taking off my pendant?"

"I don't think St. Christopher needs to be a part of any of this," he says with a wicked grin. "And I don't want to damage it. I'm not going to be gentle."

Holy mother of fuzzy ducks!

Placing the pendant on the nightstand, he winks at me before he kneels on the floor and wordlessly pulls off my socks and sneakers, then works his way up and unbuttons my jeans, sliding them over my hips and down my legs. I suck in a stuttered breath. Obviously he's fucked me before, but he told me he didn't even get halfway inside. And now we're here and Max is looking at me like a starving animal looks at its prey. He leans over me, running his nose over the damp fabric of my panties. "Fuck, Joey," he groans.

"I-I'm nervous," I admit on a whisper.

"I know, baby girl," he says with a wicked smile. He tugs my panties aside and runs the tip of his finger through my dripping folds. "But I'm going to make sure you're ready before I fuck you."

"Oh, god," I whimper as tremors ripple through my body.

"And I'm gonna need you soaking wet for the way I like to fuck." His tone is deep and soothing, and it melts into my bones. Maximo DiMarco is going to ruin me for all other men. He's barely touched me and I'm on the verge of falling apart. My entire body comes alive with spine-tingling anticipation.

"So, how about we get you naked." He peels my panties down my legs and grips them in his hand. Holding them to his face, he inhales, and my cheeks burn at the sight. Max DiMarco is a sinful sex god. And, for tonight at least, he's mine. "Your smell is fucking addictive. I'm hard as fucking stone, and I haven't even tasted your sweet pussy yet."

"Max," I groan. His dirty mouth is so hot.

He throws my panties onto the floor and pulls me up, taking off my tank top and bra in two swift moves before pushing me back down. Then he just stares at me for the longest time, his eyes raking over my body as a low growl rumbles in his chest.

"Max?" I whisper.

"Just memorizing every single inch of you, Joey. You're fucking perfect."

My skin flushes with heat at his praise. I'm such a sucker for him and he knows it. He bends his head and runs his hands up the inside of my thighs, pressing my legs flat to the bed as he trails hungry kisses over my skin—all the way from my knees to my center. He rubs his nose over my clit, and my back arches off the bed. "Fuck, Max."

"Oh, baby girl," he groans. "You're so fucking desperate for me. Your pussy is dripping onto my sheets."

"I'm sorry."

He playfully nips at my thigh. "It wasn't a complaint. I'm gonna paint this whole fucking room in your cum tonight."

Holy fuck!

He pushes my thighs down further until I'm pinned to the mattress and then licks from my pussy entrance all the way up to my clit, grunting like an animal when he does. His hot, delicious tongue swirls over the hypersensitive bundle of nerves, and my eyes roll in my head. I damn near pass out. Why the hell didn't anyone tell me sex was this good?

"Oh, fuck, Joey. You're so damn sweet, baby. Your cunt is fucking delicious."

Tangling my hands in his thick hair, I pull his head back. I'm so sensitive and on edge that I squirm beneath him, but he holds fast, licking and nibbling on my clit and causing flickers of starlight to dance behind my eyelids.

I cry out, but he's undeterred as he sucks hard and brings me to such an insanely intense orgasm, I feel like I might cry. I pant for breath as heat and pleasure fight for control of my body.

"Good girl," he soothes as he gives me a brief reprieve, peppering kisses over my thighs. "But we're gonna go again, okay?"

"No. I can't. It's too much."

He laughs at my feeble protest. "You can, baby. Your body is just getting used to something new." And to prove his point, his mouth returns to my pussy again, lapping at my opening as his tongue and lips move expertly over my flesh. "I could eat you for fucking hours," he whispers, and the vibration against my sensitive flesh makes me shudder. He's going to kill me with orgasms.

Then, when I finally get used to the feeling of his mouth on me and the sensitivity gives way to warm waves of pleasure, he slides a thick finger deep inside me and I scream his name so loudly I swear the walls shake.

"Fuck," he grunts, pushing his finger deeper and curling the tip until he rubs against that spot inside me he seems to find so easily. "Come again for me, baby girl."

Come for him? I couldn't *not* come, even if my life depended on it. A second orgasm barrels into me like a freight train, knocking all the breath from my body. Shuddering uncontrollably, I gasp for air. Max is there the whole time, stroking my neck and whispering in my ear. "Breathe, Joey."

I nod, sucking in deep lungfuls of air.

"You hold your breath when you come, did you know that?" he says, frowning.

I shake my head. "Is that bad?"

"No, but tonight, I say when you get to breathe. You got that?"

I sink my teeth into my lower lip and nod, still coming down from the epic high he gave me.

"Good. Now turn over," he orders.

I arch an eyebrow at him. Is he finally going to fuck me? Please god!

"Now."

"You're so demanding," I say with a sigh, but I flip onto my stomach and wiggle my ass in his face. He responds by slapping it hard, and I groan.

"Oh, my naughty brat likes a spanking, huh?" He smacks me again, and wetness drips from my pussy. I bite down on the pillow to stop another horny moan from escaping.

Max pushes my thighs apart and kneels between them. Then he grabs my hips and pulls me up until I'm on all fours. "Come here."

"Are you going to fuck me now?"

He pushes a finger inside me, and my back bows as white-hot pleasure sears my core. Then he adds a second and I moan at the burn of him stretching me wider. "Not yet, baby girl."

I drop my head onto the pillow and pout.

"I haven't finished eating yet." He trails kisses over my ass cheeks, soothing the sting of where he just spanked me. And then his mouth is on my ass, his tongue flicking over the seam as he moves lower until he's feasting on my pussy again. This time all the attention is on my entrance as he slides his tongue inside me.

"M-Max." My body latches onto the flickering embers of my previous orgasm to ignite another one.

He murmurs appreciatively and goes on eating, swirling his tongue inside me like he's making out with my pussy. His fingers brush over my clit, and I sink my teeth into the pillow to stop from screaming the entire house down.

He threads his fingers in my hair and pulls my head up. "Stop that, Joey. If I'm making you come, I want to hear every fucking sound you make."

I groan, and he goes back to eating me and rubbing my clit with the most perfect, delicious amount of friction and pressure until my inner walls pulse and every cell in my body trembles with the need to come. "Please, Max."

"Who has all the power now, baby girl?" He laughs darkly, and I'm too fraught and desperate to call him an asshole for it.

Instead, in my desperation, I whimper. "You do. Always."

"Now that's my good fucking girl." He groans against my flesh, slipping his tongue back inside me and causing my orgasm to go off like a nuclear warhead in my core. It tears through me, wrenching a guttural cry from my throat.

My shoulders sink to the pillow until I'm lying with my ass up in the air, trembling and gasping for air once more.

Max pushes two fingers inside me, and a loud groan of appreciation rumbles through him when they slide in easily. "Now you're ready to be fucked."

"Yes, please," I breathe, desperate to feel him. My pussy aches to be filled by him completely.

I hear the sound of his zipper opening. The crown of his cock presses at my entrance. "You remember the first time I fucked you, Joey?"

"Uh-huh."

"How you couldn't feel my piercings because I couldn't get far enough inside of you?"

"Yeah," I whisper, cheeks flushing red. It was also because I had no idea what having an actual dick inside me should feel like.

"I'm going to fit my whole cock in you tonight, baby girl,

and you know how you're going to know when I'm all the way in?"

"How?"

"Because you're going to count my piercings."

"Count?"

"Yeah, count. There's six of them, all for you, Joey. This one" —he rubs the piercing in his crown over my clit and makes me whimper with need—"you won't feel until I'm all the way in and I'm rubbing this bar against your G-spot. But the others you'll feel while I'm filling your tight little cunt with my cock. Okay?"

Holy mother of fucks! "Okay."

"Good girl. You count each one as I enter you, okay?"

I nod but wonder if Max's giant monster cock will actually fit inside me. I was barely able to take half of him last time and I felt sore for days, even though it was the delicious kind of pain that makes a girl like me smile.

Max pushes the tip inside me, stretching me wide. It burns a little, but I'm so wet that he slides in without resistance. I groan, pushing my ass back against him, but he grabs my hips and holds me steady. "Not yet, baby."

"Max," I whine, and he slaps my ass.

Then he gives me another inch, and I realize why he's going so slow. Because no matter how wet I am, he's still freaking huge. My pussy is stretched further than it's ever been, and I wince at the sting. But then one of his piercings rubs against my pussy walls, and I release a gush of arousal. "One," I cry.

"Good girl."

My toes curl as Max pulls out a little before pushing back in, drawing more wetness from deep inside me as he pushes in farther. "Two."

"That's my girl."

Two? That means we have four more to go. I have no idea how I'm going to take the rest of him.

He bends over me and presses soft kisses over my back. "You're doing so well. Such a good girl for me."

I melt under his praise, practically purring like a kitten, and he takes the opportunity to slide deeper. "Three." And then deeper. "Four," I grit out.

He rubs one hand over my back while he holds onto my hip with the other. "Almost there."

"Oh, god," I whimper as he rocks his hips and his piercings rub against my walls, the tiny barbells massaging me in the most delicious way. Jolts of electric ecstasy ricochet through me, and I almost come again.

"Fuck, Joey. You love my cock."

"Y-yeah." My eyes roll back as he keeps me balanced on the precipice of ecstasy.

He pulls out and drives in a little harder, and I feel so much more of him. "F-five!" I scream.

"Oh, there she is," he grunts, wrapping my hair around his fist and pulling me up until my back is pressed against his bare chest. "My naughty little slut."

"Yeah."

"You ready to feel the sixth one?"

"Uh-huh."

He slides his free arm around my waist, holding me tight as he rolls his hips, driving farther inside me until I feel that final piercing—and I mean I feel it in the very depths of my soul. From the tips of my toes to the end of every single hair on my head. That spot he can reach with his fingers? Well, he can damn well give it a deep tissue massage with the end of his cock. "S-six," I cry out, bucking and shuddering so hard in his arms that he has to hold me still.

His mouth is on my neck, devouring me. Covering me with

feral licks and bites as he holds me tight and thrusts into me. "Fuck, baby girl, you were made for my cock," he growls, driving deep so that every single piercing rubs against a spot inside me that's already overstimulated and sensitive. "Made for me."

My legs are already shaking as he slips his hand between my thighs and rubs the pads of two fingers over my clit. He rubs softly—his touch taunting and teasing me and so at odds with the way he thrusts into me like a man possessed.

I squirm in his arms as the sensations become too overwhelming, but he tugs me closer until I can't tell where my body begins and his ends. I feel every flex of his hard muscles as he fucks me with brutal strokes. His chest against my back, thighs against mine, teeth and lips grazing my neck, his giant arms encasing me—so huge that they dwarf my smaller frame. He is everything and everywhere. All-consuming and completely intoxicating.

Sweat covers our bodies as our breathing grows heavier.

"You feel so fucking good," he grunts.

"You fuck me so good."

Ecstasy settles over me like a heavy blanket.

I hold my breath.

"Breathe, Joey," he commands.

I suck in a mouthful of air at the same time he rolls his hips and the pierced tip of his cock hits my G-spot. Bright specks of light flicker behind my eyelids while waves of hot, electric pleasure roll through my body, converging in a spot deep inside my pussy.

"Holy shit, Max, I'm gonna—gonna come ... again. A-and I don't know if I can." This feels different from before. Such an intense build-up of pressure. Lightheaded, all I can do is whimper and moan and take what he gives me.

"You can, baby girl. Let go. I got you."

And then it happens. A tsunami of cum—at least I hope it's cum—gushes out of me, soaking me and Max and leaving a puddle on the bed.

"Jesus fucking Christ, Joey." He rails into me, his hips slamming against my ass as he gives me everything he has. Driving into me with such force that the bed rattles against the wall. I feel his abs tighten and his thighs tense seconds before his hips go still. "Motherfucking! Fuck!" he roars as he empties himself inside me, grinding against me until I'm filled with every last drop of his cum.

Then he falls forward onto the bed, collapsing on top of me as we both gasp for breath.

"Holy shit, Max," I pant.

"I know, baby." He gasps the words against my ear, his breath damp and hot against my neck.

I have never felt safer or happier than I do right now. If I died tomorrow, I could say that I lived because of this right here.

TWENTY

Holy motherfucking fuck! My legs are still shaking as I hold Joey in my arms, probably squeezing her tighter than I should because I need her as close to me as humanly fucking possible. This woman was born to be mine. I don't give a fuck what her brothers say or all the reasons why she shouldn't be mine, I'm taking her anyway.

I knew this would happen when she begged me to take her home and fuck her. I knew that saying yes would mean this. That I couldn't get a taste of her and have the strength to let her go again. And even though I was fully aware of the price we'd both have to pay, how could I say no to her when she looked at me that way? After she questioned whether she was good enough for me when that couldn't be further from the truth?

I texted her brothers and told them she was spending the night at my place because she'd had too much to drink, and then I texted Kristin and told her I wouldn't be home until tomorrow. There's one fatal flaw in my plan, but I can't think about it now. All I can think about is her. Saying yes to taking her to my bed might have seemed like a moment of madness at the time, but now I realize it was a moment of absolute fucking clarity. I have never been as sure of anything or anyone as I am of her.

She breathes hard, her eyes closed and cheeks pink, with a contented smile on her face. Yeah, she's content, I just made her come so fucking hard she drenched us both. I brush her hair from her forehead where it's stuck to her damp skin. "You okay, baby girl?"

"I'm ..." She sighs deeply. "That was amazing, Max."

I can't help the smug smile that spreads across my face. But I pushed her hard and she's so inexperienced. "Are you sore?"

"Deliciously so," she whispers, snuggling her face against my chest.

Shit. I might need to fuck her again in about ten minutes. The way her leg is draped over me has her wet pussy resting against my hip, and I'm already getting hard.

I brush over her pussy with my fingertips and study her face. She winces a little, but that smile grows wider and a soft moan bubbles out of her throat. Oh, she is so getting fucked again.

I roll on top of her, pinning her to the mattress. She gasps, but I seal my mouth over hers, swallowing the sound as I taste her. Exploring her mouth with my tongue as my hand runs over her body, seeking out every part of her so I will never forget a single second of this time with her. I squeeze one of her perfect tits, and she whimpers into my mouth, rocking her hips up as I maneuver myself between her thighs. Her heart beats fast against mine as she kisses me back with a fervor that makes my cock ache. I nudge the crown at her soaking wet hole, making her arch her back and groan.

"You took me so fucking well before, baby girl. You think you can do it again?"

"Yes," she pants, her eyes dark and full of heat. She needs this as much as I do.

"I'll take it easy this time."

"No. Max. I want all of you."

I sink my cock a little deeper into her, and her mouth falls open in a perfect O as searing pleasure spikes through my entire body. The way her tight, wet cunt squeezes my cock feels like fucking heaven. Better than heaven. I want to live and die fucking this woman. "You'll get all of me, but I need to go a little slower because you're gonna take me over and over again tonight. I'm going to fuck you until sunrise."

"Fuck, Max," she whimpers.

"You feel so fucking good." I drive in further. She's wet and ready, and that makes it easier this time, but she's still so fucking tight. "Spread a little wider for me, baby girl. I don't want to hurt you." *Yet.*

"You won't."

I wrap a hand around her throat and sink all the way inside. My eyes locked on hers, I watch her face intently as she takes every inch of me until I'm buried balls deep in her pussy. I circle my hips, and her eyes roll back in her head. "You like that?"

"Y-yeah."

I squeeze her throat a little tighter as I go on thrusting my hips, rubbing my piercing over her G-spot until she whimpers and claws at my back.

"Breathe, Joey," I remind her, and she sucks in a breath. "You need to get air while you can, baby, because I'm going to squeeze a little tighter soon and you're not going to be able to breathe. You understand?"

"Yes."

Fuck, I love how much she trusts me. "I won't let anything happen to you, but if it gets too much or you get scared, you tap me, okay?"

"Tap out," she says with a wicked smile.

"Yeah, you tap out." I seal my mouth over hers, kissing her deeply as I drag my cock in and out of her soaking pussy, and each time I slide back in, I roll my hips and make sure she feels every single inch. And when her pussy walls start to ripple around my cock and her thighs start to tremble, I squeeze the sides of her throat, cutting off her air.

I keep kissing her, stealing what little breath she has left as I slide deep into her pussy. And those few seconds right before she comes, just before her body starts to fight the lack of oxygen, I release my grip and break our kiss, letting her gasp for air as her orgasm rocks through her body.

The way her body shudders, her cunt's death grip on my cock, and the way her eyelids flutter as she sucks in deep, bone-shaking breaths send me hurtling over the edge with her. I drive into her one last time and spill my cum deep inside her as I grunt and curse in her ear.

"Holy shit, Max, that was intense," she pants, her hot breath on my skin as I slide out of her.

"I know, baby."

"Is sex always like this? Because I think I may have been missing out." She laughs softly, but I don't find what she said the slightest bit amusing.

I push myself up onto my forearms and glare at her. "What do you think, baby girl? You think if you'd have hooked up with some guy in a bar or let Toby fuck you tonight that it would it have been like this?" Her throat constricts as she swallows, her dark eyes full of defiance. "Or you think it's like this because it's with me?"

"I guess I wouldn't know, seeing as how you're the only guy I've ever been with."

"And I'm the only one you will ever be with."

She narrows her eyes. I guess she needs to be reminded who

she belongs to. I'm hard again—always fucking hard around her. Without warning, I sink back inside her, making her cry out my name.

"You think anyone else would make you feel this good?" I ask as I nail her to the bed. I'm not gentle this time. This time I will mold her tight cunt to the shape of my cock forever. She will feel me inside her until the end of her fucking days.

"No, Max," she cries, clinging to me. Wrapping her legs around my waist, she pulls me closer. "I meant sex with you."

"You did, huh?" I pound harder, burying my head in her neck and filling my senses with her smell and her taste.

"Why do you think I waited so long? I waited for you." Tears drip from her jaw onto my face.

I lift my head and brush her hair back, looking at her as I fuck her into oblivion. "Who does this pussy belong to?" I slam into her.

"Y-you."

"Will anyone else ever fuck you again?" Thrust.

"No." She throws her head back and I drag my teeth over the soft skin of her neck.

"Kiss you?" Thrust.

"No."

"Taste you?" Thrust.

"No, Max."

"Damn right, baby girl, because you're mine. I warned you that my kind of love wasn't what you were looking for, but you went after it anyway. And now that you got it, it's not the kind you can escape."

She wraps her arms tighter around my neck, tugging at my hair until I lift my head. She stares into my eyes. "It's the only kind I've ever wanted, Max." With a smirk, she arches into me. "So stop being an asshole and just make me come."

Fuck me. This woman is perfect in every single fucking way.

"An asshole?" I circle my hips again, and she moans as her hot juices flood her pussy and soak my cock. "I'm going to make you pay for that."

"I'm counting on it."

TWENTY-ONE

I rest my lips on her hair and stare out the window at the rising sun. Joey's worn out from being awake most of the night. We ate and talked, and then I fucked her again— and again—until she fell asleep in my arms. I stayed awake because I would never risk hurting her while I slept. She's the most precious thing in the entire world to me, and I would never recover if I ever harmed her.

The banging on the door isn't unexpected, although I didn't anticipate them getting here this early.

Joey's head jerks up, her eyelids fluttering open. "Max?"

"Get dressed, baby girl."

She blinks at me. "But who could that be?"

"Your brothers."

"My ... What? How? Why?"

"You have a tracker in your phone, baby. I have one in mine too."

"So, you knew? You knew they'd find out?" She shakes her head, dislodging the remnants of her peaceful sleep. "Why didn't you tell me?" She gasps, jumping up from the bed and scrabbling for her clothes. "They'll kill you, Max. No! We'll tell

135

them I slept on the sofa. No, no, you did." She pulls on her jeans, her eyes as wild as her fucked-all-night hair. "You'd never make me sleep on the sofa."

I climb out of bed and grab hold of her, putting a stop to her rambling and forcing her to look up at me. "Joey, stop. I'll tell them the truth."

"But ..." She stares at me like I've lost my mind.

"I'll figure something out, I promise."

"They'll hate you," she whispers.

"If they do, it was worth it."

"Max, no." Her bottom lip trembles.

I wrap her in my arms and kiss the top of her head. "Last night was perfect, baby girl, and no matter what happens from here on out, I wouldn't change a single second of it."

The banging on the door grows louder. If I don't open it in the next minute, at least one livid Moretti brother will bust inside. I give her a quick kiss on the forehead. After getting dressed, I leave her in the bedroom and head to the front door that rattles in its frame from the force of the banging on the other side.

I open it to a red-faced Dante, hand suspended in midair as though he was about to hammer on it again. "Where the fuck is she?" he demands.

"She's here. She's safe."

His older brother climbs out of the black SUV in the driveway and stalks toward us.

"Joey," Dante shouts, pushing past me just in time to see her walk out of my bedroom, looking every inch like the woman I thoroughly fucked all night long. He doesn't waste time asking any more questions. Instead, he punches me straight in the mouth, causing me to stagger back a step.

"Dante!" Joey shrieks.

"You piece of fucking shit. She's my little sister," he roars, raising his fist to come at me again, but this time I duck and sucker punch him in the stomach. He stumbles back. When he straightens up, he glares at me. "You've known her for her whole fucking life. I fucking trusted you, you lying fuck."

"I know, D," is all I can say. I have no defense.

He launches himself at me, knocking me back over the sofa. We tumble over the side and fall into a heap on the floor.

"Max. Dante. Stop!" Joey yells, but we ignore her, throwing punches and rolling around the floor as we try to get the better of each other. I punch him in the mouth and split his lip, and he lands a blow to the side of my head that makes me see stars.

Joey screams and hollers in the background, but neither of us pay any attention. Dante remains focused on ripping my head off and I'm occupied by my attempts to prevent that from happening.

"Dante!" another voice cuts through the air, and that's when he stops. We both do. Lorenzo stands in the open door-way, and the sun shining from behind him makes him look like a vengeful shadow. "Enough," he barks, then looks over at his sister. "Get in the car."

She folds her arms across her chest. "No. I'm not leaving Max."

Lorenzo closes his eyes and rubs his temples. "I don't have fucking time for this. Get into the car, Joey. Now."

"But—"

"But nothing. Your family needs you. Now get in the fucking car."

Joey looks to me as Dante and I haul our asses off the floor and straighten ourselves up.

I jerk my head at the door. "Go with them."

"No." She shakes her head. Tears prick at her eyes and a sob catches in her throat.

"You can't stay with me, Joey. Not right now."

"But you said!" Pain contorts her beautiful face.

"I'll fix this, I promise. Just give me a few days."

"The fuck you will," Dante says with a snort.

"The car, Guiseppina. Now!" Lorenzo shouts.

I nod at her, and with a glare, she swats the tears from her cheeks before storming out of the house. I look at Lorenzo, hoping he might see reason because at least he hasn't punched me in the mouth yet, but all I find is disappointment and anguish. Fuck! His wife is dying and he's here dealing with this instead of spending time with her.

"I'm sorry, I ..." I swallow the thick knot lodged in my throat.

"No you're not," Lorenzo spits. The venom in his tone hurts me even more than his younger brother's fists. The three of us have been best friends for as long as I can remember, and the way they're looking at me right now fucking kills me.

"No, I'm not," I admit. "But I should have done things differently."

"You could have any fucking woman you want," Dante says as he steps over to join his brother—to stand against me. "But you had to pick our kid sister. Why the fuck, Max?"

"I didn't plan this."

"How long?" Lorenzo asks.

"Was the whole date with Toby just a cover?" Dante adds.

"No. She went on a date with Toby. She was upset. I picked her up."

"So, you took advantage of her?" Dante accuses.

"No," I protest. "I would never fucking do that."

"You are a lying piece of shit, Max. Why the fuck would I trust anything that comes out of your mouth ever again?"

"Because you know me," I remind them.

"Not anymore. You're fucking dead to me." Dante spins on his heel and strides out of the house.

"Loz?"

He just shakes his head and follows his brother out.

I stand in the doorway and watch them drive away with my girl, wondering if she's looking back through those tinted windows. I knew this would happen, didn't I? And I took the risk anyway. But they're sadly fucking mistaken if they think I won't come for her. As soon as I can sort out the mess with Kristin, I'll be ready to take my girl back.

And if her brothers are intent on standing in my way, I guess I'll have to go through them.

TWENTY-TWO

JOEY—AGE 18

I stare out of the car window, my head spinning and my stomach churning as Max drives me home. I've never felt more humiliated in my life as I did when he turned up at Mo's party and literally dragged Logan Blake off me by the scruff of his neck while we were making out.

Logan is *the* hottest guy in this whole goddamn city, and I finally get a shot with him only to have it spectacularly and publicly ruined by my older brothers' attack dog. But the humiliation is nothing compared to the anxiety at facing my brothers' wrath when I get home. I was already on my last warning for sneaking out, but what's a girl to do when the two of them don't even give me room to breathe? And Max is no better. He watches me like a hawk. They should applaud my ingenuity at being able to escape their clutches occasionally.

Not that being rescued by Max usually bothers me so much. He is HOT. Man-hot, not boy-hot like Logan. Max is the whole freaking package. Dark and dangerous, with muscles on top of muscles and a body covered by tattoos. I love the way they peek out of his dress shirts, revealing a glimpse of the hidden secrets beneath.

Not that anything could ever happen between us. He sees me as his best friends' annoying kid sister and nothing more. But that doesn't stop me from staring at him every chance I get and making him feel as uncomfortable as humanly possible.

"Did you really have to do that tonight?" I ask with a sigh and an eye roll.

"Do what?" he says coolly, as though he didn't just ruin my goddamn life.

"Grab Logan like that? Drag me out of that party like a naughty teenager?"

He glances at me sideways, taking his eyes off the road for a split second. "You are a naughty teenager."

"I'm eighteen!" I snap.

"You snuck out of the fucking house with no protection—"

"Actually I have plenty of condoms in my purse," I say with a casual shrug. It's a lie, but it's way too much fun to see that thick vein bulge in his neck when he's pissed.

His knuckles turn white as his grip tightens on the steering wheel. "That's not the kind of protection I meant, Joey," he says with a snarl. "What the fuck?"

"I know." I suppress a snicker. "But why are you so bothered about what guys I might hook up with, Maximo?" I ask seductively, running my fingertips over his arm.

"Because I fucking care about you," he snaps. "And I don't want to see you hurt. You keep putting yourself in these stupid fucking situations—"

"I was at a goddamn party," I yell. "That's what eighteen-year-olds do."

"With a purse full of fucking condoms," he says through gritted teeth.

"Better that than an unwanted pregnancy, huh?" I laugh. "Can you imagine what Dante and Lorenzo would say if that happened?"

"Can you imagine what your father would say?" His cold tone is a sobering reminder of why I've never had sex with anyone. And why most guys wouldn't even dare try. A shudder runs down my spine. "Can you imagine what we would do to the poor guy who knocked you up, Joey?" he adds, his tone a little softer now.

"We?" I whisper.

"I would cut off his cock with a blunt hacksaw before your brothers even got anywhere near him," he tells me matter-of-factly.

"Well, you don't need to worry. I've never had sex. Never likely to, given that I'm basically a prisoner and now I'm going to be on complete lockdown until college starts."

Max's Adam's apple bobs as he swallows. "You've never ...?"

"Nope," I snap, going back to staring out of the window. "No guy stupid enough to fuck Joey Moretti around here."

"Joey." My name is a heavy sigh tumbling from his lips.

"Just take me home, Max. Let me listen to my lecture so I can go to bed and forget this awful night ever happened."

He opens his mouth, probably about to come up with another bullshit excuse for why he and my brothers are overbearing assholes who treat me like I'm a second-class citizen, but he closes it without saying anything, and the rest of the drive is spent in awkward silence.

TWO DAYS LATER, I find myself sitting in a car with Max again. Only this time he's driving me to the airport. My brothers were beyond pissed when I got home the other night, and I guess this is my punishment. My heart is heavy in my chest, and I fight back tears as I stare out of the window. I finger the St. Christopher pendant absent-mindedly. Apparently he's the patron saint of travelers. It belonged to my mom, and my brothers gave me it for this trip.

Never take it off, Joey! As if some crusty old saint is going to protect me. But I'll always wear it because it was my mom's. And because a part of me believes that there's something bigger than me in the universe.

"They're doing this to protect you, Joey," Max says softly.

I ignore him. He's as big an asshole as the rest of them. They can dress this up any damn way they please but shipping me off to some convent school in Italy will never be what's best for me.

"They just want—"

"Stop!" I shout. "Just stop it. You're as bad as they are."

Max sighs deeply, but at least he stops talking. I continue to stare out the window. My brothers couldn't even be bothered to take me to the airport themselves. Instead they farmed me out to Max to handle. Dealing with all that female emotion would be too much for the Moretti brothers, right? They think they're so damn tough, but they can't handle a few tears. *Cowards.*

A tear runs down my cheek, and I swat it away before Max sees. It's easier to focus on my rage toward my brothers right now. If I lose sight of that, all I'll have left is the soul-crushing despair of being sent to live on the other side of the world with people I don't even know.

When Dante and Lorenzo told me yesterday that I was going to Italy for three years and that I had no say at all in the matter, I thought they were playing a practical joke. No discussion. No consideration of my feelings at all. The decision was made, and it was final. I guess the joke's on me.

The two of them barely looked at me once after breaking their news. Not even Anya fought for me, which is so unlike her. She stands up to them on my behalf all the time, but not on this. She sat quietly by and watched while they ruined my whole life.

And here I am, headed to Italy all alone. Well except for the four armed escorts who will accompany me until I reach the convent school and receive my new security detail. No family. No friends. Nobody.

"Joey," Maximo says softly, and I realize I'm crying.

"Leave me the hell alone," I sniff. Max moved into our house when I was four. He's ten years older, and he always looked out for me like a big brother. Although for the past two years, I've fantasized about him being way more than that. I flirt with him constantly, and he pretends not to notice. His betrayal hurts just as much as my brothers' does.

When we pull up at the airport, I reach for the door handle but Maximo locks it, preventing me from leaving.

"Joey. Look at me."

"No." He doesn't get to give me some speech about this being for my own good to make himself feel better. They're getting rid of me because I'm a pain in their ass and their lives will be easier without me in it. Nothing he says can convince me otherwise.

"Joey," he says, his voice low and demanding.

I turn and glare at him.

"One day you will see that this was for your protection ..."

"The fuck I will!"

He closes his eyes and draws a deep breath through his nose. When he opens them again, he places his hand on my chin and a jolt of electricity surges through me. He tilts my head until I'm forced to look at him. "Your brothers only want what's best for you, and I promise you that one day you'll see that."

I let the tears run freely down my cheeks. Screw them all to hell. "You're a fucking liar, Max. This is my punishment and we both know it."

Shaking his head, he sighs. "It's not. But sometimes the right thing to do hurts, Joey."

"The right thing for who? Dante and Lorenzo? Because this only benefits them as far as I can see. Get Joey out of the way and forget about her, yeah?" I wipe my cheeks with the sleeve of my sweatshirt.

"I wish I could explain," he says, his brow furrowed in a frown. "But just know that they would do anything to protect you."

"I'm eighteen years old. I don't need their goddamn protection."

He grips my jaw tighter, his eyes burning into mine. "Listen to me, Joey Moretti," he commands. "Like it or not, you will always be a target. There will always be men who will want to hurt you. To make you feel less than simply because you're a woman who was born into power."

"I'm not—"

He narrows his eyes in warning, and I stop talking.

"There'll be people who will try to take that power from you using any means necessary. Do you understand me?"

"I know our life is dangerous. I know all that already. But I can look after myself. I'm not a child."

"Then stop fucking acting like one," he says, his tone dripping with anger.

"I hate all of you. I'm going to run away the first chance I get, and I will never fucking speak to any of you again."

His jaw ticks and he glowers at me. "You will not fucking run, Joey."

I narrow my eyes at him. "Watch me."

"I will be watching, Joey," he says, his tone menacing. "Know that there is nowhere far enough you can run that I won't find you."

I swallow hard as his dark eyes burn into mine. That sounds like a threat but feels like something more. "Why would you even care to look?" I sniff as another tear rolls down my cheek.

He shakes his head in exasperation.

"Max?"

His eyes narrow as they search my face. "You know why."

I don't. And this all hurts too much for me to figure it out.

"If anyone ever comes for you, Joey, you give them whatever's necessary to keep yourself safe. You have one job and that's to keep yourself alive, you got that?"

I blink at him in confusion. Why is he talking about all this stuff?

He brushes his knuckles over my cheek. "Know that I will always be looking for you, Joey. And I will always find you."

CHAPTER
TWENTY-THREE

JOEY

My chest aches. It feels like my heart is actually breaking. I stare at the backs of my brothers' heads as Lorenzo drives us home. How did my life shift from a dream come true to my worst nightmare in the space of half an hour?

Never in my life have I seen Dante and Lorenzo so angry with Max. I have no recollection of them even having an argument. And now, because of me, they hate him. *You're dead to me.* That's what Dante said.

But nothing hurts more than Max telling me to leave. After everything he said last night, everything we did, he didn't fight for us.

A sob sticks in my throat. I can fix this. I'll make my brothers see that they're being massive overbearing assholes. That they're overreacting. Then I'll talk to Max and we can figure out what to do next.

"Did you choose him just to fucking spite us?" Dante asks, his voice little more than a snarl. It's the first thing he's said to me since he got into the car ten minutes ago.

"What?"

"You heard what I said, Joey. Did you fuck around with Max just to cause trouble?"

I swear he couldn't have shocked me more if he'd turned around and slapped me in the face. The rage in my chest spreads to my arms and legs, making them tingle. "Are you serious right now?"

Dante turns in his seat and glares at me. "One hundred fucking percent serious. It wouldn't be the first time you've pulled some fucked-up shit just to piss me off."

I scowl at him. He's referring to the time I helped Kat with her escape attempt after Dante kidnapped her. That was before I knew how much she meant to him and how much she loved him. Before I knew she was pregnant with my niece. Before she became one of my favorite people in the world. But I can't fucking believe he thinks I would use Max that way. His low opinion of me hurts more than it should. "Not everything in this world revolves around you, Dante." The wrath inside me spills into my voice. It's not enough for the two of them to treat me like a child, he has to accuse me of being a complete bitch too?

"So, why him, Joey? Why not any other guy?"

I lean forward, squaring up to him as he goes on giving me that infamous Dante Moretti glare. "Like you two have ever let me be around other guys?" I yell. "Wherever I go, whoever I meet, as soon as they hear my last name, guys shrivel up and back off faster than I can blink. You think it's easy being me, Dante?"

"What about Toby?"

I shake my head. "I don't like Toby that way."

Lorenzo remains silent, eyes fixed on the road ahead while Dante practically foams at the mouth. "Someone else then!" Dante shouts.

"I don't want anyone else. I want Max. I've only ever

wanted Max, and despite your huge ass ego thinking this is about you, it really isn't. It is *so* not about you. It's about Max and me. Nobody else."

He grumbles something under his breath and throws himself back into his seat. He's acting like a petulant child, throwing a fit because I played with his best friend. And I'm the spoiled brat?

My phone rings, and I take it out of my purse, groaning inwardly. If I don't answer it now, Mo will just keep calling.

"Hey, Mo."

"Hey, girl. How was your date?"

"Fine."

"Fine?" She snorts. "Sounds fun. Did you at least pop your cherry?"

"No."

"No?!" she shrieks. "For fuck's sake, Joey. What the hell are you waiting for?"

"I can't really talk right now. I'm in the car with Dante and Lorenzo."

"Oh, I get it." She snickers. "So you did?"

"No. It's not that." I sigh.

"You're in the car at 7:45 a.m. with your brothers, and it's not because they had to come pick you up from a guy's house?"

"I'll call you later, Mo."

"Make sure you do. I can't wait to hear all the juicy details."

Then she hangs up, and I go back to glaring at the backs of my brothers' heads.

As soon as we got home, I was marched back into the house like a runaway teen. Ignoring the sympathetic glances from Kat and Anya, I stomped upstairs to my room.

I'm beyond pissed at my brothers right now. I can't even think straight. I want nothing to do with them, and that includes their wives too. I'm so over being treated like a second-class citizen in this house.

I lie on my bed, unshed tears blurring my vision as I stare at my phone. No word from Max. Not even a text. Nothing. Was last night a lie? All just a part of his possessive asshole routine? Is he like that with all the women he fucks?

I scroll through my recent calls, and my finger hovers over his name. I could call him, right? But ugh! Why should I? He told me to leave.

Someone taps softly at my door.

"Go away!" I shout.

"I would, but I can't. Your niece is demanding to see you," Kat replies.

Damn! That sneak brought the big guns. "My niece who is five months old and can do nothing but giggle and squeal?"

"And cry," Kat adds, laughing. "But, yes, that's her."

I groan, tossing my phone onto the nightstand and wiping my eyes. "Come in." Kat walks in holding Gabriella, and I sit up and grin as my niece gives me the biggest smile I've ever seen. At least one person in this family isn't constantly disappointed in me.

"Hey, smooch." I take her from Kat's arms as soon as she's within my reach. "You can go now," I say, not bothering to look at my sister-in-law.

Kat ignores me and sits on my bed beside me instead. "How are you?"

"What did they tell you?" Just how much of my sex life has been discussed by my family over the past few hours? I rest my lips against Gabriella's head, kissing her baby-soft skin and inhaling her sweet scent.

"That you spent the night with Max."

My cheeks turn pink with embarrassment, and I roll my eyes. I have no reason to feel embarrassed—my brothers and their wives can barely keep their hands off each other. I've lost count of the number of times I've walked in on Kat and Dante groping each other in the kitchen. Anya and Lorenzo are into some freaky shit. He's her Dom and she wears a collar. Yet none of that is ever talked about. It's just the way things are around here. So why is my sex life a topic for discussion?

"You want to talk about anything?" she asks softly.

"Like how it was the best night of my life until my brothers completely ruined it?"

"Yes, if you want to."

Tears prick at my eyes again, and I shake my head. It feels too raw and personal to share, even with Kat, no matter how much I adore her.

"He told me to leave, Kat. He said I should go with them." I swat a tear away and Gabriella reaches for my finger, curling her chubby little hand around it.

"Well, given how your brothers reacted, he probably thought it was for the best."

"He hasn't even called or texted me."

"Won't he be driving back? If he's on his bike, he won't be able to make a call."

"I guess," I admit with a shrug. "But he told me to go. Like what we did meant nothing."

"Joey." Kat frowns and places a hand on my cheek, catching a rogue tear and brushing it away. "Do you really think he would risk his friendship with your brothers for nothing?"

I let that sink in. Max loves my brothers. He isn't only their friend, he's a part of our family. Suddenly, an incredibly offensive smell drifts into my nostrils, and I gag.

"Wow! Smooch." I chuckle, looking down at my niece who's still holding onto my finger and smiling. "That is nasty."

She giggles at me as I hold her up to her mom.

Kat laughs too. "I guess I'll go deal with that." She puts my niece on her hip and starts to head out of the room.

I call out her name, and she pauses, looking over her shoulder.

"Thanks."

Giving me a gentle smile, she shakes her head. "I know they act like overprotective jerks sometimes, but your brothers love you, Joey. They just want you to be happy and safe."

I'm tired of arguing, so I don't say anything else as she leaves my room, closing the door behind her. Safe? Yes. Happy? I'm not so sure.

I flop back onto my bed and stare at the ceiling, and like a pathetic loser, I wonder what Max is doing. When my phone rings a few seconds later, I almost dislocate my shoulder trying to get to it. And when I see Max's name on the screen, I damn near burst into tears.

I answer it quickly. "Hey."

"Hi, baby girl. You okay?"

"No," I sniff.

"You left your pendant."

I instinctively reach for my neck, and my fingers brush over bare skin. Shit! "Will you take care of it for me? Please don't let anything happen to it."

"I'll wear it until I can give it back to you. Maybe it will protect me the way it protects you."

"You don't believe in St. Christopher," I remind him.

"No, but I believe in you."

"Max ..." I practically sob his name. This is too hard.

"I'm sorry, Joey," he whispers.

"What for?"

"For not doing this right. I shouldn't have taken you to my cabin."

Oh my god, my heart is going to split in two. "Are you saying you regret what we did?"

"No, baby girl. Not a single fucking second of it. But I do regret causing trouble for you."

"I can handle Dante and Lorenzo."

He laughs softly. "Better than anyone I know."

"I'm sorry for what they said to you. What they did." I choke back another sob as the events of this morning play through my head.

"You have nothing to be sorry for. I knew what would happen if I took you there."

"But you took me anyway?"

"Yeah. I'm a selfish prick."

"No, Max," I insist. The fact that he knew what would happen and risked it anyway makes my poor aching heart feel like it's going to burst. "But what do we do now?"

There's a deep sigh followed by a silence that seems to last an eternity. "I have something I need to take care of. It's going to take me a few days."

"What is it?"

"I'll tell you all about it, I promise. I just need to focus on this and give your brothers time to cool off."

"And then?"

"I told you, you're mine, baby girl. I'll find a way to fix this, okay? You just hang tight and let me handle it."

"But how long, Max?" I breathe. "I miss you already."

He groans loudly. "I miss you too, Joey. I can't stop thinking about how good you feel. How good you taste."

Holy fuck. My pussy throbs painfully, reminding me of everything we did last night in delicious detail. "Max?" I moan his name.

"Just a few days, baby. I promise. I can't live without you any longer than that."

"Don't leave me here alone, Max," I plead, feeling lonelier than I have since my brothers shipped me off to Italy four years ago.

"You're not alone, baby girl. You're fucking mine."

I swallow my emotions, determined not to cry.

"Whose are you?" he asks, and the deep timbre of his voice makes goosebumps prickle along my forearms.

"Yours," I whisper with a smile.

"Every fucking part of you. I'll talk to you soon, okay?"

"Okay. Can I call you later?"

"Call me before you go to sleep."

"I will."

"I love you, Joey." He hangs up before I can say it back.

TWENTY-FOUR

MAX

The elevator doors open, and I half expect Kristin to be standing in the hallway waiting for me, but the scent of bacon and eggs wafts from the kitchen. Leaning against the door, I take a moment to process the events of the past twelve hours.

I feel guilty about leaving her alone last night, but not half as guilty as I do for telling Joey to leave with her brothers. The look on her face almost broke me. But it was the only option. They wouldn't have given up easily. We would have only ended up nearly killing each other, and I don't want that either. At the end of the day, those men are my brothers. It would kill me to lose them, but I will if that's what it takes. Because I would die a thousand painful deaths before I willingly lost Joey Moretti.

At least I know she's safe with her brothers. Plus, now that I'm not welcome in their house, I can focus all my attention on finding Kristin's father. I figure I'll get some answers by following every lead I can get my hands on. Then I can tell Joey everything and stop keeping secrets from her. And hopefully Dante and Lorenzo will have cooled off enough for me to tell them that I'm in love with their sister. It will all work out perfectly, right? So why does it hurt so fucking much to be away from her?

"Max, is that you?" Kristin calls from the kitchen.

"Yeah," I shout as I walk down the hallway.

"You want some?" she asks, her back to me as she works at the stove.

"Sure."

I take a seat at the kitchen island, and she turns to greet me. Her smile fades quickly. "What the hell happened to your face?"

I brush my fingertips over the cut above my eye. Dante has a mean right hook. "Oh, it was nothing."

Hands on hips, she approaches me, and she looks so much like our mom that it takes me back over twenty years. I never think about my mom. She walked out on me, and as far as I'm concerned, she doesn't deserve a second of my time. But having Kristin here has brought back all kinds of memories I'd rather forget. How great Mom was at making pancakes. Her laugh. How she would try to scowl when she yelled at me but could never quite manage it. How she always smelled of flowers. Those kinds of memories hurt, so I bury them deep. It's easier to focus on the fact that she cheated on my father with his own brother and then left her only son when he was thirteen years old because she wanted an easier life.

It would be easy to resent my little sister, who only got the best of her. But I suppose she didn't get much; Mom died when she was six.

"It doesn't look like nothing," she says, pulling me out of my thoughts. "Was it anything to do with my dad?"

"No. It was ..." What the hell do I say?

"Was it about a girl?" Her eyes widen and she grins.

"I guess."

"Who is she?"

"Bacon and eggs, yeah?" I nod at the stove, changing the subject away from my fucked-up love life.

She grumbles and goes back to cooking.

I watch her add more bacon to the pan. She was a terrible cook a few days ago, but she seems to be a quick study. Her dad must have done all the cooking at home. I wonder what kind of father he was to her. My own dad did the best he could. It was just the two of us after Mom left, at least for a couple of years. He was never the same after she betrayed him with his own brother. He lost his edge; all the fight went out of him. He was like a shadow—drifting through life, constantly distracted by something he could never fix—so distracted that he didn't see the knife the guy pulled on him until it was too late.

"I'm gonna go to Jersey tomorrow morning. See what leads I can follow up there. Maybe I can find that safety deposit box."

Kristin turns off the stove and plates up the food before carrying it over to the kitchen island. "You want me to come with you?"

"No." I shake my head. "You'll be safer here."

She wrinkles her nose. "I don't like being here alone, Max."

"I know, but you were fine last night, right? And it will be one night. Two tops."

"I ..." Her lips tremble.

I grab her hand and give it a reassuring squeeze. "I get why you're scared, Kristin. Your dad didn't come back, but I'm not him. I'll be back soon with some answers. But I'm getting nowhere fast here, and the longer your dad is out there ..."

"I know." She gives me a firm nod. "I need to put on my big girl pants and handle it."

"Good." I wink at her and start tucking into my bacon and eggs.

"Have you had any leads about Jakob?"

"No. But I have a guy looking into him for me."

"He's not a bad guy, Max," she says with a sigh, and I realize I'm scowling. "He didn't know I was pregnant. As far as he knows, I just disappeared one day. We even used different names when we were in Philly. He knew me as Kristin Campbell."

"But he never told you where he lived. You had no way of contacting him? What guy does that unless he's playing you?"

"I did have a way of contacting him," she insists, her brow furrowed with annoyance. "I had his number until Dad tossed my phone."

"Hmm," I mumble, unconvinced of her faith in the guy.

"Look, all I'm saying is that if you do find him, you don't have to go all psycho big brother on him. Okay? He might act like an asshole when he finds out about the baby, but we won't know until I tell him."

I arch an eyebrow at her. "Psycho big brother?"

"Yeah." She laughs softly. "But I kinda like having you as my big brother."

"I kinda like it too, sis," I admit.

I HAVE my hand wrapped around some guy's throat when my phone rings. I came to talk to a few of Uncle Vito's buddies from back in the day to see if I could get any information on his acquaintances before I leave tomorrow. One of them decided to be a smart-ass and told me to go to hell, and since I was already in the mood for a fight, I punched him in the face and now I'm choking the life out of him.

I take my phone out of my pocket and smile when I see who's calling. "My girl just saved your fucking life, asshole," I tell him, shoving him to the ground. "Stay!" I warn him when he starts to scramble away.

"Hey, baby."

"Hi."

"You okay?"

"I miss you."

"I miss you too, baby girl."

The piece of shit on the floor goes to move again, so I stand on his hand, pressing all my weight onto it and crushing his fingers. He starts to howl, and I hold my finger to my lips as a warning. He clamps his mouth shut.

"When can I see you?" she asks, and the plea in her voice makes me falter. What if I just went to her house tonight and forced my way in? Made Dante and Lorenzo see how fucking much I adore her and that I'm the only man they should trust to protect her as well as they can?

Fuck, I can't. Not yet. I owe it to Kristin to give finding her father a proper shot. "A few days, baby. I told you that."

"How many is a few?"

"Two. Maybe three."

"That's too long." She lowers her voice and practically purrs, "I need you."

God, I fucking need her too. "I need you too. As soon as I've taken care of this thing, I'm coming for you."

"Will you be safe?"

"Always, baby girl. Because I will always come back to you."

"I miss you, Max."

Fuck, hearing those words from her lips makes my heart and my cock ache painfully. "I miss you too, baby. Get some sleep, okay? I'll call you tomorrow when I get a chance."

I end the call and turn my attention back to the dipshit on the floor. Taking my foot off his hand, I stare down at him as he pulls it toward his body and sobs quietly. "Should you hear anything from Vito, or any of his old associates, you tell them Max DiMarco is looking for him. You hear me?"

Snot runs down the guy's face as he nods.

I turn and walk away from him. There's no use looking for Vito here in Chicago. New Jersey is where I'll find my answers.

"You sure you don't want me to come to the airport with you?" Kristin asks as I throw my bag over my shoulder.

"No. Do not leave this apartment under any circumstances until I get back."

She arches an eyebrow. "Not even if it's on fire?"

"As long as you don't attempt any more awful cooking, it won't catch fire, will it?"

She fakes a scowl. "Hey, I made you bacon and eggs yesterday."

"Yeah, you did."

"You'll be two days at the very most?"

"Yes." I don't plan to spend any longer than necessary in New Jersey, hundreds of miles away from Joey. Being apart from her, even while we're in the same city, is the most agonizing torture. I make a mental note to call her from the cab. It's been way too long since I heard her voice.

I give Kristin a hug. "I'll check in with you as soon as I land."

"And if I don't hear from you?"

"You will. As soon as I land," I promise. "I have to go. My cab will be outside."

"Be careful, Max. My father was a very cautious man, and they still got to him."

"I'll be fine," I assure her.

The cab is on the street by the time I get downstairs. I'm just about to pull the car door open when a woman with a stroller bumps into me and drops a bag of groceries at my feet. "I'm so sorry," she exclaims.

"No problem." I crouch down to help her pick up the items that spilled out, and she ducks down beside me. Smiling sweetly, she takes hold of my hand and something pricks my skin. "Night, night, pretty boy," in a thick Russian accent are the last words I hear.

TWENTY-FIVE

JOEY

I sit on the bench in the garden, swinging my legs and chewing on my thumbnail. I need to find a way to fix this. I cannot be responsible for tearing my family apart and Max never being one of us again. If I'd known this was the price we'd all have to pay, maybe I could have fought my desire for him harder.

Jumping up from the bench, I head into the house to find Anya and Kat. I need my girls to help me out.

I find Kat and Anya in my niece's nursery. Kat is putting Gabriella down for her afternoon nap while Anya watches them from the rocking chair. I love how close they've become since Anya and Lorenzo returned home from Italy last year.

"Hey, I need your help," I say quietly, careful not to wake the baby, although that kid could sleep through a tornado.

"With Maximo?" Anya asks with a wicked grin.

"Of course."

"What can we do?" Kat says as she ushers the two of us from the room so we can talk a little louder.

"I need you to distract your husbands tonight so I can sneak out. As long as one of you can open the gate, I could call an Uber or get Max to come pick me up down the street."

"I'm in," Anya says.

But Kat chews her lip, a deep frown on her face. "No," she eventually says with a shake of her head.

I blink at her in shock. Kat Moretti is a freaking hellraiser. Dante is the head of the Cosa Nostra, but she has him eating out of the palm of her goddamn hand. She's my biggest ally in this house. She always roots for me. I can't believe she's not going to help me now when I need her most.

"Kat?" Anya scolds her.

"This is not the world I want for my daughter. Sneaking out and having to lie about what she's doing."

"But Kat ..." I whine, pouting, unable to fathom this new well-behaved version of my sister-in-law.

"You're not sneaking out, Joey. You're going to walk out of that goddamn front door." She grabs both mine and Anya's hands, and I grin at her. Now that's the Kat Moretti I know and love.

Dante and Lorenzo are in their study as usual, and their shared shell-shocked expression when I walk in with their wives makes me giddy. We might just do this.

"Something wrong, kitten?" Dante asks with a frown, directing his question toward Kat.

"Yes," she says with a sweet smile.

Lorenzo frowns. "Passerotta?" he says to Anya.

"We have something to discuss with you both," Anya says coolly.

My brothers' eyes land on mine next, and they glare at me, no doubt aware that my sisters-in-law are here to fight in my corner with me. Because it's not just my corner, it's theirs too. It's my niece's corner, and any other girl who ends up being born into this family.

"You should probably take a seat," I say.

My brothers glance at each other, but then they each take their seats behind the huge wooden desk.

"If this is about Maximo, you can all save your breath," Dante says with a deep sigh. "There is nothing any of you can say that will change what he's done."

I cross my arms over my chest and take a few steps forward until I'm right in front of the desk. Kat and Anya stand on either side of me, silent but ready to back me up when I need them. "This isn't about Max. This is about the women in this family being treated like second-class citizens."

They both scoff at that statement.

"You think this is funny?" I snap, my anger already boiling over.

"When do I ever treat you like anything less than a queen?" Lorenzo asks Anya. Trust him to go for the easy target. She's his submissive as well as his wife, and ordinarily, she would never defy him in public, although she does it plenty in private. But he underestimated her today.

"Yes, you treat me like a queen, my love." She gives him a saccharine smile. "I am your little bird in a cage."

Lorenzo's face turns beet red. "You think I keep you in a cage?"

"I do not *think* it, my love. You keep me in a cage because that is the life I want. The life I asked for when I fell in love with you. But I always thought that if I ever needed a little more freedom, you would give it to me."

His eyes narrow. "I would give you anything, you know that."

"So why is it that I'm not allowed any freedom at all then?" I demand, smacking my hands down on the desk.

"You are allowed to come and go as you please. You have every freedom that Lorenzo and I have," Dante snaps at me.

"Oh really?" It's my turn to scoff now. "Is there any way in hell that anyone would tell either of you who you could fall in love with?"

"This is about Max?" Dante gives a sarcastic laugh.

"No, this is about a ridiculous promise you forced your best friend to make, just because I was born without a dick."

"This isn't about you, Joey," Lorenzo says, sighing.

"No?" I fold my arms again. "If I was a boy, would you have cared who the hell I dated?"

Dante scowls at me, and I direct my attention to my oldest brother.

"Lorenzo, would you have ever dared to tell Dante who he could or couldn't date?"

He pinches the bridge of his nose. "This is about Max lying to us, Joey. He made us a promise."

"He only lied to you *because* of that promise. Why did you make him do that? Why?"

"Because him fucking our little sister muddies the waters," Lorenzo says, his hands steepled under his chin.

"Lorenzo," Anya chides him.

"Tell me why you're so against us being together. I'm an adult. You were fine with me and Toby, and he's half the man Max is."

They both go on glaring at me.

"If you're going to come between us, at least tell me why," I demand.

"Because you deserve better than him," Dante shouts. "He is not the kind of man you need, Joey."

"Why? Because he does bad things?" I challenge.

"You have no idea of the kinds of things he's done, Guiseppina," Lorenzo growls, his tone low and menacing enough that it sends a shudder along my spine.

"Things he's done in your name. Our family's name," I

shout as anger and frustration burn through my veins. "Why do you get to decide who or what I deserve? I love Max. I want to be with him."

"No." Dante shakes his head while Lorenzo scrubs a hand over his face.

"You know you can't really stop this, right?" Kat pipes up from beside me, earning her a withering glare from her husband.

"I think you'll find I can, kitten," he replies.

"Is this really the kind of life you want for our daughter?"

"Where she's protected every day of her life?" he fires back.

"Where she isn't given the same opportunities as her brothers?"

"Brothers? Are you ...?" He frowns at her. Dante's desperate for more kids, and considering he can barely go five minutes without dragging Kat off to a quiet room, I figure he's thinking the same thing I am—that she might already be pregnant and she's chosen this particular moment to announce it.

"I mean we might have sons one day too," she says, her cheeks turning pink. "But if this is going to be Gabriella's life, Dante, then I'm not sure I want to fill this house with children."

Go Kat! She went straight for his weak spot. The anguish that flashes across his face almost makes me feel sorry for him. But then his mask is back in place, and my sympathy dries up at the sight of his scowl. "We'll see about that, kitten."

"How can you walk away from a man who's been your brother in all but blood just because he fell in love?" Anya asks, and I turn to her, my mouth hanging open as her words wash over me.

"You think Maximo is in love with Joey?" Lorenzo frowns as he voices the same question that runs through my mind.

"You think that a man who risked everything to spend just one night with her isn't?" she asks, softening her tone.

And right there, I see my first glimmer of hope.

"I know you can't forgive him for lying right now, but please, just let me see him," I beg. "You know I'm safe when I'm with him. He would never let anyone hurt me."

"And who will keep you safe from him, Joey?" Dante asks.

Kat leaps to his defense. "Max would never hurt her."

"Not intentionally," Lorenzo adds.

"Or unintentionally," I insist. "I know the kind of man he is. He would never ..."

Dante and Lorenzo glare at me. I'm fighting a losing battle. They think they know him better than I do. He's reckless and unhinged—but not when it comes to me. I switch gears. "And what if he does hurt me? I get to choose who hurts me and who doesn't. Me. Not you. Didn't Kat hurt you when she tried to leave, Dante? Didn't Anya hurt you when she refused to have any more treatment?" I feel bad for bringing up their pain, but Kat and Anya stand beside me without flinching, their presence calm and reassuring. "Would you trade any of the pain if it cost you even a second of your time with them?"

Dante stretches his neck, and Lorenzo grinds his jaw while the air in the room grows thick with tension. But finally, after the world's longest silence, Dante speaks. "He is never to set foot in this house again."

"But I can see him?"

"You will take a security detail with you," Lorenzo says.

"What if he picks me up outside the gate? I won't need a guard then, right?" I mean, Max used to be my armed security, why do I need both?

Dante rolls his eyes. "Do not fucking push it, Guiseppina. You will have an armed escort at all fucking times. Do I make myself clear?"

I resist the urge to roll my eyes back. I can see Max. That's all that matters right now.

"Thank you." I swallow the lump in my throat and refrain from launching myself across the desk and hugging them both. "I promise it will all work out."

Lorenzo snorts as he stands up and walks around the desk to Anya. He slips a comforting arm around her waist. "You look tired, Passerotta. I think you need to lie down," he says, and the change in his tone is evident to everyone in the room. She's no longer in charge here. Anya does look tired, but she looks that way all the time now. She grows weaker and sicker by the day, and it breaks my heart to see my vibrant sister-in-law like this. I choke down a sob. She'll be okay. Lorenzo would never let anything bad happen to her.

"Yes, Sir," she says quietly and follows him out of the office.

Kat checks her watch. "I'd better go check on Gabriella. She'll be awake from her nap soon."

Dante shakes his head. "Joey can do that."

"I'm going to call Max."

He glares at me. "You can multitask, right?"

"I can go," Kat assures me.

"I don't think so, kitten. I believe we have something to discuss, don't you?" Dante says coolly, and my sister-in-law blushes deep red.

"Ugh, you two should get a room," I groan.

"We have one, and you're in it," Dante fires back without taking his eyes off his wife.

"Fine. I'll check on your child while you two do whatever it is you're about to do." I sigh dramatically, but I catch Kat's eye and smile before I leave.

My niece kicks her legs when she sees me. Picking her up, I snuggle her close while I dial Max, but his phone goes straight to voicemail. I leave him a message to call me back as soon as possible. The fact that I can see him again makes me feel like my heart's about to burst from my chest. And he must want to see me too, right? All those things he said to me when I spent the night with him weren't a lie. I know he said things were complicated, but my brothers will come around. As stubborn as they are, they love us both too much not to.

Gabriella squishes my cheeks together and giggles. God, I love this kid. "Hey there, my little smooch."

I sit down in the rocking chair and bask in the purity of her love. "Do you know what me, your mom, and your aunt Anya just did, baby?" I ask, and I swear she makes a cute little sound that makes me wonder if she knows exactly what I'm saying to her. "We just smashed the patriarchy, Gabs." I drop a kiss on top of her downy-soft head and inhale her fresh baby scent. "I promise you will never have to deal with all the bullshit that I did growing up." I give her another kiss, and she giggles. "Don't tell him I said this, but your dad is kind of cool and not a complete asshole like mine was. And I bet you're going to have a whole lot of brothers and sisters to fight in your corner too. But also, your mom, Anya, and I will fight for us girls every freaking step of the way."

An unexpected sob wells in my throat at the thought of our future. There's no escaping how sick Anya is now, and there's every possibility that my niece will never get to know her wonderful aunt.

TWENTY-SIX

MAX

The overhead light blinds me as I blink awake. My shoulders are on fire. I roll them and feel the weight of thick metal cuffs biting into my wrists. *Where the fuck am I?*

"Ah, he wakes," says a man with a thick Russian accent.

I squint, attempting to block out the harsh light, and focus on the figure in front of me, but all I can make out is the outline of an average-height man with a wide build and a shaved head.

He sneers. "You have nice sleep, pretty boy?"

Closing my eyes, I tune him out for a few beats while I take an inventory. My ankles are chained to a chair, my arms tied behind my back. Running my tongue around my mouth, I taste blood, but none of my teeth are missing.

A sharp slap across my cheek makes me reopen my eyes. The bald guy pushes his face close to mine, and I grind my teeth and suck in a breath. He's going to fucking regret that.

"Boss wants him able to talk when he gets here," another Russian voice grunts to my left, but I keep my focus on the guy in front of me. I don't recognize him at all, but given the accent, this must have something to do with Pushkin and the Bratva takeover. He appeared to have fled the city with his tail between his legs, but I knew it was only a matter of time before the snake struck back. Although why he's striking back at us rather than Dmitri, I have no idea.

"He will still be able to talk," the bald guy says with a sneer. Looking behind me, he nods, and the sound of rustling plastic has me sucking in a deep breath just before a bag is placed over my head and pulled tight. This is a scare tactic, an effective one I've used myself many times. But it won't work on me. They revealed their hand too soon. They need me alive.

So I count and I wait. It calms me, at least until my nervous system takes over. I get to ninety-nine before my lungs start to burn and my body twists and bucks involuntarily as it fights for oxygen. Then comes the lightheadedness. A blinding spark of euphoria before—

The bag is ripped from my head, and I suck in deep lungfuls of air.

"Not so tough now, are you? Vyblyadok!" He snatches the chain around my neck and yanks it off, snapping the delicate gold links and muttering in Russian as he throws it onto the floor at my feet.

That was my girl's fucking pendant, you motherfucking fuckwit. Rage burns a hole in my chest. Now that he will definitely pay for. Waiting until he edges closer, I lunge forward with my teeth bared and bite down on his nose. He screeches like an angry goat as I use my teeth to grind through flesh and cartilage, making sure to have a good grip before I yank my head back and tear his nose off his face. He staggers backward, blood gushing everywhere, leaking through the hands that cover his deformed mug. I spit the offending lump of flesh onto the floor.

One of his colleagues laughs darkly as he walks over and tends to him. "I warned you not to get too close to the dog." He calls for help, and a few seconds later, the bald guy is escorted from the room, leaving me with only two of my captors—the one behind me with the bag and a giant with a beard and ponytail who stands in front of me.

"You must be wondering why you're here," he says.

I glare at him, wracking my brain to recall any previous encounters. I've dealt with a lot of Russians in my time, but this guy doesn't ring any bells.

"Strong, silent type, huh?" The one behind me lets out a maniacal laugh and slips the bag back over my head. I count out another cycle of ninety-nine before I buck on the chair, and he removes it.

"You know why you're here?" Ponytail asks, stroking a hand over his beard.

Remaining silent, I stretch my neck until it cracks.

With a sigh, Ponytail shakes his head. "I'm sure you'll talk when the boss gets here."

Damn right I'll talk when Pushkin shows up.

The guy behind me leans close to my ear, his breath hot and sour. "You will wish you talk once he gets hold of you."

Something isn't right. Pushkin wouldn't want me tortured for information—he'd want me tortured to send a message.

"You took what was his, Maximo. You touched his girl. Tainted her," Ponytail says, confirming my thoughts. Definitely not Pushkin, but who?

Fuck! Kristin's all alone without me. Is she safe? "Where is she?" I say with a snarl, amusing them both.

Ponytail chuckles. "Pushed a button, Maximo?"

"Where the fuck is she? If you've hurt her—" The words get stuck in my throat, rage burning through my veins. These must be the men she and her father are running from. Guilt gnaws at my stomach. I promised to protect her. I should have sent her away. Far away from Chicago and from me. But she showed up at my door, alone and helpless and desperate, and even though a part of me wanted to close the door and continue to block out that part of my life, a bigger part of me wanted to save her. She looked so much like our mom, and it made me think of all the ways I failed her as a son. I shouldn't have pushed her away so hard. Maybe if I'd tried to accept her and Vito ...

The bag goes over my head again, and my hands clench into fists, every muscle in my body tense. I don't count this time. I'm too busy drowning in guilt, anger, and fear. And hope. Hope that my little sister is safe from these monsters.

Darkness encroaches, settling over my brain as my lungs scream for air, and another face appears in my mind.

Joey. This must be what heaven is like—not that I have any chance of a ticket into that place.

I begin struggling, fighting against my restraints at the thought of never seeing her again. Never tasting her. That fate is worse than any hell I can imagine.

CHAPTER
TWENTY-SEVEN
JOEY

Maybe if I glare at my phone hard enough, a dozen missed call and text notifications from Max will suddenly pop up. But of course that doesn't happen. I know the damn thing is working because Mo keeps calling me. She's desperate to know what happened after I left Toby's house with Max the other night, and although I've told her again and again that he just brought me home, she doesn't seem to be buying it.

She can speculate all she wants. I'll never tell her the truth about Max and me. Well, maybe not never. But not yet.

A groan of frustration rips out of me when I get Max's voicemail for the thousandth time. I no longer care that I'll look like a desperate stalker when he switches his phone back on. I'm worried about him. He would never break a promise like that. Not to me.

"That thing will burst into flames if you keep looking at it like that, kid," Dante says as he walks into the kitchen.

I'm too distracted to even give a snappy retort. "I'm worried about Max."

Rolling his eyes, he sighs.

"I'm serious, Dante. He said he would call me."

That gets me an even bigger eye roll, which lights the fuse of my rage. I'm aware that I sound like a lovesick teenager, but that's not what this is. "Stop with the eye rolling," I snap. "I'm telling you that something's wrong. I haven't been able to get through to his cell since yesterday morning. It goes to voicemail every single time. And I haven't spoken to him since the night before last."

He snorts. "If he has any sense, he'll be staying out of the way. Hanging his head in shame."

"Can you stop being an asshole for like one minute? This isn't like him, and you know it."

He pours himself a mug of coffee, his brow furrowed in a frown. "He's probably cooling off somewhere, Joey. At his fucking cabin in the woods or something. I'm sure he'll call you soon."

"Can I go to his place with Ash and Henry?"

"Don't make a fool of yourself, Guiseppina," he says, his tone weary. "Can't you just accept that maybe Max is not the man for you and he's doing you a favor by staying away?"

Tears prick at my eyes. My brother is an overbearing, over-protective jerk a lot of the time, but it's not like him to be cruel.

I open my mouth to respond, but I'm interrupted by one of the armed guards. "Boss, there's someone at the gate. A young girl. Says she's here about Max."

Every hair on my body stands on end. "A young girl?"

"Yeah."

Dante goes to speak, but I cut him off. "How young?"

His eyes dart from me to Dante, then back to me. "Um. Could be anywhere from sixteen to twenty. I can never tell. She's pregnant though."

"P-pregnant?"

Dante glowers at the guard. "Who the fuck is she, and what does she want?"

"She claims Max is missing and she thinks someone took him."

My heart rate kicks up several gears, and I turn to Dante, hands on my hips. "I told you I couldn't get a hold of him."

With a frown, Dante tells the guard to show the girl into his study.

I pace up and down Dante's study while he sits quietly in his chair. How can he be this calm? Max might be missing!

The same guard from before escorts the young woman in. His assessment of her age was spot on—I can't pinpoint it either. But she's definitely pregnant. *Very* pregnant.

Her eyes are bright red, and it's apparent she's been crying a lot. She rushes into the room, her hands flapping as she fidgets nervously. Something about her is endearing.

"Take a seat," Dante says, not unkindly, and she sits down. "Who are you?" he asks.

She blinks at him.

He sighs. "Your name?"

"Kristin. Kristin Campbell."

"You said Max is missing?" I ask her, dispensing with any further pleasantries.

"Y-yes," she sniffs.

"Why do you think that?" Dante asks.

"I know he is." Her eyes fill with tears and she swallows. "He was supposed to go to New Jersey yesterday, but he never got on the flight. He never checked in with me, even though he promised he would." She starts to cry again, fat tears rolling down her face.

Meanwhile I feel like I'm going to puke. Why was Max checking in with her? Who the hell is she?

"Why was he going to Jersey?" Dante asks, and I'm relieved

that at least one of us is keeping their head. That's his super-power—remaining calm when the world is in chaos. Taking a deep breath, I try to channel his energy.

Her eyes dart around the room. "He, uh, he was looking for his uncle Vito."

Dante scowls. "His uncle?"

"Who? What?" I don't recall Max having an uncle.

Ignoring me, Dante shakes his head. "Why the hell would he have any interest in that lying piece of shit?"

Kristin blanches at the venom in Dante's tone, but she leans forward, chin tipped in defiance. "Because he went missing. Probably kidnapped too. Max was looking into it."

"How do you know he didn't get on the plane?" I ask her, my feet now rooted in place.

"I called the airline."

Dante gives her a skeptical look. "Airlines don't give that kind of information."

"They do if you get a sympathetic mom of three and you cry and tell her you're six months pregnant and your boyfriend and father of your baby has disappeared."

No. That can't be true. My knees threaten to buckle under my weight.

Dante shoots me a look of concern, then returns his atten-tion to the young girl. "And is he? Your boyfriend? Your baby's father?"

"Yes," she says, her voice firm.

My whole world stops turning. I'm definitely going to be sick. I clamp my lips together because if I don't, I will wail so loudly that the house will crumble to the ground. If I open my mouth, I will shriek and I will scream. I'll call her a liar and demand she tells me the truth.

My legs tremble. I can't breathe. I can't think. I can't even be. Is Kristin the *situation* he was fixing? Bile fills my mouth. He fucked me and told me he loved me while he was with her. Did they plan a life together? Marriage and more babies while he was making me fall in love with him and promising me that I belonged to him?

Dante quietly says my name and pats the empty chair beside him. His eyes lock on mine and he gives me a subtle nod, letting me know that he has my back. Reminding me that I'm a Moretti, and this is not how we do things. I'm not going to show this complete stranger that she's torn out my heart and smashed it into a million tiny pieces.

Swallowing down the hurt and pain and rage that wants to spill out of me, I suck in a breath. Tears sting my eyes, but I blink them away. Maximo DiMarco is a lying, cheating snake. I hate him. I hope he has been kidnapped. I hope he's suffering right now.

Dante watches me until he's sure I've regained control. With a satisfied nod, he shifts his attention back to Kristin. "You think the people who took his uncle also took him?"

My hands ball unto fist by my sides.

"Maybe. I-I don't know. I know he worked for you, so maybe it was something to do with that?"

"Do you know anything about who he was meeting in New Jersey? Anything about who took his uncle and why Max is trying to find him? You know he hates his uncle, right?"

"I do know he hates him, but family is family," she sniffs. "I don't know who he's meeting or who has his uncle."

"Fuck!" Dante slams his fists down onto his desk.

I take a deep breath and try to ignore my racing heart. I am Joey Moretti. I don't wilt like some goddamn delicate flower just because things don't go my way. All that matters right now is finding Max. Then, once he's safe, I will cut off his dick with a blunt spoon and he can fuck off to somewhere far, far away and live unhappily ever after with his little girlfriend. "When was the last time you saw him?" I ask, my calm voice belying the torrent of rage that consumes me.

"Y-yesterday morning when he left for the airport."

Dante takes over the questioning again. "You were in his apartment?"

Kristin shrugs. "I live there."

She lives with him? No wonder the no-good, lying bag of shit wouldn't take me to his place the other night. God, I'm so fucking stupid.

Hold it together, Joey.

"And when did you realize he was missing?" my brother asks.

"Later that day, when he didn't call me like he promised. I checked that the flight had landed. And then I called the airline a dozen times. Late last night, I finally got someone to confirm that he didn't board the flight. I didn't know where else to go, but I know that he works for you, Mr. Moretti, so I came here."

"Max doesn't just *work for me,*" Dante says. "How the fuck do I know you're not a part of all this? He never once mentioned a pregnant girlfriend. Certainly not one who lived with him."

Her cheeks turn bright pink. "You know he's a very private person. The baby was unexpected." Looking down, she rubs a hand over her bump. "But I do live with him. The code for the elevator is his father's birthday. You don't clap once to turn the lights on because Max thought it was too boring. You have to do a two clap, three clap thing. It's so annoying when you need a pee in the middle of the night." She gives us a faint smile as though we should be sympathetic to her cause, but all I want to do is scratch her eyes out.

Assaulting my mind is an image of her untangling herself from Max's strong arms to get up and use the bathroom. I try not to think about the various intimate moments they must have shared, but the images persist like annoying little pop-up ads.

Dante pushes himself to his feet. "You'll stay here until we find him. My wife will make up a spare room for you."

I scowl at him, but I know he's doing the right thing.

"Thank you," she says, tears running down her cheeks again. "I'd like to help though. If I can do anything at all. I just want him back."

I press my lips together to avoid saying any of the hundred things that are running through my head. She just wants him back? Well, Maximo DiMarco is a lying, cheating snake. And after I'm done with him, there probably won't be much left worth having.

CHAPTER
TWENTY-EIGHT

JOEY

K at doesn't say anything when she walks into the dining room where Dante, Lorenzo, and I are sitting with Kristin. She simply sits beside me, reaches for my hand, and gives it a gentle squeeze, letting me know she's there. My brothers have been grilling Kristin for over an hour, wanting to know everything she knows about where Max was going and why. Unfortunately, it appears she doesn't know more than what she already told us.

I've spent that time quietly observing her. She's young and vulnerable, yes, but there's a quiet strength about her. She's not as naive as she looks. Maybe it's her huge doe eyes that make her look so innocent. Does Max stare into her eyes the way he looks into mine? Has he made her promises and broken them too?

Every few minutes, I remember what he's done, and a fresh wave of pain crashes over me. My heart physically hurts—a deep, visceral ache in my chest. And then I look at the girl sitting across the table. She's eighteen years old, almost nineteen, and she's six months pregnant with a boy. How could Max cheat on her too?

Dante was right, Max DiMarco is not the man I thought I knew.

"Everything okay, kitten?" Dante asks his wife.

"I'm just about to put Gabriella down for the night and wanted to let you know that Sophia made dinner. I think it's important our guest eats something."

"I-I'm okay," Kristin stammers. "I just want to find Max."

"And we will," Lorenzo replies. "But Kat's right. You must eat."

I squeeze Kat's hand in mine, steeling myself. "We'll be eating in here anyway. And we can talk while we have dinner."

Kristin gives me such a genuine smile in return that it makes my stomach roll. She thinks I'm her ally, but I'm the woman who's been fucking her baby daddy. No wonder the cheating snake wouldn't take me to his place. That anger and pain bubbles inside me once more, but I swallow it down.

Kat releases my hand and gets up. "I'll go tell Sophia to serve dinner then."

"I'll come with you. I need to kiss my daughter goodnight before she goes to bed," Dante says.

"I'll go check on Anya." Lorenzo follows Kat and Dante out of the dining room, leaving Kristin and me alone. I want to leave too. I hate her. No, that's not true. I *want* to hate her. It would be easier than hating Max because he's out there somewhere and he might be suffering. Or worse. I can't think about what I'll do if I never get to see him again.

"Do you think we'll find him?" she sniffs.

"Yes," I say with total confidence, but I don't voice the rest of my thoughts—that I hope we find him before it's too late. People don't get kidnapped for no reason. There's been no ransom or any other demands, so his disappearance is likely about revenge. And I know the kind of damage wrought by the people in our world when they want revenge. The mere thought of him suffering such a fate makes me feel like I'm going to pass out.

I refocus on Kristin. There are so many things I want to ask her. How long have they been together? Where did they meet? Does he take her to his cabin in the woods?

"Do you love him?" I ask instead.

"Max?"

No, Ryan Reynolds, I think, but I bite back the sarcastic response and nod instead.

She hesitates for a second, and the love-blind idiot in me sees a glimmer of hope, but then she smiles and says, "Yeah. He's a good guy."

Let's see if she still thinks that when Max is back here and she finds out what he's been up to behind her back. Because even if I don't tell her, one of my brothers sure as hell will.

I pick at my food during dinner, barely eating a bite.

My stomach is a giant ball of worry and fear, and anything I put in there is liable to come back up. Questions constantly buzz around my head. It feels wrong to sit here eating while Max is out there somewhere, probably suffering at the hands of his captors, but Dante and Lorenzo have every available man looking for him. There's nothing more to be done right now. Throughout dinner, they take calls and follow new leads between asking Kristin every question they can think of.

I'm staring down at my plate without seeing it when the sound of my name catches my attention. Looking up, I find Lorenzo frowning at me. "Where's your pendant?"

I brush my fingertips over my skin where it usually sits.

My cheeks turn pink. "I left it in the cabin."

If me mentioning the cabin means anything to Kristin, she doesn't show it.

He sits forward in his seat, his eyes wide. "Is it still there?"

I roll my eyes. "Is that really important right now while Max is missing?"

"Yes," both he and Dante say.

Confused, I shrug. "Then no. Max has it."

Kristin still doesn't react. I guess she trusts Max the way that I used to. Pair of fools, the two of us.

Dante pushes his chair back from the table and Lorenzo follows suit. "Joey," Dante says as they walk out of the room, so I follow them, wondering why my pendant is so important.

As soon as we're in the hallway, Dante grabs my arm. "Max has your pendant?"

"Yes. He said he was going to wear it and look after it for me."

Lorenzo doesn't often display his emotions, but I swear his eyes shine with joy. "You think he's still wearing it?"

"Only one way to find out," Dante says over his shoulder as he strides toward their study.

"Can one of you please tell me what the hell is going on?" I demand as I trail after them.

Dante's the one who answers. "That pendant is a tracker, Joey. Why do you think we gave it to you when you went to Italy?"

"A tracker? You've been tracking me?"

"We track your phone as well." Lorenzo shrugs nonchalantly. "We track each other's phones too."

"Yeah, but that's different." I don't know how it's different, but it is. "You told me the pendant belonged to Mom."

"Would you have worn it otherwise?" Dante retorts.

"You know you really need to stop lying to me," I snap.

Dante looks at the ceiling and sighs. "If Max is wearing your St. Christopher, then we can trace the signal and find him. Shouldn't you be focusing on that right now?"

"I guess," I admit with a frown.

Lorenzo reads off numbers from a file on his phone, and Dante types them into his computer. When he's done, he leans back in his chair and steeples his hands over his mouth.

"What's happening?"

"We wait for the locator to start transmitting," he says, like I understand what that means.

"Huh?"

"It doesn't transmit constantly because it doesn't have a battery to sustain that kind of activity like a cell phone does. It's activated remotely and now we wait to pick up its signal."

"Wow. That is some fancy shit. Do I have any other tracking devices I need to be aware of?"

They both shake their heads.

"You're sure?"

Lorenzo puts his hand on my shoulder. "We didn't lie to you because we wanted to deceive you, Joey. We only ever wanted to protect you."

"I know, but you've got to stop the lying. I'm not a kid anymore."

"You're here now, aren't you?" Dante says. "Not in the dining room with Kristin. We know you're not a kid, Joey, but you *are* our little sister, and like it or not, it's our job to protect you. Just like we protect each other."

"It's active." Lorenzo nods at the map that just popped up on his screen. A flashing purple dot has me leaning closer.

"Where is it?" I peer at the screen, hoping it isn't at Max's penthouse or the cabin.

"Cedar Rapids," Dante says with a frown.

"What the fuck?" Lorenzo looks at our brother.

Dante closes the laptop. "Let's go get our boy."

The two of them immediately slip into tactical mode, like generals of an army, discussing grenades and weapons.

"I want to come too," I say, interrupting their battle planning.

"No," they reply in unison.

I cross my arms over my chest and scowl at the two of them. "You literally just said you'd stop treating me like a child."

Dante grabs my arms. "This is serious, Joey. We don't know what we're walking into. This isn't about protecting you, this is about going into fucking battle with our best soldiers. I love you, kid, but in this situation, you will slow us down."

Lorenzo cuts in before I can say anything. "Part of being a grown-up is knowing when to step aside and let someone more capable do the job, Joey. We can't focus on rescuing Max if we're worried about protecting you. And not because you're a girl or because you're our sister, but because you're just not ready for something like this yet."

Yet? That's a good sign. And he's right. I would slow them down, and I need all their energy focused on getting Max back here—if only so I can kill him myself. "Fine. I'll stay here."

"I know it's not easy but stay with Kristin." Dante opens his safe and starts pulling out a variety of guns. "She's hiding something."

"You think?" I ask.

"Yeah." He frowns. "Could just be that she's scared, but something isn't quite right about her story. So keep an eye on her, yeah?"

"Of course."

Lorenzo squeezes my shoulder on his way out the door. "We should be back first thing tomorrow. Take care of Anya for me too?"

"Always."

CHAPTER
TWENTY-NINE

MAX

"Where the fuck is your boss?" I spit at Ponytail. "Because he's sure taking his sweet time if he's so desperate to speak to me about his girl."

Ponytail shrugs. "He will be here when he is here."

"Fucking assholes," I mutter, spitting a mouthful of blood onto the floor. They tried their plastic bag trick a few more times and used me as a punching bag, but they haven't dished out anything I can't handle. The waiting and not knowing what the fuck's going on is the worst part. That's the real torture. Ponytail isn't very forthcoming with information, no matter how many different ways I try to find out who he's working for, and the other guy may as well be mute. He seems to only be able to communicate in grunts.

Blood trickles into my eye, and I blink it away. Twisting my wrists, I try to work the iron cuffs off, but they're too tight. My ankles are in similar shackles, attached to chains sunk into the concrete floor. These pricks obviously need me alive for something. If I can get the two of them close enough—

None of us are prepared for the deafening explosion that rocks the room. My ears ring, and I shake my head to clear it. I need to focus. I have no idea who was behind that explosion, whether it's an ally or another enemy, but this is my shot. The force of the blast causes Ponytail to stagger on his feet. He spins around, staring at the doorway and shouting in Russian, while the mute one draws his gun and trains it on the entrance. I take my shot with Ponytail. They left way too much slack on the chains on my ankles, enough that I can kick Ponytail in the back of the knee. The sickening crunch of bone is sweet music to my ears, and he drops to the floor like a giant sack of shit, cursing and shouting something to the mute one, who comes for me.

I wrap the chain around Ponytail's neck, crossing my ankles and pulling it tight until his face turns purple. He scrabbles at my legs, fingernails pulling on the chain, but it has no effect. I squeeze harder as the mute one comes behind me and wraps his arm around my neck, trying to choke me so I'll release his buddy. But my throat is slippery with blood, and I wriggle enough to get my mouth on the meaty part of his thumb. I bite down, through flesh and cartilage and blood, shaking my head like a rabid fucking dog and refusing to let go.

He screams and curses, dropping the gun onto the floor. I guess he's not mute after all. He hits me on the side of the head, but I only bite down harder. Ponytail gets weaker, his body going lax and his eyes bulging out of his head.

Light glints off a blade in the mute one's free hand, and there's nothing I can do to stop him from plunging it into my abdomen. Burning agony has me seeing stars, but I block it out and focus on gaining my freedom. He probably thought it would make me scream and release his hand, but it only makes me channel all the pain toward crushing his hand with my jaw.

He screams louder, and the door bursts open. A cloud of smoke fills the room, obscuring the faces of the men who enter. I release Ponytail's deadweight as the mute motherfucker pulls his hand back to stab me again. Bracing myself for another strike, I flinch when a bullet whizzes by my ear. The weight of his body dropping to the floor jerks his thumb out of my mouth, and I unclench my jaw to spit out blood and chunks of flesh.

"Nice shot, Loz," says a familiar voice.

Oh, thank holy fuck. "You two took your goddamn time," I croak.

"You're lucky we came at all, asshole," Dante says. I guess they're still pissed at me about the whole having sex with their baby sister thing.

They get to work freeing me from the shackles on my ankles and wrists, and the adrenaline leaves my body in a rush, making me lightheaded, but I manage to gesture toward the floor and mumble, "Joey's pendant. They pulled it off."

Dante picks it up and slips it into his pocket.

My eyes flicker closed. "Hey, I need to ask you both something," I mumble.

"What's that?" Lorenzo asks.

"Can I date your sister?"

I don't hear their answer because everything goes black.

THIRTY

MAX

"Hey, there," Kat Moretti's soft voice penetrates the fog in my brain as light filters through my flickering eyelids. I look sideways to see her standing beside the bed, and it takes me a few beats to realize I'm in the Moretti mansion. Every single part of my body thrums with a dull ache.

I glance down at my stomach and note the bandages and the telltale signs I've had surgery. "You fix me up all by yourself, doc?"

Kat is a nurse, but we affectionately call her doc because she patches up our guys as good as any doctor I've ever met.

"Nope. Lucky for you, I got nowhere near you with a scalpel or a needle," she says, rolling her eyes. "We had to get a surgeon in. You had a little internal bleeding so we wanted to make sure ..."

"Figures," I groan as I shuffle into a more comfortable position.

I need to call Kristin and make sure she's safe, but there's someone else I'm desperate to see first. "Where's Joey?"

"Joey?" Kat blinks at me, and the look on her face makes my

stomach twist in knots. Or maybe that's just the drugs they gave me. "Isn't there someone else you should be concerned about?"

I frown, confused, but then I hear her voice. "Max?" Kristin says softly from the corner of the room, her face pale and her eyes red from crying. She rests her hands protectively over her bump.

"Kristin? Thank fuck you're safe. But ... Wait. What are you doing here?" My head throbs. What the fuck is going on?

"If it wasn't for your girlfriend here, we wouldn't have even known you were missing." Kat's voice drips with disdain, and my head pounds harder. Why do I feel like I've woken up in an alternate universe?

Hang on. What the fuck did she just say? "My girlfriend?"

"I'm sorry, Max. I didn't know if I could trust them," Kristin says.

Pinching the bridge of my nose, I suck in a deep breath that burns my lungs. This can't be happening. "You told everyone you're my girlfriend?" I ask, ignoring Kat's fierce glare.

"Y-yeah," my sister answers, her eyes wide and fearful. I guess she couldn't have known why that would be such a big deal, but the thought that for even one second Joey believed ... Fresh bile burns the back of my throat.

"Fuck, Kristin!" I push myself up and swing my legs off the edge of the bed.

Kat rushes over and tries to push me back down. "You should rest!"

"I need to speak to Joey," I insist, yanking the blood pressure cuff from my arm. Jumping off the bed and onto the floor, I groan at the fiery agony that sears through my abdomen.

"Max. You just had surgery," Kat says, sighing.

"Where is she?"

"I don't know."

"I'm sorry, Max," Kristin sniffs.

"You have nothing to be sorry for, sweetheart," Kat assures her, but I tune them both out because all I can think about is Joey and what she must think of me right now. How long have I been out of it? How many hours, minutes, seconds has my girl spent thinking that I'm the kind of piece of shit who'd do something like that?

I run out into the hallway, adrenaline coursing through me, making me stronger and more determined with each step. "Joey?" I shout as I head toward the den. "Joey!"

I see Dante first as he walks out of his study. "Keep your fucking voice down," he orders.

"I need to see Joey. Where is she?"

"She doesn't want to speak to you right now."

"I don't give a fuck. Where is she, Dante?"

Lorenzo steps up beside him, fastening the buttons of his suit jacket. They stand side by side—against me. I roll my head side to side, back and forth, prepared to go through the two of them to get to her if I must.

"She's not interested, Max."

Blood thunders in my ears. "Joey," I yell louder. I know she's here somewhere. She has to be.

Dante takes a step toward me. "I said keep your fucking voice down. My daughter is asleep," he says with a snarl, teeth bared like he's spoiling for a fight. I never thought I'd stand on this side of the infamous wall of Moretti rage, but I will take both him and Lorenzo down if they don't let me see her. And if I can't get through them, I will fucking die trying.

We glare at one another, none of us prepared to back down even a little. Each of us believing we're right.

I sense her even before I hear her soft footsteps, and I'm filled with adrenaline and anguish when I look up to see her drifting down the staircase. Her bloodshot eyes make me wonder how many hours she spent crying. *What the fuck have I done?*

"Joey?" Her name comes out like a plea.

"Shouldn't you be with your *girlfriend*?" She spits the last word like it's poison on her tongue.

"She's not my girlfriend, I swear to you."

She reaches the bottom stair and makes her way to stand beside her brothers. All three Moretti siblings glare at me like I'm the enemy. But something about her standing by their side looks exactly right. Until now, I never noticed how much she has in common with her brothers. She's equally smart, strong, and capable—and although she tries to hide her true feelings behind a veneer of sarcasm and snark, when she's hurt ... well, my girl brings the full Moretti arsenal. "She's just some poor girl you knocked up then?" she snaps, her eyes brimming with fury.

I close my eyes as a fiery poker stabs my gut, but it's nothing compared to the searing agony of Joey's contempt.

"Not my kid either," I groan, my hand pressed against my stomach. It feels like my guts are spilling out onto the floor.

"Fuck, he's bleeding," Lorenzo says and crosses the hallway, putting his hand on my shoulder. "Let's get you back to Kat."

I shrug him off. "I'm not going anywhere until I speak to my fucking girl," I shout, even as my head spins and I sway on my feet.

Joey steps forward, baring her teeth. "I'm not your girl, you lying, cheating asshole."

"Yes, you fucking are."

She stalks toward me, and her scent scrambles my senses. I don't know whether to drop to my knees at her feet, kiss her, or give into the dizziness and black out. "Tell that to that girl carrying your baby, Maximo. The one who's been sobbing by your bedside for the past six hours."

"It's not my fucking baby," I protest.

"You need to get back to Kat so she can take a look at you," Lorenzo insists, wrapping an arm around my waist.

"I *need* to speak to my fucking girl." I try to shrug him off again, but I don't have the strength this time.

She rolls her eyes. "There is nothing you can say—"

"Kristin is my little sister, Joey. That kid she's having is my nephew, *not* my son."

"What?" Joey frowns and shakes her head. "You don't even have a sister."

"I fucking knew it," Dante says.

Joey slaps her brother on the arm. "If you knew that, why the hell didn't you tell me? Asshole."

Dante sighs. "I mean ... I didn't know ..." He shakes his head. "It's a long fucking story."

"Can we do this later? Max is fucking bleeding all over the marble here," Lorenzo snaps impatiently.

I look down at the blood-soaked bandage wrapped around my abdomen and close my eyes to fight back the nausea. "I thought your wife was good at stitches, buddy?"

Dante's chuckle is cut off by his wife stomping toward us.

"She is, but I didn't stitch you up, and you're not supposed to be out of bed yet, dumbass!" Kat yells. "Get him back in the bed."

"You heard the doc," Lorenzo says as he spins me around and practically carries me down the hallway.

I glance over my shoulder, struggling to remain conscious. "Jo—"

"I'm right here, Max," she says, but I can't read her tone. Does she believe me? Does it even matter to her now? Whatever, I'll make sure it fucking matters to her. She's still mine.

Back in the makeshift hospital room, Kat gingerly peels the

wet bandage from my stomach. "Should it be bleeding like that?" Joey asks from beside me.

"He busted his stitches, is all. They weren't all that secure from what I can see." Kat looks up and scowls at Dante. "I think prohibition was in place the last time that surgeon you found operated." I try not to flinch at the glare she turns my way. "Besides, these things can happen if you go running down hallways right after major abdominal surgery."

"Major abdominal surgery," Lorenzo snorts. "It was barely a scratch."

Kat gets to work cleaning my wound with efficiency. I bite back a curse and chuckle. "Yeah, barely."

"I can give you something more for the pain?" Kat offers.

"No. No more drugs." I shake my head. "I want my thinking clear."

"Whatever you say. But this is going to hurt like hell."

Kat urges me to lie down, then quickly stitches me back up.

Only when my head stops spinning do I look up, scanning the room until my eyes lock on Joey's. I hold out my hand for her, and it feels like a goddamn eternity passes before she gently entwines her fingers in mine. "You are the only fucking girl for me, Joey Moretti." I say loudly so that there will be no doubt of that fact in anyone's mind.

"Max?" My attention goes to where Kristin still sits in the corner, a horror-stricken expression on her face, her eyes shimmering with tears. "I'm s-sorry. I d-didn't know."

I give her a weak smile. "I know. It's okay. But you can trust everyone in this room. I promise you that. Tell them who you really are."

Kristin sucks in a deep breath as every pair of eyes in the room, except for Kat's, trains on her. "I'm Max's little sister." She looks at my girl. "I'm so sorry, Joey. I can't imagine what you must have thought of me. I didn't know you and he— If I had ..."

"But why did you tell us you were his girlfriend?" Joey asks, her beautiful face pulled into a frown. "Why not just tell us the truth?"

Kristin opens and closes her mouth like a fish out of water, but no words come out.

"Because of who your father is?" Dante offers for her.

Closing her eyes, my sister nods.

"I don't understand." Joey looks between Dante, Kristin, and me. "Who is her father? Why didn't you tell me you had a sister? Why didn't any of us know about her, Max?"

I squeeze Joey's hand. So many questions, and I don't have all the answers yet. "I didn't know myself until about two weeks ago when Kristin showed up on my doorstep."

"So you've known for two weeks. Why couldn't you tell me? Is that why we didn't go back to your apartment that night?"

I open my mouth to answer, but Kristin beats me to it. "I asked Max not to tell anyone I was here," she says, standing and walking toward the bed. "My father told me that I couldn't trust a Moretti, so I made Max promise to keep me a secret."

Joey shakes her head. "But why are you here? Why now? Why couldn't you trust us, but you trusted Max? You know he's one of us, right?"

"Because he's my big brother," Kristin whispers. "My father told me if I was ever in trouble, Max was the only person I could rely on."

"You knew about Max then?" Lorenzo's eyes narrow with interest and suspicion.

She shakes her head vigorously. "No. Not until two months ago. I had no idea."

Dante pinches the bridge of his nose. "But your father is Vito DiMarco, right?"

Joey's frown deepens. "Vito *DiMarco*?"

"My uncle," I explain.

"Your uncle is also your sister's father?" Her eyebrows shoot up to her hairline.

"Yep."

Lorenzo claps his hands and gets everyone's attention. "Can someone start at the beginning and explain what the fuck is going on here?"

"Kristin? You know the whole story and Nurse Ratched here isn't exactly being gentle, ya know?" Wincing, I glare down at Kat who just stabbed the needle into my flesh with more force than before.

"I will kick your ass, DiMarco," she says good-naturedly, keeping her head down and remaining focused on the task at hand.

"A-are you sure?" Kristin asks me.

I give her a reassuring nod. "These people are my family. There's nothing you can't tell them, I swear."

"Okay." She chews on her lip for a second before she goes on. "A few months ago, my dad started acting strangely. Like he was always pretty paranoid, but he upped the ante, you know? Wouldn't let me leave the house. Always checking in on me."

"Seems like he didn't keep that much of a careful eye on you." Dante tilts his head and stares at her rounded abdomen.

Kristin flinches and rubs a protective hand over her belly. "Well, that, um. That's a different story."

My brotherly instincts flare to life. She isn't here to have her actions judged by a room full of strangers. While I know that wasn't Dante's intention—he's an asshole, but he isn't that kind of asshole—she doesn't owe them an explanation. Especially not like this, not right now. We'll need to talk about that prick soon enough, but she doesn't need to be here when we discuss how we're going to find and kill the father of her baby.

Reaching out with my spare hand, I gently squeeze her wrist. "Maybe we don't focus on the jackass who knocked you up right now?"

Kristin nods gratefully and continues. "Dad was extra suspicious, but he said he was just being careful. We moved twice in the space of six months. When I finally had enough and demanded to know what the hell was going on, he was still sketchy, but that's when he finally told me about Max. How our mom was married to Max's dad when she fell in love with him. How they risked everything to run off together."

Lorenzo snorts, and I throw him a warning look. That's clearly the version of events Vito told his daughter, and it's the story she believes. None of the choices our mother and her father made back then are on Kristin. She feels alone enough in the world right now without all of us telling her what a piece of work her father really is.

"Go on," I say, urging her to continue.

"He said that if anything ever happened to him then I needed to find Max because I'd be safe with him. He drummed two messages into me. The only person I could ever trust was Max and that I should never trust a Moretti." She pauses, letting the information sink in.

The tension in the room goes up several notches, and I'm relieved that she's intuitive enough not to share the message my dear old uncle told her to give me. That would almost certainly send Lorenzo and Dante off the deep end.

"Then, one night about three weeks ago, he didn't come home. I called and I waited, hoping I'd hear from him, but after two days I knew something bad must have happened. So I took the emergency fund and came to Chicago."

"That's when she showed up at your door?" Dante asks.

"Well, my apartment building, but yeah. I knew as soon as I saw her ..." I trail off, recalling the first time I saw her. How frightened and pale she looked. How much she reminded me of our mom.

"And she's been hiding out at your place in secret ever since?" Joey's words drip with venom. I can't blame her. She has every right to be pissed at me.

"We've been looking for Vito. I was going to tell you ..." Sighing, I shake my head. I've never kept anything like this from them before. "And I didn't want to bring any more drama to your door right now ..."

"And she made you promise not to tell us, right?" Joey snaps and turns her rage on my sister. "Never trust a Moretti, that's what your father taught you?"

Kristin looks down at the floor, her cheeks flushing pink.

"Joey, don't." I squeeze her hand tighter. "She's just a kid. She was scared. She only knows what her father told her. That's not on her."

My girl scowls at me, but she doesn't pull her hand away.

"So when you came here, you told us you were Max's girl-friend because you didn't trust us enough to tell us you were really his sister?" There's no malice or accusation in Lorenzo's tone, but Kristin's throat constricts as she swallows under the heat of his gaze.

"Y-yeah."

I gesture for her to come closer and wrap my arm around her waist. "It's okay. They just need to know what's going on."

Dante clears his throat and addresses Kristin. "You can stay here until Max is back to full strength and we find out what's happened to your father."

Her eyes widen with surprise. "I can't stay here now that Max is back."

"You can and you will," Kat says in a steely tone as she finishes off the last of my stitches. "Your father may have had his reasons for not trusting this family, but you are Max's sister, and he's our brother. You have nothing to fear from anyone in this house."

Kristin gives Kat a faint smile. Dante's wife, with her confidence and kindness, is impossible not to trust.

Still, my sister looks at me for reassurance. "You're safe here, I promise. And I'll be right here with you. Okay?"

"Okay," she says, nodding and blinking back tears.

"We'll fix you up in the guest room that's just down the hall from Joey's room. And Max, where will you be staying?" Kat arches an eyebrow at me, and the mischievous glint in her eyes has me biting back a grin. I need all the help I can get and having her on my side is more than I could've hoped for.

Dante scoffs, glaring at his wife. "He'll be in the guest room on the other side of the house."

"Dante," Joey huffs.

Dante snorts. "He's not staying in your room,"

Lorenzo puts a hand on his younger brother's shoulder and keeps his voice low. "Maybe we should let Joey decide?"

"Since when are you on her side on this?" Dante asks with a frown.

"Since I have better things to do with my time than police our adult sister," Lorenzo replies with a sigh. "Joey's a grown woman now, whether we want to admit that or not. Hasn't she proven that she's capable of behaving like an adult?"

"Thank you, Lorenzo," Joey says, giving her oldest brother a genuine smile. "It's nice to have one of you believe in me."

Dante rolls his eyes and puts his arm around her shoulder. "You know that I know you're capable, Joey. Of course I believe in you."

"Then you don't believe in Max? Is that it?"

Shaking his head, he releases a heavy sigh. "It's not that straightforward."

"Nothing worth having is," she counters.

Fuck, I wish they would all get the hell out and let me talk to her alone. I have no intentions of sleeping in her room with her, but that doesn't mean I won't be spending plenty of time in there with her. The Moretti siblings could go on arguing all night about this. I cough loudly, and they turn their attention back to me. "Can I have a minute with my girl?"

Lorenzo and Dante look at each other, but Kat ushers everyone out of the room, speaking over their protests with instructions that I need to rest. Shooting me a knowing look over her shoulder, she mouths for me to be careful and closes the door behind her, leaving Joey and me alone.

My girl props her hip on the edge of the bed beside me, her fingers still laced through mine.

"I'm sorry I didn't tell you about Kristin, baby girl. I was going to as soon as I figured out what was going on. It just never seemed like the right time."

"When she told me ... and I thought ..." A tear runs down her cheek, and she swats it away.

"I know, baby." Lifting my heavy arms, I wrap them around her, pulling her close and holding on tight. I've been desperate to touch her for so long that I'm still not entirely sure this moment isn't a figment of my imagination, but her familiar scent and the hot tears soaking my chest assure me this is real.

She nuzzles my chest. "I thought I'd lost you, Max ..."

"I'm right here."

"You almost died," she whispers, lifting her head and looking at me with tears rolling down her cheeks.

"I'd never die on you."

"You ever even attempt to get yourself kidnapped again and you'll wish you were dead, DiMarco," she says, faking a scowl.

"I promise never to even think about it."

She sits up, her dark eyes locked on my face. "I hate that you weren't honest with me."

"I know."

"If you had been ..." She wipes away another tear.

I cup her face in my hands. The fact that she even thought me capable of something like that burns me from the inside. Doesn't she, of all people, know me better than that? But I can't fight with her right now. I can feel nothing but grateful that she's here with me. "I hate that you thought I'd betray you like that, Joey. The fact you could believe me capable of hurting you that way is worse than a knife to the stomach. I regret every single second that you spent hating me."

"I never hated you, Max."

"No?"

"No. I can't."

"Not even when you thought ...?"

Joey shakes her head. "Not even then."

I brush my fingertips over her cheek. God, I want to take her to bed and stay there with her for the rest of my goddamn life. "Are we okay?"

"I guess," she whispers.

That's not exactly the emphatic *yes* I hoped for, but it will have to do for now. "I need to talk to Dante and Lorenzo."

"Do it tomorrow. Rest today. There's a room ready for you upstairs."

"The one on the other side of the house from you?"

"Well, we did make that one up for you. It was supposed to be for you and Kristin, so I wanted it as far away from me as possible."

"I'm sorry, baby."

"I know."

The fact that she was still willing to have me here, both of us, well, that reminds me how fucking incredible this girl right here is. "You were going to let me stay here? Me and Kristin?"

"Yes. Although I guess you won't want to share a room with

your kid sister?" She laughs softly, and the sound makes my heart beat faster.

I brush my fingertips over her cheek. I'd much rather share one with her, but how do I tell her that I can't, maybe not ever? How the hell do I trust myself around the one person it would kill me to hurt?

Her eyes darken as the skin on her neck turns pink. "I guess you could stay in my room," she whispers seductively.

A ball of emotion lodges in my throat. I want nothing more than to stay in her room with her. Go to sleep next to her soft, warm body and wake up with her in my arms. Fuck her every single night and every single morning for the rest of my goddamn life.

"I need to talk to your brothers, baby," I say, struggling to sit up.

She steps back, frowning at me while she chews on her lip. "Kat told you to rest."

"She stitched me back up. I'm good. Besides, I'm going to shuffle down the hallway and then sit in their office. Nothing heavy. I promise."

"Please don't get into anything now, Max," Joey pleads. I take her hand and pull her back to me, brushing my bandaged fingers through her hair. "I only just got you back," she whispers.

I press my lips close to her ear, and she shivers in my arms. "Baby girl, I promise you I'm not going anywhere, okay? But I need to speak to your brothers. I have to do this right."

She stares into my eyes, and even though I know she wants to fight me on this, her shoulders drop in defeat. "Fine. I'll wait for you in the den."

"Good girl." I don't miss the way her breath catches at those words, and my cock throbs. Thoughts of her kept me sane while I was tied up and tortured, and I'm fucking desperate to feel her again. To taste her. To claim every single inch of her as my own. But I need to make things right first.

When I reach Dante and Lorenzo's study, there's a guard outside the door as usual. I wonder if he's been given orders to keep me out, but he nods a greeting and opens the door for me, which I take to mean that the Moretti brothers didn't keep me alive just so they could kill me themselves.

"Max," Dante says with a nod.

"Take a seat." Lorenzo indicates the chair opposite them, but I remain standing for now.

"We've been thinking about who might have taken you and why—" Dante begins, but I cut him off.

"Before we get into any of that, I need to ask you both something."

They stare at me, and I suddenly realize what it must feel like to be on this side of the desk for a change—metaphorically speaking.

"I want your permission to date your sister," I say, my hands stuffed into the pockets of my bloodstained sweatpants.

Dante's eyes narrow. "And if we say no?"

I shrug. "I guess it doesn't change the outcome. I'm going to date her anyway, but I'd prefer to do it with your blessing."

"You swore, Max. Joey was off-limits."

"That was a long time ago. We were kids making stupid promises to each other. I get that I should've told you first, but it all kind of happened so fast. I tried to fight it, but I couldn't. Still, I want to do this right. You two are my family," I say, choking up on the last word.

"A family you were prepared to walk away from? Because you knew what would happen if you fucked around with Joey." Dante says, his tone cold and detached.

"I would never ask either of you to choose between me and Anya or Kat. Never. But if you make me choose, I will choose her. Every single fucking time." I step forward and place my palms flat on their desk. "I know you're worried that I might hurt her—" I stop to swallow the words that get stuck in my throat. "But I never would. I'll never drink when I'm with her. Never take so much as an aspirin if she's staying in my bed. I don't know if—"

Lorenzo holds up a hand. "You can't seriously think our problem with you dating our sister has anything to do with the Delgado girl?"

I blink at him.

"That was twelve fucking years ago, compagno," Dante adds.

"I fucking killed her," I remind them. "And I still don't remember a goddamn thing."

"You were drunk and on drugs. You weren't thinking straight," Lorenzo says, his brow furrowed in a scowl.

"I still did it. If I ever hurt Joey like that—" I drop into one of the chairs in front of their desk and scrub a hand over my face.

Dante leans forward in his seat. "We don't want you to date our sister because it's messy, Max. If you and she ..." He shakes his head. If Joey and I don't work out, it would put us all in an untenable position. "It has nothing to do with what happened with that girl."

"But it should! You should want me to stay away from her because you know what I'm capable of. The things I've done. I want to stay away from her because of them." I drop my head into my hands. "But I can't."

Dante clears his throat. "So, you date our sister, but you never spend the night together? How the fuck does that even work, Max? She'll never go for it."

"As long as I don't fall asleep—"

"Now you're going to stop sleeping?" Dante snaps.

"No," I bark. I don't know the answers. All I know is that I can't live without her. And I can't hurt her. "I'll figure something out. Maybe I could get some therapy or something?"

Lorenzo snorts. "Therapy?"

"Yes. Therapy," I repeat. "To figure out what happened. Because if I could just remember ..." I shake my head.

"You need to stop fucking torturing yourself, Max," Dante says with a sigh. "You were both so wasted, you didn't know what you were doing. She was into some kinky shit like you, and it went too far because you were both too fucked up to stop it. That's all."

I stare at him. I wish it was as easy for me to explain away, but not being able to remember what happened that night haunts my every waking moment. I've killed plenty of people— my body count is higher than both Moretti brothers' combined —but I remember them all. I watched the light go out of their eyes every single time.

Except for her.

I took her life and don't even remember doing it. How the hell am I supposed to sleep next to the most precious person in the entire world and not worry that one morning I might wake up and find her lifeless face on the pillow next to me?

Lorenzo cuts off my internal argument. "You should tell her."

"I should what?"

"Tell her. She deserves to know," Lorenzo replies with a shrug.

"You didn't think that earlier," I remind him.

"I didn't realize it still ate you up this much."

"And if it didn't eat me up? If I could just forget about the fact that I murdered an innocent girl while we were having sex, *that* would be okay? I wouldn't have to tell her then?" I snap.

"If you're making decisions about Joey's life—about the

kind of life she'll have if she chooses you, then she deserves to know before she falls for you any more than she already has."

Dante nods solemnly, siding with his brother. "He's right, Max."

"What if she hates me?"

"She won't," Lorenzo fires back.

"She deserves the truth, compagno. All of it," Dante says.

"How else are you going to explain the fact that you're not sleeping in her room tonight if you don't?" Lorenzo asks.

"I'll tell her I'm tired, or ..."

Dante shakes his head. "You'll break her fucking heart. If you're going to ask to date our sister, Max, then you will tell her the fucking truth."

I slump in my chair. I know they're right, but what if it costs me everything? What if it costs me her?

A soft knock at the door snatches all our attention.

"Come in," Dante shouts.

My entire world walks into the room, and the soft smile on her face makes me want to cut my tongue out of my mouth so we don't have to have this conversation. "It's getting kind of late, and Kat says Max should rest. We can talk about everything that happened tomorrow, right?"

Dante and Lorenzo voice their agreement.

"Good. You can stay in my room," she says to me, her eyes shining with a happiness that I worried I'd never see again. Fuck, can't I just have one more day when she still looks at me like that?

Lorenzo clears his throat. "Shall we give you the room?"

"No, stay." They know everything anyway. At least if they're here, I won't back out when I see the look of horror on her face. I'll have no choice but to tell her the whole ugly truth.

"Is something wrong?" Joey asks from where she stands beside me.

"Take a seat," Dante replies.

"Why? What is it?" she asks, an angry edge creeping into her voice. "You don't get to keep Max and me—"

"It's not that, Joey," I interrupt before she starts berating her brothers. "Sit down."

"You're freaking me out, Max." Her voice wobbles.

I take hold of her hand, curling my fingers around hers and tugging her down into the chair next to me. "I have to tell you about something I did."

"What—what did you do?"

"I killed someone, Joey."

Falling back in her chair, she starts to laugh, and I gape at her. "Max. You asshole."

"This is serious, Joey. Not just anyone. A girl."

Her laugh cuts off abruptly. "A girl? What girl?"

"Her name was Fiona. She was a ... friend of ours."

"Fiona?" She frowns.

"It was twelve years ago, Joey," Lorenzo adds.

"But why? What did she do?" Joey asks, her fingers still entwined in mine.

"She didn't do anything," I say quietly. "I don't even remember what happened. I woke up and she was dead in bed beside me."

Her face turns pale, and her nose wrinkles with horror and disgust while my heart threatens to burst through my fucking ribcage. "No." She shakes her head emphatically. "Fiona, right? The girl with those stupid pigtails?"

"Yeah. Fiona Delgado."

"No," she says again, still shaking her head.

"Joey, I know—"

"No, Max. You didn't kill her."

"I did, Joey. I woke up and she was dead. With my hand-prints around her neck."

"No!" she shouts now, pulling her hand from mine as she looks to her brothers. "Those weren't Max's handprints." Her hand flies to her mouth and tremors wrack her body.

I lean forward, placing my hand on her back. "Joey, baby?"

"Those were *his* handprints," she whispers, her eyes wide as she looks first at her brothers, then at me. "Sal's."

Lorenzo and Dante lean forward. We stare at her.

"What are you talking about?" Dante asks softly.

"He killed that girl. The night of your graduation party. I saw him."

"N-no," I stammer, shaking my head.

"He did. I saw him. I saw him and some other guy talking about getting rid of the body."

"You're sure it was Fiona? You were only ten, Joey," Dante says.

"I know what I saw, Dante!" Joey shrieks. "Dad promised me twenty bucks if I stayed out of the way of the party all night, so once you and your buddies were all too drunk to walk, I went to call in my debt. But when I got to his office, he was with some guy, and Fiona was dead on the floor. I recognized her pigtails. I knew it was her because I always hated her and the way she told me to get lost whenever I was talking to Max. But then she was dead ..."

I lean forward, dropping my head into my hands. I feel like I'm about to throw up for at least the third time today. This is fucking unbelievable. For twelve long years, I've tortured myself with the memory of that morning. With the image of Fiona Delgado, naked and dead next to me. And I've wracked my brain almost every single day since then to piece together what happened because I don't remember a single second of it. I always put it down to being so wasted on brandy and cocaine that I blacked out. And I haven't touched either of them since.

But of course I don't remember. Because I didn't fucking touch her.

"You're sure about this, Joey?" Lorenzo asks.

"I just freaking told you I am."

"What exactly did you hear Pop say?" Dante says.

"The other guy was asking what they were gonna do with her, and Dad said that he had the perfect plan for her. He called her a money-grubbing little whore, and I didn't know what it meant at the time, but I remember how angry he sounded. It gave me goosebumps all over my skin."

"Then what?"

"Then he saw me, and he was all sweet to me—the way he could be sometimes, you know? He said the silly girl in his office tried to hurt our family and that he was going to take care of it. He gave me my twenty bucks and told me to go back to bed."

"Why didn't you ever tell us, Joey?" Dante asks.

"I-I didn't really know what it meant, and it wasn't the first dead body I'd seen. He made me promise never to tell anyone and then ... well, it wasn't the worst thing he ever did."

I dry heave, and Joey rubs my back.

Barely a day has passed when I haven't thought about her and tried to remember what I did. Especially since Joey. I've smoldered with the desperate need to know what I did to that girl, so I could make sure I never repeated the same mistake again.

"B-but she was in my bed." I stand up, my head spinning. "She was there with me."

"Then he must have put her there because I assure you that she was dead when I walked out of his office."

"No." Running my hands through my hair, I shake my head. "No. He wouldn't— He let me think—"

"He would, Max," Lorenzo says, deadpan.

"B-but." I blink at him, searching his dark eyes for answers.

He looks so much like Sal. I don't think I ever really noticed that before. "Did you know?"

He scowls. "No," he insists.

Of course he didn't. He hated his father. He would never cover for him like that.

"I'm sorry, Max. If I'd known that he made you ... that he framed you ... I would have told you a long time ago." Joey's pain-filled voice makes my heart ache for her.

I squeeze her hand. "It's not on you, baby." I grind out the words as rage and sheer fucking relief course through my veins.

"I always knew there was something not right about the whole situation. The way you found her in bed that morning." Lorenzo says, appearing deep in thought.

I blink at him. "You did?"

"I've told you this many times, Maximo. But you would never listen."

"I can't ..." I shake my head. Immediately after it happened, and on the handful of occasions we've discussed it since, he questioned the events that led to Fiona being in my bed, but I thought he was just trying to jog my memory or make me feel better.

Dante stares at me. "This makes sense, Max. Fiona was never your type. She'd been hanging around you for months, and no matter how drunk you got, you never so much as brushed her arm."

"Yeah, but I was so drunk that night ..." My head spins so fast I think I might pass out. Sal gave me the last glass of brandy I remember drinking that night.

"You didn't kill her, Max," Joey says. Leaning over in her chair, she wraps her arms around my neck and presses a soft kiss on my shoulder. "I'm sorry he made you believe you did."

"Then how the fuck did she end up in my bed?"

Nobody answers—I guess because the answer is so fucking obvious.

I alternate between hanging my head in my hands and looking at my best friends while Joey holds onto me like I'm in danger of floating away in the middle of this shitstorm. "Why would he do that?" I ask when I find the words to speak. I was never anything but loyal to Salvatore Moretti. He had no reason to doubt me—to frame me for murder, if that's what happened.

"Because he was a sick, twisted fuck," Dante spits. "But we already knew that."

"I'm so sorry, Max," Joey says again. "If I'd just mentioned something. I hate that you carried this around for half your life."

"You have nothing to apologize for," I assure her.

Lorenzo pinches the bridge of his nose. "It's late and I need to check on Anya. We could spend the rest of our lives discussing the piece of shit that was our father, but nothing is going to change what he did now."

"I agree. I think we should all get some sleep," Dante suggests. He jerks his chin at me. "Is there any information about who took you that can't wait until morning?"

"No. It can wait." Sleep sounds like fucking heaven right now. Maybe when I wake up, I won't have spent the last twelve years driving myself crazy trying to remember something I didn't do. "But I should check on Kristin before I go to bed."

"I checked on her before I came in here," Joey says. "She's sleeping. I don't think you should disturb her. She hardly slept at all while you were gone."

"None of us did," Lorenzo adds, throwing his sister a concerned look.

Fuck, I should stop feeling sorry for myself and take better care of my girl. Should focus on the revelation that I'm not at risk of murdering her in her sleep after all, because as fucked up

212

as this whole thing is, the fact that I can crawl into bed with her tonight—hell, *every* night—should be compensation enough for anything her father ever put me through.

"Shall we go to bed?" Even though the way she says the words is entirely innocent, my cock still twitches to life.

I stare at her. She makes the whole goddamn world make sense. "Yeah." I guess the past doesn't matter so much when my future is standing right here.

CHAPTER
THIRTY-ONE

MAX

I manage a quick shower in Joey's bathroom, after which I crawl into her bed and wait for her to take one too. I must be exhausted because the thought of taking one together never crossed my mind.

I press my head against her soft pillow and her sweet perfume washes over me. Her sheets are soft on my skin, and I think about how these covers must have been wrapped around her last night—touching every part of her. My cock throbs, not giving a single fuck that the rest of my body needs sleep.

Joey walks out of the bathroom and heads toward me. She pulls back the covers to climb into bed, but there's something very wrong with this picture. "Um, clothes off, baby girl."

She looks down at her tiny shorts and tank top that don't cover a lot of her body, but they still cover way too much. "These are hardly anything, and you need to rest," she says as she looks at me with a devious grin on her face.

"I can still rest while you're naked. Now take off the fucking clothes."

"You are so bossy." She rolls her eyes, but then my good girl peels her shirt off over her head and throws it onto the floor. She cocks one eyebrow at me. "The shorts too?"

"Most definitely the shorts too."

"Fine." She slowly rolls them down her legs, and I enjoy the show she's giving me.

Gloriously naked, she slips beneath the covers, and I lift my arm so she can nestle into the crook of my shoulder. Her hard nipples brush over my skin as she presses her warm, soft body against mine, and my cock twitches in response. But my eyes are heavy with sleep, and my abdomen is so fucking sore, I don't think I could do anything more than talk right now. I run my hand over her back, and she shivers against me.

"I know it must have been a shock finding out about Fiona. You want to talk about it?" she asks softly.

I can't pretend I'm not a little bothered by the fact that Joey knew what her father had really done all along and could have saved me from years of torture. Not that I blame her at all—it was one incident in a long line of awful shit her father did. The fact he asked his ten-year-old daughter to keep a secret like that is all kinds of fucked up. Even more fucked up because it wasn't an unusual enough event for her to feel the need to talk to anyone about it. I should be grateful that it didn't traumatize her, but that would mean feeling grateful that she experienced such a shitty childhood. "Not especially. Do you?"

"No. Is that why you changed the subject when I asked you about staying the night with me earlier? You were worried you might hurt me?"

"Yeah." I run my hand over her back absent-mindedly, lost in thoughts of missed opportunities.

"Is that why you fucked me all night when I stayed at the cabin with you?" she says, chuckling, and I can't help but smile.

"No." I kiss her forehead. "I fucked you all night long because I couldn't stop myself from fucking you, baby girl. But when you fell asleep for a few hours, I made sure to stay awake."

"So did you never spend the night with anyone before?"

"No."

"I'm sorry," she whispers.

I cup her jaw, tilting her head so I can stare into her beautiful dark eyes. "I never really cared that much about spending the night with anyone before you."

"Never?" she blinks at me.

I can honestly say that's true. I mean, I'd have spent the night with women out of convenience more than anything else, but not out of any burning desire to be close to anyone. "Not until you. And if you apologize one more time for what your father did, I'll put you over my knee and spank your ass."

Her breath catches in her throat. "You wouldn't."

"Try me, baby girl."

"You're such a bossy asshole sometimes," she whispers, snuggling closer.

I sigh in contentment as sleep threatens to overwhelm me.

"Are you okay? I'm not hurting you, am I?"

"I'm good," I assure her. "But I'll be better when you drape that leg over me."

"Max," she admonishes me. "You need to sleep."

"I am going to sleep," I say, stifling a yawn. "But I want to feel that sweet pussy on me. When you get wet just from holding onto me, I want to feel it."

"You think I'm going to get wet just from lying next to you?" she breathes, her warm breath dusting over my bruised skin. "You're pretty sure of yourself."

I drop a kiss on the top of her head. "I know you will, baby. If I slipped my fingers inside you right now, I know you'd already be a little wet for me. Isn't that right?"

She hums. "Well, you don't have to be an ass about it."

I brush her hair back from her face and cup her jaw, tilting her head so she's looking up at me again. "I'm not being an ass because we both know it's true. Just know it's not a one-way thing. I'm gonna be hard all night having you next to me like this."

"Won't that be uncomfortable?" she whispers, and the sound of her voice goes straight to my cock.

I brush the pad of my thumb over her cheek. "I can deal with uncomfortable. Besides, I'm gonna be spending a whole lot of my life with your naked body pressed up against me, so I figure I might as well get used to it, right?"

Her eyelashes flutter as she blinks at me.

"So ..." I tap her thigh. "Leg. On me. Now."

"Yes, Sir," she whispers seductively, like a fucking sex kitten, and I have to close my eyes and take a deep breath before I flip her onto her back and nail her to this goddamn bed. I need a good night's sleep. Then, in the morning, I will fuck her six ways to Sunday.

I pull her closer and she drapes her leg over me like I asked, pressing her bare pussy against my hip. Then she rests her cheek on my chest again. "Let's get some sleep, baby."

"Hmm," she murmurs.

I'm drifting off when I feel her hot tears on my skin. I brush her cheeks with my fingertips. "That's not the kind of wet I wanted to feel, baby girl. What's wrong?"

"I called you some horrible names, Max. I even thought— just for a second, I wished ..." She chokes on a sob.

"Please don't do this to yourself, Joey. It's human nature. You were hurting."

"But then when I thought about you out there all alone— that someone had you and was hurting you ..." She sobs harder, as though she's been holding it all together for days and is only now able to let it out.

"Joey." I grind out the word because it kills me to see her torture herself like this.

"When Kristin told us you were missing, I thought my heart would shatter, but then when she said she was your girlfriend and she was having your baby—it hurt so much. I thought I was going to die."

I hug her tighter. I hate that I caused her unnecessary pain. It hurts me more than I can stand that she thought for even a little while that I want anyone but her. "I'm sorry, baby."

"But then when I thought I'd lost you ..." She pauses and takes a deep breath. "I swore I would feel that level of pain every day of my life if you could just be okay."

"I'm here now and I'm not going anywhere. Okay?"

Her hair brushes my cheek when she nods.

"Get some sleep, and we'll talk tomorrow," I mumble, losing the battle against keeping my eyes open.

"Okay. Night, Max."

"G'night, baby."

WARM PLEASURE ROLLS THROUGH ME, making my eyelids flicker open. The covers are pulled back but she's not lying next to me. Looking down, I see her beautiful lips wrapped around my cock, and fuck me if it's not the hottest thing I ever saw.

"Good morning, baby girl," I groan, my voice thick with sleep.

"Morning," she mumbles, the word muffled by my cock in her mouth.

I thread my fingers through her hair. "Fuck, baby, this is the best wake-up call I've ever had."

She breathes through her nose as she takes me all the way

to the back of her throat, swirling her tongue over my shaft as she sucks.

I wonder how long she's been working me over because I'm about ready to blow my load. I close my eyes to stave off my climax a little longer, but my horny little slut starts playing with my balls, squeezing gently and causing heat to sear down my spine.

"Joey," I groan, rocking my hips toward her mouth and pushing her head down until she starts to gag, but she doesn't stop.

I glance down at her again. Her eyes glisten with tears. "You remember to tap out or squeeze if it gets too much?"

She murmurs her agreement, and her cheeks hollow as she sucks harder.

"You look so fucking good sucking my cock. Your sexy little ass in the air begging to be fucked too."

She makes a strangled noise, but she keeps going. I grip her hair tighter, pulling at the root. "You know I'm going to fuck that ass, baby girl. I'm going to take your virgin ass the way I took your hot cunt and your pretty little mouth."

She moans, and the sound vibrates through the tip of my cock until it trembles through my entire body.

"Jesus! Fuck!" I groan, holding her in place as I come down her throat. She makes sweet little choking sounds, but her hands remain relaxed. No squeezing or tapping out. "Such a good girl the way you take my cock." I release my grip on her and she lifts her head, letting my cock slip out of her mouth.

"Thank you, Sir," she purrs, and my lips curl into a smile. Goddamn, I fucking love this girl with every single thing I have.

"Come sit on my face. Time for me to taste you."

"What?" She grins.

"Sit on my face. I want to see how wet sucking my cock has made my naughty little slut."

Her cheeks flush bright pink, and her bare pussy brushes over my chest as she moves higher, leaving a trail of her arousal.

"Oh, you're fucking soaking, Joey."

"I know."

"Come here," I growl, full of impatience, grabbing her hips and pulling her up until she's straddling my face. "Let me eat that pussy."

"You want me to sit? Like all the way down?"

"All the way. Like my face is your seat." My fingers dig into her hips.

"But I'll squash you. What if you can't breathe?"

I sigh, and she shivers as my breath dusts over her thighs. "I'll breathe just fine. Now. Sit. The. Fuck. Down." I yank her hips down until her pussy rests on my face and my senses are flooded with her scent and her taste. Darting out my tongue, I swirl it over her clit.

"Fuck, Max," she hisses my name.

"Mmm," I mumble appreciatively as I lap at her delicious juices. She's intoxicating. Everything I feel, taste, smell, hear, and see is her. Her cum drips onto my chin and makes my cock harden again in an instant. I don't care how much my stab wound still hurts, she's getting bent over and fucked as soon as I'm finished eating this sweet pussy.

I work a finger inside her hot channel while I feast on her, and her soft whimpers ripple through her body. I look up at her beautiful tits bouncing as she rides my face. Her pouty lips open in a perfect O. Seeing her on the edge makes me work her harder, sucking and licking as I finger fuck her tight pussy. I want to shower in her fucking cum.

"Max, I'm so close," she breathes.

I pull my finger out of her and she whines with frustration, unaware that I have something else in mind. Her whole body goes tense when I slide my finger along the seam of her ass until I'm circling her tight little hole.

"Max," she whimpers.

I push the tip of my finger into her. She instinctively shuffles forward, but I hold her in place, allowing her to get used to the sensation of something in her virgin ass. I graze my teeth over her swollen clit, and she shudders, arching her back and allowing me to push my finger deeper. She's so soft and warm and my cock throbs at the thought of taking her here.

"Holy fuck," she groans loudly as she rocks her hips again. I wrap my free hand around her throat and squeeze gently, hoping that will keep her a little quieter because I really don't want her brothers to hear her come. Then I eat her sweet pussy and finger fuck her perfect ass until she comes all over my face with a breathy cry of my name.

As soon she stops trembling, I lift her off my face and pull her down my body until she's lying on my chest. "Your face is covered in me," she says, giggling.

"I know. Exactly how I like it." I lick my lips.

"That was the perfect start to any morning."

"You say that like we're done, baby girl."

"Aren't we?"

I shake my head. "Not even close."

THIRTY-TWO

JOEY

"Ow," I yelp as Max slaps my ass hard, but despite the pain, I push my hips back, desperate for more. I'm on all fours on my bed, waiting for him to fuck me, but he continues to taunt me with his fingers, bringing me to the edge and then back down again. My empty pussy aches for more.

"Such a needy little slut for me." He grabs a handful of my ass cheek in his palm, squeezing roughly as his other hand coasts over my back.

"Are you going to fuck me, Max? Or just talk me back to sleep?" I snap, frustrated by his teasing.

A deep growl rumbles in his chest as he leans over me and presses his lips against my ear. "Oh, baby girl, don't think that I won't punish you for being a brat just because we're in your brothers' house."

He slips two fingers inside me, and I arch my back as pleasure rolls through me. "I'm sorry," I whimper. Damn man has me exactly where he wants me. "But I need you, Max."

"Where do you need me?" He drives his fingers deeper.

"I-inside me."

"I am inside you." He presses against my G-spot for emphasis.

"I need more."

"Tell me what you need, Joey. Beg me, baby."

"I need your cock. Please?" I plead with him, desperate and shivering and needy. "I miss the feel of you inside me. I thought I'd never get this again."

"Oh, fuck, baby, I'm sorry," he says, and then the warmth of his body is gone. His fingers slide out of me, and I drop my head to the pillow in frustration. But then his hands are on my hips and the tip of his cock pushes at my entrance. "I'm sorry I made you wait so long."

He drives deep inside me, and I scream into the pillow, flooded with relief and pleasure at the sensation of his huge cock filling me. I'm so wet and ready for him, and he's able to sink all the way inside until his piercing rubs on my G-spot, right where his fingers just were. My legs tremble violently as he brings me to orgasm so fast that my head spins.

"Oh, fuck, Max," I moan.

"That's it," he growls as he fucks me through it. "My naughty little slut."

He wraps his hands around my waist, driving harder and faster as he chases his own climax. "You make me come so fucking hard, Joey." His fingers bruise my flesh and his hips still. "Holy fuck," he grunts as his cock twitches and pulses inside me, filling me with his cum.

Max pulls out of me and falls onto the bed with his eyes closed. I cannot believe a man who underwent major abdominal surgery yesterday still has that much stamina. He pants for breath, and I watch him with concern. He opens his eyes and pulls me down to lie next to him, wrapping his giant arms around me.

"Are you okay?" I whisper.

"Baby girl, I am way fucking better than okay," he gasps, pressing a kiss on my forehead. "You?"

"Perfect." I smile as I snuggle against him.

His chest rises as he sucks in a deep breath. "I have something to tell you, Joey." His tone is even and calm, but his words freak me out.

I push myself up and lean on my elbow. "What is it?"

He brushes his fingertips over my cheeks, eyes narrowed as he searches my face. "I wasn't playing around when I said that you're mine, Joey. It wasn't the orgasms or anything else talking."

A breath catches in my throat. "Yours?"

"Only ever mine. Every part of your beautiful body. Your heart. Your fucking soul. Every orgasm you're ever going to have. Every single breath you'll ever take. Mine."

"I've only ever been yours, Max."

"My little brat," he says with a wicked grin.

I chew on my lip, and he palms the back of my head, pressing my face close to his.

"Stop chewing your lip and kiss me, baby."

I do as he asks, pressing my lips softly over his and slipping my tongue inside his mouth until heat blooms beneath my skin. He pulls back, leaving me breathless and wanting more—his goddamn superpower. "I love you, Joey."

I blink away tears. I've waited my whole damn life for Max DiMarco to look at me like he is right now and say those words. Monique told me to never tell a guy I love him unless I have his ring on my finger. She says it gives them too much power, but this man right here already has me in a choke hold and he knows it. "I love you too."

He cups my chin in his hand, tilting my head to a slightly different angle and kissing me again. And this time, he takes full control, claiming my mouth the way he's claimed every single part of me—with fire and dominance.

THIRTY-THREE

MAX

"Tell us who were these fucks who took you, and what the hell did they want?" Lorenzo asks, his face set in a grimace as he stares at me from across the desk.

His and Dante's eyes bore into mine while they wait for answers. I sit on the opposite side of their desk, but it's no longer because we're not on the same side. And I'm reminded even more of this fact when Joey reaches for my hand and curls her slender fingers around mine.

I tell them everything I know about Kristin and Uncle Vito. About my planned trip to New Jersey and the tape recording that my uncle supposedly has and Monty's suspicion that the video has something to do with their father. Finally, I describe the woman with the stroller and tell them to check the security feeds outside my building so we can ID her.

"I suspect the Russian goons you killed were the ones who actually took me off the street after she stuck me with something, but we should check it out."

"And those three guys you saw, you recognize them at all?"

I shake my head. "Nope. Did either of you?"

"No," Dante says with a frown.

"What did they want from you?" Lorenzo asks.

"They were working for someone. They made it clear their boss wanted to speak to me. But I didn't see their boss, and I don't know where he was because he didn't show his face the entire time I was there—which was how long exactly?"

"About thirty-six hours as far as we can tell," Dante replies.

Lorenzo leans forward. "Did they say why their boss wanted to speak to you?"

"Not really. But when I heard their accents, I assumed it had something to do with the takeover. But then they started talking about how I'd taken what was his and touched his girl, and it all started to make sense."

"You touched his girl?" Joey says, her brow furrowed in a frown.

"The father of Kristin's baby is Russian Bratva, at least I think he is from what she told me. I've been looking into him too, but he was less of a priority than Vito. Maybe he's the key to it all though? Maybe that's why Vito is missing? Revenge for taking his daughter away?"

"But did anyone even know that Kristin was with you in Chicago?" Joey asks. "I mean, we didn't."

I squeeze her hand at the reminder of her pain over the whole Kristin situation. "I guess if someone was looking for her ... they could have seen her going into my apartment building. She went to the deli down the road a few times." I chuckle. "Apparently they make cheesesteaks as good as any you'll find in Philly."

"You think this is all to do with your sister? They think you and she were—" Lorenzo doesn't finish the question, but he doesn't need to.

"Well, nobody knew I had a sister except for her and Vito.

She only found out herself two months ago, so she couldn't have told Jakob."

"Jakob?" Dante asks.

"He's the baby daddy, right?" Joey says.

"Yeah."

"Hmm." Dante runs a hand over his beard, a scowl on his face.

"Your uncle Vito though? He's your sister's dad? What's that about? I don't even remember you having an uncle," Joey says.

Lorenzo arches an eyebrow at me, because none of us like my uncle Vito, and I don't like to even think, never mind talk, about the reason why. But I don't want any secrets from Joey. Not anymore.

"He and my mom had an affair. It all came out when I was twelve, but apparently it had been going on for a while before."

Joey puts her hand over her mouth. "Oh, Max. That's awful."

That's not even the worst of it. "Yeah. When my pop found out, he wanted to kill Vito. He was his kid brother, they were supposed to look out for each other, but he'd been fucking his wife behind his back for years. My pop had the gun to Vito's head, but he couldn't go through with it. Vito always kind of lived in his shadow. My dad was Sal's best friend and his right hand, and Vito could never quite make it into the inner circle, which made him resent my father. Anyway, my mom left after that. She and Vito made a new life in Jersey."

"Did she try to take you with her?"

"No. Didn't even ask my opinion. Just told me to be a good boy and slipped out the door while I was eating my Lucky Charms."

"Oh, god, Max."

"I wouldn't have gone anyway." Is that the truth, though? She was my mom, and up until then, she was a good one. But it was a long time ago. I buried those feelings so deep, they'll never resurface.

"But to just leave you like that," she goes on. "That must have been hard."

"It was harder on my pop. He was never the same after she left. He lost his wife and his brother at the same time. He started drinking more. He was always distracted. He lost his edge, and a few years later he was killed." I run my tongue over my teeth and look away, unable to handle the concern and pity in Joey's eyes.

"You know he was murdered while he was on a routine money collection for our father?" Lorenzo takes over the story.

Joey nods.

"It was just some punk with a knife, but my dad didn't see it coming," I add.

"Even though Vito was long gone by then, our father blamed him for the murder." Lorenzo shakes his head. "And he made sure that he was never able to return to Chicago, even if he wanted to."

"And Max came to live with us?"

"Yeah," Dante agrees.

She lets out a low whistle. "Well, I can see why he's nobody's favorite person. And your mom and Vito never told you about Kristin? Or her about you? That's so fucked up."

"Yeah, but it's all done with now," I say, desperate to change the subject.

Lorenzo and Dante give me a knowing look, and when Joey goes to ask another question about my fucked-up family dynamics, Dante frowns at her, and she sits back in her chair and stays quiet.

"Finding this Jakob guy is the key to finding out who took you then?" Lorenzo asks me.

"And to finding Uncle Vito," I add.

229

"So the threat right now seems to be to Kristin, not to us?" Dante adds.

I shrug. "It would seem so."

"Max is one of us," Joey snaps.

Dante sighs. "I know, kid." Risk assessment and maintaining the safety of his family is a big part of what he does and the way he works. I know he didn't mean anything by it, but she doesn't. "If he was taken because of his suspected relationship with Kristin, it means it isn't a direct threat to this family. But it doesn't mean we won't kill every single fucker involved."

"Oh, okay." Appeased, she relaxes in her chair.

"Because of my suspicion that Jakob was Russian Bratva, I had Dmitri do a little digging for me." I dig my phone out of my pocket and start tapping out a text. "I'll see if he's come up with anything yet."

Dante checks his watch. "He should be here shortly anyway. I thought it was best to get him in on this, considering the whole Russian connection, but if you'd prefer to keep him out of it given what we know now ..."

"Nah, let's see what he has to say." I trust Dmitri, and I have no qualms about him learning my family history.

Lorenzo leans forward. "Until this situation is dealt with, I think you and Kristin should stay here at the mansion. This place is a fortress and you're both safer here."

"My penthouse is a fortress too."

"A fortress you got kidnapped outside of, Max." It's annoying as fuck, but Dante has a point. "You're too isolated there. At least here we have guards. Armored cars."

"You're being defensive because you're feeling vulnerable. But you're family, and we look after family."

"Don't fucking psychoanalyze me, Loz," I bark. Talking about my parents always puts me on edge, but just because he's right doesn't mean I have to like it.

"Well, our sister will remain here while there's an active threat against you," he says pointedly.

"Please stay here, Max. I feel safer if we're all together," Joey pleads.

Well, how the fuck do I refuse that? Besides, it's the truth. We are safer here with the Moretti army at our disposal.

"Of course we'll stay, baby. I'm sorry, I'm just on edge, is all."

She lifts my hand to her mouth and brushes her lips across my knuckles. "I can help you unwind if you'd like," she whispers.

"Guiseppina!" Lorenzo snaps.

"I meant we could watch a movie, Lorenzo." She wrinkles her perfect nose in disgust. "It's not my fault your mind is permanently in the gutter."

"Oh, sorry," he mumbles, glancing from me to her with a look of confusion on his face.

Dante fights a grin because, like me, he knows exactly what my devious little vixen was talking about.

"I HAVE the perfect shade for you. Cherry Bomb," Joey says excitedly as she rummages through the box containing her vast nail polish collection.

"Sounds fun." Kristin wears a genuine smile, looking happier than I think I've ever seen her as she puts her bare feet up on the sofa. "It's a pain in the ass not being able to reach my toes like I used to."

"Well, we could both use a good distraction and an afternoon of pampering, right? I have some face masks in the fridge, and Sophia is baking some of her amazing macadamia and white chocolate cookies. Anya is going to join us as soon as she wakes up from her nap. It's going to be the perfect relaxing girly afternoon."

"Thank you so much, Joey. Ugh! I have to pee real quick. I'll be right back." Kristin scurries out of the room, leaving me and Joey alone.

"Thank you for doing this for her." Cupping her chin, I tilt her head up so I can lean down and give her a soft kiss.

"Well, we really do need a distraction around here, especially while we're confined to the house."

"I haven't seen her smile like that since I met her."

She shrugs. "Well, what can I say? I'm a ray of freaking sunshine."

"You're the whole fucking sun, baby girl." I kiss her again. "I'm gonna go talk to Dmitri and your brothers. I know you'd rather be in there than in here, so thank you again. I appreciate you taking such good care of my little sister."

She smiles sweetly. "Well, I'm sure you'll make it up to me."

Damn right I will.

"I need to get some of my stuff, so I'm going to go over to the penthouse after our meeting." Worry creases her forehead into a frown. "I'll be back way before dinner, and I'll be careful. Lorenzo's coming with me. We're going to check out the security feeds, see if there's anything useful on there. Plus, Dante suggested we invite Dmitri and his family for dinner tonight, so I need to grab Kristin's things for her. She has no clothes here, and I want her to feel comfortable." Frowning, I pause. "Actually, she doesn't have much at my place either. You think you can help order some stuff online?"

"Can I online shop? Do you know me at all, Max DiMarco?"

I grin at her. I love this woman so fucking much. "Thank you."

"And Kat has some nice maternity stuff she kept hold of. I'm sure we can find her something nice for tonight if she needs it."

"I love you, Joey."

Her eyes shine with happiness. "I love hearing you say that."

THIRTY-FOUR

JOEY

Max's eyes dance with delight and mischief as he stalks across my bedroom toward me.

"What are you up to, DiMarco?"

"I have a gift for you, baby girl."

I clap my hands together and fake squeal, batting my eyelashes at him and playing up the spoiled brat persona he seems to enjoy so much. "I love presents. Did you get this while you were out earlier?"

"I did." He holds out his clenched fist and arches an eyebrow. "And you're going to love this. Promise."

"What is it?"

He turns his hand and opens it, palm side up, revealing the small round metal orb with a jewel on the end. "Max, is that a ..."

"It sure is."

"Why have you brought me a butt plug, and where did you get it from?" I whisper.

His expression darkens as he wraps an arm around my waist and yanks my body against his. His cock is hard, and he drags me over his length, making me shiver. "I came back here on the bike, and I took a quick detour to a store that sells all manner of things I'm going to enjoy using on you, baby. And I got this for you because tonight I'm going to fuck your virgin ass, and because I love you so fucking much, I'm going to let you wear this all evening to get you ready for my cock."

I look down at the plug in his hand. It's about the size of a fat nail polish bottle, and the thought of it anywhere near my ass makes my cheeks clench, but it's tiny compared to Max. "I don't think that's going to help, Max. I mean you're way bigger than that plug. I have no idea how you're going to get that thing inside me, so I don't think you'll ever fit."

He presses his lips to my ear and goosebumps prickle along my forearms. "I'll fit, baby. I'm fucking your ass tonight, and you're going to scream my goddamn name when I do."

I swallow the knot of anxiety lodged in my throat. I don't want him to see how nervous I am. "You want me to wear that all through dinner though?"

We're having dinner with my entire family, the new head of the Chicago Bratva and his wife—Dmitri and Ivanka—and his younger brother and second-in-command, Kyzen. I'm not sure I want to spend the entire evening wearing a butt plug. What if it's uncomfortable? Or what if it's hot and I'm a trembling mess at the table?

"It will make it easier later for you, baby girl. But ... if you're not up to the challenge?" he says with a shrug.

Dammit! Well played, DiMarco. "Of course I am."

His eyes twinkle as he grins wickedly. "Open your mouth."

I do as he says, and he slips the plug between my lips. "You're going to want to make that nice and wet, Joey."

I close my lips around it and suck softly, coating it in as much saliva as I can. When he's satisfied that I've done enough, he tugs the end gently until I release it and pulls it out of my mouth, a string of spit going with it. "Fuck me, you're hot," he says. His lips curl into a smile.

I lick my lips clean, suppressing a satisfied smile as I stare into his dark eyes.

"Turn around and bend over the bed."

Sucking in a shaky breath, I do as he asks, planting my palms flat on the bed. His strong hands brush over my thighs and he pushes my skirt up. I bite my lip to stifle a giggle as I think about what he's about to find. Sure enough, when his hands skim the bare skin of my ass, a loud growl rumbles through him. "Where the fuck are your panties, Joey?"

"I didn't feel like wearing any today."

"No?" He pushes my skirt up higher and smacks my ass hard. "Such a naughty little slut."

Heat sears across my backside, sending pleasure rolling up my spine. "Am not."

"Hmm," he murmurs, palms spreading the cheeks of my ass. "We may need a little more lube, baby." Then he drops to his knees, and the next thing I feel is his soft wet tongue against my skin.

"Max," I gasp as warmth pools in my core.

He only grunts in response as his tongue slips over and inside my dark hole. His beard tickles my skin as he sucks and licks. *Holy fuck!* That is definitely not what I expected him to do, but it feels so damn good.

I push my ass back against him and he laughs, giving me a playful nip on my inner thigh. "My needy little slut too."

I groan at the loss of his mouth.

He pushes the tip of the plug against my hole, and I inch forward on instinct. "It's okay, baby girl. We'll take it nice and slow," he soothes as he edges the metal plug deeper.

I whimper as it stretches me in a way I've never experienced.

He dusts his lips over my ass cheeks. "Shh. It's almost in."

"Fuck!" I groan as he pushes deeper and the widest part of the plug slips inside.

"That's my good girl," he soothes, and molten heat sears in my core. I'm such a ho for those two words. I crave his approval and he knows it. He rubs a hand over my ass again. "How does it feel?"

"Kind of strange. Like I want to push it out of me because it doesn't belong there," I admit, looking behind me, although I can't see the plug. I feel stretched but not uncomfortable. I also feel naughty knowing I'll be walking around the house with a plug in my ass.

"Keep it in. You'll get used to it soon, and I need to stretch you a little before tonight. Besides, you look fucking beautiful with that jewel on your ass." Grabbing my waist, he pulls me up until I'm standing, my back pressed against his chest as he fixes my skirt in place. "You're gonna look sexy as fucking hell with my cock in you instead."

"I'm still not sure how the hell you're going to fit."

He grabs my jaw, tilting my head back until I'm looking up into his eyes. "I promise you'll beg me for my cock by the time the night is over."

"I will, huh?"

"Hmm." His eyes twinkle, making me frown. He's up to something.

It starts slowly at first, the buzzing in my ass—sending shockwaves of pleasure rippling through my body. "Max, what have you done?" I whimper as the vibrations grow more intense, making my legs tremble. "Did you stick my bullet up there with that plug?"

"No, baby." He laughs darkly, wrapping his arm around my waist to hold me upright. Then he pulls a tiny remote control from his pocket. He presses a button, and the vibrations increase again, so strong now that I feel them deep in my pussy too.

"You're a monster."

"A monster who would do anything to make you happy, Joey. Never forget that."

My body tingles with electric anticipation. "Anything?"

"Anything," he growls, placing soft kisses along the column of my neck as he slips his hand over my hip and between my thighs. He presses the pad of his pointer finger over my clit, rubbing firmly. "I would kill any man who dares to even look at you. I'll burn this entire world to keep you safe, baby girl. I'd fucking die for you. But for now, how about I just take care of you?"

"Mmm, yes please."

THIRTY-FIVE

Whoever thought it would be a good idea to sit Joey next to Kyzen Varkov during dinner obviously wanted to torture me because she talks to him the entire evening and practically ignores me. She's not quite flirting. She isn't cruel enough to do that and he isn't stupid enough to let her, but she does give him her undivided attention, and I don't like it one bit.

I know what she's trying to do. She wants me to turn on her little toy, but as fun as it would be to watch her blush and squirm, I have no intention of alerting anyone at this table to the fact that she's wearing it—especially not Kyzen. I'm content enough with the knowledge that I could use it any time and that she knows it too.

"Don't you think, Max?" she purrs seductively, her eyes fixed on me now.

"Think about what, baby?"

"Don't you think these dinners used to be super stuffy and boring? But they're much more exciting now, right?"

I lean forward, my elbows on the table. "Exciting how?"

"Just more fun, you know?" she says, her eyes darkening

with mischief as she holds my gaze from across the table. "I was telling Kyzen that when my father was around, these evenings were all about business, and women weren't even allowed to speak."

"That is true."

"But now, well us women hold all the true power. Isn't that right?" She giggles softly and takes a sip of her wine.

My little vixen has upped the stakes. And she will regret teasing me. Joey Moretti might have me by the balls, but she's sorely mistaken if she thinks that means she has any control here.

"If you say so, baby girl."

Kyzen laughs and shakes his head. I figure he's onto the fact that she's trying to push my buttons and is succeeding.

Pushing back her chair, she dabs at her mouth with her napkin. "Excuse me while I use the ladies' room," she says politely, like the Mafia princess she was raised to be.

I push my chair back too, drawing a look from her older brothers. "I need to make a quick call."

Dante and Lorenzo nod, even though we all know that isn't why I'm leaving this table. I follow her out of the room. She turns for the stairs, but I grab her wrist and pull her down the hallway, just around the corner and out of sight of anyone who might happen to leave the dining room.

The amber flecks in her eyes glimmer with amusement. Such a fucking brat, she makes me act like a fucking animal. "Where do you think you're going?"

She rolls her lips together. "Um, to the bathroom."

I shake my head and unfasten my belt, beyond desperate for her. If I don't get inside her in the next ten seconds, I will fucking implode with pent-up sexual tension. She looks down at my hands, her eyes wide with surprise as I step forward, herding her against the wall.

"Max, what are you doing?"

"You think you hold all the power, baby girl?"

"The *true* power, yeah," she says with a wicked grin, and fuck me she's not wrong. She could make a man drop to his knees and beg for just the promise of a taste.

"You think you can tease me all night and not suffer the consequences?"

"But we're in the hallway," she whispers, her eyes darting toward the dining room. "My crazy overprotective brothers are only a few inches of drywall and plaster away."

"Then I guess you're going to have to be real quiet, Joey." Spinning her around, I press her flat against the wall. "Because if you think that being in your brothers' house offers you any kind of protection from me, then you couldn't be more wrong."

"But they'll wonder where we are if we take too long."

"Don't worry." I reach beneath her skirt and grip the edge of her plug with my fingers. "I'm so fucking hard for you, I'll only last a few minutes in your tight ass."

Her entire body shudders with the force of her gasp. She definitely wasn't expecting me to do this in the hallway. "M-Max. We can't. N-not here," she whimpers, but I ignore her, pocketing the plug and yanking up her skirt so I have access to that perfect peach.

"Spread your legs wider," I order as I tap at her ankles with my foot.

"Max." Her voice goes up an octave. "Someone might come out here."

"I'll hear them before they do." If that happens, I'll have about five seconds to make this look a whole lot more innocent —I figure I can work with that. And tough shit if I can't. I need inside her right now. She doesn't get to drive me crazy all night and then slam the brakes on now.

I put my hand over her mouth until her soft lips flatten

against my palm. "You want to show me how quiet you can be when I'm fucking you, baby?"

"Mmmf."

"Hands flat on the wall."

She does as she's told.

"You remember to tap out if it gets too much?"

She nods.

"Good girl." I take out the lube I'm glad I put in my pocket earlier and squirt a generous amount over my cock, coating my shaft. I intended to make this first time easier on her, but I should have known better. Nothing involving my girl is ever easy—and that's exactly how I like it. How I love it. Gripping the base of my cock with my free hand, I press the tip against her asshole.

She inches forward, pressing her body flush against the wall, but my body follows and leaves her nowhere to go.

I run my nose along the column of her throat. "You smell fucking delicious." I push the tip of my cock inside her, and she sucks in a breath through her nose, moaning against my palm. Sinking a little deeper into her tight ass, my cock pulses with the need to fill her. To own her. "Relax, Joey, or this will hurt more than it needs to. You can take me, I promise, but you need to relax. Need to trust me."

She nods again, and the sound she makes is muffled by my palm. Screwing her eyes shut, she allows her body to go pliant as I inch deeper. I glance at her hands, still flat against the wall.

My breathing becomes ragged, my cock pulsing inside her snug ass. I won't last long with her squeezing me. "You feel so fucking good, baby girl. You're taking me so well."

She whimpers and her eyes water, but she keeps her hands still while I feed her more of my cock.

It takes all my restraint not to bury myself balls deep in her tight ass, but there isn't a chance in hell I'll get all the way inside her this first time without hurting her. Sometimes I worry that she's so goddamn stubborn, she'd let me tear her in half before tapping out.

She continues to breathe deeply through her nose, her shuddering body sandwiched between me and the wall. Her tongue flicks out to moisten her lips, and it grazes my palm, making me groan. "You enjoying your first ass fucking?"

"Mmhmm."

Running my nose up the back of her neck, I inhale her essence. "Maybe a little too much, huh? This is supposed to be a punishment."

Her eyes shoot open as I rock my hips and sink deeper with each forward motion. The sound of talking and laughter passes through the wall, and I thrust harder. She cries out against my hand, making me chuckle.

"Better be careful, baby girl. You don't want a half dozen people walking in on you getting fucked in the ass, do you?"

For some reason, that seems to spur my girl on. She pushes back, grinding herself on me.

"Fuck, Joey." Endorphins surge through my veins, and I bite down on her neck to muffle my shout. I'm so fucking close to losing myself.

I reach my free hand between her thighs and rub her swollen clit. Her legs tremble, her muffled cries growing more insistent. Sinking a finger deep inside her pussy, I smile with victory as she crumples in my arms, her body sagging back against my chest and her knees buckling.

"You're soaking," I groan in her ear. "Have you been this wet all through dinner?"

She nods jerkily.

"Joey, you're going to fucking kill me."

I shove deeper, and my balls tighten as her ass and pussy pulse around me. Rubbing the heel of my palm over her clit, I push two fingers into her cunt, searching for the spot that makes her mewl. When I find it, I rub it back and forth until her entire body goes taut in my arms. Beads of sweat pepper her forehead, her breathing harsh and ragged. I consider pinching her nose for a few seconds and stealing her breath too, but I don't think she could take it right now. "Oh, you're fucking close, baby, aren't you? So close to coming all over me while your ass is stuffed with my cock?"

She makes a strangled moan that tips me over the edge. Filling her perfect ass with my cum, I slide my hand from between her thighs and leave her teetering on the precipice. Then I remove my hand from her mouth, and she gasps for air.

I press a soft kiss on her shoulder. "You did so well, baby girl."

"But Max ..." she whimpers, needy and desperate for the orgasm I almost just gave her.

"What, Joey?"

"I-I need you."

I take the plug from my pocket and skim my hand over her perfect ass. "You just had me."

"I didn't finish," she whispers.

I push the tip of the plug against her asshole, collecting my cum as it starts dripping out of her and using it to make slipping the plug back inside her easier. "You think I don't know that? You think I don't know your body well enough to know when you're about to come?"

"So why did you stop?" She blinks and a fat tear rolls down her cheek.

I push the plug all the way back inside her, and she moans loudly at the intrusion. I know she's sore, but the alternative is that she spends the rest of the evening with my cum leaking from her. And while I have absolutely no qualms about letting that happen, it would embarrass her in front of her family.

"Shh." I fix her dress back in place and wipe the tears from her cheeks so she can go back to the dinner table.

"Max!" Glaring at me, she tries to muster as much attitude as she can while her wrung-out body strains closer, desperate for any part of me that will bring her some relief.

I dust my lips over her ear as I fasten up my pants. "You think this was about giving you what you want? Or was this a punishment for teasing me all night?"

Her body goes rigid, her eyes sparking with indignation.

"Never forget who controls your body, baby girl. Your ass. Your pussy. Your mouth. Your pleasure. Your pain. All of it belongs to me."

I smooth the fabric of her dress over her luscious cheeks and give one a hard slap, but she doesn't flinch—she's far too pissed off to give me a reaction. "Now get your sexy ass back in there before people start wondering where we are."

She folds her arms over her chest. "I still need to pee."

Grinning, I grab her elbow. Like I would let her go to the bathroom and finish off the job I started. I straighten my expression and stare coldly into her dark brown eyes that are filled with more fire and sass than usual. "Hold it."

THIRTY-SIX

JOEY

T wo more hours we sat in that dining room, eating and drinking and chatting. I plastered a fake smile on my face the entire time, refusing to let him see that he'd gotten to me. But the whole time, my bladder threatened to explode while my ass throbbed with an irritating combination of pain and pleasure. Who the fuck does he think he is, fucking me in my own hallway and leaving me hanging? Manipulative jackass.

As soon as I get upstairs to my bedroom, I dash for the bathroom. Sitting on the toilet, I sigh loudly with relief. I hear the bedroom door close, and a few seconds later, Max kicks open the bathroom door and stands in the doorway, his arms folded over his chest.

"Do you mind?" I snap.

He smirks. "Not at all, baby girl."

I look away, finish peeing, then flush and wash my hands.

"I never said you couldn't use the bathroom for the entire night, Joey," he says, biting back a laugh.

My head snaps around, and I glare at him. "What?"

"Just while you were on the edge earlier. I didn't expect you to hold it all night." This time he doesn't bother trying to stop it. The laugh rolls out of him, filling me with rage.

"You. Are. An. Asshole!"

He steps into the bathroom, closing the door behind him and crossing the space between us in one stride. "I had no idea you were actually going to do as you were told." His voice drops an octave as he moves behind me. "It's very unlike you." He places his hand on the vanity either side of my hips, caging me in with his arms.

I frown at him in the mirror. Why did I obey him like that?

He lifts my dress and rubs a hand over my ass.

"Stop," I hiss.

He does, placing his hand back on the vanity as he looks at my reflection. Resting his chin on top of my head, he stares at me until I feel forced to speak just to fill the silence. "My ass is kind of sore."

"I know."

I swallow. Of course he knows.

Reaching back under my dress, he brushes his fingertips over my lower back. "I'm going to take the plug out, okay?"

I nod my agreement. I want to tell him to go to hell, but his fingers feel so good as they trail down the seam of my ass. Why am I this pissed at him? It was my choice to go along with his demands earlier, wasn't it?

"Breathe, baby girl," he says soothingly, his fingers gripping the metal base as he slowly slides the plug out of my ass.

I moan, half in pain and half in pleasure. Max turns and tosses the toy into the wash basin. I feel both empty and filled with relief now that it's gone.

"You did so good," he whispers in my ear.

Why does his praise always make me weak at the knees? Unwilling to give him the satisfaction of seeing me react to his words, I glare at his reflection.

He drops his head low again, pressing his mouth against my ear. "This night can end one of two ways, baby."

"And how is that?"

"You can stop acting like a brat and I'll carry you to bed and fuck you, or you can keep glaring at me like that and I'll bend you over this vanity and spank that ass."

There's a part of me, some mysterious part inside my soul, that refuses to back down from a challenge. It's probably going to get me killed some day. My lips spread into a snarky smile. "Or there's the third option."

He cocks one eyebrow. "And what's that?"

"You leave me the hell alone and I go to sleep."

Taking a minuscule step back, Max pinches the bridge of his nose and shakes his head. Oh shit. How much worse did I just make things for myself? A sick thrill makes my skin tingle as I wonder how he'll punish me this time. But when he lifts his head, the arrogant asshole is smirking at me in the mirror.

"What's so funny?" I snap.

"Oh, baby girl," he says in a voice so low and menacing, a shiver travels from the top of my head to the tips of my toes. "I am going to enjoy spanking this ass so fucking much."

I watch him in the mirror as he starts unfastening his belt, and my stomach lurches. Max is huge and strong and he's going to spank my ass with his belt. What the hell have I done? Did I finally push him too far? "I'm sorry," I whisper, shaking my head and flinching away. "I'll be good."

"Too late."

I try to escape, but he keeps me pinned to the vanity. "M-Max." I suck in a deep breath at the sound of leather sliding against the fabric of his suit pants.

He fists a hand in my hair, pulling me toward him until my back is flush against his chest. "Breathe," he says softly.

I suck in another deep breath as my heart hammers in my chest.

"Do you trust me?"

"Yes." The word leaves my mouth on instinct.

"So, relax."

Relax? When you're about to bend me over and spank me with a belt? But when Max pushes me down, bending me over the vanity, I offer no resistance. He slides my dress up over my ass, rubbing his huge hands over my warm skin and making me whimper. His hands on my body never fail to make me wet and needy.

"I love this ass, Joey," he groans. "Fucking it was a goddamn honor."

Wet heat pools between my thighs.

He dips a finger into my pussy, and to my annoyance, I moan loudly.

"And you're so fucking wet, baby. So. Fucking. Wet." He punctuates each word with a thrust of his finger, and my knees threaten to buckle. He's still gently finger fucking me when he slaps my ass for the first time, and rather than causing me pain, it sends a wave of bone-shaking ecstasy rolling through me.

"Fuck," I whimper, chewing on my lip because I'm already so close to the edge and I don't want him to stop.

He spanks me again, and his palm strikes the meaty part of my ass cheek, leaving a tingling warmth behind. He continues to spank and finger me until my vision blurs and I'm teetering over the edge of ecstasy, ready to fall into oblivion.

Then he stops.

A roar of frustration bursts out of me.

"I know, baby. Soon," he says, his tone soft and soothing.

He picks up his belt, but I don't have the energy to look back and see what he's doing, so when the sound of leather cracks through the air, there's no time to brace myself for the burning strike.

The unexpectedly intense pleasure makes me scream his name. I never thought pain could feel so good, could make my poor throbbing pussy even hungrier for him.

"Yeah?" he grunts as he spanks me again.

"I need you," I mewl, writhing on the countertop as he spanks me again and again. Each time my ass throbs a little harder and my pussy gets wetter.

"You need me?" Smack!

"Yes," I cry out as pleasure and heat burn through my skin. Tears roll down my cheeks as the tension builds inside me until I feel like I might explode. "Please, Max."

"Holy shit, I need to fuck you," he gasps, throwing his belt onto the floor.

I watch him in the mirror as he tears off his clothes. When he walks away, I want to cry. He turns on the hot water and then comes back to me. Picking me up, he carries me to the shower.

The hot water runs over my body, and with breathless anticipation, I watch him wash his cock clean. As soon as he's done, he lifts me by my ass cheeks, slams me back against the wall, and enters me before I can take another breath.

I moan at the sweet relief of finally having him inside me. Wrapping my arms and legs around him, I hold tight, allowing him to give me everything I need.

"I got you, baby girl," he grunts, driving into me again. His piercing rubs my G-spot, and he rolls his hips, dragging the tip back and forth over it. I sink my teeth into my bottom lip, the life-altering orgasm bearing down on me. If he stops me again, I might die.

"You can let go, Joey. You can come this time."

And with his permission, the orgasm rips through my body

like a black hole tearing through space. "Fuck!" I scream, dragging my nails down his back. My eyes roll back and Max just goes on fucking me through it, relentless in his apparent mission to fuck me into oblivion.

"Good girl," he growls in my ear. "Good fucking girl."

"Max, I can't take any more," I whimper.

"You can, baby. Give me one more," he grunts as he thrusts harder and deeper. My skin is on fire. My pussy and ass are throbbing. But another orgasm is already curling deep in my belly—coiling like a tight spring ready to explode like a million tiny starbursts.

My thighs tremble, and when he rubs that glorious piercing over my G-spot again, I almost pass out from the strength of my climax.

"Damn, baby, you fucking soaked me."

My head drops onto his shoulder, and he holds me tight as he drives inside me one last time and pumps me full of his cum.

I feel dazed as Max dries me off and carries me to the bed, laying me down gently on my front, which is a good thing because my ass feels like it's on fire.

"Don't move," he orders. Then he walks to my dresser and starts rummaging through my things.

"What are you doing?" I mumble, craning my neck to see him.

"I saw you had some aloe vera here."

"Huh?"

"Got it." He winks at me and walks back toward the bed. Lying down beside me, he strokes a hand over my ass.

I wince despite his gentleness.

"You sore?"

What do you think, genius? But I don't say that because I can't take any more punishment tonight and I'm too tired to be a brat. So I just nod sleepily.

"Well, you had your first ass fucking and belt spanking in the same night, baby girl. That's quite the achievement."

"And who's fault is that?" I grumble. There's only so much snark I can keep to myself.

He chuckles softly. "You tell me. Who thought she could tease me all through dinner without any consequences?"

"Me," I huff.

He leans close, mouth pressed against my ear. "Know this, Joey, there are a lot of things you can push me on, but this hot little body isn't one of them. You tease me with it, you're getting fucked. I don't care where we are or who's around."

His words send a shiver down my entire body. I shouldn't be turned on by what he just said, so why am I about ready to melt into a puddle as soon as he touches me again?

"The spanking wasn't my fault though," I protest.

He squirts some aloe vera onto his hand. "No?"

"No." I pout. Dammit. I'm never too tired to brat for this man.

He glides his hand over my ass again, this time coated in the cooling gel, and I moan loudly enough that I'm sure the entire house hears me. "That feels so good," I whimper.

"Who got spanked with my belt for being a brat, Joey?" he asks with a dark chuckle as he goes on soothing my sore behind.

"Me." I sigh contentedly, smiling as I turn my head to the side and watch him.

He catches my eye and smiles back.

"You love your little brat though, right?" I ask, catching my bottom lip between my teeth.

"More than anything in this fucking world." He leans down and gives me a soft kiss on the lips. When he's done rubbing gel onto my ass, he plants a sweet kiss on each cheek.

"I hope you haven't scarred my ass, Max. I have Monique's birthday party next week."

"And why is your ass going to be on display for that?" he asks, a dangerous undertone to his voice that makes me shiver.

"Because it's a pool party. I'll be wearing a bikini."

He places the bottle on the nightstand, lies down, and pulls me on top of him. I snuggle into him like he's my personal body pillow.

"I didn't scar your ass, but we're going to revisit you wearing a tiny bikini around a bunch of horny douchebags without me there."

"It's girls only. Although I guess they can be horny douchebags too." I snicker.

He kisses the top of my head and wraps his arms around me. "I guess."

"I'm wearing a bikini, Max," I say, yawning and nuzzling my cheek against his hard chest.

"Hmm. We'll see, baby girl."

THIRTY-SEVEN

MAX

"This is a nice place," I say, looking around Dmitri Varkov's new coffee shop on our way through to the back office where we agreed to meet him.

Dante gives an impressed nod. "Yeah, I think maybe we need to get in on the coffee shop business. You know the markup in these places is huge."

"Are you fucking for real? Haven't we got enough on our plates without adding coffee shops to the mix?"

"I was thinking of something Joey could take the lead on. I figured you'd prefer that over her being involved in the casinos."

He's got a point. The casino deals can get bloody, and I don't want my girl in the middle of all that. But I don't think I have much choice. "If you give your sister a chain of coffee shops to run, she'll just branch out and buy her own fucking casino, D."

He rolls his eyes. "She fucking would too."

"What about Kat? She's always looking for things to keep her occupied, and she's smart enough to run a business."

"My wife is going to have her hands a whole lot fuller very shortly," he says, a wicked glint in his eye.

"You've knocked that poor woman up again, haven't you?"

"*Poor woman*?" He snorts. "She has everything she could ever want or need, and she loves being pregnant."

"Gentlemen?" Kyzen says, interrupting our exchange as he steps out of the back of the shop to greet us. "Dmitri is waiting for you."

"After you, Daddy," I say with a smirk.

Dante barks a laugh and shakes his head. "Don't call me that, you fucking psycho."

"I bet you like Kat calling you that," I mumble as we head into the office.

I'm saved from a punch in the mouth by Kyzen offering each of us a seat. Dante sits, but I remain standing because it's my duty to have his back. While these men are our friends, we never know if and when something's gonna go down.

"I like your new place," Dante says.

"Yeah." Dmitri gives a small smile and shrugs. "They were my wife's idea. The markup is astronomical."

"Told you," Dante says to me out of the corner of his mouth, and I have to fight the urge to roll my eyes.

There's no way my little spitfire is going be happy managing a chain of coffee shops, so I don't bother responding. Instead, I ask Dmitri, "Did you find out anything about Vito?"

"Yes. That's why I called you here. I didn't think anything of it at first." He taps the screen of his phone a few times and passes it to Dante.

I look over his shoulder at the image of a bruised and swollen face. The guy looks half dead, but there's no mistaking that it's Uncle Vito.

"Where is he?" I ask.

Dmitri takes his phone back. "That's him? Your uncle?"

"Yes, that's him."

"I wasn't sure. Some of my men found him in the Michigan warehouse."

"The one Pushkin was using for the sex trafficking?" Dante asks.

"Yes. It was closed down as soon as Pushkin's operation was uncovered. I have some contacts there, and we had the entire building condemned by the health department so nobody would go snooping and find anything. And as far as we were aware, none of Pushkin's men went back there either. But with the search for Pushkin drying up, I had some men take a look just in case. They found this guy chained up in a cell."

"Dead?" I ask.

"Almost, but not quite. I didn't connect the dots at first. We assumed he was some guy who pissed off the wrong person, but when they sent me the photograph, I noticed a resemblance."

I nod. "There was nothing and no one else there?"

"No. My men were thorough. He was alone. Left for dead."

"And where is he now?" Dante asks.

"He's with my men. He's had some basic medical care and some fluids. I told them to wait for my word before they dropped him off at a hospital. You want him brought to you instead?"

"Have him brought to the house," Dante says.

"Of course." Dmitri says something to his brother in Russian, and Kyzen nods and leaves the room.

I thank Dmitri for his help, but he waves me off. "Anything I can do to assist either of you, you know that."

"You said the leads on Pushkin are going cold though?" Dante asks.

A shadow falls across Dmitri's face. "Yes," he grits out. "He's a slippery fucker. But I have every resource at my disposal looking for him and his sons. We *will* find him."

Standing up, Dante sighs. "He always was a snake. Keep me posted."

THIRTY-EIGHT

JOEY

"Hey." Max grabs my wrist and yanks me into the study, closing the door behind us.

"Hey yourself." I smile. "I thought you were out with Dante."

"I was," he says, pinching the bridge of his nose.

"Is everything okay?"

His Adam's apple bobs as he swallows. "We found Vito."

"Oh? That's good right?"

Max frowns, tension radiating from him in waves.

"Oh, god. He's not dead, is he?" *Poor Kristin.*

"No. He's alive, but from what we know, he's in rough shape. Dmitri's men are bringing him here now."

"Why aren't they taking him to the hospital?"

"Dante called the surgeon, and he's on his way. Kat's going to assist. We can't risk Vito going to a hospital until we know who kidnapped him and why."

"Where did you find him?"

"In that warehouse in Michigan. He was beaten really bad. Locked in a cage and left for dead."

My grief over all the poor people who were trafficked

through that place has me blinking back tears. Kat and I looked into the situation, tried to find a trace of what happened to them once they left the warehouse, but no records were ever kept and there were no leads to chase. Shaking my head, I refocus on Max. "Why not just kill him though?"

"Maybe they wanted more from him? Maybe they thought he was dead? Who knows? Anyway, I'm going to need your help with Kristin. She didn't grow up in the same world we did. This will probably be the first person she's ever seen who's been beaten within an inch of his life."

"And it's her dad."

"Exactly. Can you stay with her? Help me prepare her for what to expect when she first sees him?"

"Of course. But where will you be?"

"I'm going to be in with Kat and the doc while they're checking Vito over, in case he says anything. Dante and I are going to need answers from him. If he was found at that warehouse, maybe there's a link between him and Pushkin?"

"I know he really hurt you in the past," I say softly.

"I'm not going to fucking kill him, baby." He sighs. "You think I'd go to all this trouble to find him if I was going to do that?"

Slipping my arms around his waist, I rest my cheek against his chest. Despite his cool, calm exterior, Max's heart is hammering. "I know you wouldn't, but I also know how much what he did affects you."

"I told you it doesn't. It's all in the past."

Lifting my head, I look up into his dark brown eyes. "Don't lie to me, Max DiMarco. It's okay to feel pain."

"Not in my world, baby."

"Yes, in your world. *Our* world. In fact, don't we feel more pain than most?"

He brushes my hair back from my face. "As long as I have you, nothing can ever hurt me."

I wish that were true. "What time will Vito be here?"

"In a couple of hours. You want to come find Kristin with me and I can tell her we found her dad?"

We find Kristin sitting at the kitchen table with Kat and Gabriella. In the four days since Max's sister got here, she's managed to become friends with everyone. She's sweet and funny, and although she's only eighteen, it's clear she isn't the naive little kid Max thinks she is. I think she's fully prepared for the fact that her father won't come back in the same condition he left. In fact, I think she'll be super relieved just to hear that he's alive.

"Hey. You're back?" she says to Max.

He sits down and angles his chair to face her. "Yeah. I have something to talk to you about."

Kat stands and holds her hands out to her daughter. "I'll leave you all to it. I need to get some things ready for later." Dante must have already filled her in on the Vito situation.

I smile at my niece. "I can watch Gabs later if you're busy."

"Thanks, sweetheart. I don't know what I'd do without you." She waves Gabriella's chubby little hand at us as they walk out of the kitchen.

"You have some news about my dad?" Kristin asks. See, not the slightest bit naive.

"Yes, we found him."

"What?" Her hand flies to her mouth and tears well in her eyes. "Is he alive?"

"Yes," Max says with a solemn nod. "But he's not good, Kristin."

She frowns. "Not good?"

"I've only seen his face, but he's badly beaten. Real bad."

"But he's alive?"

"Yes."

She throws her arms around her brother's neck. "I knew you'd find him. Where is he? When can I see him?"

"He's on his way here. But maybe you should wait to see him until after Kat and the doc fix him up."

"He's been missing for over three weeks, Max. I didn't expect him to come home looking like he'd been on a vacation to the Bahamas. I know they'll have tortured him." A tear runs down her face.

Max wipes it away and wraps an arm around her. "I spoke to the men bringing him here. He's in and out of consciousness, so you can see him for a few minutes when he gets here, but then he'll have to be seen by the doctor. Maybe even operated on. You might not get a chance to talk with him until tomorrow. But Joey will stay with you while he's with the doctor."

Max glances up at me, his face etched with guilt. They're going to interrogate Vito before they let him talk to his daughter, but it needs to be done. We have no idea who took him or why, and they need to know immediately if there's any ongoing danger to our family. The safety of the people in this house is our main priority, and it always will be. I can't forget the things Kristin's father told her about us either. How we aren't to be trusted. We're the enemy.

Kristin may be innocent in all this, but I doubt her father is. Giving Max a gentle smile, I communicate that he's doing the right thing.

∼

I HOLD onto Kristin's hand while her father is brought into the house in a wheelchair. His head rests on his shoulder like he's sleeping, and his face is a mess of dried blood, cuts, and bruises.

One of Dmitri's men must have given him the huge overcoat he's wearing because it's clean.

"Dad!" Kristin lunges forward.

Vito's head lolls to the side and his eyes flicker open. "K-K..." he croaks, but he can't say her name.

"You're going to be okay, Dad. Max will take care of you. I promise. You're safe," she sobs.

"B-buh," he mumbles, and his eyes shutter closed again.

Kristin takes hold of his hand and gives it a soft squeeze. "They'll take care of you, Dad. I'll be right here when you wake up. Promise."

"We need to check him over," Kat says as she ushers the men with the wheelchair through to the room at the back of the house where she keeps all of her medical supplies. It also doubles as a makeshift operating theater when the occasion calls for it, which happens more frequently than it should.

THIRTY-NINE

MAX

K at pulls off her rubber gloves and tosses them into the trash. The surgeon left after half an hour because there was nothing for him to do. Kat Moretti is an excellent nurse and sews the neatest stitches I've ever seen. Uncle Vito lies on the bed in the center of the room, propped up by pillows. His eyes are closed, but he looks a damn sight better than he did three hours ago.

"How is he?" Dante asks her.

"He's sleeping but not unconscious. There was nothing life-threatening. All the wounds are superficial and will heal with time. Except for his two toes and his pinky finger, obviously, which are missing. He's also had a couple of back teeth pulled out. His missing digits were cauterized so there's no infection, but we've given him some antibiotics anyway. He was mostly suffering from dehydration and exhaustion. We've given him plenty of fluids and some pain relief. Now he just needs to rest."

Dante pulls his wife into his arms and gives her a soft kiss. "You are an angel, vita mia."

"Hmm." She eyes him suspiciously. "You're not going to let him rest, are you?"

"Can he talk?" he asks.

"Yes."

"Then, no. He can't rest yet."

"Can you let Kristin know he's okay but that she can't see him yet?" I don't know what Kat can say that won't send my little sister into a panic, but I trust her.

She rolls her eyes. "I'll make something up."

"Thank you," Dante says, releasing her from his embrace.

"Love you," she whispers before she leaves the room. As soon as she's gone, Lorenzo steps inside and closes the door behind him.

I wake my uncle up, and he stares at us, scratching his beard, his eyes darting between Lorenzo and Dante. He doesn't want to be here as much as they don't want him here.

"Why did the Russians take you? Was it something to do with the piece of shit who got Kristin pregnant?" I ask, ignoring the thick tension in the room. The sooner I get some answers as to where I fit into all this, the sooner Vito can leave and take his daughter with him. I've grown to care for Kristin, but her father is a snake and she's convinced that he's some fucking saint. Besides, she'll be far safer away from here.

Vito snorts, and from the corner of my eye, I see Lorenzo's hands ball into fists. "I have much better things to do with my time than try to get information from this piece of shit. If he's not going to talk, shoot him in the fucking head and let's get on with our day."

"Lorenzo," Dante says quietly, trying to defuse the palpable anger rolling off his brother. I can't blame him though. Every minute he spends in this room is another minute he can't spend with his wife.

"Talk, Vito," I snap.

"You think I'd tell these two anything, Maximo? You know you can't trust them, right? You know they're just like their father was? Lowlife scum." Vito spits onto the floor, and Lorenzo surges forward and smacks him across the face with the back of his hand, causing Vito's head to snap backward. Blood pours from his mouth and he spits again.

I frown at Lorenzo. "Let me handle this, yeah?"

He glares at me, nostrils flaring, but he gives me a subtle nod and steps back to stand beside his brother.

I crouch down in front of my uncle until we're eye to eye. "These men are my family, Vito. You ever disrespect them like that again and I will put a bullet in your head. Tell me what the fuck is going on here and I'll let you walk out of here with your daughter. You'll never have to see us again."

Vito narrows his eyes at me like he's trying to determine whether I'm telling the truth. "They know why Pushkin and his sick band of fucks took me." He nods toward the brothers.

Dante glowers at him. "The fuck?"

I hold up my hand and let them know I'll handle this. "What are you talking about? It was Pushkin who took you?"

"Yes, and they know why," Vito insists.

Dante and Lorenzo shrug.

"They don't, so you tell me."

"They had no idea what their father did? They don't know what I had on that sick fuck? You think I believe that?"

My head is starting to throb with the weight of unanswered questions. "Stop asking questions and tell me what the fuck is going on, Vito, or I swear to god I will fucking end you right here. I don't give a fuck if it upsets your daughter."

He sucks his lips into his mouth and draws a breath through his nose. "They came for me because Sal was dead. I'd have thought that was pretty obvious."

My brow furrows. "Why is that obvious? You and Sal hated each other."

Licking his lips, he flicks another glance at Dante and Lorenzo.

"Ignore them and answer my question," I demand.

"I knew about it all. Everything he and the Russians were into. That was why Sal turned you against me and your mom. Because I threatened to expose him. So as soon as he was gone, those sick Russian fucks came after me."

"He didn't turn me against either of you. You both betrayed my father, and my mother walked out on me when shit got hard," I remind him.

Dante puts a hand on my forearm and squeezes, reminding me that we have other priorities at the moment. "You knew about the trafficking?"

"All of it." Vito scoffs. "I tried to tell your father, but he wouldn't even listen to me. Sal had him brainwashed. Goddamn Moretti empire! Built on the sale of women and children. Sick fucks."

"Not on our watch," Lorenzo snaps. "That has never been our business, Vito."

Vito shakes his head.

"It's true," I assure him, but his eyes remain clouded with suspicion and anger. "But why would Sal's death make them come for you? Why didn't Sal just kill you himself if you knew?"

"Oh, he wanted to. Threatened your mom and Kristin too, but I had something on him, didn't I?"

"The trafficking?" I ask.

"No. I saw him kill that girl. I recorded it on my cell phone too," Vito says with a flicker of a smile.

"The video recording you have? It was Sal killing someone? A girl?"

"The Delgado girl. He killed her. I know everyone thought she disappeared with that drug dealer she used to hang out with, but he killed her."

The name hits me like a fist to the gut. Bile burns my throat, and I rock back on my heels. He knew too?

"You knew about that?" Dante asks.

"Yeah, I saw him."

"But how?" I ask, my head spinning.

Dante squeezes my shoulder and steps in to take over. "What exactly did you see, Vito?"

"You expect me to believe you don't know what happened? What he did to that girl?" Vito says with a sneer. "You two are just the same as he was."

"No, we don't fucking know. Now fucking tell me what you saw," Dante says, his tone low and menacing.

"He was in his office. The Delgado girl —"

I cut in. "Her name was Fiona." Her name has been burned into my brain for twelve long years.

"Fiona." Vito nods. "She was in his office. He strangled her."

Now Lorenzo gets involved. "And you saw this? You saw him kill her?"

"Yes."

"You're sure that's what you saw?" I ask.

Vito frowns at me. "Yes. He killed her, Maximo. I saw him. I have it all on video. That girl was dead. He strangled her."

"And then he put her in my bed. He let me think I killed her."

Lorenzo places his huge hands on my shoulders. "We knew this, Max. And you know he's capable of way worse than framing someone for murder."

"That twisted piece of shit killed her. And it looks like your precious Morettis made you believe you did it so you would stay loyal," Vito shouts, his hands balled into fists. "And keep you away from your real family."

"The fuck?" Dante shouts. "We had no fucking idea what

our father had done. *We* are Max's family. We are the only fucking family he needs."

"The same family who made him believe he murdered an innocent girl for over a decade? You might not have been there when it happened, but you expect me to believe his own sons didn't know what Sal did? You Morettis are all the fucking same."

Dante lunges forward, grabbing Vito by the throat. Blood thunders in my ears, so I don't register the heated exchange that ensues between the two men until Lorenzo shouts, "Enough!" so loudly that it cuts through the rest of the noise.

Dante releases his grip on Vito's throat, and we all look at Lorenzo. "Salvatore Moretti might have sired us, but *we* are nothing like him. Maximo is as much my brother as my own fucking flesh and blood, and if you ever come into our house and disrespect my family's name again, Vito, I will shoot you where you fucking stand. You got me?"

Vito's nostrils flare as he glares at Lorenzo, but after a few seconds, he nods in defeat.

"What happened? You just watched him kill her?" I ask. "What were you even doing there?"

"I came to see you, Max. An old buddy of mine was on the gate, and he let me in. There was some kind of party, and I guess security was lax because I walked straight into the house. When I couldn't find you, I decided to confront Sal. He was in his office. The door was open, and he and the girl were arguing. She was threatening to expose him if he didn't pay her to keep quiet. So I hung back and recorded the whole thing. She talked about seeing the warehouses. Said she knew what he and the Santangelos were doing. He laughed at her, and then his hands were on her throat—"

My stomach churns. "And you just stood there recording it? You did nothing to help her while you watched him kill her?"

"I was unarmed. If I'd tried to stop him, you think he would have spared either of us?"

What a fucking coward, trying to paint himself as the good guy when he watched a young girl's murder and did nothing to stop it. "And then what you left? Or did you blackmail him?"

Vito stretches his neck. "As soon as she stopped struggling, Sal left her there and walked out of his office. I ducked out of sight, but ran to check for a pulse as soon as he was gone and—"

"Checked to see if she had any other evidence on her that you could use to blackmail him instead?" Dante accuses.

"No," Vito insists. "I did what I did to protect myself and my daughter. I never wanted a penny of his filthy money."

"What happened next, Vito?" I ask.

"I got out of there before he came back. I knew I had something big. Knew I could use it to protect me and Kristin. So, yeah, I blackmailed him. Told him if anything ever happened to me or my daughter that the recording would go to the press. You see, we never felt safe in Jersey. He was always letting us know he was watching us. He blamed me for your father's death."

"I really don't give a fuck how bad you had it in Jersey, Vito."

His Adam's apple bobs as he swallows. "I came back to see you, Max. To tell you about your sister. And I thought if I told you about the warehouses and the trafficking, then you'd see Salvatore for what he really was. Then when I saw him kill that girl ... I would have told you about that too, but, well—you chose the Morettis. But I swear I had no idea what he'd done with that girl's body, Maximo! If I'd known he framed you, I would've found a way to tell you. Hell, we were supposed to meet a few days after that, and I was gonna tell you about everything I knew then. But you chose Sal. You always chose Sal, just like your father did."

I grind my teeth so hard, my jaw aches. Piece of shit trying to make me feel bad for my choices after everything he did. "I chose the Morettis because they're my family, Vito, and they always will be."

CHAPTER
FORTY

MAX—AGE 20

My jaw aches as I stare out the window, watching Dante squirt Joey with the water hose. She squeals with laughter, and the sound should make me smile, but my brain is too full of other things—secrets and lies and broken promises.

A solid hand rests on my shoulder, squeezing tightly. "You know you have always been like a son to me, Maximo."

"Hmm," I mumble, my eyes narrowed as I continue staring at the scene outside.

When he doesn't get the desired response, he goes straight for my weak spot. "I promised your father I would look out for you."

"And you have, Sal," I assure him. He took me in when I was fourteen, after my father was murdered. He and Sal were the best of friends. My father was his right hand. I practically grew up in this house even before my dad died. It was the one place other than my own home where I felt safe and wanted. Not that Sal fostered any of that comfort or familiarity. He has a violent temper and a cruel streak a mile long, but when he wants to shine his spotlight on you, he can make you feel like you're king of the fucking world. No, it was his children and staff who've always made me feel like I belong here.

"You know you don't have to meet with your uncle."

I swallow the thick knot in my throat. I haven't seen Uncle Vito in eight years—not since he ran off with my mom. She died a couple of months back, and I wonder if that's what prompted his call a few days ago when he asked me to meet with him. I hate him. But he's the only biological family I have left.

"I figure I might at least hear what he has to say."

Sal snorts. "Nothing he has to say will be worth listening to. I guarantee it. He was always a useless sack of shit. He stole your mother, might as well have killed your father himself. Because that *is* why he died, Maximo, and you can't forget that. And now he comes here looking for—what? Forgiveness? Does he want to be your uncle again now that he has nothing and nobody left?"

"I don't know what he wants, Sal."

He rubs a hand over his beard and frowns. "I can guarantee no good will come from meeting with him. *We* are your family, Maximo. We have always looked out for you. Protected you when you needed it. We've always had your back and we always will."

He stares at me pointedly and his eye twitches. Does he know what happened? No. He can't. Neither Dante or Lorenzo would have told him about what happened the other night. But maybe he saw something. This is his house and Salvatore Moretti sees everything.

"I know that, Sal," I say, trying to keep my tone even and calm even while my insides churn and I feel like I might throw up.

"If you choose to meet with Vito, just remember that he is my enemy." He pauses for a long beat. "And any friend of my enemy, Maximo ..." He doesn't finish the sentence. Doesn't need to. The threat is implicit.

What do I hope to gain from meeting with my uncle after all these years? To hear his fake apologies and excuses? For him to tell me how much my mother suffered so he can share his grief with someone else who loved her?

I check my watch, feeling torn. If I'm going to make the meeting, I need to leave now.

"Lorenzo is going to speak to the Russians. They're causing some problems at the shipyard. I'm sure he could use your help."

I sigh and nod my agreement. "Sure, Sal."

FORTY-ONE

MAX

I stare at the ceiling with my hands behind my head, my brain swimming with unanswered questions. It seems like there are a lot of pieces to this puzzle involving the Russians and my little sister, but I can't piece them all together.

I spoke to Vito again last night, just the two of us, but I didn't get much sense out of him once Kat gave him more drugs. We moved him to a guest room, and I let Kristin stay with him. He's her dad, and despite what I might think of him, he seems to have been a good father to her. Still, I'll never forgive the mistakes he made when I was a kid. I might wonder if him coming back for me should mean something, but I know better. He was seven years too late. He kept my sister from me for eighteen years, and I don't think I can ever get past that. The only thing the man has ever done for me is corroborate Joey's version of events regarding Fiona Delgado and removing every last shred of doubt that Salvatore Moretti framed me for her murder.

Joey comes out of the bathroom wrapped in a towel. My perfect distraction. Sitting up, I watch her walk to her dresser.

"What are your plans today, baby girl?"

"You know what my plans are, Max. I've been talking about them all week."

"I know you've been talking about a party, but I don't believe we agreed you could go."

"Well, luckily for me, I don't need your permission. Mo is my best friend. It's not my fault that you don't like her, and I'm going to her party, Max," Joey huffs as she tosses a black swimsuit over her shoulder in disgust before continuing to rummage through her dresser drawer for something she deems more appropriate.

I walk up behind her, grabbing her waist and pressing myself against her perfect ass.

"I thought I was your best friend?"

She stands up straight, blowing a strand of hair from her eyes and holding something blue in her hand. Turning in my arms, she gives me a snarky smile. "You are, tough guy. I just meant she's one of my best girlfriends. Look, I know you don't like her ..."

"Nope, not even a little bit," I agree.

"I'm going to her party, Max. You can even come with me if you're that bothered about it."

I take the bikini from her hands and inspect it. At least it's not one of those stringy ones and it will cover her ass and tits. "I wish I could, baby, because you will look fucking hot in this, but I have to speak to Vito some more. We still don't know who kidnapped me or why. And *that* is the only reason I don't want you going to this party today. Not because I don't like Monique, and not because you're going to spend the entire afternoon in this sexy little number."

"It's hardly sexy. I mean I can show you a much sexier one if you'd prefer?" She flutters her eyelashes at me and sinks her teeth into her plump lower lip, making me want to do the same.

I grin at her. "Definitely later."

"I'll be safe though, Max. This whole thing with you and Vito and the Russians is something to do with Kristin's baby daddy, right? Even Dante and Lorenzo agreed I could go."

"But your brothers no longer get to decide what you do and where you go, baby girl," I remind her as I trail my lips over the sweet-smelling skin of her throat. "I do."

I don't miss the shudder that runs through her body. My spoiled little brat loves to be dominated, even though she'll never admit it. She doesn't argue, but probably only because she's afraid I'd make her stay home.

Instead she tries a completely different and way more effective tactic. "Henry and Ash will be with me. I'll be gone for a few hours and then I'll be back here." She runs her hands down my chest and over my abs. "And I will be so grateful to you that I'll do anything you want."

I fist my hand in her hair, pulling her head back until she gasps. "You'll do anything I want, regardless, Joey. Because you're my needy little slut."

Her cheeks turn pink. "Please, Max?"

Why do I feel like this is such a bad idea? Her brothers think it's safe. She'll have armed guards. The threat right now is to Kristin.

"You can't keep me locked away forever. I'm a grown woman, aren't I?" she whispers.

I press my forehead against hers. She's right about that. My girl has been protected and locked away almost her entire life and I saw the damage it did to her. She deserves much more than that, especially from me. How do I expect her to be all I know she's capable of being if I don't let her breathe? If I wanted a submissive, compliant woman who obeyed my every whim, Joey Moretti wouldn't be the woman for me.

"Fine. But you stay for four hours, then you get your ass

back here. Don't get drunk because it makes you less alert. And do everything Henry and Ash tell you. Understand me?"

She throws her arms around my neck and her legs around my waist, peppering kisses all over my face. "Thank you, thank you, thank you!"

I carry her to the bed and lay us down on it. I have at least another hour before Vito's awake enough for more questions. "You want to show me how grateful you are, baby?"

She lifts her eyebrows. "What do you have in mind?"

I pull open her towel and kiss her silky skin, peppering kisses over her breasts and moving down her body, over her stomach, toward her pussy. I can smell her arousal already and it makes me hard. "First of all, you can come all over my face." Kiss. "And then my cock." Kiss. "And then ..." I swirl my tongue over her clit.

"And then?" she whimpers.

"Then you will suck my cock so you can taste just how delicious your cunt is."

"Yes, please," she says as she pushes her hips up until she can grind herself on my face.

"That's my naughty little slut."

"She'll be fine, compagno," Dante says with a wry smile as I check my watch for the hundredth time this hour.

"Yeah, well, until she's back here, I won't relax."

He laughs softly. "She's really done a number on you."

"I love her, D. I think about her every second of every fucking day. I can't help it."

He nods like he knows exactly what I mean. "Did you get anything more from Vito last night?" he says, getting back to the business at hand.

"No. Once Kat gave him some more drugs, he was making no sense at all. Kristin said he was still sleeping when I checked at lunch. I figured I'd let him sleep it off a little longer and we'll talk to him when he's lucid. I asked her to let him know we want to see him as soon as he wakes up."

He rubs a hand over his beard. "I spoke to Dmitri this morning. He's following a lead on Pushkin, thinks he might be in Miami."

"Miami?"

Dante nods. "Has some property down there in his dead ex-wife's name. Managed to keep it low-key until now."

"And his sons?"

"No sign of them yet. Rumor has it Viktor and Ivan went back to the motherland to try to drum up support to oppose Dmitri."

"Fuck, that's all we need."

"Dmitri doesn't think they'll have much success. The Pushkins don't have many allies left right now and any support they had is waning. Even the New York branch promised Dmitri their support, and they were always going to be the ones that would tip the scales. With Vlad Mikhailov's backing from the Bratva and our support in Chicago, Dmitri is set."

"Good. He's a whole lot easier to work with than his predecessors." I crack my neck and wince at the jolt of pain that shoots through my shoulder.

"You okay?" Dante asks.

The knock on the door stops me from answering.

"Come in," Dante calls, and my uncle shuffles into the room using a cane Kat must have found somewhere.

"You wanted to see me?" he asks, his eyes darting around the small space. Despite what we all learned yesterday, there's still a lot of mistrust and suspicion between us.

"Yes. Have a seat." Dante indicates the empty chair opposite his and Vito takes a seat while I perch on the edge of the desk.

"We're just trying to piece together where everything fits, and we need your help," Dante says, and Vito nods his understanding.

"You're sure that your kidnapping had nothing to do with Kristin and the father of her baby?" I ask.

Vito frowns and shakes his head. "No. I told you, it was Pushkin. He's wanted me dead for years. I knew too much about his trafficking operation, but as long as Sal was alive, I was safe."

Dante leans forward. "Because of the recording you had of him killing Fiona?"

"Yes. If anything happened to me, that would go straight to the press. So Sal kept Pushkin off my back, but as soon as he was killed, Pushkin wanted me to pay. He didn't even need me dead, he just wanted to remind me that he could do it."

"Right," I mumble, running a hand over my beard. I feel like we're still missing something. It doesn't explain who kidnapped me and why.

"Why would it have anything to do with the guy Kristin was dating? He didn't even know she was pregnant. He couldn't have. She didn't know when we left."

"Why didn't you help her find him once she did know? She told me he was Russian. Was he—"

"He was Bratva, yes. She didn't tell me much about him, but I did a little digging. He's connected, but I don't know how much. Couldn't even get his last name. He was like a ghost."

"Was he the reason you left New Jersey?"

"No. At least not entirely. We left because I started getting the feeling we were being watched. Call it intuition, but I wasn't taking any chances. And I couldn't be sure it wasn't a coincidence that my daughter's boyfriend happened to be part of the Russian mob."

"Why are you so sure that you being taken had nothing to do with her?"

"Because they never mentioned her once. Pushkin's men tortured me. They wanted to know what I knew about the sex trafficking ring and whether I had enough to put their boss away for life, I guess. And then when I told them everything I knew, they left me for dead. If it had anything to do with Kristin, they would've asked about her."

Dante voices his agreement, and I wrack my brain to remember every single thing that was said when those Russian assholes had me chained up.

"Why do you think it would be anything to do with my daughter?" Vito asks, his eyes narrowed.

"Max?" Dante says.

"Fuckers kidnapped me too. When I heard the Russian accents, I assumed it was retaliation because we were backing Dmitri for the takeover, but then they started going on about how their boss was going to kill me because I touched his girl."

"Kristin?" Vito asks with a frown.

"I assumed so. I mean nobody knew she was my sister. If anyone was following her and saw her leaving my apartment, they could have jumped to conclusions."

"*If* it was her boyfriend and it was about getting her back, why not take her too?" Vito asks.

"I know. That part didn't make sense to me either, but at the time I didn't know if they did have her. After Dante and Lorenzo got me out and I found out she was here, I knew they never could have gotten to her here."

Vito shifts in his seat, wincing. "Could it have been about the dead girl? Fiona?"

"That is one long ass time to wait for revenge." Dante

shakes his head. "And her father died a few months after she did. Who would take their revenge?"

A fucking lightbulb explodes in my brain. "The girl. They weren't talking about Kristin or Fiona ..."

Dante frowns. "Then who?"

"Joey, D. They were talking about Joey." My heart starts racing so fast that it feels like it's going to burst right through my chest at any second. I fish my cell from my pocket and bring up the tracking app.

"Joey?"

"Your father promised her to Viktor."

Horror dawns on his face. "But that was four years ago, Max. We smoothed it over. He married someone else."

I glare at him, pissed at us both for not realizing it sooner while Vito stares at the two of us in confusion. "And his wife mysteriously disappeared two years later—because he never fucking wanted her. He wanted his Italian Mafia princess. You think he gives a fuck that it was four years ago?" I snap. "They said I had my hands on his girl. We assumed they were referring to Kristin, but they were talking about Joey. She is the girl."

He gapes at me in horror. "Fuck! Where is she?"

I look down at the screen and close my eyes, flooded with relief. "She's at Monique's house, where she's supposed to be."

"Wait." Dante shakes his head. "Nobody knew about you and Joey. She didn't even tell her friends."

"Maybe someone saw us?"

"Where?"

I pinch the bridge of my nose. Nowhere. I was extra careful with her. Even the night I screwed her outside the club, I made sure we were in a secluded spot that nobody could get to. "I don't know. Maybe she told someone?"

"She said she didn't though, and why would she say that now that it's all out in the open?"

"I don't know, D." I continue to watch the blue dot on the tracking app. I need to call her, then I need to bring her home. My gut tells me she's the one in danger. And I let her go to that fucking party without me. Fuck!

"Who's with her?" Dante asks.

"Ash is watching her, and Henry's outside. It's a small party. Monique and a few of the girls from high school." My mind races, but I can't process everything quickly enough. "Toby!"

"I thought it was girls only?"

"No." I shake my head. "Toby knew about me and her."

"He did? How?"

"That night she went on a date with him. I came for her. I was fucking raging when I saw her crying. He must have figured it out."

"Toby?" Dante repeats.

"I can't think of anyone else who even saw us together, D. Not like that. I had my arm around her. Maybe it was obvious ...?"

"Then we go pay the little fuck a visit," Dante says, taking his gun from his desk drawer.

"I'll tell Joey to come straight back here." I bring up her number and call her cell. I'm vaguely aware of Vito asking if he can help while I listen to Joey's phone ring several times before going to voicemail. Not bothering to leave a message, I hang up and dial Ash's number instead. I shove aside the violent swell of rage and panic swirling in my gut and remind myself she's at a pool party. Her phone's probably in her purse.

Ash picks up on the third ring. "Yup?"

"Do you have eyes on Joey?"

"Sure do. She's floating around the pool on a giant pink flamingo."

"And you're with her? You can actually see her?"

"Yeah. I'm looking at her right now, Boss. Standing about twenty feet away from her."

Relief washes over me, and I nod to Dante who's watching me intently for any sign of distress.

"Everything okay?" Ash asks.

"I need you to bring her home, right now."

"Okay. And, um, what shall I tell her?"

I rub my temples. He's one of the scariest men I know, but I guess even he doesn't relish the thought of dealing with Joey after she's told to do something she doesn't want to do. And I don't want him having to carry her out of there—because then I'd have to break every finger he touched her with. "Put her on for me."

"Sure, boss."

I wait for him to pass the phone to her. The sound of her voice puts a huge smile on my face. "You missing me?"

"Always, baby girl."

She giggles. "Aw, you're so sweet." She's obviously been drinking, which is only going to make this more difficult.

"I need you to listen to me, baby. You need to come home with Ash. Right now."

"But Max ..." she whines.

"Now, Joey."

It must be the tone of my voice that makes her pay attention. "What's happened? Is it Anya?" she says, sounding afraid.

"No. Everyone is fine, I promise. But I need you to come back to the house."

"But we just made a fresh batch of margaritas."

"Joey, if you don't get your ass back here now, Ash will have to carry you to the car in your bathing suit. And you know if he does that, I'm going to have to fucking kill him for putting his hands on you. So get your ass dressed and get home."

"You're freaking me out."

I suck in a breath. "I'll explain later. Just get dressed and go straight home with Ash, okay?"

"Why can't you come and get me? Where are you?" I hear the panic in her voice.

"Joey, for the love of god, do as you're fucking told for once," I snap. I don't have time for her questions right now.

"Fine." She sighs. "I'll be home soon."

"Put Ash back on."

There's another dramatic sigh from my girl before Ash is back on the phone. "Get her out of there and back home as fast as you can. And do it quietly. Don't take your eyes off her for a second."

"Okay, but—"

"But what?" I bark.

"She just got out of the pool. She's in her bikini, boss."

Fuck! I don't want him watching her change. "Stand outside the room while she changes. No pit stops. No margaritas for the road. She gives you any hassle, you pick her up and carry her ass out of there. You understand me?"

"Yes, Boss."

"Good. Call me when she's home."

When I look up again, Vito has left the room and Dante is still staring at me. "She bitching about leaving the party?" he asks.

"She'll get over it," I say with a shrug. She can spend her whole goddamn life pissed at me if she wants to. I don't care, as long as she's safe.

FORTY-TWO

JOEY

I hand the phone back to Ash. "Do you know what's going on?"

He shakes his head. "Only that I need to get you home, like now."

"Oh, you're not leaving, Joey." Monique slips an arm around my shoulder, her lips pulled into a dramatic pout.

"I'm sorry, I have to," I say with a roll of my eyes, annoyed at being called away from my best friend's birthday party with no explanation other than Max ordered me to.

"Is something wrong?" Monique asks, her eyes wide with curiosity now.

"I have no idea." I shrug. "But I need to go."

"Aw, Joeeeey," Monique whines, clinging to my arm. She must have had way more margaritas than I thought because she's never this clingy.

"Oh, stop. You have a dozen friends here, you won't even know I'm gone."

"We need to move," Ash says, nodding toward the house.

"I'll just go get changed. I'll meet you out front."

Ash shakes his head. "Not allowed to take my eyes off you for a second."

I frown. "What?"

"Except when you're changing out of your wet bathing suit, obviously."

"Maximo is worse than my brothers," I mutter under my breath.

"I'll come help you," Monique says. "Just let me grab our drinks."

"I'm fine, Mo. Enjoy the party and I'll call you tomorrow."

She opens her mouth, feigning indignation. "If my best friend in the whole world is leaving my birthday party early, the least she could do is let me have one last drink with her."

"No margaritas for the road." Ash shakes his head. "We need to go. Now."

"Oh, we can drink while she changes, Ash. Go on through and I'll follow you in." She wanders over to the poolside pop-up bar.

"If we move quickly, we might get out of here before she even has time to fix another drink and find us," Ash says with a grin and hands me a towel from the locker beside him.

"Don't be mean," I say, nudging his arm with my elbow.

He laughs as we head toward the house. "I know she's your friend, but you have to admit she's a bit full on."

"She's just vibrant, is all. She lives life to the fullest."

He arches an eyebrow at me. "Uh-huh. Sure."

I'm drying my hair with a towel when someone knocks on the door of the small shower room. "Come in."

Monique walks through the door with a margarita in each hand and a grin on her face. Ash holds the door open, covering his eyes with his other hand. "You got two minutes before I come and grab you out of there, Joey."

I roll my eyes. "I'll be out in one."

With a nod, he shuts the door.

"One last birthday drink?" Monique says, holding up a salt-rimmed glass.

"I have to go," I remind her, pulling my dress over my head.

"It's my freaking birthday." She stomps her foot on the floor for effect.

I sigh, taking the margarita from her. "See how much I can drink in thirty seconds."

"I bet I can down mine way faster than you, Moretti."

Narrowing my eyes, I scowl. "You really think?"

"I know."

"Huh." I lift the glass to my lips, tip my head back, and down the entire cocktail in one gulp. When I look at her, she's grinning at me, her drink still untouched.

"You not even going to try and beat me?" I ask, but my words sound like they're coming from underwater. Now Monique sways on her feet. Or is that me?

"W-wha?" My legs buckle and I drop to the floor. The glass tumbles from my hand. The sound of shattering glass comes from a distance as my head smacks the marble.

"Never could resist a challenge, could you, Joey?"

My eyes flutter closed, but I manage to reopen them long enough to see her take a gun from a small locker. *No!* I try to shout for Ash, but my mouth won't open.

Everything goes dark but I can still hear.

The door opens. "Is everything okay?" Thank God! Ash is here.

A muffled gunshot is followed by a sickening thud.

I try to move, screaming at my body to get up and run, but I'm paralyzed. My heart races. Where's Ash? What the hell is Monique doing?

Drifting in and out of consciousness, I can't make sense of the snippets of conversation floating above me.

"Hey, baby, it's me ... move fast ... take her home ... don't know ... he's dead ... there's another one outside ... as soon as you can."

Then nothing.

CHAPTER
FORTY-THREE

MAX

Michael Fiore's face is a mask of shock when he opens the door to me and Dante. Maybe it's our fierce expressions that communicate our willingness to ruin lives to get what we want. Either that or the fact that I just threatened to shoot the guard at the gate if he didn't let us through.

"Where's Toby?" I demand.

"T-Toby? He's here. Why?" Michael stammers.

I pull my gun from the waistband of my suit pants and hold it against Michael's temple. "I can shoot you right now and go inside and get him. Or you can call him out here." I press the cold metal into that little indent at the side of his forehead, and his lip starts to tremble.

"D-Dante?"

"Don't fucking look to him for help, you piece of shit. You have five seconds to get him out here or your brains are going to decorate this porch."

"Call him, Michael. You know he'll do it. If Toby's here, there's every chance you'll both get out of this alive."

Michael keeps his eyes focused on Dante. A man he's worked for ten years—a man he trusts.

"Toby. C-come out here, son," he shouts into the house.

I remove the gun from his temple and take a step back, bouncing on the balls of my feet while we wait.

Five seconds pass. "Where the fuck is he?" I snap.

"He's coming from upstairs. He'll be here in just a minute," Michael assures me, his face as white as the walls of his house.

A moment later, Toby comes to the door, all smiles and wet hair. He opens his mouth to speak, but I don't let him utter a single word. Grabbing his hair, I force him to his knees.

His father lurches forward, and under different circumstances, I'd admire his instinct to protect his child.

"Don't!" Dante snaps. Michael freezes, rooted to the spot.

"Dad? Maximo?" Toby pleads. "What is this? W-what?"

I press the cold steel barrel between his eyes.

"Dante? Please?" Michael begs.

"If the kid's done nothing wrong and he tells us what we need to know, he has nothing to fear." Dante stands, watching me impassively.

"W-what?" Toby asks again.

"Who did you tell about me and Joey?"

"Y-you and Joey?"

I shove the gun against his forehead, pushing his head back. "Don't stall on me, you little fuck. Answer the question or I'll blow a hole in your head. Those are your only options."

"I don't know what you mean, Maximo. I haven't told anyone anything."

"That night I came here to pick her up, did you tell anyone about that?"

"N-no."

"You sure about that?"

He squeezes his eyes shut.

"Toby?" I demand.

"I'm thinking," he cries. "It's kind of hard to do with a gun in my face."

Dante chuckles. "Now, you see I woulda thought that would help matters, wouldn't you, Max?"

"Sure would."

A bead of sweat rolls down Toby's temple.

"You either did or you didn't, Toby. It's not fucking rocket science. Now, I'll give you ten more seconds to come up with an answer, or your dad here will be wearing your entrails on his suit."

The boy nods, his eyes still screwed tight and his mouth clamped shut.

I start counting to ten in my head. When I get to four, he speaks. "Monique," he spits the name, and I drop my arm, glaring at him.

"What did you say to her? Did you tell her Joey and I were together?"

"No!" He fervently shakes his head. "I didn't know you were. I told her what happened, that's all. That you picked her up on your bike."

Dante clears his throat. "Monique called Joey in the car while we were driving home from the cabin. Said she was on her way to our house, but Joey told her she wasn't home. She knew Joey left with you and didn't come home."

"Monique." The name burns my tongue like battery acid, and I give Dante a look filled with apprehension. "D. Joey's at her house."

Taking a deep breath, he checks his watch. "She should be almost home by now."

Stepping to the side, I dial her number while Dante helps Toby up and smooths things over. Her phone goes straight to voicemail and my heart rate kicks up a few gears. I dial Ash next and his phone rings out and now my blood is thundering so fast around my body I sway on my feet. I can't fucking breathe. When Ash's phone goes to voicemail, I can barely see straight for the pounding in my head and adrenaline thundering around my body.

"Joey and Ash didn't answer, D."

"Call Henry."

I dial Henry's number, and it rings and rings until voicemail kicks in. Dante stares at me like I have the answers to the meaning of life. I shake my head, and the pain on his face makes me want to puke my guts up. Holy fucking fuck. We dropped the ball.

"Let's go," he orders, and the two of us race back to his car, leaving Michael and Toby standing on their doorstep.

Tires spin, spitting gravel as Dante guns the engine and heads toward Monique's house. "I never should've let her got to that fucking party, D."

"Try their numbers again," he barks.

I call each of them again and the response is the same. "Drive faster," I snap at him when he slows down for a red light.

"You think I'm not as fucking terrified as you are, Max? I'm driving as fast as I fucking can," he shouts at me.

"She's my whole fucking world, D. If anything happens to her—if I let something happen to her because I was too focused on Vito and Kristin—" I can't finish the sentence.

"We're going to fucking get her," he insists. "We'll speak to Monique, and she's gonna tell us Joey is drunk on cocktails and wouldn't get out of the pool. It's going to be okay."

Despite knowing Henry and Ash would never miss a call from me, I cling to his words, trying to convince myself that my girl is perfectly safe and that I haven't let her down in the worst possible way.

"There's Henry's car." Dante nods at the black sedan in Monique's driveway. "Maybe they're all inside?"

But as we draw closer, I see the figure of Henry slumped over the steering wheel and my heart almost bursts through my ribcage. My lungs stop being able to take in air and my stomach twists into such a tight knot that I think I'm going to throw up all my internal organs. My door is open before Dante brings the car to a grinding stop. Scrambling out as quickly as possible, I run toward Henry's car. The driver's side window is open, and even before I pull Henry's head back, I see and smell blood. The blood spatter is consistent with a sliced jugular, which is confirmed when I place my palm on his forehead and the gaping wound grins back at me.

Henry Jones was a good man and an experienced soldier. This wasn't the work of an amateur. Straightening, I take deep breaths. I need to hold it together. I'll be no good to Joey if I fall apart. "He's dead, D."

"Fuck! Henry." Dante nudges me out of the way and leans forward to close Henry's eyes.

With a nod, Dante follows me to the front door of the house. Not bothering to knock, I draw my gun and shoot through the lock. Silence greets us.

"Joey?" I shout.

As expected, there's no answer. Because she's not fucking here. I would know if she was. We stalk through the house toward the back patio and find the pool empty except for a giant inflatable chair and a floating pink flamingo. My girl sat there only an hour ago. My heart is splitting in two. If I didn't believe my own eyes, I'd be sure someone had their hands inside my chest and was tearing it apart. This can't be real. She can't be gone. Because I cannot fucking breathe without her. There is a deep, visceral ache in my chest that makes me heave for breath. I hold onto the door frame before I fall on my ass and can't get up again. Half-empty cocktails sit on tables and towels are draped over the sun loungers as though everyone left in a hurry. I look at the inflatable flamingo again and my heart almost stops beating. If I could only travel back to that moment, the moment Ash told me she was safe ... before my whole goddamn world fucking fell to pieces. If I could go back, I could keep her safe.

"Max?" Dante calls me and I spin around. "Here." He disappears, and I hear him mumbling. I find him crouched over Ash's body. There's a bullet hole in the center of his chest, and Dante places two fingers on his throat, checking for a pulse.

Eyes wide, he slaps his hands down on Ash's chest. "Call 911!"

"He's alive?" The question is rhetorical, so I don't wait for an answer. Ash might know something that can help us find Joey, which means we need to get him medical attention immediately.

After I call the ambulance, I take over from Dante, applying pressure on Ash's wound while he calls Lorenzo and tells him what happened. "Hang in there, buddy. Help's coming."

Dante finishes his call and crouches beside me, taking back over trying to stem the flow of blood from Ash's bullet wound. "Lorenzo's on his way. He's coordinating reinforcements. All the men we can spare and Dmitri too. While we go to the hospital with Ash, he's going to tear this place apart and find something to tell us what happened here."

I can tear this place apart while we wait for him. Noticing a scrap of blue fabric on the cabinet, I stand up and cross the room. It's Joey's wet bathing suit. I pick it up and hold it to my nose hoping for her sweet scent, but all I smell is pool water. I keep it in my hand though because it was on her skin not so long ago and that makes me feel closer to her.

"We'll find her, Max," Dante assures me.

"Hmm," I mumble as I pick up the cocktail glass nearby. It's full. I sniff the contents and confirm it's a margarita. Glancing around the room I see the small dustpan and brush. Inspecting the contents reveals shattered glass. I pick a piece up and hold it to my nose. More margarita.

"She was drugged," I say.

"You think?"

"She told me Monique had made a fresh pitcher. There's a full one and this glass had margarita too. My guess is Joey drank hers, Monique didn't, and she dropped the glass onto the floor when she passed out. Then Ash came in and Monique shot him."

"Likely," Dante agrees, his eyes scanning the room. "Joey's purse is gone?"

"Looks like. They probably dumped it somewhere."

"Her St. Christopher?" he asks.

"It's broken, remember? When they took me. It's on her nightstand."

"Fuck!" he snaps. "I promise you we will find her."

"I know, compagno, because I will tear this goddamn country and everyone in it to pieces until we do."

FORTY-FOUR

JOEY

O w! There's a reason I don't drink a lot. Hangovers are hell. A hell of a lot of fun while you're getting one, not so much when you actually live through it. My head throbs as I open my eyes. Damn margaritas.

Except I'm not in my room. Not in my bed. These covers aren't soft like mine. They're rough and scratchy against my bare calves.

Holy shit! Where the hell am I? Where is Max? Where's Ash?

Bile burns my throat. My headache has nothing to do with the margaritas. I banged my head. But Ash was there. He told me we had to go home.

What the hell happened? *Think, Joey!*

I was changing out of my bathing suit. Monique gave me a cocktail.

Monique! That bitch fucking drugged me. And then she shot Ash. Bile surges up from my gullet.

I survey my current situation. My dress is dirty, but I'm still in it, my underwear too. My knees are scraped from when I fell. My wrists and ankles are bound together with zip ties. I twist against them, but the plastic only tightens, pinching my skin.

"Hey! Where the hell am I?" I yell, but my voice is little more than a croak, my throat raw and dry. "Hey!" I try again, and this time it's loud enough to send someone walking through the door.

"Morning, princess," Monique says, wearing a saccharine smile. *Bitch!*

"What the hell, Mo?" I shriek. "Is this some kind of joke?"

"A joke?" She throws her head back and laughs like the psycho she so obviously is. "What exactly do you think is funny, Jo? Although seeing you all trussed up like a turkey is kinda funny."

My stomach rolls. She's unhinged. "What the hell, Mo? You're supposed to be my best friend!"

"Your *best friend?*" She whines the last two words in a mocking tone. "You have any idea how fucking infuriating it is to be your friend, Joey? Watching you get every single fucking thing you want just because you're *Joey Moretti*." She rolls her eyes and sticks her index finger down her throat.

I blink at her. Where the hell is this coming from? "But ... you and me ... we were ..."

"You never liked me. You were only ever my friend to make yourself feel good and we both know it."

"That's not true. You're rewriting our entire lives."

She stalks toward the bed and leans over me. "You are a spoiled little bitch, Joey. Snapping your fingers and getting whatever you want."

"You have everything, Mo. Any guy you want. Money." Those are the only things that have ever been important to her. "What more do I have that you don't?"

"Money?" She snorts. "I have nothing, Joey. My mom has burned through it all. Every last cent."

"I didn't know." I frown.

She sneers. "Of course you didn't. Because you wander around in your own little perfect Joey world."

"Are you out of your freaking mind?" I scream. "My world is far from perfect." My mom died when I was three. My father was a maniac. I was sent off to Italy for three long years—for reasons I still can't fathom—and she knows all of this.

She folds her arms across her chest and looks down at me like I'm something she just stepped in.

"Mo? Please?" I plead with her. Surely she has to see reason. "Why are you doing this?"

She sighs dreamily. "For Viktor."

"Viktor?"

"Hmm. He's my ticket out of here."

I only know one Viktor, but it can't be him, right? "Tell me Viktor Pushkin isn't Mystery Guy?"

Her only response is a smug smile. It makes a sick kind of sense. Her man was always disappearing for weeks on end and more recently seemed to have gone completely off the radar. "But why? What does Viktor Pushkin want with me?"

She runs a finger through one of my curls and I yank my head out of her reach, making her laugh. "Poor little naive Joey. Nobody ever tells you what's going on, do they? Even screwing Max didn't make him open up to you."

My stomach rolls again. "What the hell are you talking about?"

Before she can answer, the door opens and a heavyset man with tattoos on his face and a shaved head walks into the room.

"Hey, baby," she squeals when she sees him. This must be Viktor.

He doesn't smile. There isn't even a flicker of affection for her in his eyes. He lifts his arm, and it's only then that I see the gun in his hand. I close my eyes and shrink back. *Dear god, he's going to kill me.*

A deafening gunshot rings out and I'm splattered with warm stickiness. Opening my eyes, I take a deep breath, and something drips into my mouth. Blood. Is it mine?

Refocusing on my surroundings, I see Viktor standing directly in front of me. On the floor is Monique, face down with a huge hole in the back of her skull.

I lurch forward and vomit onto the floor.

"We meet at last, Guiseppina," Viktor says in a thick Russian accent. He smirks, not in the least bit bothered by the dead body or the puddle of puke at his feet.

"You're a psychopath."

"Maybe." His smirk transforms into a full smile. "But I am your husband also. At least this time next week I will be."

FORTY-FIVE

MAX

"I can't fucking stand this, D," I snap, pacing up and down the corridor. "We need to be out there doing something, not sitting around waiting."

"Doing what, Max? Lorenzo has a team of men ripping Monique's house apart. Dmitri has half his army scouring the city. I got all my tech guys searching every traffic camera for Monique's car. But our best lead is in that fucking room having his chest sewn back together." He nods in the direction of the operating room. "This is where we need to be. But if it makes you feel better to be out there busting some heads open, you go do that."

I glare at him, hating him for being right. "It's been six fucking hours, and nothing." I rake my hands through my hair. My ability to think logically or rationally has fled. I'm consumed with rage and terror. My girl is out there somewhere, and they could be hurting her right now. They could be—

A woman in scrubs steps into the waiting room. "Mr. Moretti?"

Please, fuck, let Ash have made it.

Dante steps forward. "Yes."

"Your friend is out of surgery and he's stable. He's in recovery."

Thank whatever god or devil is responsible for saving that lucky fucker's life.

"When can we talk to him, Doctor?"

She frowns. "He's had major surgery. He needs his rest."

"I understand that, but I need to speak with him. I assume you've been informed of our particular circumstances?"

She winces. "I have."

The Morettis pay for this hospital's discretion and cooperation in the form of millions of dollars in donations each year. This nurse knows she's unlikely to work in another hospital in the entire tri-state area if she refuses to comply.

He lifts his eyebrows. "So when can I speak with him?"

"You can wait in his room and speak with him when he wakes," she says reluctantly.

"Which room is he in?" I ask.

"Follow me."

Ash is hooked up to a dozen machines, but he looks pretty good for a guy who was shot earlier today and almost died.

"Please don't wake him. You won't get any sense out of him if you do. He should start coming around in about half an hour when the anesthesia wears off."

Dante thanks the nurse and she leaves us alone to stare at Ash, lying motionless in the hospital bed.

I cough, breaking the long silence. "What now?"

Dante takes a seat in one of the bedside chairs. "We wait until he wakes up."

With a deep sigh, I sit next to him and stare at Ash, willing him to wake the fuck up and hand us the key to finding Joey.

"Why the fuck would Monique drug her?"

"Money," he answers without hesitation. "You know her mom has all but burned through what her dad left them?"

"I figured as much."

"I knew though. I should have seen it, Max. It should have been a huge fucking red flag. I know people like her. They will do anything for money."

"So, she what? Delivered Joey to Viktor Pushkin? Why?"

"Because Monique is his girlfriend," Ash croaks.

I jump out of my seat. I could fucking kiss him. "Ash, you tough-as-nails son of a bitch!"

Nodding, he winces.

"What else did you hear?"

"Not much. I was in and out ... wherever he's been hiding ... they've taken her there."

"If she's his girlfriend, why did she help him take Joey?" Dante asks with a frown.

"Revenge," Ash answers, coughing.

"No." I shake my head. "The guys who took me said their boss was furious with me for touching his girl. They very much implied she belonged to him. He took Joey because he wants the Italian Mafia princess he was promised. He wants her to be his wife."

"Twisted fuck," Dante says with a snarl.

"This is good news, D. It means that Monique is dispensable, but not Joey."

"You know my sister though, right? Never backs down from a challenge. Never runs from a fight. She will run her mouth as soon as she finds out what the fuck is going on. He'll kill her."

"No, she won't. She's smarter than that," I assure him.

"I fucking hope so."

I take Ash's face in my hands and kiss his forehead, making him groan with disgust.

Everything's falling into place like a puzzle that I just found the last, most important piece of. "I fucking love you, but we have to go to Racine."

"Why are we going to Racine?" Dante asks.

"Because I know where his place is."

"What? Where?"

"Above a sex club called Elena's Erotic Arena in Racine."

"How the fuck do you know that?"

"I'll explain in the car. Now, can we please go get my fucking girl?"

He turns to Ash. "Get some rest, buddy and thank you."

"My pleasure. Tell her I'm sorry I let her down," he whispers as his eyes close.

"You didn't, Ash," I tell him, but I doubt he heard me.

I call Lorenzo and bring him up to speed while Dante drives as fast as possible to Racine. When I'm done, I tell Dante how a complimentary tin of breath mints is going to lead us to his sister.

CHAPTER
FORTY-SIX

JOEY

Viktor brushes his fingertips over my face, almost reverently. I force myself not to flinch at his touch.

"Your father promised you to me a long time ago, Guiseppina."

My father what now? "I don't understand," I say, shrinking back. Making myself appear as small and weak as possible.

"That is why your brothers sent you away. They thought they could keep you from me."

"That's why they sent me to Italy?"

"Yes."

I blink at him. I can't believe those assholes never told me. I can't believe Max never told me. I am so over them treating me like a goddamn foolish child. "They never told me that."

"I figured as much. But you were always meant to be mine. I have waited a long time to claim you."

My stomach lurches and I swallow the bile that burns my throat. Just how the hell does he intend to claim me? My face must show my fear and disgust because he laughs. The sound is cruel, and it raises the hairs on the back of my neck.

"Don't worry. I won't take you until we are married. I won't touch you until you are intact again. No longer tainted by that animal, Maximo."

Every cell in my body screams for me to rage at him, to break out of these restraints and kill him with my bare hands. But logic reminds me that I would get about as far as scratching his face. He's much stronger than me, so I'll have to use my intelligence to get out of here.

"Intact again?"

"There is an operation." He shrugs. "To replace the hymen. Tomorrow we leave for Russia, and you will have it as soon as we arrive."

"L-leave for Russia?" I try to appear calm, but my heart beats so hard, I'm sure he can hear it.

"Hmm. It is too dangerous to stay here."

"Where is here?" I ask.

"You don't have to worry about where you are, only where you are going. Just know that nobody will hear you scream."

"Why would I scream?" I say with a shrug. "I'm just trading one prison for another, right? My brothers never let me go anywhere. They sent me to Italy, for god's sake. They'll be happy to see the back of me and the feeling is mutual."

I lie back on the bed, my mind racing with escape scenarios.

"And Maximo?"

"He was just a little fun. Nothing serious. Someone to pass the time because I was bored." The words burn me to say them, and they seem to anger Viktor rather than appease him.

He grabs hold of my face, squeezing my cheeks roughly. "I do not want to marry a slut. Are you a slut?"

"N-no! Maximo was the only one. It was only a couple of times, I swear. I'm not a slut."

He snorts and kicks Monique's lifeless body. "She was a slut. Could not wait to suck my cock and offer all of her dirty used holes to me."

I tremble at the venom in his voice. There goes my idea of offering to suck his cock and biting it off.

"She thought that helping me get you, the thing that was rightfully mine anyway ..." He laughs maniacally as he paces the floor.

Thing? I need to get out of this fucking room and away from him.

"Then I would forget that she was a filthy little cock whore and marry her instead. When it is you, Guiseppina. *You* are the only one I ever wanted."

I turn sideways on the bed, my feet hanging off the edge as I prop myself up on my elbows. "I had no idea I belonged to you, Viktor. If I had ..." I let my words trail off and flutter my eyelashes.

Shaking his head, he snorts like he doesn't believe me.

"I've never really fit in. I think it might be kind of nice to belong to someone." I keep my tone soft and sweet and pray that he buys it. "Will we live in Russia?"

"Yes."

"My sister-in-law tells me there are many beautiful places to see in Russia," I say with a sigh. "Will you take me to Moscow?"

He edges closer but not quite close enough. "Maybe. If you are good."

"I'll be good." I give him the most genuine-looking smile I can muster. "I've spent my life learning how to be a good wife to a strong man." I'm lying through my teeth now, and I have no idea if he's buying any of it. But then he takes another step toward me.

I smile up at him, pulling my knees up to my stomach as he draws nearer, as though I'm making room for him to get closer to me. He runs a hand over my bare leg, and I swallow back the urge to vomit. Leaning down, he kisses me. He tastes of cigarettes and vodka, and I want to retch into his mouth. When he pushes his tongue inside, it feels so disgustingly big and slimy that tears prick at my eyes. But I must focus.

Toni said go for the nuts, right?

With every ounce of strength in my body, I aim both of my heels at his groin. He wasn't expecting it. Underestimating me as most men do. He doesn't just double over, he drops to his knees with a sickening bellow.

I jump off the bed and bunny hop across the room faster than I've ever moved in my life. If I can just find a weapon, I'll stand a chance. I open the door and jump out into the hallway, completely shocked to find that I'm in a regular-looking apartment. I grab the door handle, and sweet mother of Jesus, there's a keypad lock on it. Of course there is. He was keeping me prisoner in there.

He curses loudly in Russian and clambers around the room. Holy shit. Blood rushes in my ears. My fingers tremble as I scramble to close the door behind me. I hear his fingernails scratch against it a fraction of a second after I yank it closed.

I suck in deep, bone-shaking breaths. I'm out. Now I just need to get these damn zip ties off and get out of here. Viktor pounds against the door, making me flinch. "I will break this down, Guiseppina, and I will make you suffer far more than your little slut friend." Viktor is a big guy, and I figure he can get through that piece of wood in a minute—two if I'm lucky. I need to move fast.

"Fuck you!" I shout, hopping down the hallway, looking for the kitchen and the biggest knife I can find.

I try two doors before I find the kitchen. The sound of Viktor trying to burst through that bedroom door makes my heart race faster than a Ferrari. I can barely breathe. Adrenaline thunders through my body. Everything feels sharper and clearer even while every part of my body trembles with fear. When he gets through that door ... If he takes me to Russia ...

"Guiseppina. I am coming for you," he sing-songs while he continues to slam against the door. Psychopath!

I need to get out of here. Now. Scuttling through the kitchen, I frantically search drawers and cabinets until I find the knives. Grabbing a thick black handle, I almost pass out with relief when I see the long, sharp blade. I quickly cut the zip ties off my hands and feet, then I run, knife in hand, straight for the front door of the surprisingly ordinary and spacious apartment.

I saw other buildings through the window in the kitchen. We must be in a town, which means Viktor lied about no one being able to hear me scream. There are people around. If I can just get outside into the open space—

"You fucking whore!" he roars, venom dripping from the words. His toxicity seeps through the bedroom door and surrounds me, but it only makes me move faster.

There are at least half a dozen bolts on the front door, and I struggle to get a grip on the first one, but my sweaty hands slip right off. I quickly dry them on my dress and manage to get it on the second try. My head swims, my heart pounding so hard I can barely hear Viktor's thuds and curses. Maybe the drugs are still in my system? Maybe I'm going to pass out again?

Fuck. No.

I won't let him win. *Work faster, Joey!*

The crashing sound of Viktor trying to break down the door grows more persistent, louder than the sound of my own heartbeat. Holy fuck! My fingers tremble and slip on the bolts. Then I hear wood splinter from down the hall, and my heart stops beating for a long moment. Shaking my head, I scrabble at the remaining bolts, keeping the knife between my legs, certain Viktor is seconds away from grabbing me.

Just as I turn the last one, Viktor crashes through the door.

Heavy footsteps clamor down the hallway. I can't look behind me. If I see him, I might crumble to pieces. Taking the knife from between my legs, I throw open the door and make a run for it.

My legs tremble, almost giving way as I bolt down the flight of stairs, but sheer terror lends me strength and hastens my escape. Footsteps thunder right behind me, and I scream and drop the knife, watching helplessly as it clatters to the bottom of the stairwell. I scan the floor below, but I'm unable to find it in the dim light. He's going to get me before I can get out of here. He's going to take me back to that room. He's going to—

"There's no way out of here, you fucking whore," he yells, and his voice is so close now, footsteps even closer. I can smell his stale breath, and it makes me heave. Tears stream down my face.

No. Please no. I'm almost there.

I stumble on the last few stairs, falling against the exterior door. There are bolts on this one also. Only two, but still too many. I fumble with the first one, heart racing and blood rushing in my ears.

His breath is on my neck. Fingers in my hair. I suck in a shaky breath. Tears blur my vision. His body slams into mine, sandwiching me between him and the door and knocking all the air from my lungs. I gasp for breath.

"Caught you, little whore," he whispers harshly, his mouth pressed at my ear. Saliva drips from his lips and onto my neck, and my flesh crawls like a million tiny ants scurry beneath my skin.

"No!" I scream, praying that someone might be passing by. Somebody, anybody, might hear me. Opening my mouth to scream again, I gag when his huge meaty hand covers it, choking on his foul stench. Out of desperation, I slam my head back and hit his chin. He mutters curses in Russian and grabs my hair, yanking my head back.

"You will pay for that, you little bitch," he says with a sneer as he pushes my body flat to the door. Pressing his hard cock against my ass, he grinds on me and groans. Bile fills my mouth and burns my throat as I'm forced to swallow it back down.

Tears sting my eyes.

"You know I said I was going to wait until you were pure?" His sour breath washes over my face, and I screw my eyes shut. I need to think. "I have changed my mind. You let that animal, Maximo, defile you. I think I will also fuck all of your filthy, dirty holes. Then I make you pure again."

I try to block his vitriol, his taunts. I *will* get out of here. I'm smarter than he is. The knife! It's here somewhere.

I mumble against his hand, pushing my ass back and gyrating against his cock. Swallowing another mouthful of vomit, I summon my courage. I can do this. I must do this.

"Oh, is this what you wanted all along? You like it rough, little whore?" he says with a sneer, licking a path up my neck to my ear. My entire body shudders, and I guess he thinks I'm enjoying myself because he moans loudly.

"Mmhmm," I murmur, continuing to grind against him.

"Well, let's just see how rough you can handle it, because I like when you whores fight back." Throwing me on the floor, he laughs darkly.

I look up at him, a fake smile on my face as I watch him unfasten his belt while I spread out my hands and search the darkness for my weapon.

He leers at my open thighs, focused on my panties rather than what my hands are doing. "You really are a dirty little whore, Guiseppina."

"I never said I wasn't," I purr as my fingertips creep over the cold tile floor, and a genuine smile spreads over my face at the same time Viktor pulls his dick out of his pants.

He leers at me. "Oh, you want this?"

"Yes." I lick my lips and he drops to his knees. Men like him will always have the same weakness—underestimating women like me.

He leans over me, nudging my legs apart and sliding a hand between my thighs. "I hope you bite and scratch, little whore."

"Oh, I sure do." With a feral grin, I plunge the knife into his side, right below his left armpit. His face twists with agony. He roars, flopping onto his side and allowing me to scrabble out from under him. I dive for the door while he's still immobilized.

My hands are no longer shaking as I pull back the bolts. Who does that sick fuck think he is, thinking he can take me to Russia and make me his fucking bride? I am Joey fucking Moretti.

Jerking the door open, I fall out into a large parking lot. The bright sunlight shines directly in my eyes, making me shield my face from the glare, and I barrel directly into a broad chest.

FORTY-SEVEN

MAX

She runs straight into me like a gift from the fucking heavens.

I pull her close, wrapping my arms tight around her. "Baby girl, I got you." I breathe out a sigh full of relief, my lips pressed against her hair as she buries her face into my chest.

"M-Max," she gasps, her heart hammering against my chest.

Dante steps toward the open doorway, gun drawn.

"He's at the bottom of the stairs," Joey says. "He's injured and I don't think he's armed. But be careful."

A smile creeps over her brother's face as he looks through the open doorway and puts his gun back in the waistband of his pants. "You did this, kid?" he asks proudly.

"Of course," she sniffs.

The sunlight illuminates Viktor Pushkin as he pushes himself to his knees, a kitchen knife sticking out of his side. He goes to pull it out, but Dante stops him, dragging him to his feet and pinning his arms behind his back. If Viktor pulls that knife out now, he'll likely bleed to death on the way home. That would be a death far more merciful than he deserves. Dante pushes him into the parking lot, and Viktor blinks at the bright glare of the sun, screaming Russian curses.

Joey takes a deep breath and wrenches herself from my arms. Before I can pull her back, she launches herself at Viktor, raking her nails down his face. "You evil, disgusting piece of shit!"

Dante holds onto him, keeping his arms firmly behind his back.

"Let him go so I can kick his ass," she rages. "Let him fucking go."

Her brother shakes his head. "Calm down, kid."

She turns her wrath on him. "Don't fucking tell me to calm down. Let him the fuck go and let me kill him, Dante."

Dante shoots me a look and I step in, wrapping my arms around her. Fury pulses through her body and she kicks out, still trying to get to him.

I hug her tighter. "You can kill him later, Joey."

She snarls, wrestling to free herself from my arms.

I press my mouth against her ear. "Slowly. Painfully. But right now, we need to get out of here."

Immediately she stops struggling, appeased by my promise.

Dante laughs as he secures Viktor's hands. "Yeah, you can kill him later, kid." He shoves a rag soaked with fast-acting sedative into the prisoner's mouth. Within seconds, Viktor slumps over.

Only when he passes out do I let her go, allowing her to walk away from me. I want to carry her out of here, take her to some faraway fortress where nobody will even get to look at my Mafia princess ever again. With a sigh, I shake my head. That will never happen. She's Joey Moretti, the most stubborn woman I've ever met.

Dante and I haul Viktor into the trunk, and we're about to climb into the car when Joey speaks, hands on her hips. "You know it's about time you all started treating the women in this family with some fucking respect."

Dante has his hand on the car door, holding it open, and I see the instant shift in his mood. "Get in the car."

"If you'd just told me about your little scheme, I could have been prepared. Maybe I would've ..."

"Get in the fucking car, Joey."

She folds her arms over her chest. "Not until you admit that you treat me like an idiot just because I'm a girl. You know I'm right. If you'd told me about the stupid pact between Pushkin and our father, this all could have been prevented."

Tension ripples through the parking lot like the aftershock of an earthquake. Joey keeps glaring at Dante with her arms folded. His hand stays on the door handle.

I glower at him. *Just get in the car, D.*

He doesn't. He shuts the door with a soft, deliberate click and turns to face her. "You were eighteen years old."

"I deserved to know. You had no right to keep that from me."

"We did what we had to do," he insists.

"No, you did what was easy for you. Anything to avoid dealing with the fact that I might have an opinion about my own fucking life."

"You were just a kid," he says, the vein in his temple throbbing.

"I wasn't a kid! And you had no right to make decisions about my life without consulting me."

He scoffs. "Like you would have listened to anything Lorenzo or I had to say?"

"You didn't give me a fucking choice," she shrieks.

"We gave you plenty of chances to prove you could be trusted, Joey, and you threw every single one back in our faces."

"Bullshit!"

"You constantly whined and pouted because your mean big brothers wouldn't let you do whatever the fuck you wanted. But how many times did Max have to haul your ass home after you snuck out to some party? How many fucking times did I have to clean you up after you got wasted on vodka and weed?"

She balls her hands into fists, clenching them at her sides as she rocks on the balls of her feet. "I had to do those things because the two of you would never let me out of the goddamn house."

"Because our own fucking father wanted to marry you off to a Russian psychopath, Joey," he screams at her.

"And you should have fucking told me," she yells louder, and I run a hand over my face. This argument has been a long time coming, but I wish they were having it elsewhere. "You should have consulted me."

"I couldn't consult you Joey, you were ..."

"I was what?"

His jaw ticks. He shakes his head. "Get in the car."

"I was what, Dante?" she demands. "At least be man enough to say it to my face."

Don't say it, D.

"You were a spoiled little bitch!" he snaps.

She steps back as though he slapped her in the face. Looking devastated, he scrubs a hand over his face and sighs.

"That's why you sent me away? Not to protect me, but to make your life easier?" The pain in her voice makes my chest ache.

"No, Joey. We sent you away to protect you," he insists.

"Don't fucking lie to me. No more lies. I'm sick of them," she screeches.

All I can do is stand back and let her vent some of the rage she's bottled up inside for years. She has so much pent-up frustration inside her, and it has to come out sometime. I tried to fuck it all out of her, but I obviously missed some.

Dante steps forward. "It's the truth, Guiseppina."

"No, it's bullshit! You sent me away because it was easier for you all. Admit it, Dante. You wanted me out of your hair."

"Why would I want that, Joey? You're my kid sister."

"You just said I was a spoiled little bitch."

"You were, but that's not …"

My girl doesn't let him finish what he's saying. Instead, she pulls back her arm and punches him in the jaw. Gaping at her, he staggers back.

He rubs a hand over his chin and glares at her, and fuck me if she doesn't gear up to clock him again.

Looks like it's time to step in. He'd never hit her, but he might defend himself if she punches him again, and if he touches her—well, then he and I would come to blows. I grab hold of her, and she lashes out at me too, but this time there's no getting away from me. I carry her around to the other side of the car, locking my arms around her like a cage when I set her down.

Her eyes shoot daggers at me. "I hate you all."

"I know, baby girl. Now get in the damn car."

CHAPTER
FORTY-EIGHT

MAX

As soon as we're all safely in the car, I call Lorenzo.

"Yeah?" he barks.

"We got her, Loz. She's okay. We're on our way home."

I hear the deep sigh of relief. "Thank fuck. And she's okay?"

"Yes."

"And Viktor?"

"He's in the trunk. Sedated."

"I'll make sure to get a room ready for him."

"Yeah, do that. And Kat might need to stitch him up a little." We don't want the piece of shit to die before we can kill him.

"I'll let her know. Get her home soon."

He ends the call, and I sit back against my seat, casting glances at Joey every few seconds to make sure she's okay.

We've been driving for a few minutes when she speaks. I guess the adrenaline seeping out of her body is allowing her some space to think. She sits in the back seat with me, as far away from me as possible. Although I'm burning to touch her, I give her the space she needs.

"Is Ash ...?"

"He's fine. He'll be in hospital for a few days, but he'll be okay."

"Oh, that's good," she says with a sigh and sinks back against the seat.

"Henry didn't make it though, baby."

She stares at me, eyes brimming with tears. "Henry? No." She shakes her head.

"I'm sorry."

She sobs quietly, and I stare out of the window because her body language screams *do not touch me*, and I'm not getting into a fight with her right now and definitely not in the back of her brother's car.

"What happened to him?"

"Viktor slit his throat."

She wipes the tears from her cheeks and glances back at the trunk where Viktor currently lies, sedated. "Evil fuck," she mutters.

Joey barely speaks for the rest of the journey home, and as soon as we arrive at the mansion, she jumps out of the car and runs to Kat and Anya who stand in the driveway with Lorenzo, awaiting our return.

"Joey!" Kat throws her arms around her, hugging her tight. My girl clings to her, sagging against her sister-in-law, finally showing vulnerability. Anya hugs her too, and the three women stand in the driveway embracing. Tears are shed, but no words are needed.

When they pull apart, Lorenzo tugs his sister away and kisses her head. "Are you okay?"

"Yeah." She nods.

"Let me deal with this sack of shit." He nods at Viktor as Dante and I take him from the trunk.

"No. I want to," Joey insists. "I need to, Lorenzo."

He nods his understanding. "Of course, but it's late. Everyone's tired, and he's not going anywhere."

"Kat can stitch up that knife wound. Then we leave him chained in the basement tonight and we can handle him tomorrow," Dante adds.

Joey opens her mouth to argue but sways on her feet. Kat wraps an arm around her. "Your brothers are right. You need to rest right now, and then tomorrow you can decide what to do."

Joey looks at her eldest brother. "You won't do anything without me, will you?"

"No. I swear."

She glances at me. She's barely spoken a word to me since she told me she hates me.

"Let him wake up alone and cold and wondering when someone is coming for him and how he's going to die," I suggest.

"Okay," she finally agrees.

My heart is racing, and my stomach is a twisted knot of emotion as I walk inside my bedroom. Max follows behind me and closes the door. The click of the lock makes my breath hitch in my throat. I told him that I hate him. I punched Dante. And all they did was come to rescue me.

The tension in the room is thick enough to taste. My skin bristles, sensing his closeness as he draws near. He steps up behind me, his warm breath tickling my neck, and a shudder runs the length of my entire body.

"So you hate me, baby girl?" he says, his voice is low and full of danger, and it makes my knees tremble. Max presses his lips against the shell of my ear, and my flesh breaks out with spontaneous goosebumps. "Or do you want to take that back?"

Of course I don't hate him. But I'm still beyond fucking angry. Pissed off at everyone. At him and my brothers. Monique. But mostly, my incandescent rage is directed at the Russian sack of elephant shit who thought he could force me to become his wife. His *thing*.

Turning around, I look up at Max as he towers over me. "I

hate when you don't trust me enough to tell me the truth. Like I'm some sort of idiot who would fall to pieces if I had to deal with reality."

His eyes blaze into mine and the heat that surrounds me does nothing to stop the tremors rippling through my body. Tucking my hair behind my ear, his fingertips graze my skin and make me shiver. "I'll never keep the truth from you again."

Tears prick at my eyes. That was the last thing I expected him to say. "You promise?"

"I promise."

He dips his head low, dusting his lips over my neck. "I love you so fucking much, Joey."

I close my eyes, trying to savor the moment with him because this is all I dreamed about when I worried that I'd never have it again. But all I can think about is Viktor. His hands on me. His smell. His kiss. His vile little cock. Bile surges up from my empty stomach and I reel backward, but Max puts his hands on my hips, holding me steady.

"I-I'm filthy. I need to ..." I look down at my dirty clothes and my scraped knees.

"Of course. I'll run you a bath." Dropping a soft kiss on the top of my head, he turns and disappears into the bathroom.

Sitting on the edge of the bed, I listen to the water gurgle out of the pipes and think about Mo. How could she betray me for a man she meant nothing to?

My thoughts shift to him—alone in our basement—and all the ways I'm going to make him pay for taking me. For killing Henry and hurting Ash. For making my family worry. For making Max look at me like I'm broken.

"Tub's ready." Max's deep voice cuts across the room, snapping me from my thoughts.

With an absent-minded nod, I stand and peel off my clothes. I leave them in a pile on my bedroom floor. Max steps back from the bathtub and doesn't even try to touch my naked body. I fight back tears as I step inside the tub. The water is hot and bubbly and soothing, but all I want to do is curl into a ball and bawl. Why do I feel this messed up?

It's only when I lie back that I notice Max getting undressed. I watch him strip off his clothes, revealing his toned muscles and beautiful ink, and I relish the sight of his glorious naked form.

Noticing that I'm watching him, he frowns. "I can take a shower if you'd prefer?"

"Would you prefer?"

With narrowed eyes, he wastes no time climbing into the steamy water that sloshes over the sides as he positions himself behind me. Wrapping his huge arms around my waist, he pulls me close. "I let the hating me comment go, Joey, but don't push it," he growls, and the sound rumbles through my back.

I lean against him and rest my head on his solid chest. "I punched Dante in the mouth."

"He deserved it."

That makes me laugh, but I still owe my brother an apology.

Max runs a washcloth over my legs, gently cleaning my scraped knees. "Did he hurt you, baby?"

"No."

"Did he touch you?"

Would it matter if he had? Would that make you see me differently, Max? I don't voice those thoughts though. "He kissed me."

His entire body tenses. "Where?"

"On the mouth."

Max grips my jaw, tilts my head back, and seals his lips over mine, sliding his tongue into my mouth and kissing me so deeply that wetness pools between my thighs. He pulls back, his dark eyes blazing. "Where else did he touch you, baby?"

"Nowhere else, Max. You don't have to worry."

I swear the thunderous sound he makes is like nothing I've ever heard before in my life. He lifts me, spinning me around until I straddle his hips. "You think I'm worried about me?" I avoid his gaze, but he grabs my jaw again and forces me to look at him. "Do you?"

"I just meant ... you're still the only one."

"It would break my fucking heart if he hurt you, baby girl. But not because of that. Not for a second because of that."

Reading the tender look in his dark eyes, I believe him.

"Did he touch you anywhere else?" he asks again.

"No. He tried when I was escaping, but before that ... He said I wasn't intact. He was going to make me have an operation to have my hymen replaced before he—"

"Sick fucking fuck," he mutters.

Wanting to forget about Viktor, I wrap my arms around Max's neck. "I don't hate you, Max."

"You don't, huh?"

"You know I don't."

"I should turn your ass a pretty shade of red for saying it though."

"Probably." I chew on my lip. "So why don't you?"

"I can find plenty of things to punish you for any time I want, baby girl. Tonight, I just want to take care of you."

I grin at him. "You want to *take care* of me?"

He brushes his lips over my collarbone. "Whatever you want. Whatever you need."

"I want you to touch me like I'm not broken. Max."

He blinks at me. "You think that I think you're broken?"

I swallow the ball of emotion that jumps into my throat. "You're looking at me differently."

"Because I almost fucking lost you, Joey. I was too focused on looking elsewhere when I should have been focused on you. You are the only thing that matters. If anything had happened to you, that would've been on me. If he'd hurt you ..."

"It would be on him."

"If I'm looking at you differently, it's because I'm thanking whatever god or devil I prayed to today that brought you back to me. Maybe I'm looking at you differently because I'm scared you'll realize that I let you down and that I don't deserve you."

"You didn't let me down, Max. You never could."

"I never will again." He pulls me closer, and my pussy nudges his stiff cock. "But don't think I'm giving up any control here, Joey. I still know what you need. I still know exactly what's going on in that head of yours."

"And what's that?" I ask as I rub myself over his cock, trying to distract him.

"You're scared because Pushkin got to you. It makes you feel vulnerable and you hate that. You feel betrayed by Monique and naive for trusting her the way you did, even though none of us saw what she was doing. And despite what she did, you're sad she's dead, and that confuses the hell out of you. You're blaming yourself for Henry and Ash, even though logically you know it's not your fault. You're still full of anger and you feel justified in the things you said to your brother today, but you also feel guilty for saying them."

"Wow! That's quite the summary," I snap, irritated that he was able to verbalize what I feel better than I could have.

"I'm not quite done."

"No?" I tip my chin up, daring him to go on.

"You're still pissed at me too, even though you won't admit it. But you're also wondering whether you can use sex to distract yourself from all the things you don't want to feel."

I stop grinding against him. Asshole. "You think?"

He grabs my hips, dragging me over his stiff cock. My core

contracts with need. "I know it, baby girl. And you know, I could use a distraction too."

I bite on my lip as I stare at his handsome face, etched with anger and guilt. Maybe this is exactly what we both need.

"And I know you've had a rough couple of days, but I hope you know that doesn't mean I'm taking it easy on you. Because you're mine, Joey. I own you and I always will. Never forget that."

"Show me."

His eyes narrow as his fingers dig into the soft flesh of my hips. Then he shifts his hips, lifting me up at the same time. His cock nudges my entrance, and, without any further warning, he pulls me down, slamming into me. My toes curl, shockwaves of pleasure surging through my body. This man knows exactly what I need when I need it. But he's wrong if he thinks I'm incapable of taking control.

FIFTY

MAX

S oft fingertips trail along my forearms and I shift in my sleep, stuck in the space between dreaming and waking. The place where anything is possible.

The sound of the cuffs snapping around my wrists jolts me back to reality. Opening my eyes, I sigh with relief when I see Joey straddling me, her long dark curls cascading over her shoulders and a wicked grin on her face. "Morning," she purrs seductively.

I try to pull my arms from above my head, and the cuffs clang against the metal bed frame. Little brat cuffed me to the damn bed. "What are you doing, baby girl?"

"You think you're the only one in control here, Max?"

"Take these cuffs off me and we'll see who's in control."

"Oh, Maximo." She tuts, raking her fingernails down my chest as she rolls her hot, wet pussy over my hard cock. "You can give it, tough guy, but you can't take it. Is that it?"

"I can take whatever it is you have to offer."

"You sure about that?"

"One hundred percent." My eyes roam over her delectable body. Apart from a few scratches on her knees, there's no outward sign of yesterday, but the psychological scars will affect her much deeper than any physical wound. That sick fuck kidnapped her and tied her up. He was going to take her to Russia and force her to marry him. She stabbed him and got away, all on her own. I'm beyond fucking proud of her for that. But what if he'd gotten up and come after her again? What if we hadn't got there when we did—

I close my eyes and focus on taking deep breaths. Pushkin is in the basement, and I'll have my time with him soon enough. But first, my girl clearly has some control issues she needs to work out.

"Do you trust me, Max?" she breathes, probably mistaking my deep breaths and the scowl on my face for unease over her having me in cuffs.

I open my eyes. "Yes."

Raking her eyes down my body and licking her lips, she hums with pleasure. Her pussy is already wet as she moves over me, and I fucking love how hot she is for me. Her fingertips graze my abdomen and she scoots back, running the pad of her pointer finger over the crown of my dick and collecting the drops of glistening precum. She places that same finger into her mouth, her eyes darkening and her eyelashes fluttering as she sucks it clean. "You taste so damn good, baby," she says with a soft laugh.

"Wrap your lips around me and I'll taste even better," I groan, rocking my hips upward, rubbing my piercings over her clit and making her moan. "You like that?"

Her eyes return to mine and she bites her lip. "Not as much as you do," she says. "And I'm going to make you beg for my pussy."

Holy fuck, this woman is going to be the death of me. "You think?"

"I know, tough guy." She rocks her hips, coating my shaft

with her slick heat and grinding her sensitive pussy on me. I shift my hips, trying to slip inside her, but she pulls back, giggling.

"Take my cock, baby girl," I order. She drops her hips lower again, until I feel her wet heat on my skin. My cock throbs with the desperate need to be inside her. "Pussy or your mouth, I don't care as long as I'm inside you."

She laughs and scoots back farther, dropping her head and running her soft, wet tongue the length of my shaft, flicking the tip over each of my piercings before focusing on the one in the crown. She licks it softly, coaxing the barbell to the very edge of my skin and sending jolts of hot, searing pleasure through me.

"Fuck, Joey," I growl, pulling on the cuffs and rattling the bed frame.

She looks up at me with a wicked smile on her face. "Who owns you, Max?"

"You do, baby," I groan. "Let me get my cock in you."

"Not until you beg, tough guy."

"Please?" I drive my hips upward, trying to get inside her.

She sits back up, settling her beautiful pussy directly over my length. "That really doesn't sound like begging to me."

"Joey," I order. "Sit the fuck on my cock. Right now, baby."

"Beg me, Max," she moans, her head tipped back as she rubs herself over me. "Because I can get off just as easily like this."

Fuck me, she could too. "But how much better would it be with my cock stretching your tight cunt?"

She bites her lip, her skin flushed. She's every bit as desperate for me as I am for her, but she continues to hold out on me. "You tell me, Max. How good would it feel to slide that huge cock inside me? Fill me up until my soaking wet pussy is wrapped tight around you?"

My chest heaves with the effort of keeping my hands off her.

I need to be inside her more than I need my next breath. "Please, Joey." Now I beg. "Please ride me, baby girl."

"You want this?" She maneuvers herself until my cock presses at her entrance.

"You know I do." I drive my hips up, but she's ready for me. Pulling away, she laughs wickedly like my spoiled little brat.

But now I'm frantic for her and I can't keep this up much longer. "I'm going to tear this fucking bed in half if you don't sit on my cock, Joey."

Her narrowed eyes question whether I'm capable of carrying out my threat, but she knows without a doubt that I am. She holds my gaze and slides down, taking every inch of me, every single piercing until I'm balls deep inside her. The relief that washes over me almost makes me pass out. Her pussy squeezes me tight, shooting pleasure through every nerve in my body. My thighs and my balls are on fire, burning with the need to come inside her even as I try to hold off and enjoy this.

"Holy fuck, Max," she whimpers as her arousal slicks my cock.

"I know, baby girl. You feel so fucking good."

She rocks her hips back and forth, using my cock to stimulate her G-spot over and over again. We both teeter close to the edge. Her eyelids flutter, her mouth open, jaw slack as she chases her climax. And when she comes, she milks my cock with her ravenous cunt, drawing every drop of cum and pleasure from me as I empty myself inside her with a roar of her name.

While she struggles to catch her breath, she looks down at me, cheeks flushed from her release and her tits shuddering with each heavy breath.

"Come here," I demand, and in her compliant, post-orgasmic state, she leans forward, thinking I'm going to kiss her. Quickly lifting my head, I suck one nipple into my mouth before she can move away.

"Oh, Max," she whimpers as I release it with a wet pop and rest my head back on the pillow.

"You done?" I arch an eyebrow at her.

"Yeah," she pants, her hands planted on my chest. "Let me find those keys."

With a grin, I pop the lock on the cuffs with ease.

Her eyes widen. "W-what? How—?"

I flip her onto her back before she can finish her question, nestling myself between her thighs. Her tits jiggle against my chest as she sucks in air.

"You ever need me to give up a little control, all you have to do is ask. Okay?"

She blinks at me, her eyes wet with tears. "Okay."

"Because you fucking own me too, Joey. Every single part of me. I am and always will be all yours, baby girl."

"Fuck, Max," she breathes.

"But"—I glare at her—"if you ever cuff me in my sleep again, I will make you regret it in so many ways."

Not saying anything, she chews on her lip.

"You think that's a challenge, baby?" I press my already-hard cock against her pussy.

"Maybe."

I sink myself balls deep into her tight, wet cunt until her back arches. Throwing her head back, she gives me access to her neck, and I drag my teeth up the sweet column of her throat until I reach her ear. "Just try me."

FIFTY-ONE

JOEY

Max's hand rests on the small of my back as we walk into Dante's study, where we find him and Lorenzo deep in conversation.

"He's tough as fuck," Lorenzo says with a pleased nod that makes me think they're talking about Ash.

"Is Ash okay?" I ask.

"He'll be out of action for a few weeks, but yeah, he's going to be fine," my oldest brother confirms.

"Nothing a long vacation and some sunshine won't fix," Dante adds. "But how are you, kid?" He holds his arms wide open, inviting me in for a hug.

I step into his embrace. "I'm good, thanks."

He hums his approval.

"I'm sorry I punched you in the face," I whisper.

"Don't be." Stepping back, he runs two fingers over the cut on his lip and winks at me. "I deserved it. And I'm sorry about what I said."

I shrug. "I guess it was true." I *was* a bitch back then, but I hope both he and Lorenzo see how much I've changed.

"No," he says with a shake of his head. "You were never a bitch, Joey. Just a survivor."

Lorenzo wraps an arm around my shoulders and plants a brief peck on my cheek. "D says your right hook is something to be proud of."

Dante laughs. "Those lessons with Toni are paying off."

"Hey, I taught her how to throw a right hook," Max interjects.

"He sure did." I smile over at him. "It was lesson number one."

"Well, you did a damn good job teaching her, compagno," Dante replies, and my face flushes pink with pride.

"She's a fucking powerhouse," Max says matter-of-factly, and my cheeks flame brighter.

"Are you going to let me deal with Viktor then?" I ask, deflecting their attention.

"Not alone," Max says, and my brothers nod their agreement.

"Maybe you and Max can handle him, if that's what you want. But you don't have to. Nobody would think any less of you if you let us deal with this. We all have plenty of blood on our hands already. There's no need for you to get yours dirty too," Lorenzo adds.

"I need to do this, Loz. And I'm not scared of a little blood or doing what needs to be done. I'd have killed him in that house given half the chance."

My oldest brother gives me a subtle nod of approval. "Of course you would've, because you're a Moretti to the core, Joey."

Having their endorsement makes me feel invincible. As though they finally see me as a woman and a true member of this family rather than a little girl who needs protection.

∼

STANDING outside the room where Viktor's being held, Max asks me if I'm okay.

I've always hated the basement and the way it smells of damp and decay and death. But I guess I've changed more than I thought because right now all I can think about is getting inside that room and making Viktor Pushkin pay for everything he did to me. Everything he did to my family, to Henry and Ash —even to Monique.

I nod and lick my lips, tasting blood in the air like a snake senses its prey. I will never be anyone's prey ever again. I am Joey Moretti, hear me fucking roar. Adrenaline thunders through me as Max draws back the deadbolt. Reaching in, he flicks on the light before we step inside. A single bulb hangs from the ceiling in the center of the room, illuminating the cold concrete cell that's empty except for the Russian chained to the floor.

Viktor pushes himself to his knees, groaning and blinking in the bright light as his eyes adjust after hours and hours of nothing but pitch-black darkness.

Upon hearing us enter the room, he begins cursing in Russian, spitting words full of hatred and venom.

"Now, is that any way to speak in front of a lady?" Max says.

"She is no lady," Viktor says with a snarl, spitting at my feet. "Filthy whore."

I roll my eyes. Yeah, I'm such a filthy whore he wanted me for himself. But Max does not appreciate his outburst and he kicks Viktor full force in the stomach, causing him to double over. He groans loudly, his forehead resting on the cold concrete floor for a few seconds before he grunts and pushes himself back up. He glares at Max, his eyes bulging in their sockets and every vein in his neck tightening as he tugs at his restraints.

"You ever call her that again and I will cut out your fucking tongue. And the only reason I'm not doing it right now is because I want to hear you beg my girl for mercy when she carves you open," Max says with a satisfied smirk. Then he hands me the hunting knife from his pocket. "He's all yours, baby."

My hand trembles as I take the knife from him, but his fingertips brush mine and his touch grounds me. He winks. *You got this*, he mouths.

My hand closes around the handle of the blade, and my heart thumps wildly as I step closer to Viktor. "Hey, asshole."

He lifts his head, pulling on his chains and foaming at the mouth. "Silly little girl." He laughs loudly, showing his teeth, stained with fresh blood.

"Maybe I am, but you're the one chained up in my basement, fuckface."

"Chained!" he yells, pulling them taut. "You wouldn't dare challenge me if I was not in chains. Pathetic." He spits again and a blob of bloody saliva lands on my shoe. I feel the tension in Max even from here, but he stands back and lets me handle it, and I love him even more for it.

I circle him slowly, looking for the places he's already injured so I can use them to my advantage. "Maybe you're right about that," I admit. "Although I did beat you yesterday, didn't I?" His face turns purple with rage. "But I guess I wouldn't stand a chance against a big guy like you if you weren't chained to this floor." I already know about the knife wound beneath his left arm that I gave him, and I recognize my sister-in-law's neat stitches. I note the large purple bruises over his kidneys. The deep gash on his shoulder and the laceration to his left ear. My brothers really were gentle with him before they tossed him down here and left him for me to deal with.

I come full circle until I'm standing in front of him again. "But you *are* chained to my floor." Smiling, I slice off his left ear and toss it onto the floor at his feet. He doesn't scream or yell.

Instead he clamps his lips together, breathing heavily and trying to hold all the pain inside him.

"And I seem to remember you needing to keep me tied up. Pathetic little girl that I am," I say with a shrug.

"Bitch," he eventually spits. "You were promised to me."

Max growls loudly from behind me, but I remain focused on Viktor. "But I was never my father's to give away," I remind him, slicing through the middle of his left nipple and causing fresh blood to run down his chest.

He cries out, but the sound doesn't affect me. I thought it would, but it doesn't even make me flicker. I think about Monique and how he manipulated her. How scared my family and Max must have been when this piece of shit took me. Ash in the hospital. And Henry who will never get to take his own revenge. It all bubbles inside me like a tiny volcano of rage. I force the knife into the freshly stitched wound beneath his armpit, and this time he screams. "That was for Ash, you asshole."

He lunges for me, but his chains hold him back. Max warned me about this, about how adrenaline and survival instinct kick in and can give someone an unexpected burst of energy. Asshole had that coming. Then I picture Henry's face. Grumpy but sweeter than sugar. Henry who was killed just because he was protecting me.

"And this"—I plunge the knife into Viktor's chest—"is for Henry, you twisted sick fuck."

He roars with anger and pain and defeat, and I take a few steps back, bumping into Max. He wraps his arms around me, and I realize I'm trembling.

"You're doing so good, baby," he says against my ear. "But this man has been trained to endure physical pain. I've got a much better way to hurt him. You think you're up for it?"

I stare at the monster on the floor. "Yes."

CHAPTER
FIFTY-TWO

MAX

"My girl is really something, huh?" I ask Viktor as he lifts his head again, his eyes narrowed. Blood pours from the wounds in his chest and the wound on his head where his ear used to be.

He spits blood onto the floor. "She was promised to me." I have to admit it, the guy has balls the size of boulders and he can handle pain better than most of the men I've tortured. "That makes her mine."

I grab hold of his hair, tipping his head back. "Yours? You really think so?"

"Mine!" he snaps, his body shaking as he tries to wrench out of my grip and jerks against the chains that bind him.

"No, Viktor." Walking over to my girl, I grab her by the hips and yank her toward me. "She is mine. All fucking mine." My cock is already semihard from watching Joey using that knife on Viktor, but at the feel of her body brushing against me, it stiffens like an iron bar. "Every fucking inch of her. Isn't that right, baby girl?"

"Yes. All yours, Max," she says sweetly, throwing our captive a wicked grin.

He curses in Russian while I place my hand beneath her dress and slide it into her panties, making her eyes darken with heat. "Every." I force my hand further into her underwear. "Fucking." I pinch her clit between my fingers, and she moans loudly. "Bit of her."

"Oh, fuck, Max," she hisses, grinding herself on my fingers.

I push her back against the wall and drop to my knees, tugging her dress up and pulling her panties off before I stuff them into my pocket. Satisfied that my back obscures Viktor's view of her, I spread her thighs wider and brush my lips over her waxed mound. She smells so fucking good. So ready for me. Always ready for me. Viktor curses in Russian again and spits my name as though it's poison.

I slip two fingers between her folds, smiling when I find her dripping for me. Using the pads of my thumbs, I part her wet lips, exposing the swollen bud of sensitive flesh. Her scent is thick in the small windowless room, and I wonder if Viktor can smell her. I certainly fucking hope he can. I want him to know exactly what he's missing before he dies.

Viktor's chains rattle as he struggles to free himself, but all my attention is on my girl. "Hey, Viktor, you're about to get to watch while I eat what's *mine*."

"I need you, Max," Joey groans.

She threads her fingers through my hair, pulling my face closer until she can get my mouth where she wants me. My naughty little slut.

"I know, baby." I flick her clit with my tongue and her legs tremble. "Shall we show Viktor how hard my girl can come for me?"

"Fuck, yeah." She grinds that beautiful pussy on my mouth, but I can't get enough of her like this. I need to spread her wider.

"Hold on to me, baby girl, I'm gonna lift you up, okay?"

"Uh-huh," she pants.

I grab her hips and lift her until she's seated on my shoulders with her back pressed against the wall.

Much fucking better. I suck on her sweet, swollen flesh and her cum coats my lips and tongue, making my cock throb. "You taste fucking incredible, baby."

"You're so good at that, Max," she moans. "So good."

I murmur against her skin, letting her taste and scent flood my senses as I eat her sweet pussy. I could do this every minute of every day and never get enough of her.

"Holy fu-oh!" she cries, coming all over my tongue. She pulls at my hair and gyrates on my face, rubbing out the last of her orgasm. But it's not enough. I'm desperate for her. I lower her to the floor and stand up, pulling my cock out of my sweatpants.

Viktor shouts obscenities, but I tune him out. This might have been about him a few minutes ago—about showing him what he'll never have and teaching him a lesson for daring to touch what belongs to me—but now it's only about her and the burning need to be inside her.

"Fuck me, Max," she pleads.

I wrap her legs around my waist and sink inside her, giving her every single inch. Her breath hitches and her eyes flutter closed as she squeezes around me, sucking me deeper.

"Look at me when I'm fucking you, baby," I growl. Her eyes lock on mine and I smile at her. She's fucking perfect. "That's my good fucking girl."

"Yes, Max," she groans, raking her nails down my back. "I'm your good girl."

"Tell this thick fuck who you belong to, baby," I grunt as I slam into her, nailing her against the wall with each thrust.

"Yours, Max DiMarco. I'm y-yours," she gasps as I roll my

hips, rubbing the tip of my cock and my piercing over her G-spot.

"Damn fucking right you are," I groan as heat sears through my thighs and gut, coiling in my balls as I drive harder and come inside her—hot, heavy, and all-fucking-consuming, I spill every drop I have into her cunt.

"Fuck yes, Max," she rocks her hips, chasing her own orgasm as I grind mine into her. I bury my face in her neck, sinking my teeth into her skin and pushing my cock deeper and allowing her to get herself off. When she comes a few seconds later, her pussy clamps around my cock like she'll never let me go.

I keep her legs wrapped around me, my face buried in the crook of her neck and my cock deep in her pussy as I catch my breath. My heart beats wildly against hers and she runs her fingers through my hair. I don't want to pull out of her. I'd much rather carry her out of here like this and go on fucking her for the rest of the day and night, but Viktor needs to die first. The sound of his constant grumbling and cursing is almost drowned out by the blood pounding in my ears.

When I can breathe normally, I pull my dick out of her and the rush of cum that comes with it makes her blush. I catch some on my fingers and push it back inside her before bringing my fingers to her lips. "Open."

She parts those juicy pink lips and I slip my cum-soaked fingers inside her mouth. Her tongue swirls over my skin as she cleans up every drop. And when I pull my fingers free, I replace them with my tongue, tasting us both as I kiss her hard. By the time I pull back, she's panting and her dark eyes are full of fire. I have to look away and remind myself that we have a job to do. I tuck my cock into my pants and pull her dress down so Viktor won't see her bare pussy. That's only for me.

I grab the knife from the floor. "Are you done with him, baby? You get all you needed?"

She glances at him, her nose wrinkled in disgust and one hand on her hip. She looks every inch the Mafia princess she was born to be. No, fuck that princess nonsense. She's a queen —my fucking queen.

"Yeah. Take care of him for me, would you, baby? Then we can get out of here."

"My pleasure." I wink. I could drag this out for a few more hours—days even. The old me would have. But the old me didn't have something much better to do with my time. I walk over to him, grabbing a handful of his hair and yanking his head back again.

"Pig!" He spits at me.

"Goodbye, Viktor." I slice his neck from ear to ear and let his head roll back so he can choke on his blood. Just to make sure my girl has no doubt that this piece of shit will never bother her again, I stick the tip of my knife into the wound in his gullet and pull out his tongue until it protrudes through the gaping hole in his neck like a tie.

When I look at her, she's watching him twitch while the life drains from his body, her lips stretched in a satisfied smile. Not even a flicker of unease or discomfort on her beautiful face. That's my fucking girl.

FIFTY-THREE

I smile as I look at the faces gathered around the dining table. Kristin and her father are still here, and Vito's almost fully recovered now. Anya sits close to Lorenzo, and he has a protective arm draped around the back of her chair but not on her shoulder. I think she might buckle under the weight of it now. Dante and Kat sit close, constantly touching each other. They're so sweet together. And then there's my Max. He sits beside me with his hand resting possessively on my thigh.

While everyone is discussing plans for Gabriella's christening in a few days, Max leans close to me, his lips pressed at my ear and his warm breath sending goosebumps prickling along my forearms. "I forgot to tell you how fucking beautiful you look tonight, baby girl."

My cheeks flush pink at his praise. I didn't realize we were having company tonight, so I'm dressed in a pair of ripped jeans and a tank top. My hair is piled on top of my head in a messy bun and I don't have a scrap of make up on, but Max makes me feel beautiful no matter what. "Thank you," I whisper.

His hand slides down my thigh until it settles on my knee,

which is a much safer place for it to be when we're in this room, but I pout anyway, which makes him laugh softly. "My hands will be exactly where you want them later, baby. Promise," he whispers.

"I'm gonna hold you to that, DiMarco."

He gives me a soft kiss on the cheek and rejoins the conversation without missing a beat.

Dmitri and Kyzen are here tonight too, and while they're not blood, they've been here so often the past few weeks, they've practically become part of the furniture. Our two families have formed a solid alliance that my brothers seem confident will be good for us all.

Once dinner is over, Dante abruptly returns the conversation to business. "Pushkin is dealt with?" he asks Dmitri.

Dmitri gives a solemn nod. "I know you wanted to deal with him yourself, but he was expecting us. He would have killed Kyzen, and I had to take the shot."

Dante nods his understanding. He would have done the same if it had been Lorenzo.

"But we have made it clear that he was killed in revenge for the murder of your father and that we took him out as a sign of respect for you."

"It's not ideal. I would have preferred to deal with him myself, but we can work with it," Lorenzo replies.

Kyzen leans forward. "Also, Ivan was killed in Russia last night. My cousin put a bullet in his head. I've seen the pictures. He is dead."

"Then there's no further challenge to your leadership?" Max asks.

Dmitri and Kyzen nod.

"Good. No more Pushkins." Dante smiles and raises his glass of whiskey in a toast that we all join.

Shifting the conversation, Lorenzo turns to face Max's uncle. "What's the plan for you and Kristin now?"

"We thought we might head back to Jersey. Now that there's no longer a threat from the Pushkins, I don't see why we can't go back to our old lives." He looks over at his daughter who nods excitedly. I figure she's more than keen to get back to her old life and try to find her baby daddy while she's at it. "We'll be leaving the day after tomorrow if you don't mind putting us up until then?"

"Of course. Any family of Max's is welcome here," Lorenzo says.

"Thank you for everything you've all done for us." Kristin's eyes shine with unshed tears. "It means so much. And I know it was awful the way we met, but I'm still glad that we did."

"Me too," I agree, and she smiles at me.

"Especially you, Max. I had no idea I needed a big brother until I found you."

Max laughs. "Well, you're not all bad, sis."

Vito looks down at the table and Kristin puts an arm around him. "It's okay, Dad. I understand why you did what you did."

"It's water under the bridge now, right?" Max adds.

Vito looks up at his nephew. "You are a more gracious man than I, Maximo," he says as a tear rolls down his cheek. "Your parents would have been very proud of the man you've become."

Max's grip on my thigh tightens, but he keeps a faint smile on his face. Before the awkwardness becomes unbearable, Dante suggests drinks in his study. I go to stand but Max takes my hand and pulls me back down, indicating I should stay in my seat, so I remain at the table and watch everyone else file out of the room. Dante turns and looks at Max and me before he leaves. The look he shares with Max must appease him because he walks out of the room, closing the door behind him.

"Come here, baby girl," Max says as soon as we're alone, lifting me onto his lap until I'm straddling him.

"Someone could come back in here."

"They won't," he assures me. "Besides we're not doing anything wrong."

I bite my lip but wrap my arms around his neck. His cock is already getting harder. "Hmm. Not yet."

His eyes narrow as he stares into mine. "Not now, Joey."

I swallow the hurt that unexpectedly bubbles up at his rejection, but he brushes his fingertips over my cheek before I can voice my annoyance. "I just wanted to check in with you," he says softly.

I frown at him. "Check in with me? Why?"

"Because we killed a man today."

I roll my eyes. More sexist bullshit! I'm about to shuffle off his lap, but he tightens his arms around my waist, holding me in place. "Just because I'm a g—"

"No," he says with an exasperated sigh. "Because I fucking love you, Joey. You don't think I checked in with your brothers the first time they took a life?"

"You did?"

"Of course I fucking did. Dante threw up all over my shoes the first time he killed someone."

I blink at him. "He did?"

"Yeah. Had to throw them away and the fucker still hasn't replaced them sixteen years later."

I do that math in my head. Dante was only fifteen when he first killed a man? Sadly, that doesn't surprise me. The fact that he threw up after certainly does though. He's like ice when it comes to business, but I guess he wasn't always that way.

"I'm sorry, Max. I guess the defensive thing is kind of my default response."

"Hmm," he murmurs as he presses his forehead against

mine. "For the sake of your beautiful ass, I suggest you find another one soon, baby girl, or you'll be spending a whole lot of your time wincing when you sit down."

I cannot stop the soft moan that escapes my lips at the mere thought of constant spankings from Max, and it makes him laugh. "But you like the sound of that, don't you?" His deep, velvety tone melts my insides.

"Yes," I admit, rocking my hips against him and delighting in the delicious friction caused by the seam of my jeans and his hard cock.

He runs his nose over my jawline and an animalistic groan rumbles through his chest. "What the fuck am I going to do with you, Joey?"

I run my fingers though his hair, tugging his head back so I can stare into his dark eyes. "Spank me? Fuck me? Spread me out on this dining table and eat my pussy until I scream? I mean the possibilities are endless."

Those dark eyes blaze with fire now and I can tell he's considering all those options right now. But the man has way too much self-control for my liking. "Tell me how you're doing, baby girl?"

"I'm okay, Max. I promise," I assure him. I may not have killed a man before, and technically I didn't today—although that doesn't make me any less responsible for his death—but I was born and raised a Moretti and this life is in my blood as much as it's in my brothers'. As much as it's in Max's.

He brushes my hair back from my face. "You sure? Because it's okay not to be. I'm right here for whatever you need."

"I know that, but I'm okay. Are you?"

He frowns at me.

I arch an eyebrow at him. "I'm allowed to be concerned about you too, aren't I?"

"Of course you are." A smile tugs at the corners of his lips.

"So, are you okay? You need me to do anything to make you feel better?" I whisper.

"Oh, there are many things, baby," he says with a groan. Standing, he sets me on my feet. "But not right now." Then he gives me a soft kiss on my forehead. "We should join the others before your brothers come in here to check on us."

"You're such a tease." I giggle as we walk out of the room, earning myself a hard smack on my ass. God, I am the happiest girl in the freaking world right now.

FIFTY-FOUR

MAX

"**M**ax? You have a minute?" Dmitri asks me quietly as we head out of Dante and Lorenzo's study.

"Sure." I step aside with him while the others disappear down the hallway.

"I found out who your sister's boyfriend is."

"Yeah?"

"You heard of the Mikhailovs in New York?"

I nod. Vlad Mikhailov was the second-in-command to Alexie Ivanov. His boss got taken out by the Irish, and despite the rumor that Alexie's daughter, Jessica, is still alive and should've taken over the reins, Vlad stepped up instead. He's well respected and runs the New York branch of the Bratva much better than his predecessor ever did. His sons are his trusted enforcers, and their reputations as vicious and ruthless men precede them.

"Well, Jakob is Vlad's son."

"His son?"

"Yes, and apparently he's been pining for his Italian princess since she left. He's been trying to find her this whole time, but he didn't know about Vito's connection to Chicago, so he hasn't looked in this direction."

"Wow. Seems like our alliance with the Bratva keeps getting stronger, eh?"

"Seems like," he says with a smile. "And while Jakob's enemies might describe him as an ..." He rubs his jaw, searching for the right word.

"Animal?" I offer.

Chuckling, he nods. "But my sources tell me he's respected among his peers. Both he and his brothers even managed an alliance with the Irish, and we know that would not be easy."

"The Irish who took out their father's former boss and allowed him to step into the role," I remind him.

"Yeah, but they're also the same men who married the true Bratva heir, Jessica Ivanov, although she goes by Jessie Ryan now. They do their best to keep her identity a secret and have every reason to cut all ties with the Mikhailovs, but they haven't."

"They're all married to her?"

He nods. "It's a complicated setup."

"Sounds it."

"If nothing else, a friend of the Ryans is a good ally to have, Maximo. They own half of New York."

"You're suggesting I use my sister to make connections in New York?"

"No." He laughs. "I'm saying that Jakob Mikhailov is a solid guy, despite his reputation, and that there could be much worse families for your sister to become a part of."

"Noted. And thanks, Dmitri."

"You're welcome, my friend."

∿

STARING AT THE CEILING, I hold Joey in my arms. Her leg drapes over my stomach, her sweet pussy resting on my hip. This is my favorite position in the whole world. Well, almost—having her bent over while I'm balls deep inside her is probably my all-time favorite. But this comes in a pretty close second. Freshly fucked and sleepy, snuggling into me like I'm her personal pillow.

I grab her chin and angle her head up so I can look at her. "I need to talk to you about something, baby."

That cute little spot between her eyebrows pinches together with a confused frown. "What is it?"

"I love being here with you and I know that this is where we needed to be, but now that Kristin is heading back home and things are a lot more settled ..."

"Yeah?"

"I have a perfectly safe and functional apartment in the city. I know we have Gabriella's christening in a few days, but after that, I want to go home."

She blinks a few times. "Oh, I see," she whispers. "I can stay over though, right?"

Shaking my head, I laugh softly. "No, baby girl. I'm not leaving here without you."

Her frown deepens.

"You think I could bear to spend even a single night away from this beautiful body?" I skim my hand over her perfect ass to emphasize my point. "I want you to come with me."

She pushes herself up, resting her forearms on my chest. "Like move in with you?"

"Yes."

"For real?"

"Can you think of a better alternative? I can't be apart from you, but I'm over having to hold back when I fuck you, Joey."

She arches one eyebrow. "This has been you holding back?"

349

I brush her hair back from her face and grin wickedly. "There's so much I want to do with and to you that I can't do in your brothers' house. And it's not all sex related, baby. I want to eat breakfast with you—granted, you will be naked, but still. I want to watch TV with you. While you're naked. Cook dinner with you—"

"While I'm naked?"

I wink at her. "You catch on quick, baby girl. But I'm serious about this, I just want to be with you. I want to share every part of my life with you."

"I want to be with you too, Max. It just seems like such a big step. What if I drive you crazy?"

"You do drive me crazy," I remind her.

"True," she says, giggling. "But I will miss Gabs. And Anya and Kat. And even my jackass brothers."

"I know."

"Not as much as I'd miss you though."

Thank fuck for that.

"Can we visit every day?"

"Every day," I assure her.

"But then every night ...?" She chews on her bottom lip, fluttering her eyelashes and making my cock twitch.

"You're all mine."

FIFTY-FIVE

MAX

"He's the one who should be nervous, Kristin." My little sister sits in the chair beside me, fidgeting with her clothes.

"You think?" She laughs nervously. "What do I say, Max? Oh, hey, I know we haven't spoken for six months and I just disappeared without a trace, but I'm having your baby."

I look down at her huge pregnant belly and lift my eyebrows. "I think he'll figure out that last part fairly quickly."

She swats me on the arm. "Stop!"

"When he gets here, I'll give you two some privacy, but I'll be right at the next table if you need me."

"I won't need you." She rolls her eyes. "Jakob's a sweetheart."

I almost choke on fresh air. That's definitely not what I've heard. But men like him—men like me—can still be good fathers and husbands. I'm willing to give him the benefit of the doubt, which is why after Dmitri gave me his name, I contacted him and arranged this meeting.

Suddenly, Kristin grabs hold of my arm. "It's him," she whispers. I look up to see a tall, heavyset guy with dark hair and a thick beard walk into the empty restaurant. His two guards hang back by the door, and as soon as his eyes meet hers, I get it. I understand why my sister insisted he would never do anything to hurt her because he looks at her the same way I look at my girl.

I stand and greet him first. "Jakob?"

"Maximo?" He holds out his hand and I shake it.

"I'll leave you both to talk." I turn to Kristin and give her a soft kiss on the cheek before I whisper, "Say the word and he's dead."

"Stop it." She laughs, pushing me away and looking at Jakob.

I shake my head and take a seat at a table a few feet away. They stand and look at each other for several seconds.

"I'm sorry. My dad ... he ..." she starts to ramble.

"I know. They told me," he replies in a thick Russian accent.

She rubs a hand over her swollen belly.

"It's mine?" he asks, and I wince at the hurt on her face. But what else is the guy supposed to say? He hasn't seen her for six months.

"Of course he's yours."

"He?"

"It's a boy, yeah." She looks down at the floor, and I shake my head. Jakob's blowing this, and I'm going to be forced to slap some sense into him if he doesn't up his game soon.

He says something in Russian, and the words must mean something to her because she looks up and smiles. And then she's in his arms and he's kissing her like there's no one else in the room.

Uncomfortable, I look away, feeling like a voyeur and making a mental note to limit Joey's and my displays of affection in front of her brothers. Well, I'll try at least, but it's too damn hard to keep my hands off her.

When I look up, they're still kissing, so I clear my throat to remind them that I'm still here. Fortunately they pull apart and sit down, spending the next hour talking and smiling and staring into each other's eyes. Even a blind man could see these two are made for each other.

"Thank you for looking after Kristin and arranging this, Maximo," Jakob says as he gets ready to leave the restaurant.

"Any time," I assure him.

He looks back at my little sister. "I'm not leaving here without you both. I'll be staying in Chicago until you agree to come home with me."

Kristin blushes to the roots of her hair. "I know. But I have to speak to my father. And you have to meet him. We have lots to organize."

Jakob nods. "Come to my hotel later. You and your father. We can talk about everything?"

"Okay. We can do that," she agrees, a huge smile on her face.

"I'll be outside in the car." With a nod to them both, I walk away, giving them privacy to say their goodbyes.

Stepping outside into the sunshine, I smile. I'm glad Kristin was right about him. Whatever else he may be, he seems to adore her. That's all I can ask, not that I have much say in her life given that I've only known her for a few weeks. But I guess my relationship with Joey has taught me that the people we would choose for those we care about aren't necessarily the people they belong with.

Kristin climbs into the car a few moments later, a radiant smile lighting up her face.

I laugh as I start the engine. "That went well then?"

"Better than well, Max! He wants me and the baby to live with him in New York. He has his own apartment. His brother lives there as well, but the place is huge and we won't be in his way, and he's fine about having a baby there. And Jakob is super excited about the baby too ..." She continues to ramble excitedly for the entire ride home, talking about their plans for the future and how happy she is.

"I'm happy for you, sis."

"You are?"

"Of course I am."

"Did you like him, Max? It means a lot to me that you do."

It means a lot to me that she cares about my opinion. "I do," I admit. "But I'm going to miss you when you go to New York."

"I'll miss you too. But you and Joey will come visit, right? I mean you'll have to come meet your nephew."

I grin over at her. "Try and stop us."

Kristin goes to find her father when we get back to the house, and I shower and change into my suit. It's Gabriella's christening day and the house is a flurry of activity. Joey's busy organizing caterers and balloons for the party afterward, and I head down to the garden to find her.

"Maximo?" Anya's soft voice calls as I pass the den.

"Everything okay?" I ask as I walk toward her. She's dressed in a soft pink dress with her hair and makeup done, but she still looks so pale and weak that it stops me in my tracks. With everything going on, I haven't seen much of her these past few weeks, and I regret that. Anya is a woman I deeply admire and respect. Life is too fucking cruel sometimes.

"I need to ask you a favor," she says with a smile that is still capable of lighting up a room. Slipping into the den, she beckons me to follow.

"Of course. What is it?"

I watch her perch on the edge of the sofa, my curiosity well and truly piqued. I'm surprised she's even here alone. It's rare that Lorenzo isn't by her side these days.

"Won't you sit?" she asks.

Unable to figure out what she could possibly want to talk to me about, I sit across from her. She takes a sip from the glass of water on the table beside her. Reaching under the sofa cushion, she grabs a small white envelope and hands it to me. It has Lorenzo's name written on the front in her delicate hand-writing.

"What is this?"

"It's for Lorenzo."

"Yeah, I can see that, so why are you giving it to me?"

"It's a letter," she says softly, her eyes brimming with tears. "For after I'm gone."

Jesus, fuck! "Anya. Don't talk like that—"

"Maximo!" she admonishes me. "I am dying. We all know it. There is no miracle cure around the corner. In a few months' time, I won't be here. That's the sad truth, but I've come to accept it." She gives a slight shrug of her shoulders. Even talking about her own death, she's dignified and resilient.

"But this ..." I hold up the letter.

"If I give it to him myself, he'll tear it up." She shakes her head. "Besides, it is not for him to read yet."

"When should he read it?"

"That's for you to decide. I trust you to make that call."

A heavy weight presses on my chest. "How will I know that, Anya?"

"It's not sealed. Read it."

I open my mouth, but no words come out.

"Please, Maximo?"

"Why not Joey? Or Kat? Or Dante?"

She shakes her head. "They're too close to him. They won't be able to bear his pain and they'll give in too soon just to make him feel better. It will all be wasted."

"And you think that I can stand to see him hurting? They should be the ones, Anya. Not me," I argue. Staring at her, I silently plead for her to reconsider. I don't want this fucking letter. Already it feels like a lead weight around my neck. How the fuck do I know when the right time is? I don't understand why I'm the one being trusted with something as important as whatever this is.

"You are the right man, Maximo. You love him like a brother, but you see him for the man he is and the man he can be. Read the letter, and then one day I hope you will know when to give it to him."

"I-I can't read your private letter to him. It's fucking wrong."

She frowns. "It's not private if I give you permission."

"Anya? Please? This feels too important. What if I fuck it up?"

Her frown shifts into a beautiful smile. "You won't. I promise you that."

I stare at her, the white envelope scorching my hand. I don't want this, but what choice do I have?

Anya stands and brushes the creases from her dress. "Read it now and we will never speak of it again. You will know when the time is right."

"Anya?"

"Promise me you will give it to him when the time is right, Max."

I stare at her face, etched with anguish and pain—not for herself though, never for her. It's all for him. He will break when she dies. He will lose himself, and who knows if he'll ever recover? "I promise."

"Thank you," she whispers, and then she walks out of the room, leaving me alone.

My fingers actually tremble when I unfold the top of the envelope. Carefully, I pull out the pale pink pages, unfurling

356

them gently so I don't damage the precious contents in any way.

Sitting back on the sofa, I read the words a dying woman wrote to the man she loves more than anything in the world. I am not an emotional man and I never have been, but tears stream down my face as I accept the enormity of what she's asked me to do.

FIFTY-SIX

JOEY

I slick on a final coat of lipstick right as Max storms into my bedroom. I figure he's here to tell me that we need to leave and I'm about to tell him I'm almost done, but I'm distracted by how good he looks in his suit. I mean he looks good in anything, but there's just something about this man in a finely tailored suit that makes me want him to nail me into next week.

He strides over and stops directly in front of me. His eyes look a little red and his brow is furrowed in a frown, but like he's angry at the whole world rather than at me.

"Everything okay?" I ask.

"I need to fuck you," he breathes, dropping his head and running his lips over my neck.

My body shivers in anticipation. "We can't. The cars will be leaving in fifteen minutes."

"I need to fuck you, baby girl," he repeats, gliding his hands over my hips and palming my ass.

I giggle, slapping his hands away but he's undeterred. "There's no time." He pushes me backward until I'm pressed against the wall.

"I'm not asking, Joey," he growls, his hot breath sending a shiver of pleasure up my spine.

He tugs my dress up, and I almost lose my breath and my resolve. "Max, It's Gabriella's christening day. We're her godparents. I can't stand at the front of the church with your cum dripping out of me," I whisper as I wrap my arms around his neck.

"Your panties will soak it up."

I bite my lip as his hands tug at the expensive fabric and he drags his teeth over the sensitive skin of my neck.

"I'm not wearing any." My cheeks flush with heat.

That certainly gets his attention. He stops and stares into my eyes. "You intended to go to church with no panties on?"

"Yeah."

"Such a naughty little slut." Frenzied, he yanks my dress all the way up until it bunches around my waist. His hand gropes between my thighs, his fingers sliding through my folds and making me groan.

"Max. What are you doing?"

"I already told you. I need to fuck you." He unzips his pants and frees his thick cock.

"And I said there's not enough time."

He presses his lips to my ear, his beard tickling my skin. "And I told you"—he lifts my legs and wraps them around his waist—"that I'm not asking." As the final word leaves his mouth, he drives into me, making me gasp for breath. My arousal coats him as he rubs his piercing over my G-spot. I groan loudly, like the needy slut he makes me.

I feel every single piercing as he slowly pulls out before driving into me again, nailing me against the wall.

"Max," I whimper, wrapping my legs tightly around him as my pussy sucks him deeper.

"Fuck. That's it." He hisses a breath and rests his forehead against mine. "This is all I need, baby girl."

I place my hands on his face, trying to focus on his dark brown eyes as he fucks me so hard mine want to roll back in my head. "You couldn't have waited like two more hours though?" I gasp as he rocks into me.

"Couldn't wait two more fucking seconds." He hammers deeper, hitting my G-spot over and over again.

I bite down on my lip, stifling another moan. "Then you'd better hurry. Dante will be pissed if we keep him waiting, and he'll take one look at my face and know what we were doing."

Grabbing my throat with one hand, he squeezes gently as he pins me to the wall with deep, punishing thrusts. His other hand slips between us, his fingertips working my clit. "Then I'm gonna need you to come for me, because we're not leaving until you do."

"You don't have t—" He pinches my clit and squeezes my throat, cutting off my sentence. Shockwaves of pleasure rocket through my core.

"You'll come on my cock or we don't leave this room, Joey."

There's something in his eyes, something I can't quite figure out. All I know is that he needs me right now, and I love being what he needs. Giving him whatever he needs, whenever he needs it, just like he does for me.

I nod as much as I can, and he releases his grip on my throat, allowing me to suck in a deep breath. He presses his forehead against mine. "I love you so fucking much, baby girl. I need you so fucking much." He grinds the words out as though they pain him.

I whimper as the first waves of my climax start to roll through my core. "I love you too, Max."

"You coming for me?"

"Y-yes," I moan.

"Good fucking girl." He thrusts into me with each word, sending us both over the edge into sweet oblivion. When he's done, he lowers my legs to the floor and uses his pocket square to wipe between my thighs.

I giggle. "You're such a gentleman."

He puts the cum-stained fabric back in his pocket, making me blush.

"I think you'll still need to wear some panties though or you'll have a wet patch on the ass of your beautiful dress when you get out of the car," he says, smirking.

"I'll grab some." I wrap my arms around his neck and pull him close. "Are you sure everything's okay?"

"Everything's perfect, baby girl," he assures me.

I arch an eyebrow at him. "So what was that?"

"I hadn't felt your pussy squeeze my cock for almost twelve hours. I wanted to make sure I hadn't forgotten what it felt like." He winks at me and takes my breath away. This man has no right to be as goddamn hot as he is.

"Don't lie to me, Maximo."

He pushes his body against mine, pressing me into the wall again. "I'm not lying, Joey. Sometimes I get an overwhelming urge to fuck you, is all."

"Oh?" I chew on my lip.

"Oh." He kisses me hard, stealing all the air from my lungs, and I melt into him, giving him everything I am.

CHAPTER
FIFTY-SEVEN
JOEY—FOUR WEEKS LATER

"Joey?" Max's voice echoes through the apartment.

"In here," I call out as I survey my handiwork.

A few seconds later, he walks into the bedroom.

"Dammit, baby," he groans.

"I hope you don't mind, I bought some new things," I say, looking at the new throw, cushions, and vanity with the huge mirror that I ordered for our bedroom. Everything was delivered about an hour ago, and I've spent my time since arranging all my things. Max said I could do whatever I wanted to make the apartment feel more like home, and I missed having a place to sit and do my makeup in the mornings.

"I'm not talking about the things, baby girl," he says as he steps up behind me, sliding his cool hands over my hips and bare stomach and making me shiver. "Tell me you didn't take the delivery wearing these?" He snaps the band of my pink panties, which is all I'm currently wearing.

I lean against him, enjoying his hard muscles against my back. "Well, of course I was wearing these." I giggle and rub my ass against him, feeling his cock grow hard. A possessive growl rumbles in his throat, making me laugh harder. "But obviously I

362

had all my other clothes on then too. I only took them off fifteen minutes ago."

He dusts his lips over my neck, making me shiver. "Because you knew I was on my way home?"

"Yes."

"Good girl, greeting me in your panties." He nips my neck, slipping one hand into them. "Although I believe we agreed that naked is my preferred choice."

I shrug. "I can't always give you everything you want. What would be the fun of that?"

"Hmm. Lucky for you these happen to be my favorite panties of yours.".

"They are?" I know they are. They're vibrant pink and have a frill on the butt, which drives Max wild for some reason.

"Mmhmm. They showcase your incredible little ass to perfection." He circles a finger over my clit and wetness pools in my core. "And everything looks great. I'm glad you finally got yourself a vanity too."

"Thank you. I'm glad you like it."

"I like that more of your things are here, baby girl. This is your home too."

"Our home," I whisper as I grind against his hand.

"My little slut need taking care of?"

"Yeah." I always need taking care of. The man fucks me at least three times a day, and I still can't get enough. I crave him constantly. I'm not happy when he's around unless his hands are on me. The week after I moved in, I got my period and was so annoyed because I thought it would mean we couldn't have sex for a few days. But Max wasn't the slightest bit bothered, and I learned that orgasms, especially the ones he gives me with his fingers, are the perfect cure for cramps. Go figure.

He pushes a finger inside me, and I hiss out a breath as a rush of heat slicks his hand. "How was your day, baby?"

"G-good. I found the casino a new cleaning company that ..." My head drops back on his shoulder when he adds a second finger. Holy fuck, he's a magician with those hands.

He prompts me to continue. "That?"

"They pay their employees a fair wage and have health insurance. They're much better than the company the previous owners ..." My thighs tremble as he rubs the heel of his palm against my clit while thrusting his fingers in and out of me. "Had in place."

"You're a good boss, Joey."

That makes me smile. Kat cleaned offices for a while after she left her job as a nurse, and I know how hard she worked. Plus, it's important to me that every single person my family employs has decent pay and benefits. It's not like we can't afford it. And treating employees well fosters loyalty and hard work.

"And afterward I went with Kat to her prenatal checkup, then I watched some TV with Anya and read her a little William Blake."

"You're a good sister too, baby." He adds a third finger, and my knees buckle but he holds me up. "Your cunt is so fucking tight. I have no idea how you're able to take my cock the way you do."

"Oh, god." My orgasm is only a breath away. "How was y-your day?"

"Good. Pretty uneventful. Although I broke someone's hand because he gave your brother the finger."

"W-which one?"

"The middle one." He chuckles as he twists his inside me, causing specks of light to cloud my vision.

"I m-meant which brother, asshooo—" My orgasm washes over me, stealing my ability to finish the sentence.

364

"That was close, baby girl. You almost called me an asshole."

Panting to catch my breath, I giggle. "No, I was just coming."

"Hmm," he murmurs. "I need you naked."

Crouching down, he shoves my panties down my legs, and I step out of them. Within seconds, he has me pressed against the window, and I shiver at the sensation of cool glass on my warm skin. My stiff nipples brush against the hard surface, making me moan.

"You see that?" Max asks, his hot mouth brushing my ear as he unzips his pants. "Look at this city while I fuck you. The city that your family owns. Does that make you feel powerful?"

I push my ass back against him, feeling his hard length against the seam of my ass. "Not as powerful as knowing how desperate you are to fuck me."

A dark laugh rumbles through his chest. "Careful, baby girl," he warns.

Then he sinks into me, and I moan his name, relieved to be full of him. My body aches unless he's inside me.

"You like being fucked while the city watches you, Joey?" he asks, even though nobody can see through these windows.

"I'd let you fuck me anywhere in front of anyone, Max."

"Fuck, baby." He drives into me, lifting me off my feet with the force of his thrusts. "Such a naughty slut for me, aren't you?"

"Yes."

"So wet for me too. You hear that pussy slurping on my cock?"

"Y-yes."

He places his palms flat against the window. "Play with yourself. Let this city watch you come for me."

Reaching down, I rub my clit while Max sucks and nibbles

on my neck and fucks me against the glass. The muscles in his thighs and abs tense as he nears the edge.

"You gonna show this city how hard you make me come, Max?" I tease him, pressing more firmly on my clit as he picks up his pace.

"Damn right, baby girl," he says, yanking my hand away so he can take over. The pads of two thick fingers circle my clit while he rolls his hips, dragging that barbell on the crown of his cock over the sweet spot inside me.

"Fuck, Max."

"Your cunt takes my cock so fucking well. Fuck!" He bites down on my neck as he fills me with his cum, bringing me along with him. My climax bursts through me and I squirt all over his cock and his hand, splattering the window too. At one time, I probably would have felt embarrassed, now it's just part of living with my very own kinky sexual genius.

He lets out an exaggerated sigh. "I'm gonna have to clean those windows again."

"You could stop fucking me against them," I suggest.

"Not a fucking chance, baby."

We lie in bed facing each other, Max still in his shirt and pants and me completely naked—just the way he likes me.

"I spoke to Kristin today too."

"You did?" he asks.

"Yeah. She said she's gotten so fat that Jakob has to help her put her sneakers on. She can't wait for the baby to arrive."

"Well, it shouldn't be much longer for her," he says with a soft smile.

"She thinks Jakob is going to propose."

"He is."

"How do you know that?"

"He told me."

"You think she'll say yes?"

"I don't think Jakob will take no for an answer if she doesn't."

"Probably not," I agree.

He goes quiet, and I wonder what he's thinking about. Max never wants to get married. He told me that once at Lorenzo's wedding, although that was a long time ago. But he told me again at Dante's, when he'd drunk too much whiskey, and that was only last year. I guess people can change their minds though, right? Because I told him I'd never get married either. I had no desire to do the whole settling down thing. I wanted to experience freedom and explore my options, but Max gives me an entirely different type of freedom. One that lets me be exactly who I am with no judgment or constraints.

"Where are you, baby girl?" he asks, dusting his fingers over my cheek.

Not wanting to ruin the mood of the evening, I decide to lie. "Thinking about dinner."

"It's my turn to cook."

"I know. But I wanted seafood linguine, so I picked up some fresh pasta and made the sauce earlier. I can finish up while you grab a shower."

"You have had a busy day."

"Hmm. I'm very skilled and efficient when I need to be."

"Yes, you are *very* skilled."

"I'm also very hungry." I give him a soft kiss on the cheek. "So I'm going to finish dinner."

Groaning, he rolls out of bed and starts to undress. "I guess I'll grab a shower and then I'll come help."

I lie back and watch him get naked, enjoying the show. He's perfect. Every muscle perfectly toned and tight. Tattoos cover almost every inch of flesh from his neck to his knuckles, all the way down to that perfect V beneath his abs. Each one is a work of art. No matter how long I stare at them, I find something new every time. But his arms are my favorite part about him—aside from his huge pierced dick, obviously—curled up in them is my favorite place to be in the world.

FIFTY-EIGHT

MAX

W alking into the kitchen after my shower, I find my girl wearing my shirt from earlier, sleeves rolled up while she stirs the pasta sauce. Her wearing my clothes makes me hard as fucking stone for her and she knows it. Something about her being wrapped in my scent and the way it lingers on her skin makes me feel something primal that I've never experienced before in my life. I fucking love when she smells of me. But everything about this girl makes me feel like an animal. I thought that us living together might curb my insatiable appetite for her just a little, but it's ramped up even further. I can barely look at her without wanting to mount her like some oversexed hound dog.

She turns and gives me a sexy half smile before she goes back to the stove. Fortunately for me, Joey is as insatiable as I am. I don't know how this girl manages to walk with the amount of time I spend inside her.

"You hungry, tough guy?" she asks sweetly as she turns off the burner.

"Always."

She giggles softly. "I meant for food."

369

I grab the silverware and go to the fridge for a bottle of wine while she plates the food. We move around each other as though we've been doing this our whole lives, each of us fitting seamlessly into the other's space. I don't know how I survived so long without her in my life this way. But I do know I wouldn't survive losing her. Not today. Not ever.

"THAT WAS DELICIOUS, BABY GIRL," I tell her as I push my plate away.

"Thank you," she says with a huge smile, her cheeks flushing at my words.

She's such slut for praise.

She takes a sip of her wine, her mind elsewhere.

"You okay?"

"Huh?" She blinks at me.

"You seem distracted."

"Just thinking about stuff," she says with a shrug.

"I've been thinking too." I slide off my stool and walk around the island until I'm standing in front of her.

She grins cheekily. "You thinking? That sounds dangerous."

"Careful."

She flutters her eyelashes. My brat is looking to get spanked. "What were you thinking about?"

"I had a whole plan for this, baby girl, but—" I drop to one knee and take the box out of my pocket, pulling it open to reveal the platinum ring with a 4-carat pink diamond. "Will you marry me, Joey?"

"W-what?" She stares, open-mouthed. "But you ... you never wanted to get married. You said ..." Her eyes dart from me to the ring.

The truth is I never had any desire to spend eternity with

anyone—but that was before her. That was before I realized there was a person out there who I didn't want to call my girlfriend, my casual hookup, or my partner, or anything else other than my wife.

Mine.

I want a ring on her finger so that every man who looks at her knows that she belongs to someone else—that she belongs to me.

The silence between us stretches out for an eternity as she goes on blinking like she's in a daze. Fuck! Maybe it's too soon.

"Any chance I could get an answer? You're killing me here, baby girl."

She blinks at me, her eyes wet with tears. Then she drops to her knees in front of me, wrapping her arms around my neck. "Yes. Yes! So much freaking yes."

She smothers my face with kisses, and I wrap my arms around her, trying to calm her down long enough to get the ring on her finger, but her lips are way too distracting. I kiss her back and we fall onto the floor into a heap. She giggles, threading her fingers through my hair and guiding my head lower as I nip at her neck and run my hand over her ribs.

"Can I get this damn ring on you first?" I ask, holding up the box.

She holds out her left hand. "Please."

The ring fits perfectly and looks fucking incredible on her finger. "I think from now on this is the only thing you get to wear in this apartment."

"I love it, Max," she squeals. "It's beautiful."

"You make it look fucking beautiful, baby." I start unbuttoning her shirt, trailing kisses over the soft tan skin I expose. Pushing it open and revealing her naked body, I gape at her. She is beyond perfect. Sucking one of her hard nipples into my mouth, I bite down onto the creamy flesh and she moans, arching her back and pressing herself against my mouth.

I fist my hand in her panties, working them off her as I keep sucking on her tits. She wriggles her legs to help me and the scent of her arousal in the air makes me desperate. I lick a trail from her breasts to her stomach. Her skin smells of me. Her pussy reeks of sex. She makes me feral.

"Fuck me, Max," she pleads, her breathing fast and shallow.

I reach for my cock, pulling it out of my sweatpants and giving it a quick tug before I drag the crown over her soaking folds. My piercing grazes her clit, making her whimper and claw at my skin.

"I need you," she cries, wrapping her legs around my waist and pulling me closer. Needing her just as much, I drive into her pussy, sinking all the way inside her hot, wet heat and feeling like I might fucking pass out from the sheer relief of her hugging my cock the way she does.

"Jesus. Fucking. Christ, Joey," I growl as I pull out and slam back into her. "Always ... need you ... so fucking much."

"It's the same for me, Max." Her pussy squeezes me tighter, like it will never let me go. "I always need more."

I roll my hips, driving deeper and rubbing my piercing over her G-spot, making her tremble. "That not enough for you?" I grunt as I watch her eyes roll back in her head.

"You're an asshole," she groans, pulling me tighter and digging her heels into my ass to keep me deep inside her pussy.

"Don't make me spank your ass on our engagement night, baby girl."

"Holy fuck." Her tight cunt milks my cock, squeezing and releasing as her orgasm edges closer.

"Or maybe my naughty little slut wants a spanking, huh?"

"Y-yesss." She arches her back, throwing her head back as she comes on my cock. I drive into her even harder, burying myself so deep inside her cunt that she'll feel me and think about this moment every time she moves tomorrow.

I take her to bed after I finish fucking her on the kitchen floor. Dinner dishes can wait until morning because I don't want to be anywhere except directly next to her naked body. My future wife.

We lie face-to-face, her leg draped over mine and my arm around her waist with my hand on her ass. I squeeze it and she moans contentedly. I think I'm going to fuck it in about five minutes.

"Max?" she whispers.

"Yeah, baby?"

"I'd like Anya to be one of my bridesmaids. You think we can make that happen?"

"We can get married tomorrow if that's what you want." I would marry her anytime and anywhere.

"Well, maybe not tomorrow because I want a nice dress and a party, but soon?"

"We can speak to Father Michael tomorrow and see when he can fit us in."

Her radiant smile melts me. "For real?"

"Of course, Joey. The sooner I get to call you my wife, the happier I'll be."

She presses her cheek against my chest. "I can't wait to call you my husband too."

A knot of emotion balls in my throat. I never thought I'd want this. "And how do you feel about Daddy?"

She giggles. "I'll call you Daddy any time you want, tough guy."

I smack her ass. "My belt is right there, baby girl."

"Is that supposed to be a threat, Daddy?" she asks, making my cock twitch. "Because you know it only makes me super wet and super needy."

I cup her chin in my hand and tilt her head so she can look at me and know that I'm serious. "Joey?"

"One day, yes. Most definitely I want to have lots of beautiful babies with you, but not yet."

I nod my agreement. I just needed to know if it was on the table, but I get that she's still young and we have plenty of time. "I'm more than happy to have you all to myself for a few years first."

She pushes me onto my back and straddles me. "I like the sound of that."

She leans forward, her dark curls falling onto my chest as she peppers soft kisses over my skin. "Does my girl want to be in control this round?" I ask, brushing her hair back and allowing me to see her beautiful face.

"Sweet Max," she whispers seductively. "I am *always* in control."

"Oh, baby girl," I shake my head. "You were doing so well."

I flip her onto her back, and she squeals as I press her into the mattress, pinning her hands above her head. "And now you're about to have your ass spanked hard." I nip a trail across her collarbone and she mewls as she wriggles beneath me. "And then fucked even harder."

"Holy fuck. I love you, Max," she breathes out the words.

"Love you too, baby girl. I'll need you to remember that in a few minutes when I'm fucking you like I don't."

She bites her lip and those amber flecks in her dark brown eyes sparkle with mischief and joy. "I'll try my best, but I'm sure you can remind me if I forget."

"I will, baby. Every single fucking day for the rest of my life."

EPILOGUE

JOEY—FIVE MONTHS LATER

"You need anything, Mrs. DiMarco?" Ace asks as we walk into my office alongside two of his colleagues, Ash and Romeo. I have four armed guards with me wherever I go these days. Unless I'm with Max, of course.

"No thanks. I'm good."

"I'll be outside then." He gives me a polite nod and walks out of the room to stand guard in the hallway with his buddy, Jenson. Ash and Romeo take their usual seats. They've perfected the art of being in the room but not disturbing me, and half the time I forget they're even here.

Leaning back in my chair, I look around the space and can't help but smile with pride. Since Dante and Lorenzo gave me the casino to run four months ago, I've doubled our profits, and we're currently in negotiations to open a new one in Atlantic City.

My office. I will never tire of saying those words. It took a lot of convincing for Max and my brothers to allow me to make my base here, but it makes good business sense. I don't live at the mansion any longer, and Max and I obviously don't want to conduct business at our penthouse, so I needed a space of my own. The corner office suite at our newest hotel casino was the perfect solution.

I chose all the furniture and the single piece of art on the wall. It's an erotic yet tasteful original by a young up-and-coming local artist. The whole room is all me and I love it.

I feel Max walk into the room before I look up and see him. My breath catches in my throat. The sight of him will never ever not give me butterflies in my stomach and an ache between my thighs. Especially when he's wearing one of those finely tailored suits that hugs his body like it was painted on him.

"Can you give us the room?" he says to Ash and my newest guard, Romeo.

The two men nod and leave the room, closing the door behind them.

Oh, shit! I'm in so much trouble. I roll my chair back as he steps toward my desk, his dark eyes burning into mine as that thick vein bulges in his neck.

"Did you forget something today, baby girl?" he asks, his cool tone disguising the anger bubbling just beneath the surface.

"I'm sorry. I was busy—"

"You think being busy is an excuse to make me worry about you? Wondering if you're okay?"

The ensuing eye roll is more out of habit more than anything else. Dammit!

"I know you did not just roll your fucking eyes at me, Joey."

"Well, I know you always know where I am, Max. I have no doubt you would've called Ash when I didn't check in. He would've told you that I'm fine," I insist. There's no chance in hell that Max didn't make sure I was okay after I forgot to check in with him after my meeting with the Strauss brothers today.

He plants his hands on my desk, leaning his face close to mine. Damn, he smells so good I want to jump his bones. "That is not the fucking point. You want to do this, then you follow the fucking rules."

"Your rules?" I arch an eyebrow at him.

He stands straight, running a hand over his beard and dragging his tongue over his bottom lip. Without another word, he shrugs out of his jacket.

"I'm sorry," I say, even as warmth builds in my core.

"Now that would've been the appropriate thing to say when I first walked in here, wouldn't it?" I bite my lip as I watch him roll up his shirt sleeves. My pussy quivers with anticipation. "Not *after* the eye roll and the snark?"

"Yes," I whisper.

He goes on glaring at me, making heat sear through my core. When he's finished rolling up his sleeves, he unbuckles his belt and slides it off slowly. My legs tremble while my pussy clenches with need. He's so skilled at building tension and anticipation. I'm going to be dripping wet for him before he even touches me, and he knows it.

"What do you think the appropriate punishment for making your husband worry like that should be, baby girl?"

I press my lips together and look toward the ceiling, pretending to be deep in thought. "Three orgasms and a cinnamon roll from the bakery in the lobby?"

He narrows his dark brown eyes at me. "You really are bringing the spoiled brat out to play today, huh?" He palms the buckle and wraps the belt around his hand. Holy shit. He's going to spank me hard enough that the guards outside will hear, and he won't give a single fuck. In fact, he'll make it his mission to make me scream. Not that I'm overly concerned about that. I actually kinda like when people hear us fuck. I adore this man and I want the entire world to know it.

"I am really sorry though," I whisper. "Let me make it up to you." I lick my lips and my eyes drop to the outline of his huge cock straining at the seam of his pants.

"Oh, you'll be doing that later when we get home, I promise," he says as he steps toward me. "Now, get your ass off the chair and bend over the desk."

I swallow a knot of trepidation that bubbles up my throat. "Max?"

"Now!"

With no other option, I stand and move my laptop and papers out of the way before bending over and resting my face against the cool wood. Max steps up behind me, rubbing his hands over my ass and making me shiver.

His hands move lower until he reaches the hem of my pencil skirt. When his fingertips brush against the backs of my knees, goosebumps prickle over my forearms and I whimper.

"You like working here?" he asks.

"Yes."

"You want to keep working here in your office or do you want to go back to a desk at your brother's mansion?"

"Here."

"Tell me, why do I have rules, baby girl?" he asks, his voice so deep and commanding, it rolls through my bones and makes me shiver.

I guess I'm in the mood to push him today because the words come out before I can consider the consequences. "Because you're a possessive asshole."

He slaps my ass hard and I squeal. "Don't fuck with me, Joey, because I will carry you out of here and we can do this at home. And if we do that, you won't be coming back. Ever." I suck in a stuttered breath as he yanks my skirt up over my ass and hips. "You want to try that answer again?"

"Because you love me and you worry about my safety," I

pant. He's so possessive and stubborn, he actually would stop me from coming back here. Well, he'd try.

"Better." His fingers brush over the edge of my panties, and when he tugs them aside, I stifle a moan.

"Are you wet for me?"

I pout. "No."

He slides two fingers between my folds, coating them in my arousal. "Lying to me too, huh? My brat really wants her spanking today." I moan softly as he pushes a thick finger inside me. "Unless this isn't for me?" He laughs darkly.

"It's only ever for you, Max."

"Damn right." He slips out of me and then spanks my ass with the flat of his palm.

"Ow," I whimper, wriggling my ass.

"You know that wasn't even the warm-up, baby girl, now stop squirming."

"It hurt," I say, pouting.

He leans over me, mouth pressed against my ear. "Not even close to how I felt when I thought something had happened to you," he growls, and a shudder runs the length of my spine. "And nowhere near as much as I'm going to make it hurt very soon."

He stands straight again and peels my panties off, running his hand down the inside of my thigh as he tugs them down my legs and helps me step out of them. I look back to see him holding them to his face, breathing in my scent. "Have I ever told you how fucking good your cum smells, baby? I should wear it like fucking cologne."

"Yes to both," I say with a satisfied smile as I lay my cheek back on the desk.

He spanks my ass again, warming me up for his belt. Heat and pleasure coil up my spine.

"Max," I whimper, rubbing my pussy against the edge of my

desk for relief, but he stops me and nudges my legs apart with his knee.

"Stop trying to get yourself off and spread your legs so I can see my sweet cunt."

I groan as I shuffle my feet along the floor. Then Max slides two thick fingers inside me and my knees almost buckle. "Oh, fuck."

"You're soaking already. So greedy for me," he groans the last part before pulling his fingers out and making me moan from frustration. "Let's see how much wetter we can make that pussy with my belt though, huh?"

I don't get a chance to answer before he brings it cracking down over my backside. It stings like hell, but it also makes my pussy ache for his cock.

"Holy shit, Max." Before I've recovered from the first blow, he spanks me again, and the leather landing on my ass cheeks makes such a loud thwacking sound that I blush. "Everyone will hear," I whimper.

"Good," he grunts as he spanks me again. "They'll all know who this ass belongs to, won't they?"

"Think they already do," I yelp as he spanks me again.

"Will you call me when you're supposed to next time?"

Smack!

"Y-yes." I suck in a breath as tears roll down my face and the deep throbbing ache in my pussy ratchets up even further. I need him inside me so bad it makes me want to scream. There's something so primal and hot about him when he's like this. I'm desperate for him and the bastard knows it.

"Please, Max. I'm sorry," I whimper.

He pushes two fingers inside me again. "Fuck me, baby. I love how wet being punished makes you." When he slides them out, he holds them near my face to show me how they're covered with my arousal. "You see that?"

Before I can answer, he places them in his mouth, sucking them clean before he spanks me again. Over and over. The leather slices through the air before cracking against my flesh.

By the time he's done, my ass stings like I've been sitting on an open fire, and I'm all but begging for him to fuck me.

He throws his belt onto the desk beside me and nudges the crown of his cock against my clit, rubbing his piercing over the hypersensitive bundle of nerves.

"Please, Max?" I whimper again.

"Tell me what you need, baby girl," he pants, breathing heavily from the effort of spanking me.

"Your cock inside me. Now," I moan loudly.

He presses it against my opening, and I push back against him. "You're so fucking wet, Joey. You make it too easy for me to get my cock in you. You want me all the way in on the first thrust?"

"Yes!"

"Yeah?"

"Please?" I beg now, tears pooling on the desk under my cheek.

"Fuck, baby," he grunts, grabbing hold of my hips and driving into me. I feel each piercing as he slides in deep, rubbing against my pussy walls as they squeeze around him. "I love your tight cunt."

He fists his hand in my hair. Pulling my head up, he leans over me and presses his wickedly sinful mouth at my ear. "This pussy belongs to me."

"I know."

"This ass." He rubs his hand over the welts he left there. "Belongs to me."

"Yes."

He turns my head. "These lips ..." Then he kisses me. It's brutal and dominating, and it makes my insides melt. "You belong to me,

Joey. The next time I tell you to call me after your meeting with a pair of misogynistic douchebags, you call me. Okay?"

"Okay," I pant.

"You want to come?"

Is that a rhetorical question? "Yes, please."

He rams into me harder. "Then come all over my cock, baby girl. Squeeze me with that hot little cunt until I fill you up."

"Fuck!" My walls ripple and squeeze around him, and that makes him work harder, fucking me like a man possessed. His animalistic grunts and growls in my ear make my head spin. I'm an addict and he's my only drug of choice.

"I can't ever sate this fucking need to be inside you. Every single time I fuck you feels better than the last. I'm addicted to you. You're driving me fucking crazy."

Oh, dear holy mother of all that is divine. "M-Max."

"That's it, come for me. My good fucking girl."

"Yes," I breathe as I fall forward against the desk.

Max lies on top of me, driving into me one more time. "Motherfucking Christ, Joey," he grunts before he bites down on my shoulder through my shirt. His entire body tenses as his cock pulses inside me, filling me with his hot cum.

I can't help but smile. Spanking me makes him come so hard and I love it. Making him lose control like that makes me feel invincible.

He places his hands over mine, pressing them flat to the desk as he sucks in deep breaths. His wedding ring clinks against my own, and I choke on a sob. He has the sexiest hands, and I could look at them all day, but that platinum wedding ring makes them look a hundred times hotter.

"What was that for?" he asks, rubbing his nose over my neck.

"I saw your ring," I sniff.

"My ring?"

"Yeah, whenever I see it, it makes me feel all warm and happy."

"So, that was a happy cry?"

"Yeah." I sigh. "I'm sorry I forgot to call you."

"I know, baby girl."

"I love you so much."

"I love you more. You're fucking everything to me, Joey. Everything. Do you get that?"

"Yes, Max, because you're everything to me too."

"Yeah? So the next time I ask you to check in with me and let me know you're okay ..."

"I'll check in. I promise."

"Good girl." He kisses the top of my head and I push back against him, seeking the comfort of his body.

"Is my punishment over?"

"No." He nips at my ear, and I giggle. Then he stands up straight again, pulling me with him while his cock is still inside me. "When I get home tonight, I want you naked and on your knees. I want to fuck that pretty little throat."

"Hmm. That's doesn't sound like much of a punishment. I love sucking your cock."

"I know you do, my naughty little slut. But when I leave you dripping for me afterward, then we'll see how much you're enjoying yourself."

"Monster," I hiss, even though I'm already melting at the thought of being home alone with him later. Max's punishments only ever end one way, and that's with our mutual pleasure. The longest he's ever been able to deny me an orgasm was twelve hours. Twelve torturous hours, but when he finally made me come, I swear I saw the Pearly Gates.

He slides out of me and a torrent of our cum drips down my

thighs. "I wish I could fuck you some more, but I have to go back to work."

"So do I," I remind him.

"I know, baby. You're doing an amazing job. I'm so fucking proud of you." He refastens his suit pants and I turn around to face him.

"Where are my panties?"

"In my pocket." He shrugs.

"Can I have them back?"

He pulls me into his arms, sealing his mouth over mine and kissing me so hard I almost come again. I rub myself against him like a bitch in heat until he breaks our kiss, looking down at me with a devious glint in his eyes. "Will you be good for the rest of the day?"

"Yes. I promise."

He pulls my panties from the pocket of his suit pants before crouching down on the floor to help me. "You'd better put them on before Ash and the new guy come back in here."

I step into my underwear. "His name is Romeo."

Max pulls them up my legs, securing them in place before pressing a soft kiss against my pussy through the fabric. Then he smooths down my skirt and stands. "Romeo, huh?" He arches an eyebrow at me.

"Yep."

He rubs his hand over my ass and squeezes. "I should have fucked this too."

"Maybe tonight. If you're good," I whisper.

"I'm always good, aren't I?"

Wrapping my arms around his neck, I offer him my sweetest smile. "You, sir, are incredible."

He drags his bottom lip through his teeth, like he's contemplating throwing me back down on my desk and fucking me again right now.

"We both have to work," I remind him.

"I know." He sighs, annoyance flashing in his eyes. "I wish I could take you home right now instead of having to wait until later."

"I think my butt needs a break from your punishment."

He smooths his hands over my behind, soothing the raw skin. "No more spanking tonight, baby. And after you've sucked my cock, I'll run you a bath and you can soak this beautiful ass while I make you dinner."

"You're still making me dinner?"

"It's my turn," he says with a shrug. Then he gives me a quick kiss on the tip of my nose, puts his belt and jacket back on, and opens the door to my office. Sticking his head out, he tells the guards to come back inside. Ash walks in and sits in his usual seat in the corner of the room. Romeo follows, and as he ducks into the room, he looks toward me and smirks. Unfortunately for Romeo, Max sees him too.

Grabbing him by the neck, Max throws Romeo across the room, and he crashes into the wall. "What the fuck was that?"

"What?" Romeo asks, feigning ignorance as his face turns an unnatural shade of gray.

Max stalks toward him. "Don't play fucking games with me, dipshit. What was the smug grin on your face for when you walked in here?"

"I-I—"

"I just fucking saw you, so think very carefully about what I'll do to you if you lie to me," Max says, the timbre of his voice so low and menacing that it even gives me goosebumps.

"I just ..." Romeo squirms under the heat of Max's glare.

"You just?"

Romeo's Adam's apple bobs as he swallows. "We heard you," he whispers, and his cheeks turn a deep shade of crimson.

"You heard me fucking my wife?"

Romeo nods.

"You hear me spanking her bratty ass too?" Max asks with a grin.

And that poor deluded asshole grins right back. "Yeah."

Max has him by the neck before Romeo can even blink. Pressing his face close to the younger man's, he snarls. "She is Joey fucking DiMarco, Cosa Nostra royalty, and your fucking boss, you smug little prick. You only get to work, walk, breathe, live, and die at her say so, do you understand me?"

Romeo's eyes bug out. He tries to nod, but Max has him pinned to the wall by his throat, his feet dangling an inch off the floor.

"Don't you *ever* mistake my wife's submission to me as anything but a reflection of my utter fucking devotion to her. I would crawl through fire and broken glass on my hands and fucking knees if she told me to. If you ever disrespect her like that again, I will rip out your fucking tongue and use it to choke you to death. You got that?"

Romeo nods as best he can, and Max releases him. He slides down the wall, gripping his throat as he gasps for breath and glancing at Ash as if seeking back up. Ash knows Max all too well, and he didn't once glance up from his cell phone throughout the entire exchange.

Max turns to me. "What do you want me to do with this stupid fuck, baby?"

I consider the guy panting for breath on the floor. Despite what just happened, he's usually respectful. He's worked here for three weeks now, and he knows how to blend into the background when I need him to. I don't have the energy to break in another newbie.

"I think he's learned his lesson."

"You sure?" Max scowls.

"I'm sure."

"You're so fucking lucky she's such a good influence on me," he barks at Romeo, teeth bared like a wolf guarding his mate. Then he turns back to me. "I'll see you tonight, baby."

"Can we have those fancy cheeseburgers you make for dinner?"

"Of course. Anything you want." He winks at me and walks out of my office.

I lean back in my chair and watch his fine ass disappear down the hallway. I am the luckiest girl in the whole damn world.

MAX

"How was she after I left?"

"She was fine. She didn't say much, but that was because she was working. Had her head bent over her computer all afternoon," Ash replies. He's worked for the Morettis a long time, and out of all the men assigned to Joey's personal security team, he's the one I trust most with her safety. I know that she trusts him too. The guy has literally taken a bullet for her, and he'd do it again without a second's hesitation.

"Did she eat?" I ask with a frown.

"She did."

"And that fuckwit, Romeo. Did he behave himself?"

Ash laughs softly. "He did."

"What's your read on him? Can I trust him to protect my wife? Because the way he fucking looked at her, Ash ..." I clench my jaw. He's lucky I didn't tear his fucking head off earlier.

"He's good at what he does, Boss. He's usually very respectful, but he's also young and I think he was probably trying to impress you."

"Impress me? Then he should learn that the *only* fucking way to do that is to impress my wife."

"Yeah, I think he gets it now." He laughs again.

"For his sake, I hope you're right."

"Pretty sure you conveyed your message loud and clear, Boss. She's getting in the elevator now. She'll be with you in less than a minute."

"Thanks. Talk soon."

I end the call and quickly change out of my suit and into a pair of gray sweats, the kind that make my girl drool.

"Max, are you already home?" she shouts from the hallway.

I step out of our bedroom to see her walking toward me, and my cock hardens instantly.

Her hair is pulled up into a ponytail, her heels already discarded near the elevator, and her shirt hangs off one arm. She shrugs it off and reaches back to unzip her skirt. I remember that I told her I wanted her naked and on her knees when she got home. She's always submissive after a punishment. It lasts for all of about two days before she's back to her usual Joey Moretti self, but I love her like this. I love her every way she is; when she's hard and strong and when she rolls her eyes and runs her smart mouth, but when she's compliant and does anything I say with no resistance, I don't like to waste a second of it. Neither of us will get much sleep tonight.

"I know you said ..." She pulls her skirt down and kicks it off until she's standing in just her underwear. "But I didn't think you'd be home this early ..." Her bra is off now, and my eyes drop to her beautiful tits and hard nipples. I want to bite them. "I'm ready though ..." she says breathlessly, shoving her panties down and kicking them off her feet.

My eyes roam over her naked body, every curve, every line, every fucking inch of her. Mine.

Her knees bend slightly as she goes to sink to the floor, her eyes fixed on my cock, but I step forward and scoop her into my arms, carrying her into the bedroom. She wraps her arms around my neck. "But I was supposed to suck your cock."

"Not now."

"Is this another punishment? Because you were home early and—"

"It's not, but I do love the fact that you consider not sucking me off to be a punishment, baby girl," I say, laughing.

"Max?" she gasps when I carry her through to the bathroom and she sees the room lit up with candles, and the huge tub full of bubbles. She takes a deep breath through her nose. "Is that my favorite candy cane bubble bath?"

"Yup."

"But they discontinued it."

"I had someone recreate it." I kiss the tip of her nose. "Just for you."

She places her hands on my face, her eyes shining with so much happiness that it makes my heart race and my cock ache. "What did I ever do to deserve you, Max DiMarco?" she whispers.

"I have no fucking idea, because you're a giant pain in my ass." Winking, I lower her into the tub.

She doesn't give me a smart comeback. Instead, she leans back, resting her head on the ledge of the tub and closing her eyes with a contented sigh. "I actually do have a pain in my ass," she murmurs. "And this feels so damn good."

"I know, baby." I climb in with her, and she scoots forward, allowing me to slide in behind her. I wrap my arms around her so she can settle against me. "How is your ass?"

"Stinging like a mother, but not in a bad way." She smiles. "I loved having you visit my office today. You should stop by more often."

"I stop by all the time."

"Not often enough. I could do with a visit like that every damn day." She giggles and pushes her ass against my cock.

I press my lips against her ear. "I'm going to have to think up alternative punishments for your bratty ass. I think you like my spankings way too much."

"Oh, I can't wait," she says.

I nip at her ear. "Masochist."

"If I am, it's only because you've taught me to be one."

That makes me smile. I love being the only man who's ever touched her and the only man who ever will. All fucking mine.

I run my nose along the back of her neck. "You smell so fucking good, I could eat you."

"Please do," she whimpers, rubbing herself over my cock. It aches to be inside her.

"You going to be a good girl?"

"Yes. Always. I promise."

"Liar." I slide my hand between her thighs, and she opens wide for me, hooking her legs over mine. When I slip two fingers inside her, her back bows as she tries to take more of me. "So desperate for me, Joey. You're fucking soaking already, baby."

"I always am around you," she moans.

I push my fingers deeper into her and she starts to make those sweet little mewling sounds that drive me crazy. "Fuck, you're gonna taste so good. But not now, baby girl. Later."

"Max?" she whines.

"I can't have dessert before dinner," I taunt, brushing my thumb over her clit until her body bucks against me. "And I want you to sit dripping for me all night. We're going to watch a movie after dinner, and I'm going to kiss your neck and play with your sweet cunt without getting you off. And you'll be so fucking wet, because you know that I'm going to eat you so fucking good when I finally take you to bed."

Her walls squeeze around me, milking my fingers as I rub against her most sensitive spots. "Max, please?" she pleads, grinding herself on my fingers.

"I know," I soothe, rubbing my nose over the back of her neck. "I'm gonna let you come now though, because you took my belt like such a good fucking girl today."

"Oh, fuck."

"Yeah, I'm gonna fuck you now too," I say in her ear. "Because I'm not going to last the entire fucking night if I don't. Now take a deep breath."

She sucks in a breath, and I clamp my hand over her mouth and nose as I work my fingers deeper inside her, rubbing the heel of my palm over her clit. She approaches the precipice, her cunt milking me. Her heart pounds against my bicep as I pull her body closer to mine. Her chest heaves as she struggles for air that I won't give her, and her skin scorches with heat. She's so close. I know her body as well as I know my own, and I love the control she allows me to have over her. She is too fucking perfect.

A deep guttural moan ripples through her entire body, and I release my hand, letting her gasp for breath as her climax hits her. She roars like my warrior princess, her body completely overwhelmed by the strength of her orgasm as she trembles and shudders in my arms. Before she can fully recover, I spin her around and impale her on my cock. My tension melts away at the sheer fucking relief of being deep inside her, and my cock pulses in her tight, wet center.

Her head drops onto my shoulder as she goes on panting, and I palm the back of her neck, holding her in place while I rail into her.

"Catch your breath, Joey, because I'm not coming in your pussy, and you've already got me close."

"Okay," she pants her agreement, sucking in deep breaths

like I taught her as I drive my hips upward and pull her down onto me, getting as deep inside her as I can.

"I could fuck you all day every day and still not get enough," I whisper, my lips against her ear. She shivers at my words and a soft smile tugs at her lips. Her hot breath dances over my skin as she regulates her breathing, readying herself for what I have planned next. "You drive me crazy, baby girl. I love you more than I can ever put into words or even show you, but if I can even make you feel a fraction of it, I'll be a happy man."

"You make me feel all of it, Max," she pants. "All of it. I swear."

"Yeah?" I rock my hips, rubbing my piercing over her G-spot as I suck one of her hard nipples into my mouth.

"Y-yeah." She throws her head back, walls rippling as she comes for me again.

My hand still on the back of her neck, I tilt her head so she looks into my eyes. Her cheeks are pink, her lashes wet with tears. "My turn."

I slip out of her, and she sucks in a lungful of air just before she disappears beneath the bubbles. Her hands wrap around the back of my thighs and her soft lips slide over the tip of my cock, making me groan loudly. She gags when I hit the back of her throat, and it makes my balls churn with the need to fill her.

My knuckles turn white as my grip on the bath tightens. I'm fucking desperate to hold her head down, but I'm about to come and I can't see her properly. I'm not confident I'll feel her tap out while I'm blowing my load because this woman makes me nut harder than I ever have in my life.

"Fuck, Joey," I grunt. My eyes roll back, and every muscle in my body tightens as I come hard down her throat. She sucks and licks me through it, my limbs trembling with the force of my release. Then her soft mouth is gone, and she breaks through the bubbles, gasping for air as she straddles me again.

"That was fucking amazing, baby."

The smile she gives me in response reminds me what a slut for praise my wife is. She has me wrapped around her little finger and she pushes my buttons constantly, but I wouldn't have it any other way. I fucking love it. But as a man who thrives on control, I enjoy knowing that I can always keep her in line one way or another—if punishment won't work, praise surely will.

I wrap her in my arms, and she rests her head on my chest while we both catch our breath. Palming one of her ass cheeks, I squeeze gently and she moans. I can't feel them, but I know my belt marks are there. Later she'll have my bite marks all over her too. The thought of her covered in me—my marks, my scent, my cum—makes me feral and possessive. She's lucky I don't keep her chained to my bed twenty-four seven.

"You think maybe this is what heaven's like?" she whispers as her fingertips brush up and down my arm.

"Every single second I spend with you is heaven, baby girl."

She snuggles closer and I feel her smiling against my chest. "I think you might be right."

IF YOU WANT to know if Max keeps his promise about that movie, then you won't want to miss the exclusive extended epilogue available via my newsletter - contact me on any social media platform to sign up

ARE you ready for more of the Moretti's? You can order the other stand alone books in the series on Amazon now

Dante

Lorenzo

Also by Sadie Kincaid

Want to know more about the Irish Mafia in New York and their connection to the Bratva? If you haven't read New York the series yet, you can find them on Amazon and Kindle Unlimited

Ryan Rule

Ryan Redemption

Ryan Retribution

Ryan Reign

Ryan Renewed

New York Ruthless short stories can be found here

A Ryan Reckoning

A Ryan Rewind

A Ryan Restraint

A Ryan Halloween

A Ryan Christmas

A Ryan New Year

If you'd prefer to head to LA to meet Alejandro and Alana, and Jackson and Lucia, you can find out all about them in Sadie's internationally bestselling LA Ruthless series. Available on Amazon and FREE in Kindle Unlimited.

Fierce King

Fierce Queen

Fierce Betrayal

Fierce Obsession

If you'd like to read about London's hottest couple. Gabriel and Samantha, then check out Sadie's London Ruthless series on Amazon. FREE in Kindle Unlimited.

Dark Angel

Fallen Angel

Dark/ Fallen Angel Duet

If you enjoy super spicy short stories, Sadie also writes the Bound series feat Mack and Jenna, Books 1, 2, 3 and 4 are available now.

Bound and Tamed

Bound and Shared

Bound and Dominated

Bound and Deceived

ACKNOWLEDGMENTS

As always I would love to thank all of my incredible readers, and especially the members of Sadie's Ladies and Sizzling Alphas. My beloved belt whores! You are all superstars. To my amazing ARC and street teams, the love you have for these books continues to amaze and inspire me. I am so grateful for all of you.

But to all of the readers who have bought any of my books, everything I write is for you and you all make my dreams come true.

To all of my author friends who help make this journey all that more special.

Super special mention to my lovely PA's, Kate, Kate and Andrea, for their support and honesty and everything they do to make my life easier.

To the silent ninja. Thank you for continuing to push me to be better. And to my amazing editor, Jaime, who helped me take Joey and Max's story to that next level.

To my incredible boys who inspire me to be better every single day. And last, but no means least, a huge thank you to Mr. Kincaid— all my book boyfriends rolled into one. I couldn't do this without you!

About the Author

Sadie Kincaid is a dark romance author who loves to read and write about hot alpha males and strong, feisty females.

Sadie loves to connect with readers so why not get in touch via social media? Follow links below.

Sign up to her newsletter for all the latest news and releases here

Join Sadie's reader group for the latest news, book recommendations and plenty of fun. <u>Sadie's ladies and Sizzling Alphas</u>

Made in the USA
Monee, IL
16 October 2023

44234508R00236